MAELSTROM

America's year of hell!

by

Michael B. Dodd

An Author's Request

I enjoy writing in the same way a painter likes to paint or a sculptor likes to sculpt. My overriding desire for any of my works is that it be read and enjoyed by others. I've tried not to price my books too steeply, and while I'd be lying if I said I didn't want to become successful enough to quit my job and write full time, my great desire is simply to know that my books are being read by others.

To that end, in this modern age of electronic media, and particularly, Kindle publishing, it is paramount in any author's career that his books be reviewed on Amazon.com. If you enjoy this book, or have constructive criticism for my edification, I'd greatly appreciate it if you could take a small amount of your time and review this book on Amazon.com. It is from these reviews that I believe most people choose their reading material.

Thank you in advance for your kind attention.
Sincerely,
Michael B. Dodd

Chapter One

Lisa Martin had no idea that she was moments from death. The man who would be the instrument of that death was happily oblivious of his target's identity. She was, simply, fodder, no more important than the bullet that would soon enter her brain. Act one of an international play in which he was but a bit player. Not important enough for a cameo role, yet, when the credits rolled, his name would be there—Allah would see to that.

Raheem Milani was happy to be in this position. The bastard son of an Islamic mother who had actually divorced her husband—his father, and a man he'd never met—Raheem was raised with little or no religious dogma. While technically a Muslim and son of a technically Muslim mother, Raheem was the product of a purely American lifestyle.

His mother was a prostitute and crack addict, allowing her son to be raised in a one-bedroom pigsty above a sleazy bar that catered to ladies of the night. After 36 years of debaucherous living she died of Aids when Raheem was only sixteen years old, leading him to spend the next ten years of his woeful existence selling drugs and pimping.

After his arrest and conviction for drug trafficking, Raheem was sent to Florida's criminal-vacation spot, the Florida State Prison in Stark, where he continued to barter in drugs and prostitutes for six years until meeting the man who would change his life.

Tariq Haqqani was a fellow prisoner at Stark and the man who led Raheem to give up his life as an infidel and embrace the Koranic teachings. It was this influence that led him to apply himself to chastity, self-control, education, and

3

the kind of behavior that led to an early release at the age of forty-five.

Tariq was the man that Raheem credited with his enlistment in the American version of the Islamic Brotherhood, or Ikhawan, with its motto: "Allah is our goal; the Messenger is our model; the Koran is our constitution; jihad is our means; and martyrdom in the way of Allah is our aspiration."

Raheem adopted this philosophy as a way of life and a means to atone for his sins and those of his whore mother. Always remembering the words of his new Islamic father, Hasan al-Banna that it is the nature of Islam to dominate, not to be dominated, to impose its law on all nations and to extend its power to the entire planet, Raheem would fight the good fight and do his part to bring America to its knees.

He had spent many a day in a remote area of Mexico, practicing with this…contraption—he still didn't like the feel of its contours—which was supposed to give him the power to strike terror into the hearts of these godless Westerners. Just give him an old Kalashnikov, he thought, and he could single-handedly rid the world of the Jews and the Christians—and it wouldn't cost nearly as much as this European-made, brazenly put-together sniper rifle that they had requisitioned him. Jihad was not what it used to be.

No matter; quickly done and he would be on his way home to the delights of a wife who had taken seriously the directive to "immerse yourself in western culture"— evidently to allay any suspicions of un-decadent, i.e. un-American leanings.

Through her great desire to obey Allah, she had become an avid Victoria's Secret customer. This coincided well with the body she had sculpted at the local women's fitness-center. In American parlance, "she had a body that wouldn't quit". In that, she was not unlike the woman converging in

4

the cross hairs of the scope of Raheem's German-made GOL-Sniper rifle.

Through the scope's necessarily enhanced view, he had not neglected to inspect the woman's physical attributes: shoulder-length sandy-blonde hair, parted in the middle; she seemed to have pretty brown eyes that, at least as far as Raheem could see, were wet with tears; her figure was very attractive in that it more than filled out the light-blue scrub clothes that she was wearing when she got into her car. American women seemed to have much larger breasts than Arab women did, but he supposed that, as a rule, Islamic dress code tended not to highlight a woman's shape. Undercover work in America did have its advantages. Not the least of which was the "need" to project a lifestyle to his "fellow" Americans that would assure them that he had no need for 72 virgins in the next life—he'd have them right now, thank you.

Raheem was forever thankful that the leaders had chosen him for this assignment. He supposed that it was largely due to his graduating magna cum laude at Stanford (the school he attended after his release from prison), as well as his long and comfortable relationship with the complexities of American English—a continually changing montage of illiteracies, long ago disowned by the British.

Raheem was now one of twenty-four "soldiers" with similar, if not comparable skills—or so Raheem thought—and spread throughout the contiguous United States to affect nothing short of a national paradigm change. His job was to travel haphazardly within the two-state area of Florida and Georgia, randomly killing anyone that Allah put into his sights. Each of the other 23 men would have similar two-state assignments. This would allow each man to "hunt" in a largely slapdash manner and in a relatively vast region. It would permit each long-distance murder to be committed by

5

a man with no ties or motives, with each victim being equally untied to the shooter by any ways or means.

With at least 24 random American sniper victims per week splashing across Fox News and CNN—well, it would be a thing of beauty. In coordination with multiple other modalities of murder, Allah would soon be the master of even so despoiled a land as America.

It was almost 9pm on a rather humid and quickly fading September evening as Lisa "Doc" Martin attempted to put her cell phone back into her scrub top after another sad conversation with her soon-to-be ex-boyfriend. It was becoming tiresome and not a little embarrassing to submit herself to these daily lamentations of regret by a man who, by all rights, should be parking her car.

It was the most foolish of relationships. She was a physician and her "boyfriend" worked in the housekeeping department of the hospital. He was handsome and well-spoken, and when Lisa ran into him at the previous year's hospital Christmas party, she became somewhat enamored. With feelings of loneliness urging her on, she began dating the seemingly charming rogue.

The relationship was never consummated and consisted of only a few dinner-and-a-movie type dates; but, Robert had thought them a pledge of undying love and pursued Lisa for more, even after she had made it clear that she considered the relationship over. Now, he was calling her at all hours and usually inebriated, to boot. Physicians, she thought, really ought to be above this kind of sordid business, unless they were working at Chicago Hope.

As she opened her car door, lost in thought, her beeper suddenly started chirping. Unbeknownst to Lisa, Raheem, wet with the sweat of the Florida heat, was, at that very moment, slowly squeezing the trigger that would end all of her relationship woes. As the beeper's sudden detonation interrupted her sullen mindset, Lisa's hand jerked back and it slipped from her grasp. It was at that precise moment, as she bent to retrieve it, that Raheem's calling card passed her head with a high-pitched whiz and hit her car door with a low-pitched thud. Unsure what had happened, but sure that whatever it was wasn't good, Lisa burst from her car and ducked behind an old Ford pickup truck. She was filled with adrenaline but unsure what had happened.

By this time, the sound had brought the hospital's security guards scurrying in her direction. Raheem realized he would be unable to take another shot without being detected. As the security guards reached Lisa and hustled her back to the hospital, Raheem jumped back into his Pontiac Grand Am and drove slowly away.

Pure dumb luck had saved Lisa Martin's life and sent Raheem home to massage his wife, and his somewhat bruised ego. He would not make that mistake again.

•

The city of Tampa, Florida was fast asleep. A raucous Saturday night of revelry had drifted into the slumbering peace of a Sunday morning; even the crickets had given way to silence.

Kevin O'Brien was fast asleep in his man-cave of an apartment. Haphazardly scattered around his rumpled bed were dirty clothes on the floor, dirty dishes on the tables, and an empty bottle of Captain Morgan Rum sitting on its side on the nightstand.

To call his "apartment" Spartan would be an affront to all those who had attended Michigan State University. The blandly painted walls were dressed with the obligatory picture here and there, none un-tilted and all tasteless. There was a small writing desk on which sat an old laptop computer, an unmatched couch and chair facing an old, console television and an odor of unknown origin emanating from somewhere, although Kevin couldn't smell it. It was an apartment to challenge even the most daring interior decorator, though surely none would get the call to try.

Suddenly, Kevin's head shot from his pillow, eyes wide and adrenaline coursing, *What is that God-awful sound?*

It was the phone.

Still more in touch with his very pleasant dream but conscious enough to realize where he was, he reached for the phone—*If only to stop that incessant noise!*

"What?" Kevin said angrily as he put the receiver to his ear. Even as he said it, the better part of his mind was scuba diving off the coast of Aruba. Unfortunately, the man on the other end of the line had been awake all night, and his last few hours had been spent anything but scuba diving.

"Don't take that tone with me, O'Brien! I'll have you doing body cavity searches at Kabul International Airport!"

It was Special Agent in Charge Sam Waters. He ran the Tampa office. He was a gruff, if fair boss but Kevin doubted that anyone had ever made him laugh. "I'm sorry, sir, I guess I was still asleep," he said.

"Well, wake up and smell the coffee, kid. The dream's over and the nightmare is waiting for you at the office. Get your butt in here!" he added, before hanging up the phone in Kevin's hung-over right ear.

The FBI established the Tampa division on June 1, 1960. The Miami division—previously in charge of the Tampa Bay area—had become too busy to cover such a large geographic area. Now, well established in its own right, the office was a welcome assignment for "upwardly mobile" young agents. It assured an environment that provided an aspiring agent with the opportunity to see some real action, while adding the obvious advantages of Florida coastal living.

When Kevin finally arrived at the office, he was petulantly greeted by the graveyard shift—they'd been up all night and were rightly assuming that they wouldn't be leaving anytime soon—and the groggy band of special agents with whom he worked on a daily basis.

The office was typical Government Issue: heavy, matted-green metal desks that couldn't be moved and made one wonder who had put them there in the first place; matching chairs that screamed, "Uncomfortable and Hemorrhoid-producing!"; the obligatory pictures of the President of the United States and the Director of the FBI, and an air of excitement that only a trip to the dentist could match.

"Alright, let's get them caught up!" Special agent in charge Waters announced, a little too loudly for the newcomers. "Austin, give them the rundown," he said, after all seven agents were seated and caffeinated.

"Good morning, everyone," she began. Special agent Diane Austin was only 30 years old but she was the epitome of professionalism. She had risen meteorically to become second in command to Agent Waters who both trusted her and relied on her to keep him from shooting someone. She was also a very attractive woman by any standards; ironically, this didn't create a problem in the workplace because of her professional manner of dress and deed.

Rather "smallish", even for a woman, Diane had chestnut-brown hair of medium length, though now in a ponytail, wide brown eyes that were one-part serious and one-part vulnerable, a trim figure that accented her dark-blue pants suit and an engaging smile, sure to melt the defenses of any man.

"I'm sorry we had to interrupt your beauty sleep, gentlemen. From the looks of some of you, it's clear that a few more hours would have done a world of good." She didn't smile but her comportment implied humor.

"Well, the scenario we've been waiting for has finally occurred. It seems that Al-Qaeda has begun a terror campaign throughout the United States which is sure to unnerve even the most jaded of Americans. Over the past 24 hours, 32 people have been killed and 5 have been injured."

Diane ignored the agent's audible gasp as she continued, "All 37 were the result of sniper fire from a high-powered and quite expensive montage of rifles. In addition, these clearly semi-coordinated attacks were spread over 32 states from Maine to California, Oregon to Florida."

Agent Bennett interrupted with, "Why do you say, semi-coordinated?" Doug Bennett was the only African-American in the office. He was 47 years old, midriff expanding and temples graying. He was overweight, at least by FBI standards, but was usually trying to diet, although with mixed results. Never dressed in a professional manner, Agent Bennett was allowed to wear his blue jeans and tee shirts to the office because he was such a valuable member of the office and a difficult one not to like. There was no pretence about the man and although he seemed intent on changing his outward appearance, at the same time seemed most comfortable in his own skin.

"Because," she explained, "while the shootings were clearly the work of some coordination, the odd range of attack times lends itself to the supposition of what I call, 'free-lance organization'. While it would appear the snipers were given their marching orders from a single entity, they were probably given a modicum of discretion as to target and time, probably with each sniper given a two to three state area in which to…hunt, as it were."

Kevin, now awake and alert, piped in, "Oh, you've got to be kidding me!? This is going to be a nightmare!" He did a slow head turn towards Agent Austin as he continued, "There is nothing to tie any of the shooters to any of the victims. There is no motive, except to create terror, and it would seem that each shooter has a large area in which to move around. This is a thousand times worse than the Washington snipers. They never left the area and look how hard it was to find them?"

(The Washington snipers were John Allen Muhammad and Lee Boyd Malvo. They killed 10 people and critically injured 3 others in the Washington DC Metropolitan area during a three-week rampage in October of 2002.)

Kevin cocked his eye toward Waters and said, "Sir, I have a couple months of vacation time I'd like to take...starting right now!" He arose in a mock gesture of exit. "Let me know how this all turns out, will ya?"

Special Agent in Charge Waters was not in the mood for levity. He was well aware that Diane's, as well as Kevin's assessment was correct. Finding even one of these terrorist snipers, if that's what they were, would be dumb luck at best. Finding all of them would be impossible. "O'Brien, sit down!" he said, half joking. "Nobody's going anywhere! Once the damned secretary answered the phone this morning, our whole 'wrong number' ploy was out the window. Washington knows we're here and we can't get out of this."

Kevin sat back down. Diane joined the others in subdued laughter before she continued addressing the room. "Agent O'Brien is quite correct; however, the first stop on his whirlwind vacation will be Tampa General Hospital. One of their physicians was a likely sniper target last night. Ballistics has shown the bullet that inexplicably missed its intended victim to be a .338 Lapua Magnum cartridge. So, unless there's a sniper who just happened to be sniping at the same time as our terrorist friends, I'd say we've got a lead."

Kevin again rose to his feet, a little slower than before, and headed for the door.

"Don't forget Agent Forbes, Kevin!" Diane called out. "You seem to keep misplacing him, don't you?" she added, sending all those seated, except Agent Forbes, into a laughing jag.

Sheepishly, the young Agent Forbes ambled towards the door, red-faced and stopping only to turn momentarily when Agent Rodriguez reminded him not to forget his secret-decoder ring.

•

Falah Mohamed had been out of Folsom prison, near Sacramento, for only seven days. Raised in the south Los Angeles area known as Watts, he was born, Terrique Johnson, son of a mother long ago dead of Aids and of a father, never identified. More famous for its 65' riots than anything else, Watts is considered by most to be an African-American ghetto, yet the Hispanic population is almost double that of African-American.

Terrique was raised in an old Spanish Mission for destitute boys, where Padre Juan Fernandez had been a loving and faithful custodian until his death when Terrique was only fifteen years of age. In the ten years that he resided there, Padre Fernandez had seen to it that Terrique immerse himself in Catholicism, even to the point of Confirmation and Alter-boy duties. The Padre's needless death in a drive-by shooting had sent the young man away from the mission and into the brutal LA gang known as the Bloods.

Five years of hatred and violence later, Terrique was arrested and convicted of the murder of a Korean convenience-store owner and sent to Folsom for twenty-five years. It was there that he found Imam Amir Muhammad, chaplain of Folsom prison and recruiter for Allah. Finally, he had found a god for the "black" man! Jesus was the white man's god, always telling the black man to turn the other cheek when "whitey" gave it to him up the wazoo: Never again!

After shedding his slave name and taking the Islamic name of Falah Mohamed, he became engulfed in Islamic teachings, gravitating to the Wahhabi sect: a strict form of Islam practiced in Saudi Arabia, home to 15 of the 19 September 11 hijackers.

Paroled after ten years in prison, Falah, now 30, was ready to fulfill his duty to Allah. His whole life had been one of chaos: now it was time to inflict some of it on the blue-eyed devil.

When a young American embraces the Islamic Fundamentalist creed and actively seeks to become involved in terrorist activities, he will not have to look far to find those who will assist him, even in America.

Within months, Raheem had been given his own personal "weapons-of-mass-destruction kit" and set loose on an unsuspecting public, eager to wreak havoc and inflict death on anyone who represented the culture that had turned its back on him.

Today, Raheem was nestled within a wooded area outside LAX and equipped with Russian-made and Iranian-purchased devastation. Finally, he would be allowed to exact revenge for a lifetime of neglect and abuse at the hands of Christians and Jews.

The IGLA 9K38 MANPADS (Man-Portable Air Defense System) is a man-packable fire-and-forget surface-to-air missile launcher. Created for use as an idiot-proof weapon of mass destruction, the IGLA-S system allows for proximity detonation of the missile warhead (in the event of a mishit) with optimization of the detonation point. In English, if you can point the weapon and pull the trigger, you can't miss.

Falah, who was well and stealthily positioned in a wooded area with easy access to his Jeep Cherokee for a swift egress, did not intend to return to prison. If they caught him, he would take out as many infidels as he could before entering Islamic paradise.

Although, well acquainted with LAX's runway layouts (he had played around here as a child), Falah was taking no chances. He selected a pair of flights that he knew would bring them in close enough proximity to his position, and in short enough intervals, to both fire and escape before anyone knew what had happened. Both were American Airline's flights: one, a non-stop to New York—sure to be fully fueled— and the other; a flight to Phoenix that would never arrive.

Twenty minutes later, Falah watched as the first plane lifted off for its long trek to New York. If he had calculated correctly, this flight would go directly over his head while the Phoenix flight would take off almost simultaneously at his 10 o'clock position.

His IGLA at the ready and two 72mm stinger missiles at his side, Falah waited for the deafening sound of a 767 overhead. The New York bound flight began to scream its powerful cry as it battled the laws of physics and nature with thunderous technology. Falah, already locked and loaded, winced as the earsplitting jumbo jet overshadowed his location. At about the 12 o'clock position, he leaned back, pointed his weapon to the heavens and fired.

5 seconds later, a fireball erupted which lit the evening sky as though it were daylight. Falah knew he didn't have much time. Quickly, he grabbed the second missile, jammed it into the IGLA and waited for flight number two. He did not wait long as the clamorous sounds and bright rocket jets lifted the jumbo jet skywards for its long flight to Phoenix. He pointed a bit to his left, lifted the IGLA and fired. The resultant explosion scattered fiery debris over a wide area, surely killing many people on the ground, as well.

He had done it! He was now the instrument of death for the enemies of Allah! For the first time in his life, he felt important. He was no longer a loser from the neighborhood. He was now a warrior in an epic battle against the infidels who had lied to him all his life.

Back in the Jeep Cherokee and headed in the opposite direction of the planes, Falah knew that his future was bright and his eternity assured. He raced back to his hotel room to watch the carnage on TV.

Chapter Two

Jim "Jimmy" Forbes had only recently completed his 16 weeks of field training at Quantico, Va. The written examinations had never been difficult for him, as he'd always had an easy acumen with the written word, lending grudging credence to his academy nickname of "Brain". It was a sobriquet which applied to both his intellectual prowess, as well as the fact that his short-cropped curly hair, parted down the middle, looked to those with an eye for parochial humor—i.e. every agent-in-training at the FBI academy—as if Jimmy's brain was on the outside of his head.

Although these types of "ribbings" were not welcome, Jimmy had endured them for so long that he would, forlornly, miss them if absent. Yet, it was in the area of physical aptitude in which he was most often left wanting. A pudgy build and cruel feelings of inadequacy made physical conditioning, let alone physical exchanges, an almost comical undertaking. If not for his intellectual and linguistic ability—and a father with enormous influence— he would likely not be accompanying Agent O'Brien on this interview.

Yet, here he was, riding shotgun with the agent that he most respected, and with whom he felt the least self-conscious—an incongruity with which Jimmy would often psychologically wrangle.

Kevin O'Brien, at least to Agent Forbes' opinion, was everything that he was not. He was handsome, and strikingly so, intelligent, macho—in what Jimmy considered a good way—and most astounding to him, at ease with others in a way that Jimmy knew he could never be.

16

However, rather than the expectant jealousy and resentment that Jimmy might otherwise assume, he felt a closeness to Agent O'Brien that belied the outward appearances. It gave him the courage to ask questions that he would be terrified to ask of others in this most testosterone-packed business.

"Agent O'Brien...?" Jimmy sheepishly began.

Kevin interrupted him with, "I told you, Jimmy, you don't have to call me, Agent O'Brien. Call me Kevin, if you don't mind?"

"Sorry," Jimmy gave him an appreciative glance, "Kevin, do you really think I can cut it out here on the street?"

"What is this, the Hill Street Blues?" Kevin said. He had a tendency to use humor to mask his emotions. He had a soft spot for Jim Forbes and truly wished to put him at ease. "Jimmy, look, you went to the same academy I did; you passed the same tests that I did, and you have an FBI I.D. card with your name and picture on it, just like me. You just need a little seasoning and a little confidence, and you can't get one without the other."

"I know, but we both know I wouldn't be much good to you if the situation were to escalate into an exchange of blows." Jimmy was not well versed in street vernacular. Kevin ignored it.

"No, Jimmy, you probably wouldn't, but I'll tell you what; I'd much rather have a partner who's quick on the uptake. Contrary to television dramas and the 6'o'clock news, there is very little physical violence involved in this job. Mostly, it's a combination of paperwork and fine details, with a large dose of boredom thrown in.

"To put it another way," Kevin continued, "I prefer an agent like you to an agent who fancies himself as some kind of patriotic superhero. That kind of agent gets you killed.

Just let me handle the rough stuff and you handle the details; we'll make a great team."

Agent Forbes felt an indwelling-warmth for Agent O'Brien as they pulled into the parking lot of Tampa General Hospital, quickly finding a parking space reserved for the police.

Both men extricated themselves from Kevin's aging automobile with contrasting results: Kevin, lithe and athletic, turned off the ignition, popped the keys out and into his pocket, while at the same time, opening the door and almost leaping to his feet; Jimmy was a little less artistic in his movements, swinging his legs out the door and lifting his more than stocky frame from the car with a grunting sound usually reserved for elderly men.

Kevin was just over six feet in height and ruggedly built. His light-brown hair was parted on the side but not held in place with mousse or gel, leaving it to seem unkempt at times, but pleasingly so. Blue eyes, a square jaw and an eternal 5 o'clock shadow made him quite popular with the ladies, when he had the time. He wore the standard black or dark-blue FBI "uniform" most of the time, but when left to his own devices, he was a walking garage sale. Maybe someday he'd meet a woman who could pick out his clothes; most who knew him thought he shouldn't wait; his last girlfriend threatened to call 911 and have the fashion police make an emergency run. Kevin's not dating her anymore.

•

Kevin and Jimmy were shown to the doctor's lounge of the first-floor radiology department. Upon entering, Kevin was struck by the posh furnishings and ample supplies of food and drink that were apparently an everyday part of the life of a modern physician. There were comfortable looking couches and chairs, a large-screen TV-tuned to Fox News, two large circular tables with surrounding chairs, and a number of small wall niches with Dictaphones.

The room was empty of people with the exception of one rather angry-looking, but quite beautiful physician, seated at one of the circular tables; she was eating an apple from a large fruit basket at the table's center.

"Hello," Kevin said, stepping toward the stern-looking, white-lab-coat clad figure, now glaring at him, "I'm Agent Kevin O'Brien; I'm here to ask you some questions about the shooting incident last night."

Dr. Martin was not quite as cheerful as Kevin had expected. People who barely escape death are usually much more upbeat, or so went Kevin's irreverent wit.

"I don't know what you want me to tell you?" Dr. Martin howled, "I already told that other policeman everything I know! What do you people want from me?"

The doctor was obviously in a bit of a snit. "Look, Miss Martin..." Kevin said, as he began his attempt to assuage her angry demeanor.

Lisa corrected him. "Doctor... my name is 'Doctor' Lisa Martin."

Kevin understood her anger and didn't wish to exacerbate it, but, *"Doc Martin? Oh, that's too easy,"* he thought. Kevin wasn't going there. "Excuse me, Dr. Martin," he said, "I just need to ask you a few questions about last night. I'm sure it will only take a few minutes and I can probably ease your mind a bit as well."

"Ease my mind?" Dr. Martin howled, "How in the hell are you going to do that?" Lisa hesitated a moment and then said, "Oh, don't tell me you're one of those agents from "Men in Black"? What? Are you going to use one of those laser pencils to erase my memory? If you do, would you be so kind as to erase my memory of this particular meeting?"

"Wow!" thought Kevin. *"She's a pistol! I like her already."*

"Actually, Doctor Martin," Kevin went on, "I'm not with Men in Black but I am with the FBI. What happened to you last night was not a personal attack on you; per se, it was part of what we believe is a coordinated terrorist attack on our country. You were not targeted because you are Doctor Lisa Martin, but because you were an American citizen in the wrong place and at the wrong time and a terrorist sniper took a shot at you. It was nothing personal," Kevin added with his unique flair.

Lisa, although overwrought from a combination of work, personal issues and assassination attempts began to see that Kevin was trying to be kind to her. She'd been too untoward, she realized. Besides, he was kind of cute. "I'm sorry, Agent..." she left it hanging there in hopes that he would...

"Kevin," he replied with a flirtatious grin. "Call me, Kevin."

"Bingo!" she thought. "Well, Kevin, I'm sorry if I was a little overbearing. It hasn't been a very good 24 hours, as you can imagine." she said, coquettishly. *"I must be in shock"*, she thought. *"I'm flirting with an FBI agent who's here because someone tried to kill me."*

"A 'little' overbearing?" Kevin said, joining in, "I thought I was going to have to call for back up." He then turned to a quiet-as-a-mouse, Agent Forbes and said, "Slap the cuffs on her, Jim! If she tries to resist, don't hesitate to use your taser!"

Lisa and Kevin both laughed and drank in their most excitingly mutual, and awkward, feelings of attraction. Kevin finished with his short interview (there was nothing she could tell him that he didn't already know), rather inappropriately and clumsily got her telephone number (in case he had other questions) and left with an air of anticipation at the possibility of seeing her again.

●

"It is truly a work of art, Sadad." replied the President's closest friend and First Vice President Ali Rajsanjani. "We have seen only the implementation of the most trivial elements of our North American jihad and already the Americans are in a panic. Glorious!" he shouted, ending with a flourish.

Sadad-Hasan Habibi had been the Iranian president for only 6 months. Following the surprising death of Mahmoud Ahmadinejad to a cerebral hemorrhage, he had won the presidency in a landslide—or so it was announced. In actuality, he had received less than 37 percent of the Iranian Universal suffrage vote, but when the Supreme Leader and the Assembly of Experts for the Leadership— a congressional body of 86 Ayatollahs which select the Supreme Leader and supervise his activities—are in your corner, you have a very good chance of winning. Needless to say, President Habibi had the full support of Iran's version of the "Religious Right".

Just 2 months after assuming the presidency, Habibi introduced his master plan, which he had secretly promised to the Majlis—Iran's version of Parliament—in order to garner their support.

Like Ahmadinejad before him, Habibi and Rajsanjani are Twelver Shī'a's, or so it was thought. They believe that Muḥammad ibn al-Ḥasan al-Mahdī, born in 869AD and hidden away by Allah, will soon return as the twelfth Imam, or Mahdi, the savior of the world. They believe that this twelfth Imam will return with Isa (Jesus Christ) to destroy all the Christians and Jews and bring justice and peace to the world. It is said that the Mahdi will reappear when the world is in the throes of a great human conflict, and some, like Ahmadinejad and Habibi, seem to believe it is their duty to start such a conflict in order to expedite the Mahdi's return.

In a super-secret meeting of the Supreme Leader, Assembly of Experts for the Leadership and a few well-chosen Majlis, "Jihad America", as he called it, was wholeheartedly approved and fast tracked into action.

The plan was brilliantly uncomplicated, if eventful. It called for the temporary end to the planning of colossal made-for-TV events like 911 in favor of a more diverse approach. Why make complicated, risky and over burdensome preparations for one great assault, when hundreds of smaller, more "personal" attacks could create an even greater and more profound apprehension among the infidel horde? If fear and dread were brought to what the Americans called, John Q. Public, then the word "terrorist" would begin to take on the meaning it has for too long lacked. No one in America would be allowed to feel safe!

"Planes are coming down all over America," vice-president Rajsanjani continued, "At last count, there had been 27 planes destroyed with all passengers and five greatly damaged with some survivors. Along with the sniper attacks, which, if I'm not mistaken, have killed or injured over 125 people in these last two weeks, America is frantic."

President Habibi smiled at his old friend, beside himself with euphoric optimism. "Allah is feeding the infidels a most distasteful supper," he said, "Let us hope they still have room for dessert."

"Allah be praised, Sadad! God is great!" Ali cried out, literally.

Sadad was used to seeing tears in Ali's eyes. His emotions had been close to the surface since the death of his wife. He was glad to see his old friend so happy.

•

The President of the United States was enjoying a small respite from what had been a tumultuous proceeding 2 months. With hundreds of his fellow citizens falling victim to sniper attacks and thousands more killed in attacks on passenger airlines throughout the country the level of angst in the White House was palpable.

"Harry," the President quietly whispered to his Chief of Staff, Harold R. Cummings, "What the hell are we gonna do? Nobody's wants to fly for fear of being blown out of the sky; nobody wants to drive for fear of being shot while pumping gas (an activity shared by 47 sniper victims) and nobody wants to re-elect a President who can't protect the public from being killed while driving to the grocery store."

"Well, Mike," (formalities were dropped when President Hamilton was sailing on his yacht) "It's a hell of a mess, that's for sure, but the FBI says that short of stopping every automobile in the country and doing a body cavity search on everyone in the car, we don't have much chance of stopping this."

The President groaned.

"As far as the airplane attacks;" Harry went on, "Bernie (the director of the FBI, Bernard Freed) seems to think that they're running out of SAMs (surface-to-air missiles). There hasn't been an attack on an airplane in 2 days." Harry was being a bit facetious but he knew that the President preferred diffident humor to morose particulars. Besides, there really wasn't anything he or anyone else could do about it, at least, not yet.

Michael Hamilton reached into the cooler and drew out another Budweiser. It was a Sunday morning and he was sailing on the Chesapeake Bay with his best friend and most trusted personal aide. Ok, so maybe he'd get a little schnockered; what the hell! He'd probably be long sober by the time they got to shore, anyway. "It's a sad state of affairs when the good news is that no one has blown up an airliner in 2 days. Is there any other good news?" the President joked, "Are Jennifer Aniston and Brad Pitt getting back together?"

Harry and Michael shared a short but cheerless laugh before Harry looked up to see a small dinghy heading toward their boat. "Perhaps that's the good news you were waiting for, Mike." Harry said, tongue and cheek.

"Not likely, Harry." the President lamented, tossing his empty into the trash. "They don't usually send the director of CTD to the President's yacht to tell him things that will make him happy."

"Unless," Harry added, engendering the last laugh either of them would have for some time, "Jennifer Aniston and Brad Pitt really are getting back together."

"From your lips to God's ears," replied the President, sensing calamity's approach. "Let's see what he's got to say," he said, as they both arose and stepped to the portside ladder where Assistant Director Terry McCarthy was unsteadily climbing aboard "Katie's Clown"—President Hamilton's self-effacing name for his yacht.

President Michael Robert Hamilton was in the third year of his, hopefully, first term in office. He celebrated his seventy-third birthday just two weeks prior. Although, one of the oldest men ever elected to office, President Hamilton was in extraordinary physical shape. He drank moderately, didn't smoke, exercised every morning and, according to his mother, "came from good stock".

He was happily married to the only woman he'd ever really known, the former Katherine Ann Case, love of his life and the only person whom he trusted "unconditionally". The father of two, both of whom died untimely deaths, he was a man acquainted with grief and steeled by a hard life, not that he would complain; Katie wouldn't let him.

The FBI's Counterterrorism Division (CTD) is a division of the FBI that deals with terrorist threats inside the United States. The International Terrorism Operations Section (ITOS) I and II deal with international terrorists, with the latter focusing on Palestinian groups, Iran, Hezbollah, Syria and other global terrorist groups.

It had been understood from the beginning that Iran was the likely instigator of America's recent series of attacks— with the probable help of Russia and/or China—but proving it was the Iranian government and not some rogue Islamic entity was more problematic. Ballistics had confirmed that the weapons systems used to bring down the aircraft were of Russian origin, and likely Iranian employ; nevertheless, it was not a demonstrable fact, as yet.

"Mr. President," Assistant Director McCarthy began as he shook his hand, "I'm sorry to interrupt your holiday…"

The President interrupted him with, "The President doesn't get a holiday, Director McCarthy; didn't you know that?"

Assistant Director McCarthy was a very capable and trustworthy civil servant, but he was not what you would call a "funny guy". "Yes, Mr. President, I'm sure that's true. Nevertheless, I must inform you of a rather disturbing development in the financial community." McCarthy was a slender man whose short, black hair was combed over and glued to his head. His face was wan and splotched with "way-post-adolescent acne", leaving the President to wonder if this was the first time the sun had ever hit this man's face.

"Well, Director McCarthy," the President said as he turned and headed toward the yacht's cabin, "Why don't we go below and cool down, huh? Would you like a beer?"

"Oh no, Mr. President, I shouldn't." McCarthy stuttered. Both Harry and the President got the feeling that McCarthy not only shouldn't, but wouldn't and probably couldn't.

"Teetotaler, ah?" quipped the President.

McCarthy was in over his head. "Excuse me?" he replied, confused.

Hamilton eased off. "Nothing…what have you got for me?" he said as they all sat down at a central dining table.

Director McCarthy reached into his briefcase and withdrew a file marked, Top Secret. Every time someone took something out of a briefcase in front of the President, it said, Top Secret. *"Just once I'd like someone to take out a few pictures from a family vacation, or something."* the President reflected.

Director McCarthy began, "Mr. President, there has been a significant increase in online banking frauds perpetrated within the last month or so. I say, significant, but the word which more aptly describes it is, 'startling'."

The President perked up. "Doesn't this sort of thing go on all the time? What makes this so pronounced?"

"Well, sir, it's not just the frequency but the amounts that have taken a quite massive turn. Just within the last two weeks, we have seen amounts, either stolen or confusingly transferred, in excess of two trillion dollars." McCarthy put great emphasis on the last three words.

"Two Trillion dollars? How could that be?" Now President Hamilton's eyes were aglow.

"Well, sir, as you said, this kind of thing happens all the time, to the tune of millions per month, but this is rather titanic. It is clearly the work of a foreign government; highly focused on the United States with little or no disruption of Europe or our other allies."

"Director McCarthy," Harry inquired, "how can money just be taken away like that? Don't we have protection for this kind of thing?"

"We do indeed, Mr. Cummings, but as I'm sure you know it is an ongoing battle with everyone from the Chinese government to a 12 year old kid in his mother's basement. The moment a virus is defeated, another virus crops up. There can never be an end to it, per se, but so far we've held the high ground," McCarthy finished shyly, "as it were."

McCarthy went on to explain that the usual scenario involves a company employee—usually without their knowledge—clicking on an infected e-mail or visiting an infected website. If the employee has the ability to transfer funds, the virus simply steals the logons for the company's bank accounts. Once that information is compromised, it is a tiny step to making wire transfers.

He went on to explain that not all the monetary fund transfers were for the purpose of thievery. In fact, over half of the monetary amount had been for the obvious purpose of financial chaos, in that; it was transferred into other company or citizen's accounts. This led to the obvious conclusion of espionage; this was the work of a government whose intent was subterfuge. Thousands of companies believe that money paid to them has not been paid and thousands of citizens seem to have amassed fortunes overnight; most being completely oblivious until their next month's bank statement.

Who owns what?

Who owes what?

President Hamilton looked over at Harry and with a sardonic tone said, "Well, if Jennifer and Brad don't get back together soon, we're all done for."

Terry McCarthy just looked bewildered.

"Well", the President thought, *"I guess that puts the kybosh on this little excursion."* "Harry," the President said to his friend, "Can I get a rain check?"

Harry smiled at Michael Hamilton and gave him one of his patented smirks, "I'm ok with it, Mike, but the Secret Servicemen are going to go ape shit. They need the vacation more than we do."

"I don't doubt that at all, Harry," the President said in all seriousness, "Maybe when we get to the bottom of this, we can go on a nice hunting trip; I'm sure they'd enjoy that."

The President picked up the phone and informed the Secret Service that his (and their) short, but sweet vacation was over. It was time to head back to Washington.

Chapter Three

"Agent O'Brien, can I see you for a moment, please?" the disembodied voice insisted. When Special Agent in Charge Sam Waters requested your presence in his office, you did not delay. As bosses go, he was tolerable, but boss he was and it was not something you'd likely forget.

"Yes, sir?" Kevin said as he entered Agent Waters' austere office, "You wanted to see me?"

Waters motioned toward one of two Government Issue, olive-green metal chairs in front of his similarly government-issue desk. "Sit down, O'Brien, I've got something to discuss with you."

Waters was a large man. He was the kind of man that had physically piqued in high school. There wasn't enough hair on his head to have use of a comb, but the heavy-black hair on his arms and chest could go up in flames at any second, especially with the sparks that constantly fell from the cigarettes of the chain-smoking Agent in Charge. He seemed to possess all the stereotypical mannerisms of the gruff, tough boss; like an old, ex-military drill sergeant; however, as much as he tried to put up the icy exterior, Kevin saw that he was a good man at his core and he was actually quite fond of him.

Kevin sat down, unsure as to which direction the meeting would take; with Waters you could never tell. He could be promoting you or telling you that you were fired. His personal assortment of emotional expressions was not exceedingly wide-ranging.

"I received a call from Assistant Director McCarthy this morning. McCarthy, in case you don't know, is the director of ITOS II. He's taking the lead on this terrorist business." Waters was almost matter-of-fact about it. "For some reason," he continued, "and one that I can't fathom, I might add, he has requested that you fly up to Washington for a briefing."

Kevin was more surprised than Waters. "A briefing, sir? What kind of briefing?"

"You know as much as I do, O'Brien. You're flight leaves at 0800 tomorrow. I'd suggest that you brush up on all the recent terrorist activities as much as possible. You can get most of the info from Carolyn (the office's senior-most secretary and the one with the highest security clearance).

"Sir, if I may ask, why me? What possible reason could they have for requesting me?"

Waters smiled. "Like I said, kid, you know as much as I do. Get the info from Carolyn and take the rest of the day off to familiarize yourself with whatever data there is."

Kevin got up and headed toward the door.

"Hey kid," Waters' voice was raised, "Make us proud!"

Kevin got the files—the two boxes of files—and packed them into his yellow 1999 Toyota Celica. Kevin refused to have one of those "new-fangled" cars from the 21st century; most people who knew him assumed that he felt the same way about clothing.

Feeling a bit frightened at the prospect of a briefing in Washington, Kevin wished for something to ease his anxiety. Booze was out of the question; he would need to be at his bright and shiny best for what could be a seminal day in his life. He didn't know any women or he'd…wait a minute.

Kevin reached for his notebook; the one he used to jot down things he wanted to remember. *"Let's see,"* he thought, *"when was that sniper shooting? Oh yeah, here it is…Dr. Lisa Martin."*

•

When her cell phone started humming, Dr. Lisa Martin had just finished reading her third CT Abdomen/Pelvis in the last 5 minutes. She was well paid for her medical knowledge but rued the monotony of incessantly routine interpretations. Even the most esteemed and lucrative rut is still a rut, she thought.

How many times can one say, "The heart, lungs, and mediastinum are within normal limits for the patient's age", or "No significant visualized abnormalities"? She could say it in her sleep, and had many times. Not that she was complaining, it just seemed that after seven years as a working radiologist things had become routine; predictable in some way. Lisa knew, for the most part, the entire day that lay ahead of her before she had had her morning coffee.

As a radiologist, she was the one that all the other physicians looked to for guidance. She was the interpreter of all the X-ray, CAT scan, MRI, Ultrasound, PET scan and Nuclear Medicine modalities that were an everyday part of modern medical diagnoses. She was earning well over five-hundred thousand dollars a year, highly respected in her field as a virtual phenom (having graduated med-school and finishing her residency before the age of 23) and supermodel beautiful. Only an American could complain about a life like that, she had often lamented, guiltily. Yet, sad she was; unfulfilled she remained.

"Hello, this is Lisa," she said, having seen the name Kevin O'Brien on her caller ID but not recognizing it.

"Lisa, my name is Kevin O'Brien. I'm the agent who interviewed you the day after your...incident with the sniper."

Lisa's eyes lit up. She had indeed remembered Agent O'Brien—though perhaps not his name—and had spent many a wandering notion on scenarios with him as a central character. Nevertheless, it would not do well to advertize the point. "Well," she said, "I can see you still have an economy with words, Agent O'Brien. Are you calling to warn me of impending danger or are you still upset that your little minion was never able to 'slap the cuffs on me', as you put it?"

"Oh, now I wasn't all that dreadful, was I?" he said. Kevin thought Lisa was superb. What a quick mind, she had. "Actually, this is a personal call, and I seem to remember asking you to call me, Kevin. Am I interrupting anything?"

"Nothing that I'm not thrilled to be interrupted from," she said, "particularly, if it's personal."

"Well," Kevin initiated, *"might as well swing for the fence"*, he thought, "I'm leaving for Washington tomorrow morning. It's just a briefing but I'm very nervous about it. I guess I just wanted some company and I couldn't think of anyone I'd rather spend time with than you." Kevin paused a moment and added, "I suppose this is a little presumptuous of me, but I thought you and I really hit it off and I've thought about you a lot since then. Would you consider having dinner with me, tonight?"

Lisa was dumbstruck with awe. She was not sure why, but this took her completely off guard. Nevertheless, she was delighted. "Kevin, that's one of the sweetest things I've heard in a long time. I'm not sure how my presence will serve to alleviate your anxiety over your meeting, but yes, I'd love to have dinner with you."

Kevin was overjoyed. "I'll pick you up at seven, if that's ok?"

"Don't you think I'd better give you my address?" Lisa said.

"Welcome to the FBI, Lisa." Kevin said with a flourish. "I'll see you at seven." And he hung up.

•

Hamid Kazemi was at the end of his rope. His boss was more than his usual aggravating self that day; besides, Hamid had troubles at home that prayed on his mind. His wife, Suha was becoming more and more Americanized by the day. Her penchant for "empowerment", as she put it, was becoming more worrisome all the time.

Hamid had worked on an assembly line at the Ford Motor Company in Detroit, Michigan since he had come to America ten years before. It was not a complicated job, but it was taxing; the assembly line kept moving all the time and you always had to keep up. In that sense, it was quite stressful. He was one of many Muslims who worked at Ford but he had always had the distinct impression that his boss didn't like or trust them; nothing overt, but you could see it in his eyes and sense it by his tone.

Now, at least, the work day was over and he was headed for home. He and Suhu lived in Dearborn, the city many call "America's Muslim Capital": Muslims make up about 40% of Dearborn's 100,000 residents. It was a good life but Hamid was troubled by his wife's recent desire to get a job. He could feel that the temptations of America were becoming more than she could handle. Most of the Muslims he knew were only Muslims in the general sense. They went to Mosque but didn't live their lives according to Mohammed's teaching. He did not want that for himself or his family. *"Don't even get me started on my children"*, he thought, just as his cell phone went off.

"Hello," he said, distracted by his thoughts.

"Is this Hamid Kazemi?" the voice on the other end said.

"Yes, it is." Hamid answered.

"The Detroit Lions are a sure bet to win this Sunday. You can still get tickets online," the voice stated. Then the line went dead.

Hamid immediately called Suhu to tell her he would be late for dinner. What he understood; however, was that he would never see her or his children again.

Hamid was what the CIA would call a "sleeper agent". He was sent here 10 years ago to blend into the American culture and await instructions that would "activate" him.

His instructions were simple: Upon hearing the correct code, as he just had, he was to proceed immediately to an internet café, a commercial enterprise that gave him access to computers and the internet without any ties. Naturally, Hamid had a number of suitable establishments in mind at all times. The one he chose on this occasion was just outside Dearborn; it was called, Carla's Coffee and Computer World.

After paying a nominal amount to use a computer, and buying what Americans called "coffee", Hamid logged on and went to an innocuous pre-determined website where he received coded instructions regarding his assignment. He knew it would be big because "deep-cover jihad", as it was known in Lebanon, was far too expensive and time consuming for use as a minor annoyance; he'd always known that when the day came he would kill scores of infidels and most likely die in glory. He was not only prepared, but considering the way his life was going, he was looking forward to his seventy-two virgins. They would not want a job.

•

In the over three months since the first sniper attack on September 16, America had settled into a kind of controlled panic. To date: 325 people had been randomly shot by snipers, killing 286; 72 planes had been attacked by surface-to-air missiles while either attempting to take off or land, resulting in over 13,000 deaths. Hundreds more were injured.

The only snipers to have been "apprehended", killed themselves rather than be taken into custody, and in a variety of ways: gunshot, cyanide pills and high-speed automobile "accidents". In all, seven were dead.

Only one of the "missile-men"—as the press was pleased to call them— had been apprehended. He was of little help to authorities, as most terrorist "cell" members tend to have knowledge of only their part in the plot.

With most Americans deathly frightened of airplane travel—for good reason—the airline industry sank into a financial and technical morass. The cost of patrolling the perimeter of all the airports was prohibitive. With the over 70% drop in flight patrons over the last two months, most, if not all American carriers were on the verge of collapse; saved only by the international fares.

The financial state of affairs was unraveling with alacrity. With American corporations, as well as citizens, depending on digital monies, trust in the accuracy of debits and credits was essential. Without the assuredness of "who owns what and who owes what" the stock market went belly up. European, Asian, Arab and even South American interests were withdrawing from American companies in droves. The G-8, minus the United States, determined to make the new Euro and Yen into the new reserve currency of the world; news that could prove catastrophic.

The power of the dollar comes from its position as the world's reserve currency. If Germany wants to buy a barrel of oil, for instance, it must do so in dollars. That means they must buy dollars with Euros in order to make the transaction. This power has always given America the ability to keep oil prices down. In addition, if another country's money were to devaluate, the cost of buying dollars (in order to buy the oil) would increase. If American's money devaluates, it simply prints more money; no other country can do this because no other country has dollars. America's current financial crisis was looking to make the stock market crash of 1929 look benign, by comparison.

Both blue and white-collar crime had skyrocketed. Every Wall Street financier with a lack of capital and a lesser abundance of morals had found newer and more lucrative ways to swindle the public. With unemployment at 28% and rising, people who would not normally have even contemplated criminal activity were jumping in with both feet. Domestic violence was rising, juvenile delinquency was rampant and drug and alcohol abuse was the order of the day—what better time to escape reality than when reality sucked.

•

Kevin and Lisa had become more than fast friends. The night they spent together before Kevin left for Washington was like a tonic for them both. Since his return, they had spoken on the phone everyday and seen each other as much as possible, given the circumstances.

Kevin's meeting with Assistant Director McCarthy was as enigmatic as it was thrilling. Apparently, Director Freed requested him because of his sparkling record, as well as his contribution with a previous case involving a Muslim terrorist-leaning Professor at the University of South Florida. Assistant Director McCarthy said that the Director told him, "We need a young man with a level head on this one. I liked the way the kid handled himself on that case." Kevin was flattered to say the least, until McCarthy cautioned him not to "get a big head" over it. "The Director may be looking for someone to use later on as a scapegoat," he reminded him.

Nonetheless, Kevin felt this was his big chance to shine. The stakes could not be higher and the country was truly in need of some relief. Even a minor victory against these terrorists would be a welcome occasion for a despondent and worn-out populace; he meant to give it to them.

Kevin was assigned as "point man", nationally. He would work out of his Tampa office but oversee the coordination of all relevant matters that pertained to what was believed to be the Iranian threat. Kevin was promoted to Special Agent in Charge and given complete hegemony pertaining to the case, now officially designated as, "Maelstrom".

His fellow agents in Tampa were quite impressed by Kevin's promotion and added responsibility, quickly showing their newfound respect by slipping a whoopee cushion under his seat pad and gluing his office equipment to the ceiling.

Two weeks later Kevin had reorganized the case in order to maximize his agent's efficiency. He selected three agents from his office and ordered 2 others reassigned to the Tampa office under his command: Agent Diane Austin— eminently capable and highly organized; Agent Douglas Bennett—a real pro and always a calming, stable influence, and for good measure, Agent Jim Forbes—ok, maybe Kevin was trying to throw him a bone but Jimmy was sharp as a tack and eager to prove himself. There is a lot to be said for an agent who is "hungry".

The two "outside" agents Kevin requested were Robert "Bobby" Wang from the San Francisco office—an expert on weapons systems of all kinds and Ali Hussein from the New York office—expert on Muslim religion and culture; hailing from Iran.

The Tampa office was large enough for Kevin and his team to commandeer a five-room section for use as a command center. Diane and Doug shared one office; Ali, Bobby and Jimmy shared another. Their new secretary, Jennifer, who oversaw all communications, had a small office with an even smaller waiting room; Kevin's office abutted hers. There was also a moderate sized conference room for meetings and presentations.

The group quickly broke Maelstrom down into categories of crimes from which to better approach: sniper attacks, airline attacks and computer fraud. After a couple of weeks with all six of them reworking the case from many angles, some basic concepts had arisen.

These snipers could not have been recent émigrés to America. They must have established residence, if not citizenship itself in order to be enlisted for such work. Each assassin must have a home base from which to travel back and forth without suspicion.

Ali was quick to chime in: "These men have jobs and probably families; I'd bet on it. What they do takes more than just financing; it takes stability, or at least the appearance of it. This is probably why most of the shootings take place on a weekend; they work during the week!"

"Yeah, but how many people leave their homes every weekend? You'd think the neighbors would begin to notice something like that, particularly if they were Muslims,"

Doug Bennett added, quickly glancing at Ali and saying, "No offense, Ali."

Ali had obviously dealt with this kind of thing before. "It's ok, Doug, I know better than anyone that we are looking for Muslims; I'm looking for them too. Please remember; I have rejected Islam and have embraced Christianity. They may be my race, but they are no longer my people."

"I know we're all glad that you're here, Ali," Diane assured him and then addressed the room. "I believe we have the right angle, gentlemen. What we have to do is focus on what is sure to be an anomaly in at least 16 neighborhoods nationwide (16 now that eight assassins had been killed). How many Muslim men are leaving their homes every weekend? If the public knew what to look for they could be of enormous aid in catching these shooters."

"I agree," Bobby said, "We should get the word out as soon as possible. The American public is already wary of Muslims, especially in areas with high Muslim populations. We'll get a lot of overly suspicious psychos calling every five minutes but it could lead to something."

"And remember," Kevin added, "these shooters don't seem to have been replaced. The areas in which they were killed have been largely assassination-free. That also lends credence to Ali's assertion that these men have homes in the areas in which they hunt. It just wasn't so easy to replace them.

"Alright, moving on," Kevin said, "These missile-men are a different story. The airline attacks were pretty willy-nilly, weren't they?"

Diane looked up from her notes. "That's true, gentlemen, they might not be so conspicuous. The airplanes have come down in no discernable pattern, either chronologically or geographically."

"We do have the specs for the SAMs, though." Bobby answered, "They are IGLA fire and forget systems: Russian made; 72mm Stingers and all traced to an arms deal in Iran. They were shipped into New Orleans and transported throughout the country by automobile. I believe we've put the kibosh on any future shipments, though."

Agent Robert "Bobby" Wang was the group's weapons expert. He was born in Chinatown, San Francisco, USA, raised by his step-father and deserted by his crack-addicted mother, who'd left her husband and son for the exotic life of crack-whoredom. Bobby never saw her again. His biological father was of no concern to him and, frankly, he hoped he'd never meet him, if he was still alive; if either of them were.

His step-father, a former gang member and recovering addict, himself, had raised Bobby with the love and nurturing that gave him the self respect and personal aspiration to stay on the straight and narrow until he could eventually follow his childhood dream of becoming an agent of the FBI.

Now, 37 years old and excruciatingly single, Bobby leapt at the chance to fly to Tampa and join the newly formed, Maelstrom Task Force. With his expertise in weapons platforms, and what his instructors described as "a cool hand", Bobby Wang was on top of Kevin's wish list when he put his task force together.

"Sir, if I may?" young Forbes squeaked.

"Go ahead, Jimmy, I need all the input I can get." Kevin said.

"Well, it seems to me, if Agent Wang is correct and we have irrefutable proof of Iran's culpability in this matter...well, it would seem to be an actionable offense. The President would be within his international rights to launch an attack on Iran...or, at least threaten it."

Kevin looked to Agent Wang and asked, "Well, Bobby, are we irrefutable?"

"I'm not sure we're actionable, at this point, Kevin, but I think we're close." Bobby said with a hint of insecurity.

"Jimmy, what have we got on the internet fraud?" Kevin said, readdressing Agent Forbes, the computer geek. "That may be the most dangerous problem we face. I cannot believe the Iranians are capable of such a sophisticated computer swindle. They must be getting help!"

"Well, sir," Jimmy said, "I was just about to address that conundrum." The other team members subtly glanced at each other, as if to say, *"What's up with this guy?"*

"I believe you are correct," Jimmy continued, unaware of their quiet communications, "the Iranians are far too backward to propagate such a convoluted virus. It is obvious that they have employed the services of a rather stylish systems hacker—perhaps to their detriment."

Diane jumped in. "What do you mean, 'to their detriment'?"

Jimmy rolled his eyes a bit, suggesting curiosity. "Well, had this virus not been so…entailed, we might have had a harder time tracking it to its source…"

Again, Diane broken in. "You mean we've got a lead on the virus's origins?"

"I would say," began Jimmy—he was surprisingly confident; clearly in his element, "that we have much more than a lead, Agent Austin; we may well have a definitive source."

The sound of five people simultaneously inhaling has a palpable air. Their next question was obvious: Who?

"This may be a bit disturbing, but I see the obvious use of the 'pinyin', the system that the Chinese use to transcribe Chinese characters into the Roman alphabet. This could only have originated from the Chinese government. Their computer systems use the Cangjie input method, which assigns different "roots" to each key on a standard computer keyboard. I'm afraid they could only have come from the Chinese. The results are quite conclusive." Jimmy finished with an air of haughty snobbery. It was not intended, as such; nevertheless, it did not always endear him to those who did not know him.

Diane looked from Jimmy to Kevin with an expression of staggered, if not dumbfounded feelings. "That doesn't make any sense, Kevin. Are we expected to believe that the Chinese have picked this time, when America is under terrorist siege by what must be an Iranian plot, to launch a cyber-attack? I can't imagine the Chinese and the Iranians coordinating such an enormous venture, and even if they could, why would they?"

Bobby chimed in, "Maybe the Chinese have had this computer thing under wraps for a while and were waiting for the right moment to activate it. What better time than when we're reeling from a series of terrorist attacks? Maybe they're just opportunists?"

"That may be," Ali added, "but it all seems a little too coincidental, doesn't it? It also makes the Chinese come across as conspirators in the terrorist attacks, which could conceivably lead to nuclear war. The Chinese aren't stupid. If they wanted to launch a cyber-attack on the United States, I don't think they would make it so obvious; they would want plausible deniability."

"Nevertheless," Jimmy said, "here it is. Have someone else check it out if you don't believe me."

"Nobody doubts your capability, Jimmy," Diane said, "but it could be possible that someone wanted to make it look like the Chinese in order to throw us off their scent." She looked at Agent Forbes, "Isn't that possible?" she added.

Jimmy didn't look at Diane. He didn't look at anyone. He just stared at the ceiling and said, after a slow exhale, "I suppose it's possible," he said.

"Gentlemen," Kevin said, then after an appreciative nod to Diane, "Lady," he sighed, "I think our lives just got a whole lot more complicated. Let's take the rest of the day off. If I look like the rest of you do, then it's clear that I need a break."

Chapter Four

For many years, Christmas had not been much of a time of celebration for Lisa. While she did like the general atmosphere of the season and had always had a fondness for the old Christmas movies, the lack of family had made the holidays a bit glum.

As a child, however, things were much different. Her father would always make Christmas into a memorable occasion by creating "Christmas Corners", as he called them, for both she and her little sister Mary—yes, her name was Mary Martin; the Peter Pan references went on ad-nauseam. An older brother, Joe, had died when she was very young; her parents had never spoken much about him. Lisa assumed it was just too painful for them and never belabored the point.

These "Christmas Corners" were delightful memories for Lisa. Her father would fill their stockings during the night (after they had fallen asleep) which were then nailed to the bedpost. This would give them something to do until Mom and Dad decided to get up on Christmas morning. The rule was absolute: No one goes downstairs until Dad says it's ok!

However, when he did give the ok, both she and Mary would race downstairs to see all of their presents neatly arranged in separate corners: Lisa's corner and Mary's corner. What made it so exciting for them was the fact that Dad would never wrap anything. There was never the obligatory "opening of the presents, one by one". All of their dolls, doll houses, toy kitchen appliances, games, bicycles and yes, even their clothes would be neatly arranged and "set up" if the need be. This made their first glance after descending the stairs a moment of pure, unadulterated avarice. But, what the heck, it was Christmas.

Shortly after her graduation from medical school, her parents and Mary were killed in a car accident on Interstate 4 at the junction of I-275; generally referred to by Tampa residents as "Malfunction Junction." Lisa always tried to avoid the area whenever possible, taking the Cross-town instead. For Lisa, Christmas' appeal died in the accident.

Now, however, Lisa was beginning to warm up to the season. The reason was as obvious as the strong but gentile blue eyes on Kevin's face. She was unquestionably in love with the man she referred to as, "honey", while he called her his "little tweety pie". They were both aware of how syrupy it all sounded, but such was uncontaminated love.

"I don't suppose you're going to tell me what's in the package?" Lisa coyly queried.

Kevin looked down at the face of an angel and said, "Only if you tell me what's in the back of your trunk that's so mysterious I can't look inside."

"I haven't wrapped it yet," she said, "I've never been much of a Christmas wrapper. I'm hopeless." She giggled like a little girl. She felt warm and protected in his arms as they lay together on the couch, the fireplace aflame before them.

"Lisa," Kevin gently whispered, "I can't believe how happy I am right now. I have only known you for about three months and I feel as comfortable and as trusting toward you as I have ever felt, even toward my mother. I keep thinking that the alarm is going to go off and I'm going to wake up and you'll be gone."

"Oh, that's so sweet," Lisa cooed, "but don't you worry, I unplugged the damn thing. I plan on keeping you asleep for as long as I live." She slowly turned onto her back and with a smile that would light up any man's libido, said,

"Speaking of which, why don't we go up to the bedroom. I'm suddenly getting a great desire to remind myself of why I'm so happy."

Kevin was never quite at ease with Lisa's beauty. He had always had an easy time with women; never really feeling uncomfortable or timid; yet, Lisa made his knees weak. It was something he was willing to live with. "You go turn down the bed," he said, "I'll turn out the lights and get the whips and chains."

Lisa leapt to her feet, sat her wineglass on the coffee table and said, "You've got a deal, mister." As she headed for the stairs, she turned and added, "Don't forget the midgets!"

•

Ali Hussein's wife was an American beauty. It had been her influence that led him to fall in love with America, and with its "decadent" culture. Ali, like few Muslins (at least, it seemed that way to him), could separate the mindlessness of American popular culture with the American lifestyle of home, family and God; the latter being the real bugaboo.

You see, Ali, although "officially" Muslim had never really given much credence to Allah or the Koranic teachings. He had avoided the Madrasahs—Islamic schools that do not necessarily teach anti-Western rhetoric, but in the case of the one in his home town of Qom, Iran, did— thanks to a forward thinking father who was fascinated by the West. He, of course, followed the Islamic way of life in public in order to avoid any "difficulties", but when the opportunity came to flee to America, by way of England, he took it with all speed.

Ali became a New Yorker and fell in love with all things American. He grew up and went to school in the Bronx, graduated from NYU and then signed up for the Academy in Quantico, Virginia. His American life was not a particularly happy one until he met a woman.

Karen Hussein was a petite brunette with chestnut brown eyes that, to Ali, were incapable of deceit or malice. She was just as she appeared, and she appeared to Ali like an angel of God. This was the woman who had, he believed, saved him from a life of selfishness and emptiness. It was through Karen's counsel and a few visits to the Community Christian Church on Broadway Avenue in New York that had Ali not only embracing Christianity, but becoming "born-again", to boot.

To someone who had known only anger and self-interest, the concept of living for others was a novel one. He had found that it worked just as well in practice; personally experiencing the inner peace and joy that came with caring for others. Needless to say, Ali was very happy.

"When are you coming home, darling?" Karen whined into her new iPhone. "I miss you so much that I can't sleep at night."

Ali felt a lump in his gut. "I know, sweetheart, but you know I'm involved with trying to stop these terrorists. I can't leave until we've rid the country of them all!"

Ali could tell that Karen was hurting; so was he. He and she had rarely been apart for more than 8-12 hours. It was an onerous burden on them both. "I'll tell you what," Ali suggested, "why don't you fly down to Tampa. We can stay in Clearwater beach; it'll be like a second honeymoon," he added exuberantly.

Karen hadn't heard a more exciting and appealing idea in her whole life. "Are you serious? Could I really?" she said, her voice becoming more falsetto, as it usually did when she was excited.

"I'll make you a deal, sweetheart," Ali said, "I'll make reservations at the Hyatt Regency on Clearwater beach. They have these nice little Tiki huts where you can wile away the day listening to a steel band. It's great!"

This was the answer to Karen's dream. "Oh, sweetie, that's the best news I've heard in…" Karen didn't finish her statement. She, along with 500,000 other New Yorkers were instantly vaporized from the fervent heat of two backpack nuclear devices detonated just 36 feet from her location on Broadway.

Those that didn't die instantaneously would die soon enough from radiation burns, heat and later, radiation poisoning. None were expecting this to be their last day on earth…except one, Hamid Kazemi, of Dearborn, Michigan. He and his fellow backpacking-buddy Mustafa were taking in the sights of Broadway with a bent toward seeing them destroyed; they succeeded brilliantly.

With a simultaneous detonation of two 5 kiloton "backpack" nuclear bombs, Hamid and Mustafa had essentially ended New York's existence, certainly as a major world city.

For those not incinerated at the speed of light, a blinding, split second flash foreshadowed a quickly approaching death. Expanding rapidly, the fireball vaporized anything within 500 feet of ground zero with temperatures reaching 10,000,000° C. The World Trade Center, by comparison, probably never exceeded 5,000° C.

Lower Manhattan was a radioactive wasteland, never again to be inhabited by a living thing.

The news reports of the attack came quickly, but not from the usual sources. ABC, NBC, CBS, Fox News and a multitude of other media outlets were no more. Twitterers, tweeters and texters were the first to get the news out, albeit from a distance, as cell phone coverage was necessarily interrupted.

A frantically scrambling Media Empire whose connection with its "mother ship" was abruptly severed began a frenzied attempt to reattach the umbilical, to no success. Within a half hour, surrounding areas in New Jersey and Connecticut were broadcasting images of the mushroom cloud hanging over Manhattan like an already fallen Sword of Damocles.

Ali was unable to reconnect with his wife and completely oblivious of the attack. He assumed that the cell phone coverage was down for some technical reason; things like that happened all the time. He plopped down in his La-Z-Boy recliner and flipped on the TV. Channel 8, WFLA was just beginning to receive footage of the conflagration.

•

In the weeks and months that followed the devastating attack on New York, all the resources of the Federal Government were activated, mostly for evacuation, clean-up and prevention of future attacks. The damage to America was incredible!

Besides the obvious loss of life—over 3 million people, including many nationally known politicians, news people, movie stars and sports stars—were the horrific financial consequences of the destruction of Wall Street.

After 911, the American economy had taken a 1 trillion dollar hit; and that was because 2 buildings fell down. This was Wall Street itself. The monetary tribulation that would ensue was mind-boggling. The media capital of the world had been reduced to a pile of rubble, both literally and figuratively. Millions of Americans, as well as those still foolish enough to invest in America, had lost everything.

The words Armageddon, End of Days and Apocalypse were being thrown around like never before. Prices skyrocketed, crime increased to new highs, riots were commonplace in most of America's larger cities, sporting events and television were almost totally gone from American culture and unemployment jumped to a frightening 35%.

Fringe religious groups, as well as many mainstream churches were warning of the end of the world. The Anti-Christ was spotted behind every tree. Many cult groups sprang up within weeks to "guide" their confused followers to a new enlightenment; many requiring the blissful peace that only suicide could afford them.

Nevertheless, there was a certain sanity that began to re-infuse itself into what the media would later call "the Neo-Empathetic Age". Much of the superfluous nature of modern American culture had been set aside. The mind-numbingly dim-witted entertainment was being rejected due to the serious nature of the nation's woes, and a new sense of community swept across the land.

Neighborhood watch groups were active in most areas, church attendance was exponentially elevated, television— what was left of it—was airing, along with news, weather and religious programming, many shows designed to teach self reliance. The seemingly ironic twist to what appeared to be America's downfall was an ever increasing sense of patriotism. The general feeling seemed to be one of righteous indignation towards whomever or whatever had caused this. The United States government was put on notice by an ever serious and attentive public: Find out who's doing this and stop them.

Kevin and his team were, of course, unprepared for the attack on New York. Ali had been a basket case for weeks, but had recently found the strength to continue—if only to make sure that no one else felt the pain he was now going through. Kevin urged him to take some time off, but Ali would have none of it. He intended to redouble his efforts to root out those responsible for murdering his wife and the millions of others who had been as innocent as she had been. The very idea that it was the work of his native country of Iran filled him with anger and shame. A vacation was the last thing on his mind, besides it gave him something to do instead of sitting around thinking of his wife.

Lisa was needed, seemingly, on a continuous basis at Tampa General. Accidents, illnesses, altercations, suicide attempts and a variety of pseudo sicknesses (usually for the purpose of acquiring drugs) were inundating the hospital, 24/7. She and Kevin spoke via cell phone often but rarely got the opportunity to see each other in person.

The Tampa FBI office was buzzing with activity, most of which was unrelated to the terrorist attacks. Sam Waters was running himself ragged with calls involving everything from bank robberies to kidnappings—desperate people were trying anything to make a buck.

As Kevin, Diane, Ali and Doug were going over some data pertaining to Maelstrom; a rather odd phone call came in.

Due to the enormity of the situation, the President had authorized the FBI to not only monitor incoming phone calls but trace them as well. It was a preemptive measure in case someone called with information but chose not to identify themselves; no stone could be left unturned.

When Maelstrom's secretary, Jennifer, alerted Kevin to the incoming call she prefaced the announcement by stating that the origin of the call's whereabouts was being obscured, by what she could not say.

"That's interesting," Kevin said with raised eyebrows, "Put the call through."

Kevin's phone chirped. After waiting the obligatory amount of time—even the FBI doesn't want to appear too anxious—he picked up the receiver and identified himself. "This is Agent O'Brien, may I help you?"

The voice on the other end of the phone belonged to either an elderly man in respiratory distress or Kevin was getting his first x-rated phone call. As luck would have it, it was the former. "Agent O'Brien, forgive me for jamming your tracking equipment, but for now I'd like to remain...unidentified."

Kevin was intrigued. Call it a gut instinct, but he felt he should listen to what this man had to say. "Well, sir, what can I do for you?"

"I have come across some information that may be helpful to your case. I'd like to be of assistance, if I may," the apparently elderly man announced, with some trouble.

Kevin wasn't going to pass up anything in the way of information from any source; nonetheless, he was wary of this man's knowledge about a situation that was not generally known to the public. "What case is that, sir?" Kevin replied, then, sensing the trouble the man was having, added, "Are you alright?" Kevin was genuinely concerned over the man's breathing patterns.

"I'm not in the best of health, Agent O'Brien, but all that can be done has been done." He paused a moment to take a raspy breath before continuing. Kevin could sense not to interrupt. "Please don't ask me how I know the things I know. Suffice it to say, I am an extremely well-informed person. The confidentiality of the source of this information is the price I will require of you for its disclosure. Does that sound reasonable?" he asked, sounding more and more like an approaching train.

"It's a bit unnerving to keep calling you, Sir. What name may I use in our conversation?" Kevin asked, amiably. He didn't want to scare this guy off.

After another hard breath, he said, "Call me, Deep Throat, for obvious reasons. Now, let me continue before I need another breathing treatment."

Kevin remained silent in deference. Moments later he would be glad he did. Deep Throat, or whatever his name was, was about to drop a bomb.

"I'll call you Kevin, if that's ok?" he began, "Kevin, I have unmistakable proof that the Iranian government is directly responsible for the sniper attacks, the attacks of the airlines, and the nuclear attack in New York. The computer attacks were not of their doing, but I believe they were well aware of those who perpetrated them. Would you like to hear more?" the man said as though dangling meat in front of a hungry dog.

The call was now on intercom so the whole office could hear. All were stunned, but all knew to remain silent. Kevin assented with a nervous anxiety. "I very much want to hear more, Deep…I don't think I can keep calling you Deep Throat with a straight face. I'm going back to, 'Sir', if you don't mind," Kevin said, "Now, sir; I'd very much like to hear more and to see the proof…which I'm sure you have. Am I right?"

"You are quite correct, Kevin," the man said, adding, "Of course, I wish to see you in person. I wish to see you, you alone, and no one else. Is that agreed?"

"Agreed," Kevin nodded to the phone, "Where may I find you?"

"After I hang up the phone, which my health requires of me," he began, "call that lovely lady-friend of yours, Lisa. Tell her to reach into the right pocket of her white doctor's jacket. The instructions are written there. I hope to see you soon, Kevin."

The line went dead.

The fear that entered Kevin's heart was unknown to him. He'd never much worried about his own safety, even during gunplay, but the idea that this unknown man, with obviously powerful tentacles was involving Lisa, brought Kevin's ire to a boil.

Immediately, he phoned Lisa at the hospital. She was ok, she said, and was unaware of any contact with anyone all day, save for her patients. After Kevin told her where to look for the instructions she reached into her right pocket and found an envelope marked, "Agent Kevin O'Brien, F.B.I.". Kevin hurriedly left for the hospital.

Chapter Five

Since becoming the Iranian President, Sadad-Hasan Habibi had become very popular with those he needed most. The Supreme Leader, in particular, was quite taken with Habibi's "devout and faithful leadership", as he called it. This made President Habibi's relationship with the Majli's—Iran's version of Parliament, and the Assembly of Experts—86 "virtuous and learned" clerics elected for eight-year terms, a much smoother one than would otherwise exist.

Habibi, however, was not the pious devotee of Allah that he had led everyone to believe. In fact, he didn't even believe in God; his lack of faith buoyed by what he considered to be "obvious" proof of evolution. Nonetheless, he was the epitome of faithful Islamic virtue, holding steadfast to the Five Pillars of Islam: His testimony of Allah's and Muhammad's rightful place in worship; the offering of daily prayers; the payment of Zakat (charity); the Hajj (at least once in a lifetime Pilgrimage to Mecca—he had done it twice) and the observation of the Ramadan fast. Even his best friend and 1st vice-president Ali Rajsanjani had no idea of Sadad's faithlessness.

Always suspecting that he was not alone in his "realistic view of the world", Sadad Habibi was the consummate politician. He told people what they wanted to hear and did what was expected of him. This seemingly Western political trait was publicly unknown in the Islamic world but Sadad thought it was probably prevalent in all of international politics. The problem was; if you wanted to get anywhere, politically, in the Islamic world, you'd better be sure that everyone was convinced that you loved Allah, hated Jews and wanted to kill Americans. Habibi was batting a thousand.

Though he was President of Iran, Sadad lived a modest lifestyle (naturally), in a simple two-story home. His wife, ChalipA, was the only person in the world who was aware of his true point of view. In fact, it was one of the things that drew him to her; she was an independent thinker.

They had no children, but ChalipA was always feeding the poor or comforting the bereaved. Both she and Sadad lived lives that smacked of Godly faith and charity; however, ChalipA was the only one whose actions came from a kind heart.

The recent death of Ali Rajsanjani's wife, Azar—her closest friend— had given ChalipA much to ponder. Why would Allah allow such a loving woman to spend 6 months suffering and then take her life? Not personally religious, anyway, ChalipA made a clean break with whatever possibility was left for reconciliation with Allah.

While she was happy with her husband's position as President, she thought the Supreme Leader was full of falafel fritters; likewise, the Assembly of Experts; never had a description been more misapplied, she thought. It just seemed like the people in charge, notwithstanding her husband, were mostly out for themselves; actually, ditto for her husband.

Contrary to popular belief, Muslim women, even in the strictest sects are permitted to be "women" at home. Most upper class Muslim wives have a wardrobe which includes a wide variety of garments purchased at Victoria's Secret.

While Muslim men are raised in a society that decries Western decadence, the lack of visual stimuli—aka attractively dressed women—can cause its own special problems. While Western men see erotic images on a daily basis, Muslim men do not. With the advent of computers, the Muslim men have been no stranger to internet porn. This can lead to sex crimes and a general dissatisfaction with societal norms; however, it can also stimulate a young man to national service, if only to expedite the attainment of those 72 virgins.

In the hands of the women, however, the computer is a window on the world: how other women (Western women) live; the latest fashions (forbidden by her sect) and fascinating literature and ideas. Also, as in ChalipA's case, one could actually have "pen pals".

ChalipA's latest "chat room" pal was an American who called himself, Deep Throat; a simply diabolical name, she thought. She was intrigued by the erotic nature of their conversations; conversations that would probably end her life had they been discovered, likely at the hands of her husband. Yet, she couldn't help herself.

She knew that her internet traipsing was not monitored—one of the advantages of being the wife of the Iranian President, so she approached it with her usual devil-may-care attitude.

She, like most women, even in erotic hijinks, craved more than just smutty talk. She wanted to get to know the person and them to know her, even though they were ignorant of each other's actual identity. Deep Throat was, in fact, quite an intelligent man, and by all she could deduce, worldly in a way she would never be. This was the attraction to internet friends; vicariously visiting exciting and exotic people and places.

"DT," ChalipA typed, shortening his pseudonym, "how long have you been living in Hawaii? I hear it's beautiful there."

"Well, Catherine," he typed back, (she wanted her name to sound elegant and Western), "I have lived here in Maui only a short time. I have a small bungalow on the beach. In the summer I stay at the main house in Palm Beach, California. Perhaps you could come visit me in Maui? The bungalow is quite private, if you know what I mean."

"Oh, this is exquisite", ChalipA thought *"if he only knew!"*

He did.

Over the weeks and months that followed, Deep Throat was able to play on ChalipA's disquieted heart. She knew that it was the Iranians, and more precisely, her husband who had caused all this death and destruction in America. While not divulging her identity, she was able to imply that she had special knowledge of the situation—not that he'd believe it anyway. She knew that telling Deep Throat about it wouldn't do any good, but it felt good to get it off her chest, as long as he promised not to tell anyone.

He did.

•

Agent Douglas Bennett had been with the FBI for over 20 years. He wasn't the upwardly mobile type, but he was an emotionally steady and dogged investigator. Since the assembly of "Task Force Maelstrom", Doug's main focus had been on the sniper attacks in the Florida-Georgia area.

Diane Austin's initial supposition proved to be correct, or so it appeared. Each assassin had a two state area in which to hunt, with slight alterations arising from the loss of what were now 13 of their fellow shooters. Florida and Georgia seemed to be the responsibility of one sniper.

Doug had spent a great deal of time studying this man's patterns to date. He seemed to alternate between Georgia and Florida. There was no recognizable pattern for which area of each state was attacked, but using a little deductive reasoning Doug was able to surmise that the shooter probably lived in Florida and more precisely, the Tampa Bay area.

Agent Bennett's breakthrough was immediately funneled to the other Agents across the country. So simple in its logic that one would think it obvious; yet, no one else had thought of it.

By going on the assumption that the shooter had a home base, Doug correctly pointed out that it is likely that the man's first attempted assassination would have taken place close to home. Further, there had been four attacks in the Tampa-St. Petersburg-Clearwater area, leading to the likely conclusion that the shooter lived nearby.

To Agent Bennett's mind, the shooter was, to some extent, lazy. He had an obvious cycle of Georgia, then Florida, and then Georgia...and so on. The victims in Georgia had all been within a 20 minute driving distance of the Florida border, leading Doug to infer that this man was not only living in the Tampa Bay area, but very happily. He seemed to be willing to do his "job", but wanted to get back home as soon as possible.

There had been 4 local sniper shootings believed to be the work of the terrorist: One, an elderly woman in St. Petersburg, had been shot in the head as she fueled her car at a local gas station; the second was a 26 year old man sitting in his car on Clearwater Beach—this shooting was late at night and the victim had been smoking crack-cocaine; thirdly, a businessman was shot in the chest while exiting Bern's Steak House near Ybor City—Tampa's historic and Hispanic pride, and the fourth was Agent O'Brien's new love, Dr. Lisa Martin, in the parking lot of Tampa General Hospital.

Since the first shooting attempt was targeted at Lisa Martin, Doug began there. He checked the ballistics reports and found something interesting. First pointed out to him by

Agent Wang, who'd been helping him sort out the details, was the fact that the bullet's trajectory implied an elevated position. After studying the hospital's surroundings and correlating it with the bullet's path, Doug concluded that the shot was fired from the TGH parking garage. The interesting point made by Bobby Wang, was that all vehicles entering the parking garage were not only photographed but registered via license plate number. Needless to say, Doug and Bobby had a lead.

●

Kevin nervously scurried to Tampa General Hospital to check on Lisa and retrieve the note that was left in her pocket. After seeing that Lisa was ok, Kevin raced back to the office to have the note examined by experts. There was virtually nothing of consequence that could be determined by laboratory examination, he was told; no fingerprints, hair fibers, salivary DNA or paper origin. Deep Throat was a thorough man.

The contents of the note were as follows: *"Kevin, a rather indistinct, white automobile will arrive at your residence at 0800 tomorrow. You will be transported to Tampa International Airport where you will be escorted to my private jet. As you can imagine, I am too ill to meet you at the plane. The pilot will fly you to my home where we can continue our discussion. I would appreciate not being tracked by satellite or other means. I assure you my desire for privacy is not malevolent. See you tomorrow, DT."*

After spending a most enjoyable evening with Lisa at her condo in Tampa, Kevin made sure he was home in time to "catch his ride" to the airport. The indistinct white automobile that Deep Throat had referred to was in fact a Hummer H2 Limousine. Upon entering the vehicle, Kevin was unsure were to sit down. It looked more like someone's apartment than an automobile.

Finally, Kevin seated himself in one of the 24 leather seats. As he looked around, awed by the amenities of flat-screen televisions, DVD and CD players and a well-stocked wet bar, Kevin could only comment to the driver, "Roughing it, huh?" to which the amiable driver replied, "You should see the other one, it's got a dance floor with strobe lights."

The drive to the airport was a pleasant one; Kevin fiddled with the TV for a while and calmed his nerves with a rum and coke. As he began to relax in the spacious luxury that surrounded him, Kevin was convinced that "Deep Throat", whoever he was, was actually trying to help him. He couldn't explain to himself why he felt this way, but he was sure that this trip would benefit the investigation, as well as his career; something Kevin got the distinct impression that "Deep Throat" was interested in facilitating.

After a relatively short drive to the airport, the limo pulled up to within 10 feet of the most expensive private jet in the world. It was a Gulfstream G550 business jet. Deep Throat had gotten it on sale for 60 million dollars; a pittance of his net worth. When he entered the plane, Kevin quickly realized that he was the only passenger. The pilot was in the cockpit and other than a steward—apparently, there to see to his every need—Kevin was alone. He sat down in one of four large captain's chairs facing a large Mahogany table.

It amazed Kevin that something he considered a useful tool, like an airplane, could be turned into a lush living space comparable to the finest luxury apartments in the world—not that Kevin had any experience with such things, he just assumed it.

Everything on this plane must have cost a fortune. There was a rich brown Persian rug covering most of the floor, paintings that looked to Kevin to be "originals" and, he assumed, very expensive, and even vases, sculptures and other "knick-knacks" that he rightly guessed were each worth more than he made in a year.

"Well," Kevin thought, *"I might as well enjoy this; I'll probably never get the chance to live like this again."* He looked over the short, exotic menu, ordered the Wine-Poached Salmon with Black Truffles, and then sat back in his comfortable chair and contemplated the situation.

As the jet raced through the sky his thoughts vacillated between Deep Throat's cryptic messages and Lisa's beautiful face. It was with the latter that he spent the more agreeable time.

•

Lisa had just gotten out of the shower when the phone rang. She had been meaning to get rid of her "land line" for some time but simply hadn't gotten around to it. Since her cell phone was always with her and she had unlimited minutes throughout the United States, a home phone seemed a bit redundant.

The last few months had been a combination of horrible and thrilling at the same time. First, she was attacked by some lunatic, for no reason, and then she meets Kevin— definitely the thrilling part— followed by this whirlwind series of attacks on America which has led to a great deal of chaos, and chaos always visits the medical industry; needless to say, it had been a rough couple of months.

So, Lisa decided to take a week of vacation to relax a bit and; hopefully, spend some time with Kevin. The flight that he was taking this morning made her a little anxious. She was well aware that Kevin was an FBI agent and fully capable of handling himself but even Kevin had seemed a little apprehensive before he left. Lisa supposed that her concern for Kevin's safety was just proof of her deep feelings for him and it was something that she would have to get used to, given his line of work.

At just under $500,000, Lisa considered her beach-front condo to be a great purchase. It had well over 5,000 square feet of space, with its five bedrooms occupying the second floor while the spacious living room (with a red brick hearth), the dining room and the large kitchen (with an island, something she'd always wanted) were nestled snuggly on the ground floor.

Her living room, where she spent the most time with Kevin, was covered by a terra cotta- brown, Berber carpet on which sat a comfortable Sha-Shou-Cocoa sofa and loveseat, both giving an excellent view of the 52 inch television which rested on an Ellenton Credenza, nestled between two Pier cabinets. There were Antigo coffee and end tables, decorative lamps, throw pillows, knick-knacks on the tables and tasteful pictures on the light-blue walls.

The couch was Lisa's favorite place to sit. It faced the fireplace; allowed her to watch television and provided enough room for cuddling with Kevin. The phone rested on the table at the arm of the couch, ringing itself silly, until a bath towel-clad Lisa sat down on the sofa and picked up the receiver.

"Hello," Lisa said upon answering the phone. She knew it was polite phone edicate to identify one's self when answering the phone, but being a single woman, alone, she thought better of it.

She recognized the voice on the other end as that of Doug Bennett, an FBI agent and one of Kevin's colleagues at the office. "Is this Lisa?" Doug asked. She acknowledged that it was before Doug asked if Kevin had left for the airport.

"Yes, Doug," she said, "he left about 2 hours ago. Can I give him a message when he returns?"

Agent Bennett seemed a bit nervous to Lisa. "I'm not sure..." he slowly drew out his words, as if in deep contemplation, "Are you alone?" he suddenly asked, a bit more abruptly than Lisa would have thought the situation called for, and an odd thing to ask, at any rate.

"Yes, Doug, I'm alone," was all she could think to say. "Is there a problem?"

There was silence on the other end of the line long enough to elicit another question from Lisa. "Doug?" she asked, fearing they'd been disconnected.

The next words out of Doug's mouth were not ambiguous. He shouted through the phone with force and certainty, "Lisa, lock all your doors and windows! Check that! Just lock your doors and stay away from the windows! I'm on my way!" He hung up the phone.

Talk about panic mode! Lisa wanted to ask Doug what the hell he was talking about! Why does she need to lock her doors? Stay away from the windows? What's that all about? Nevertheless, the urgency, and to some extent dread that Lisa sensed in Doug's voice was all she needed to heed his warning.

She jumped off the couch and raced to the front door and double bolted the lock; she then darted through the living room, as if on air, towards the back door in the kitchen. When she reached it she noticed that it was ajar. *Did I leave that open?*

Suddenly, she heard an unfamiliar noise behind her. She turned instantly and was shocked to see a man standing in her living room, apparently looking for her, unaware that she had seen him.

She slipped off her shoes, so as not to make a sound, and tiptoed back toward the still ajar back door. She could hear the floor creak under her feet as she eased her way to what she hoped was a silent exit. When she reached the door, sure that he had heard every step she'd taken, she reached out and slowly pulled the door a bit more open, hoping she could slip out undetected. Unfortunately, the door had not been oiled for some time and the squeak that it emitted sounded like someone dragging their fingernails along a blackboard. It was a noise that no one could miss.

Knowing that this intruder, whoever he was, had undoubtedly heard the sound of the door squeaking, she knew that it was now or never, so she pulled the door open with all her might and lunged for the screen door. However, just as she got her hand on the door's latch, the assailant reached her and pulled on the only thing she was wearing, her bath towel, jerking her back into the kitchen and onto the floor. The force of the man's grip had torn the towel from her body, leaving her completely naked.

She looked up to see a man of obvious Middle-Eastern decent staring at her with wide, frenzied eyes. He was dressed in blue jeans and a hunter-green sports shirt. His hair was neatly trimmed and he sported a heavy black mustache. Except for the fact that he had broken into her home and his eyes were "crazy", she would not have considered him an international terrorist.

"Well," he said, "it looks like I've hit the jackpot!" The man began to laugh as he stood there staring at her nakedness and lusting after her with a malevolent gaze.

Lisa slowly rose up, horrified at this man's ogling eyes, and now fixated on her nude form. *"How can this be happening? Haven't I been through enough?"* she thought.

As he slowly approached her he began to unbutton his shirt. Lisa knew what that meant. "I suppose I should be glad I missed you the first time," he said with a lustful sneer, "Now, I can enjoy the fruits of my labor."

"So, this was the man who had taken a shot at me! And now he plans to rape me before he kills me? Not without a fight!" She vowed.

Lisa had forgotten about being naked and stood up in defiance. As she stood, she eased open the drawer behind her that stored the pots and pans. She was determined to get a hold of something that could be used as a weapon.

Raheem freed the last button on his shirt and began to remove it, all the time fixated on Lisa's trembling body and the delights that it held in store for him. He pulled on the shirt with both hands in a quick shoulder shrug and it dropped to the yellow-brown tile of the kitchen floor. He stepped toward Lisa again, this time with a more determined gait.

Feeling around in the drawer, she came upon something that felt heavy enough to be of use. She suddenly turned and reached into the drawer, retrieving a cast iron skillet. She pulled on the handle of the heavy skillet and jerked it into the air. Raheem, realizing that Lisa had gotten a weapon, dove at her, one hand reaching for her arm and the other for the skillet.

She was not aiming at anything when she swung the heavy pan through the air with all her might; she was just hoping it would hit something. As luck would have it, Raheem's head was right in its path. The sizable pan crashed into his head with a sickeningly mushy sound as it turned the bone of his skull into pulp. The impact sent him crashing to the floor in a heap, blood streaming from his forehead. The skillet clanged against the floor tile with a metallic thud, cracking the ceramic tile with its weight.

Dazed, but not unconscious Raheem wobbled to his feet and stormed toward Lisa with revenge in his eyes. There was no longer the lustful continence in Raheem's approach.

He just wanted her dead. He started towards her, stumbling and shuffling like the mummy.

Lisa turned back to the drawer behind her. Even she was surprised at how she was handling the situation. She wouldn't have thought herself capable of resisting an assailant in such a violent way, but here she was; she'd already made mince meat out of his skull, she was sure of that, but it wasn't over yet. Lisa was determined to stop this man from raping her, if for no other reason than because he had pissed her off. She was determined to find another weapon. There was very little time.

Out of the corner of her eye, she spotted a pan of hard boiled eggs on the stovetop; they were still simmering. She must have forgotten to take them off the stove when she took her shower. She wasn't sure she could get to them before this swarthy psycho could get to her but she was sure as hell going to try.

In one fell swoop, she pulled the drawer that held the pots and pans completely out of its runners. It crashed to the floor with a multitude of loud bangs and clangs. Raheem was startled just long enough for her to sprint to the stove and grab the pan of boiling eggs and whip it backwards toward Raheem. Her aim wasn't as perfect as she'd hoped as the scalding water splashed across Raheem's legs, leading to a blood curdling scream and a renewed desire to seek vengeance.

Now, with the blood streaming down his angry, sweaty face and chest, Raheem, head tilted slightly forward, looked into Lisa's eyes with a cold determination that would be a regular part of Lisa's nightmares for years to come. He took a dogged step in her direction before suddenly, and unexpectedly, beginning to quiver and wobble as if someone had hit him over the head with a cast iron skillet, but no one had, at least not in the last 10 seconds. Lisa reached down and picked up the pan, prepared to swing it a second time, when abruptly, her assailant simply dropped to the floor like a bag of bricks.

As Lisa stood there, stunned but overjoyed at having survived, Doug walked through the door, his gun was drawn and smoking and he had the look of a man who had just ended the life of another human being. In all the commotion, Lisa hadn't heard the report of Doug's Glock 23 as it saved her life. Raheem lay in a heap on the floor with two bullet holes in his chest; ending a murder spree that totaled 24 people.

Still trembling from shock and overcome by enormous relief, Lisa was still unaware that she was naked. Doug, a gentle and compassionate soul, immediately grabbed a blanket from the bedroom and threw it over her, and then he guided her into the living room and sat her on the couch. Raheem was long past looking after.

"I'm sorry, Lisa," Doug began in earnestly humble explanation, "I should have been here earlier." His eyes were moist with the tears of regret.

This was not the first time Doug Bennett had felt this kind of pain and regret. He still had vivid memories of what he considered to be his failure to protect his sister from a similar attack.

He was only 12 years old, living with his mother and 18 year old sister in a ramshackle house in Baskin, Louisiana. His mother was working as a maid for one of the town's well-to-do families and was forced to spend the night at her employer's home because of a family crisis.

These were the days just following the civil rights movement and racial tension was still simmering, if not boiling on the surface of Baskin society. Doug and his sister were too young to remember Martin Luther King and had never felt much concern over the things that their mother's generation had taken for granted: Under no circumstances is a black male allowed to talk to a white female unless respectful and witnessed; Coloreds sit at the back of the bus, the balcony of the movie theater and nowhere in a restaurant; be respectful of whites and keep your head down, never looking them directly in the eye.

Doug and Monika didn't grow up feeling they were inferior to whites. Doug's hero was Mohamed Ali; he didn't take no shit. Monika was oblivious to skin color and filled with coursing hormones and the wisdom of an 18 year-old valley girl.

Monika used the absence of their mother to invite a white boy over to the house. When the boy arrived at the house, he had a friend in tow. Both were scruffy and vile in appearance and action. Doug stayed in his room. The music was loud and the foul language flew more freely than feathers in a hurricane.

After a while, Monika began to scream. Doug knew immediately that her screams were of a serious nature, having seen and heard every action and sound she'd ever made. This was the scream of Monika in trouble. Doug burst from his room only to witness his sister, naked and bleeding, being raped by one of the guys and held down by the other.

He raced to his sister's aid, but he didn't get far. The young thug who was holding her down got up and leapt on Doug, beating him into unconsciousness, before returning to Monika and taking his turn with her.

When Doug regained consciousness, he found his sister lying naked on the couch, blood still dripping from her ears, eyes fixed and dilated. They had killed his sister and there was nothing he could do about it. Not long after, Doug vowed to become a police officer and stop people from committing such crimes; the FBI made him a better offer.

Now, here he was, seeing the frightened look of a young, beautiful woman and it all came rushing back to his mind, as if a dam had burst in a river of disturbing memories.

Lisa, for her part, was still trying to figure out what had happened. She looked up at Doug and as tears now began streaming down her face, said, "That's the man who tried to shoot me a few months ago. He told me so."

Doug knelt in front of her, feeling the burden of "what if". He gently said, "I know, Lisa, that's why I told you to lock your doors."

He got up and moved to the chair just in front of the couch. "Bobby and I identified him yesterday. We traced his license plate to a small home in Ybor City. He wasn't home when we went in but I found a letter on his computer saying that he wouldn't rest until he'd finished the job he started. That got me thinking of you."

"So I'm the unfinished business?" Lisa moaned.

"I'm afraid so. It's actually very unusual for a terrorist," Doug added, going on to say that Raheem's wife was happy to give him up. She had told Bobby that her husband was going after "that girl he missed the first time". Apparently, she had become quite a fan of the American way of life and had no desire to undermine it. She was; nevertheless, jailed for complicity, but with a good lawyer she may see the light of day before her old age.

"Is there any way I can speak to Kevin?" Lisa asked with a longing tone, "I'm afraid he could be in danger, too."

Doug was sympathetic to Lisa's concerns, he had them, as well, but Kevin was definitely unreachable, at least for a while. "I'm afraid that Kevin has gone dark, Lisa," he told her, "there won't be any way to contact him until he returns from…from wherever it is he's gone."

Chapter Six

Kevin arrived at his destination after what seemed to be a short flight. When he exited the plane, another limousine waited to whisk him off, he assumed, to Deep Throat's home. From the looks of the local topography he must be in the Appalachian Mountains, probably North Carolina; maybe southern Virginia; lots of rolling hills.

After a relatively short drive on an ascending and winding mountain road, the limo came to a stop in front of what could only be called a mansion. The circular driveway wended through an immaculately groomed lawn with ornate shrubbery that would have made Edward Scissorhands proud. There were lush gardens, a second-story wrap-around porch and grand columns that reminded Kevin of the White House, only bigger.

The driver instructed Kevin to approach the front of the "house" and ring the bell. So, Kevin did as he was told, waiting about 1 minute for the door to swing open. *"I guess butlers don't like to seem too anxious, either",* thought Kevin.

The man who opened the large front door was right out of central casting. Kevin had to resist the urge to smirk. "Good day to you, sir," the man said, doing his best Jeeves impression, English accent and all, "If you will come this way," he said, turning slowly and plodding his way through the atrium, down the hall and into a grand room that Kevin assumed was a study of some kind, but much larger. Kevin thought the flight over took less time. *"This guy needs to buy a Rascal",* Kevin thought, relaxing himself with a little private humor.

As he tuned into the vast room the view was astounding. Above his head were 6 brass chandeliers; under his feet was a rich chocolate-brown Victorian-style carpet. The huge fireplace, brightly ablaze with what could have been an oak tree, was a spotless white marble surrounded by intricately ornate molding.

There was a large Mahogany desk on which nothing rested but a green desk lamp. Behind the desk was a large brown-leather chair. It was empty.

"Kevin, I'm glad you could make it. Did you have an enjoyable trip?"

The question came from the other side of the room. The raspy voice announced its owner with stirring clarity. There, seated in a comfortable-looking easy chair was a man who appeared to be in his eighties, if not older. He was smaller than Kevin imagined, but his presence exuded confidence and power. His hair was snow white, but full and luxuriant. His face was reddened with many years of sunlight and he had what looked to Kevin like spider veins on his nose. Kevin was pretty sure it was a sign that Mr. Throat had spent a fair amount of time drinking alcohol. Kevin's father was an alcoholic and, as a boy, he had seen those marks on his father's nose.

Kevin walked over to the man's chair which was resting snuggly on a maroon Persian rug. "Are you Deep Throat?" Kevin asked, knowing the answer.

"I am, indeed, Kevin, but let's dispense with the cloak-and-dagger, shall we?" He extended his hand to Kevin and said, "My name is Reginald Townsend. Perhaps you've heard of me?"

That was an understatement, Kevin thought. Reginald Townsend is generally regarded as the richest man in America. Oddly, he is also widely assumed to be dead. "I assume that you know you're dead?" Kevin quipped.

Mr. Townsend took a deep breath and said, "A condition that awaits me sooner than I would wish, Kevin. Please, come and sit down." He motioned Kevin to the chair facing his.

As Kevin seated himself he noticed that Mr. Townsend didn't have oxygen. "I would have thought, given your obvious condition that you'd be on oxygen."

"I just finished my breathing treatment, so I'm reasonably well aerated," he said, "I hate the oxygen because after a while it hurts my throat."

So much for the small talk.

"So," Kevin began, "I hear you have some information for me."

Mr. Townsend reached up and pushed a button on a chain around his neck. Shortly, a man that Kevin had not previously seen walked quietly into the room carrying a briefcase. While the man who led Kevin to this room was clearly a butler of some kind, this man looked anything but. He was well over six feet in height, jet black hair, closely cropped, wearing a spotless and creaseless black tuxedo. His dark brown eyes were stern and full of purpose, and his movements were smooth and unambiguous.

Without saying a word or even making eye contact, he walked over and handed the briefcase to Kevin. Then, just as stealthily, he turned and was gone. Kevin didn't even notice him leaving.

"Everything you need to know about the terrorist attacks is contained within that valise, Kevin." Mr. Townsend said this with an almost grandfatherly tone. "Again, due to the furtive nature of my, shall we say, contacts, identities of those I wish to keep safe have been omitted."

"With all due respect, Mr. Townsend, couldn't you have simply faxed these to me?" Kevin was not upset, only curious.

Townsend gave Kevin an appreciative smile. He looked upon the young FBI agent with endearment; Kevin could see it in his eyes. "Kevin, I have done my homework on you. I believe I am an astute judge of character; you don't get very far in my business if you are not. It has given me an almost fatherly appreciation for you." He leaned forward with a concerned look. "I hope that doesn't disturb you, Kevin. As I said before, there is nothing unnatural or malevolent. It's simply that as an old man, soon to leave this earth, and with no children of my own, I like to help young men who impress me. You have impressed me."

Kevin was taken aback, though flattered by this man's obvious affection for him. "It's not disturbing, Mr. Townsend, just a little surprising. Did you just wish to meet me, face-to-face?"

"That's about it," Townsend said, "I wanted to see if you were the man I thought you were, and now that I know that you are, I can leave this place."

Kevin's curiosity concerning the cryptic nature of Mr. Townsend's statement took a back seat to his sudden and pressing concerns for his health.

Townsend's breathing began to labor. The struggle he had to aerate his lungs was almost frightening. Quickly, Kevin reached over and grabbed the device around Mr. Townsend's neck, pushing the button as he did so.

Within 5 seconds the man who had delivered the briefcase, entered the room and walked over to Mr. Townsend's chair. Kevin was struck by the almost poetic way this man moved. He seemed to glide across the floor with a rhythm that he had not seen before.

The man could see that Mr. Townsend was in respiratory distress, but strangely, he did not seem panicked or even in much of a hurry to come to his assistance. He knelt down in front of him and smiled, as if he expected this to happen and was not greatly opposed to its occurrence.

The man then turned to Kevin and said, "Agent O'Brien, would you please step into the foyer for a moment. Mr. Townsend wishes to die alone."

Why wasn't anyone helping this man? "Shouldn't you do something?" Kevin called out. "Why aren't you getting him to a hospital?"

Townsend's breathing became more and more labored. Soon, under the watchful eye of this mystery man, Reginald Townsend appeared to give up the ghost and slump forward into oblivion. Kevin stood stunned, unable to understand this man's lack of concern.

The man calmly went about his business, neatly arranging Mr. Townsend's arms across his lap and then covering his head with a blanket. Then, he surprised Kevin by standing up, leaning over Mr. Townsend's corpse, and kissing him on the head. He then turned, and with tears in his eyes, said, "Because, Agent O'Brien, Mr. Townsend didn't wish it."

The man then walked stoically passed Kevin. As he passed him, he said, "Come with me, Agent O'Brien," to which, Kevin, after retrieving the briefcase, turned and followed him out of the room. When they had reached the entryway the man opened the door and turned to Kevin. "Agent O'Brien, as Mr. Townsend alluded, everything you need is in that briefcase."

"You mean everything about the terrorist attacks?" Kevin said, matter-of-factly, not expecting anything but a yes.

The man then said, "Let me put it this way, Agent O'Brien, death did not take Mr. Townsend by surprise." Then, as Kevin passed him out the door, he looked him up and down as if assaying him. "Yes," he said, "I believe Mr. Townsend chose wisely." And he closed the door.

Kevin walked to the limousine in a more confused state than when he had arrived. Mr. Townsend had just died in front of his eyes, after essentially telling him that he thought of him in an almost "son-like" fashion. It created an almost mourning state of mind for Kevin. He travelled home the same way he'd arrived, but with heaviness in his heart that he'd not previously had or expected.

On the flight home, Kevin was feeling morose. It was a combination of Mr. Townsend's death and the absence of Lisa. He couldn't wait to get home to see her. He'd almost forgotten about the briefcase when he accidently kicked it with his foot as he stretched out in the chair. When he saw it, he thought to himself, *"Some FBI agent, huh?"*

"Well," he said, to no one there, "there's no time like the present." He then reached down and raised the briefcase to his lap, "Might as well get some work done," he said, and began sifting through the enormous amount of materiel that the "late" Mr. Townsend had given him.

As he did so, his thoughts began to swirl with images of Mr. Townsend's death interposed with the vivid memories of watching his father die of lung cancer when he was only sixteen. These long dormant reflections of what seemed to be another life filled Kevin with a dread he hadn't felt since childhood.

Michael Patrick O'Brien was born in Dorchester, a suburb of Boston, Massachusetts in the early 1950s. His father, Paddy O'Brien, was right off the boat from County Cork, Ireland. The son of, you guessed it, a police officer, Michael was raised in a very poor section of the city he called, Dot. Strangely, although Paddy was a tough-as-they-come Boston beat walker, he had the heart of a poet and the wisdom to raise his son with "good Catholic morals".

Kevin had fond memories of listening to his father recount his time spent with Martin Luther King, Jr. in the early fifties. King attended Boston University, where he received his PhD, and was quite a celebrity in the area, long before anyone had ever heard of him nationally. He and his roommate, John Bustamante were inundated by visitors anxious to hear the words of King and to discuss civil rights. The Baptist community of Boston was particularly fascinated with him.

Strangely, Paddy O'Brien, an Irish Catholic policeman, spent an inordinate amount of time hanging around his friend and the man he called, Marty. He had known firsthand the effects of racial prejudice when he arrived in New York as a child: Irish need not apply! He had no intention of allowing his son to adopt a mindset of hatred simply because his neighbors were ignorant.

Michael, Paddy's son and Kevin's father, was raised to be blind to all things racial. He marched in Selma and Birmingham as a young man and actually got to meet his father's old friend, Dr. Martin Luther King Jr., who not only remembered Paddy when reminded, but gave Michael an old picture of he, Paddy, Coretta, his future wife and John Bustamante drinking beer on the porch. Needless to say, Michael grew up with a heart for giving and a soul for understanding. Unfortunately, he didn't grow up with lungs for breathing and was diagnosed with lung cancer at a very early age.

Kevin watched him go from a virile and vital man to a scrawny, weak epidermal-clad skeleton in a very short and anguishing time. Seeing Mr. Townsend's life fade from his body brought back painful memories that Kevin would just as soon forget.

He shook off the feelings and tried to concentrate of Mr. Townsend's material.

The Singer Castle on Dark Island was built in 1905 as a hunting lodge for the family of Commodore Frederick Gilbert Bourne—he was Commodore of the New York Yacht Club. The original castle, then known as "The Towers" was designed by Ernest Flagg with inspiration from a Sir Walter Scott novel about the "Woodstock Castle" in Scotland. Although over 100 years old, the Singer Castle—as it was later named, for the company for which Frederick Bourne worked—is one of North America's many attempts to capture the grandeur of European "Dark Ages" history.

Sitting on the St. Lawrence River between New York and Ontario this Italian stonecutter-shaped four-story granite edifice is complete with a large boathouse and a four-story clock tower. It is also filled with secret passages, a dungeon and a large medieval entrance where Knights of Armor stand guard on either side of the massive entryway. Most importantly to those who now own the island is the simplicity of its privacy.

It is surrounded by a plethora of oak, elm, birch and maple trees, all of which restrict the view of the castle from the prying eyes of boaters and binocular carrying landlubbers. The windows have been treated with a glare restricting polymer that allows those inside to look out but not the reverse.

Within its environs sits a massive library with walnut paneling, brass lamps, oak cabinets, lithographs, paintings and a rather substantial Italian hand-carved center-room table, easily seating twenty.

On this day, however, the seating arraignment called for eight. These eight men would have lunch served to them by highly skilled and loyal servants who presented dishes prepared by their equally consummate chefs. After lunch, they would all sit around the table with cigars and brandy until their need for high stakes wheeling and dealing took over, then they would then get down to the business at hand.

Each of these men had a net worth that would put them in the top one-percent of the top one-percent of the richest people in the world, that is, if anyone actually knew their net worth. The Forbes 500 would not have listed these men in their magazine; yet, each of them could probably buy and sell most of those who were. Their fortunes are considered by each of them as a solid and sacred trust, not to be used for personal aggrandizement or flippant emotional urgings. They would not be found in People magazine, basking in the sun with a beautiful movie starlet, nor would they allow themselves to be photographed by the paparazzi, not that most paparazzi would even recognize them.

These men are the ghostlike after images of conspiracy theory. They are the bullet that you don't hear coming; the hidden derringer up the sleeve; the silent scream of a comatose man. They are not the Illuminati or the Bilderbergers. They have no affiliation with the Trilateral Commission or the Council on Foreign Relations. None of them have shown up in any of the pedantic conspiracy theories inundating the internet, but they undoubtedly should. These are the Shadow Men of Dark Island and they have a plan.

"Gentlemen, this meeting has come to order," announced the de-facto chairman of the "Elite Eight", as they called themselves. "The doors have been secured, the electronic monitoring system has been activated and the room has been thoroughly swept for visual and listening devices.

"Now, there are two items that we need to address, right off the bat. First, I have been assured that there will be no radioactive fallout on Dark Island. New York City is too far away; otherwise, we would not have chosen it.

"Secondly, I would like to introduce you to our newest member, as if he needed an introduction; Amal Singh, hailing from Agra, India." He gestured toward Mr. Singh, leading to short, respectful applause.

The man introducing Mr. Singh and chairing the meeting was well into his eighties. He was slightly built with a full shock of white hair seated above a benign countenance. If he were the "Grandpa" on a Mutual of Omaha commercial you would believe him to be perfectly cast. His name is Arthur Swift. Arthur is from Chicago, Illinois and is a second-generation member of the Elite Eight. In all, three of its current members are the sons of prior members: Sir Harold Covington of London, John C. Devaney of Castlebar, County Mayo, Ireland and of course, Arthur Swift.

The remaining members, other than Mr. Singh, are Aldo Veneto of Genoa, Italy; Antoine Rousseau of Marseille, France; Wolfgang von Graff of Hamburg, Germany and Michael Grant of Atlanta, Georgia. All are wealthy beyond what is necessary for world manipulation and none are well-known, even in financial circles. They perform business through intermediaries in order to remain anonymous.

"The floor is open for discussion, gentlemen," Mr. Swift announced as he reseated himself. The meetings were not formal but they wanted a modicum of structure.

"Has President Hamilton responded to EU (European Union) proposals?" inquired Mr. Covington, "One would think the old man would see it as his only way out?"

Wolfgang von Graf answered him. "Well, Harold, America will be difficult to persuade. They have a rather stubborn streak when it comes to their sovereignty. They'll come around, though, I should think."

Arthur interjected while peering down through his bifocals, "It looks as if the United States economy has taken a more than 4 trillion dollar hit since we introduced the 'China Virus' just over 4 months ago. Naturally, we've eased up a bit. We don't want to tank their whole economy, just get them to see reason."

"Are they still convinced that it came from the Chinese Government?" asked Mr. Rousseau.

"By all indications, as well as our friend in the FBI, they bought it hook, line and sinker," Arthur replied. Then he turned to Mr. Singh and asked, "Amal, have there been any disruptions within the Iranian leadership? Are they still fully supportive of President Habibi?"

"Let me say, gentlemen, it is an honor to sit at this table, and in answer to your question, Mr. Swift, no, there have been no disruptions. The Parliament, as well as the Ayatollah, is drunk with success. Give them a weapon to strike 'the Great Satan' and they won't ask who gave it to them or why. They fancy themselves as quite sophisticated but are as pliable as clay; easily steered in almost any direction."

"That's good," Arthur said, "where would we be without the useful idiots."

Aldo Veneto was the same age as Arthur Swift. In fact, Amal Singh, their newest member, was the only man at the table under 70. Aldo wasn't in the best of health, fighting pancreatic cancer and a fading will. "Arthur," he asked, "would it be possible to either meet once a month—it was now once a week—or consider teleconferencing? This is becoming quite fatiguing."

Arthur looked around the table for the other's reactions. Sensing they were in agreement he answered Aldo, "I believe, at this point, there is no need to meet as frequently, Aldo. Once a month will, I think, be sufficient.

Teleconferencing, however, is out of the question; there would be no way for us to guard against interception."

Aldo nodded his approval as Michael Grant piped in. "Gentlemen, I'm an American, as is Mr. Swift, and although I wholeheartedly approve of our plan I would like some clarification, if possible."

Michael Grant was a southern gentleman of the first order; at least that's what everyone who knew him thought. In actuality, he was born poor-white trash in Biloxi, Mississippi. The money he'd made over the years had allowed him to rewrite his personal history, even to the point of altering his family tree, pruning here and grafting there; in one case, loping off a whole branch and completely eliminating the fact that his grandmother was black.

Rather small—five foot eight—his comportment suggested a larger man. He had followed the example of George Washington and reinvented himself from the inside out. After furtively attending a posh European "finishing school" for men, where he was exhaustively trained in all things refined, he returned to American, changed his name and moved to Atlanta, where his shipping and media empire led him to this table.

There was a short pause caused by the subtle glances of each man around the table but it was understood that Mr. Grant had the floor. "I love my country, as I'm sure does Arthur, so while I wish for my country to join a larger community, I want it clear that we are not attempting to eliminate the United States."

Harold Covington, the only Brit in the group was as proper in posture as he was in speech. Just under seventy-six years of age, he looked much younger. With Sir Harold, there was no pretense; he was, and always had been, just as he appeared to be.

Born the son of a previous "group" member, Harold Covington's blood was so blue that oxygen couldn't make it turn red. He had never had a "job" and except for most of those in this group, had never met anyone who had. To the uninitiated, Harold would most certainly come across as "snooty", but in essence, he was nothing of the kind. Acting "high brow" was his occupation, like that of any carpenter, lawyer or blacksmith. His job was to be the lord of Kensington Manor, as his father before him, and on and on for over 800 years. His eye was sharp and his observations spot on.

"I shan't worry about it, Michael, ole boy, America is not our enemy. In fact, in the end, it will be essential to restore her to her prosperous ways, just a bit more humble and a bit less stubborn. Our goal has always been clear; we wish to build a Union of Nations, stemming from the EU, that will be powerful enough to resist aggression, economically vibrant enough to sustain its people and military, and of course, influential enough to assure its will isn't challenged by those foolish enough not to join. What could be simpler?"

"That is most reassuring, Sir Harold," Mr. Grant said, "May we have a list of those countries that will form this Mega-State?"

Arthur had a folder in front of him which contained the only documentation, of any kind, concerning the "America plan", as it was euphemistically called by the group. He listed for Mr. Grant the nations currently within the Euro-Union, "The list includes the current members of the European Union, obviously, India, Saudi Arabia, Iraq, Jordan, Russia, Canada, Mexico, Brazil, Japan, Australia, Greenland and Iceland, South Africa and soon, we hope, the United States. China hasn't seen fit to join with us; perhaps that will change.

"It was felt that most of Africa and South America have little to offer that can't be taken by force and they are no threat to anyone, militarily. We will likely add others until we have a whole world in which wars have no purpose and economic prosperity will have no adversary." He looked at Mr. Grant and added, "Does that alleviate any qualms, Mr. Grant?"

"It does, indeed, Mr. Swift." Michael Grant sighed with contentment. He looked around the table, reasonably sure that their business was concluded and added, "Perhaps this would be a good time for some more brandy, gentlemen?"

After a few mumbles signaling mutual agreement, Arthur pushed a button on the table to summon his personal valet. Upon entering, the dutiful servant was told to bring brandy for everyone and cigars for those who wished them.

These men were the kings of the universe, at least that part of the universe that they were aware of. While there were the occasional personality conflicts, these eight men were part of the most exclusive club in the world, and they were the only ones who were aware of it. There was no need for posturing because each of these mysterious Masters of the Universe were quite content with their positions as equal partners in an enterprise that would astound even the most paranoid conspiracy theorist. Even these men's wife's and children had no idea that they were married to, or sired by, men with power and influence that could not be matched; the secrecy just made it all the more fun.

John C. Devaney, the Irishman and only member who hadn't spoken in the meeting, loudly announced, "If you don't mind, gentlemen, we may be world manipulators but we are not uncivilized!" He shouted to the valet, "Don't forget the whiskey!"

If you've ever seen the movie, The Quiet Man, with John Wayne, then you've seen John C. Devaney. Everyone who knew him agreed that he was the spitting image of Ward Bond, the actor who played Father Peter Lonergan. He was boisterous, sometimes a bit too loud, well-liked for his outgoing personality, and a man that, in his younger days, would slit your throat for a ha'penny. He'd made a bundle in weapons sales throughout the Middle-East, Asia and South America.

Popular with all in the group, he had a stereotypical Irish brogue which he loved to accent as much as possible. "You know," he began, "my pappy used to say, 'an Irishman is never drunk, as long as he can hold on to a blade of grass and not fall off the face of the earth.'"

The meeting ended with laughter, followed by a few bouts of inebriation and a slew of naps. In the morning, all returned to their homes; they would meet again one month from today.

Chapter Seven

The return trip was uneventful but quite informative; the information within the briefcase—only a portion of which Kevin was able to sift through—was eye opening to say the least. Townsend contends that there is an uber-secret group of men who are orchestrating all of this chaos from behind the scenes. He goes on to say that China is not involved in cyber-warfare, and that while Iran's intentions are still hostile, it is this secret cabal that has ignited Islamic ambitions and made the attacks possible.

Much of the data would seem to suggest that this "secret" group of men believe they are beneficent and wish only for America to join the European Union; with the obvious long term goal of a united and stable planet.

Kevin was dubious, to say the least. This kind of thing was old news. Everyone knows the stories of the Illuminati—the evil masterminds of a plan to create a one-world government through careful maneuvering of people and events. They are blamed for everything from the Kennedy Assassination to the UFO "landings" in Roswell, New Mexico. How could Mr. Townsend really expect him to believe that this was actually happening? The concept itself seemed flawed, to say the least. There were far too many variables in world events for a small group of people, no matter how rich and powerful, to orchestrate them to a desired outcome. It simply strained credibility.

Upon his return to Tampa, Kevin was informed of the attack in Lisa's condo. He immediately called her, anguishing over her trauma and his not being there when she needed him. Lisa was still pretty traumatized but didn't want Kevin to feel remorse for something he had no control over, so she lied and told him she was fine. Kevin could tell she was more affected than she let on but he had to get to the office with this material. He promised to come by later.

Back at the Tampa office, Kevin met with his team and let them pour over the wealth of material contained in Townsend's briefcase. There were no names divulged; no locations to search and no direct proof of the allegations; yet, the preciseness of the data was alluring.

There were descriptions of the precise steps taken to accomplish each tactical move in which this group would venture. The routes for smuggling the SAMs and Nuclear Backpacks into the port of New Orleans, the apparent "suggestive" element that had the ear of the Iranian President and the sophisticated software program that was developed to convince the U.S. they were under Chinese cyber-attack, were all included.

"What do you think, Jimmy?" Kevin asked Agent Forbes, who was speed-reading his way through much of the info, "Does any of this sound feasible?"

Jimmy, his eyes still furiously darting back and forth over some bit of text, held up his left index finger—the universal sign for, *"Don't bother me now, you moron! Can't you see I'm reading?"*

"Feasible?" Jimmy asked, after pulling himself away from his papers, "I'd say it's possible. I'd say it's doable; but, likely? I think not. The amount of power and influence these men would have to wield in order to perpetrate an enterprise of this magnitude...well, I just can't see it."

"Why, man?" Bobby Wang asked, "You don't think this kind of stuff goes on? Are you kidding me?" Bobby was a big Star Trek fan. "I've seen pictures of the aliens from Roswell! That ain't no fluke, man, that's a fact!"

Kevin leaned toward Bobby and said, mockingly "Bobby, stop helping." He then asked the rest of the team for input, to which Diane responded.

"This Mr. Townsend would seem to be a rather serious kind of guy. From what Kevin describes in his visit, he would also seem to have been an extremely wealthy and powerful man. Also, it seems that the man was moments from death and not only knew it, but apparently planned Kevin's visit around it. That, to me, doesn't sound like the resume of a practical joker."

"Well put, Diane," Doug said, "the details are so intricate and the plan so in sync with what's happening...it's got to be true. We just have to find this unnamed group of conspirators."

Ali added, "I'd believe anything at this point. Who would have believed that New York would be destroyed? All this sh...Excuse me...stuff, makes perfect sense to me. Why would the guy lie? He was dying, for God's sake!" Ali's emotions were close to the surface.

Doug raised his hand to about half mast, just to let everyone know he had something to say. "Let's just assume, for the moment, that this is all true. The question then becomes, how does Mr. Townsend know all these details about something so 'hush-hush' and why does he feel the need to tell us about it, posthumously, of course."

"I may have found the answer to that question, Doug," Diane said, rustling through a few papers, "The reason Mr. Townsend knew so much about this Illuminati-type group is that he was one of them!" Diane rested the manuscript down on the table and read from it. "It says here, 'having been a proud member of the Elite Eight for most of my adult life, I could not in good conscience betray the men to whom I have given and received such honor'. What do you know? He was one of them!" Diane ended with an ironic smile.

Now things began to make a little more sense to Kevin. Mr. Townsend had seemed to show the signs of a man who was about to face his maker and wanted a bit of absolution to increase his chances of an upwardly-mobile afterlife. "Well, that settles it," Kevin said, "we need to begin an investigation into the, who, what, when, where and why of this group. This could be the key to everything. Let's get on it!"

•

When Lisa opened the door and saw Kevin, all pretence of fearlessness went out the window. She threw herself into his eagerly awaiting arms and buried her face in his neck. "Oh, honey, you wouldn't have believed it. I was so scared," she sniffled, "You need to give Doug a medal or something. He saved my life!"

By now they had adjourned to the sofa, Lisa's face still investigating Kevin's shoulder. "I know, I know," Kevin said, trying to comfort her. "Doug told me what happened and I read the report. As you can imagine, I let Doug know how grateful we both are, but the important thing right now is that you're ok?"

Lisa was feeling warm and protected now. She was calm enough to throw in a little humor to ease the tension that she knew Kevin felt. "Why shouldn't I be ok? Being marked for death is nothing new to me. I'm actually becoming quite fond of it."

Kevin appreciated Lisa's attempt to assuage his concerns but it had little effect. Kevin couldn't get the scene he'd imagined out of his mind. The woman he loved, with a face that would make the angels jealous, fighting for her life against some Muslim psycho, in her own home. It was more than he could do just to keep from bursting with rage, but he knew he needed to be supportive, not saddle Lisa with his fear and anger.

"I'll tell you what," Kevin said, suddenly bright eyed, "the team's taking the rest of the day off to recharge. What if I give the rest of the day and night to you? We can go to dinner anywhere you wish, see a show or a movie, walk on the beach or just stare at the wall. What would you like to do?"

Lisa's smile had returned in earnest. Kevin was heartened to see its warmth. "Alright," she said with a naughty look, "let's order a pizza and grab a bottle of wine. We'll take them upstairs and not leave the bedroom until, at least, tomorrow morning!"

Kevin couldn't say no to her, so he relented, acutely aware of the horrors that awaited him upstairs. *"What I do for victims rights!"* Kevin thought.

•

By March, the country was not in the best of shape. It had been just over six months since the first sniper had set off a series of terrorist attacks. Although, the SAM attacks on airplanes had all but ended, there were still frequent sniper attacks in various states and the cyber-attacks were still disrupting commerce.

The aftermath of the attack on New York was somewhat under control, thanks, in part, to America's friends in the European Union. They provided assistance in cleanup and decontamination, medical expertise and most importantly to a staggering economy, lots of money. In fact, the EU made what seemed to be a quite magnanimous offer to America, particularly in light of recent events, to join the EU. This would strengthen America's financial system and bond it with its Western allies in Europe.

Most of the economists in America considered this proposal to be a win-win situation. Many, if not most in Congress thought the President should seriously consider linking America with Europe in a more profound way than just NATO. Most, it seemed, felt that it was time we realized that the 21st century would not be the same as those that had come before. As a race, we needed to grown up and accept that the world had gotten too small for the continuation of nation-states and the conflicts that arose from them.

The President of the United States was not among them.

President Hamilton was busy with his taxes when his wife, Katherine, walked into the Oval Office. Only she and Chief of Staff Cummings were permitted to simply "walk in" to the President's office when he was in there. She was well-known as her husband's equal, both intellectually and chronologically, having turned 73 just two weeks after the President. "Good afternoon, darling," Katie said upon entering, "how's it going here in the salt mines?"

Katherine Hamilton was a woman of pure class, but not a pretentious one. Her silver-gray hair was always well coiffed, above the shoulders and stylized in a way that gave one the impression of a woman that cared about her looks…but not that much. Her manner of dress was elegant, in the way she felt a First Lady should be, but never ostentatious or off-putting; she was perfectly comfortable in a pair of blue jeans and a sweatshirt.

She kissed him on the forehead, but he didn't even look up. He was knee-deep in his tax forms, "Afternoon, sweetie," he said, "Same old crap, as usual."

"Michael Robert Hamilton, you are the President of the United States; can't you find someone to do your taxes?" Katie ribbed.

Michael looked up to see Katie now sitting on his desk. "Hey, you're the First Lady of the United States! You have access to some of the finest chefs in the world and half the time you won't let anyone eat unless you've prepared it, personally! The Israeli ambassador is still recovering from those Chitterlings you fed him last week." She had done nothing of the kind but Mike Hamilton's wit knew no bounds. It would get him in plenty of political hot water and then pull him right out with its likeability.

Katherine and Michael Hamilton met at the annual Yale-Harvard football game when they were both twenty-three. She was a Yale cheerleader and he was a Harvard student who liked to look at Yale's cheerleaders. He ogled his way right into her heart.

Shortly after graduation, they married and have been happily enmeshed for almost 50 years. Michael has always relied on Katie's opinions and advice, both of which she will offer free of charge and often, much to the distraction of a man trying to do his taxes.

"What are you going to do about the EU's offer, darling? It sounds like a pretty good way to go, if you ask me?" she chirped. "I'm sure you could persuade Congress of the importance of our ties to our European friends. It's not like we'd lose our sovereignty; it's like joining NATO, for God's sake!"

The President dropped his pen on his W-2 form in disgust. "Maybe your right," he said, "I need to get someone else to do these damn taxes." He reached over and took his wife's hand, "What did you say, sweetie? You think we should join NATO?"

"No, silly!" she said, "I said joining the EU would be like joining NATO; we wouldn't lose our national sovereignty. Don't you think it's the only answer?"

"As a matter of fact," the President said, "I believe we would do just that, lose our national sovereignty. They're talking about doing away with the Dollar in favor of the Euro, or whatever else they've come up with. The people of America aren't ready to become a satellite of Europe. And I can tell you one thing; the people of this country will never stand by and allow our troops to fight under EU command anymore than they'd give up the Bill of Rights."

"I see your point, darling," Katie said, "but what else can we do? Our economy is about as bad off as it's ever been. At some point, we may have no choice but to take them up on their offer. Better to exist in the EU than not to exist at all."

The President stood up, leaned over and kissed Katie on the cheek. "You know what really bothers me about it, honey," he said, "it's that I have a sneaking suspicion the EU leaders know more than they're telling. They seemed to be very conveniently ready for our admittance into the EU, and just in the nick of time, I might add."

Katie's eyes grew to saucers. "You're not suggesting that they had something to do with these attacks, are you, Michael? That's crazy!" she added with incredulity.

President Hamilton plopped back down into his office chair behind JFK's old desk. He somberly offered, "Half the Congress thinks we should join the EU; hell, even the Vice-President thinks we should join." He looked up at his wife, best friend and closest advisor and said, "I don't know, I just don't like the smell of it. It's like this whole thing was orchestrated to tank our economy and force us to have to join the EU and give up our independence. Not if I have anything to do with it!"

"Well, that's the point, isn't it?" Katie said, "If you have anything to do with it. You know, most of the polls show that the American people are in favor of the move. You may end up out of office if you don't go along with this."

Michael laughed at the thought. "Katie, you know I don't care about things like that. What do I care if I get a second term? Frankly, I'm not sure I want to run again, anyway."

Katie knew better. "Oh, poop, Michael, you'd drop dead of boredom if you didn't run for re-election. You're difficult to live with when you've had a few days off; I wouldn't even try to imagine the pain in the neck you'd be if you didn't have all the problems of the world to worry about every day. As a matter of fact, after you finish your second term, I'm planning to divorce you, or shoot you, whichever one leaves me with the most money."

"You're a riot, Katie. Have you ever thought of taking your show on the road? You'd be a big hit in Iran."

Katie went over and sat on the President's lap. "I hope no one comes in, this might not look very Presidential," she said.

Michael kissed Katie and patted her knee while he spoke, "I'm just worried that this would be like trying to get the toothpaste back in the tube. America has been the envy of the world for well over 200 years; do we really want to be like the Europeans?"

Katie rested her head on the President's shoulder, like she'd been doing for almost 50 years, "Darling, I think you should do what you think is right. I've always trusted your instincts and I think the American people do to, besides Americans can't stand soccer, they like to bathe every day and nothing will ever get us to accept the metric system."

Katie got off the President's lap and kissed him on the forehead. "I'll leave you to your taxes, honey," she said, and walked to the door. After opening it, she turned and said,

"You know I'm meeting Juanita Espinoza (the wife of the Spanish president), would you like me to spit in her tea?"

The President loved his wife and her irreverent humor. "I wouldn't go that far," he answered back, "but if the opportunity arises, you might consider kicking that dorky little dog of hers when she's not looking."

•

Doug was busy doing what Doug was always busy doing, investigating leads. He was busy going through some of the material that Kevin brought back with him, while Jimmy was seated across the table doing some calculating, or so Doug assumed.

Doug leaned back in his chair with a sigh suggestive of fatigue. He removed his bifocals—which he needed because he couldn't put contacts into his eyes—rubbed the bridge of his nose and sighed again as he said, ostensibly to Jimmy, but anyone would have sufficed, "This is like mowing the lawn in a snowstorm! Most of it doesn't make any sense!"

Jimmy felt that Doug had addressed this statement to him. Feeling the need to respond, but unable to master the nuances of human interaction, he replied, "Actually, it would make no sense at all to mow your lawn in a snowstorm. I think the proper analogy would have been, 'mowing your lawn in a rainstorm'. It makes very little sense, but at least it makes some sense." He paused for an uncomfortable moment. "I understand your point, though."

"Jimmy, you're a trip." Doug said, shaking his head in mockery.

"Agent Bennett, forgive me, but I'm not familiar with African-American street language. Was that a compliment?" Jimmy actually asked this with all sincerity.

"Yes, Jimmy, it's a compliment," the ever compassionate Douglas Bennett told him, and in some ways, he meant it.

After a few more minutes of perusing the data in front of him, Doug spotted something odd. On a small Post-it note were written the words, *"Aldo's back in Genoa."* It seemed to Doug that perhaps Mr. Townsend had missed this in his attempt to erase this "group's" identification.

Not being a rocket scientist or a brain surgeon, Agent Bennett used what came natural to him; he used his common sense. Whoever these guys were, they were rich and powerful, that much seemed obvious. He did a quick check with Google for a man named Aldo in Genoa, and bingo!

"Hey," Doug called out, "I think I've got something!"

"What is it?" Jimmy Forbes asked with some curiosity.

"Well," Doug said, "after I found a note that mentioned a man named Aldo going back to Genoa, I Googled it and, voilà, his name is Aldo Veneto of Genoa, Italy. He's well-known as one of the richest but most private men in Europe. Doesn't that sound like the resume of one of our Euro-perps?"

"I would imagine," Jimmy suggested, "that the name Aldo in Italy is comparable to the name John in America. How could you be sure it was the right one?"

"I don't know, but it's a start!" Doug said, and he went right on researching a man named Aldo Veneto of Genoa, Italy.

Chapter Eight

March gave way to April, and as they say, "April showers bring May flowers." Kevin was discovering, to his slight discomfort, that April showers bring May weddings.

On an evening in mid-March when both he and Lisa were feeling an overabundance of affection towards one another, Kevin proposed marriage. She, of course, accepted and began plans for showers, receptions and other wedding-type stuff.

Kevin; however, had a bit of buyer's remorse. It wasn't that he didn't want to marry Lisa; he did, it's only that the timing was not good. He knew he couldn't leave on a honeymoon while he led a national FBI task force during one of the most tumultuous periods in American history. It simply wasn't done!

After Kevin spent the morning stewing about it, he and Diane decided to have lunch at Genaro's Italian Restaurant around the corner from the office. Diane was not only a good friend, but also sensible, calm, and what he needed most, a woman.

"What am I supposed to do, Diane? She's so excited about the wedding and all the planning that goes into it; I don't know how to tell her I can't get married!"

Diane was always empathetic, particularly with someone she knew well, but she did have a sense of humor. "You know what they say, Kevin, beware the Ides of March."

Kevin just looked at her. "I hope that isn't advice," he said.

"It might have been had I told you on March 14th, but I suppose it's of little value now," she said, smirking. Then she thought better of it, "Kevin, who says you can't get married? That's not the hard part; the hard part is telling her that you can't go on an extended honeymoon. Am I right?"

"I suppose so," Kevin moped, "but what woman wants to get married without a honeymoon?"

The waiter arrived with the food and the two began unwrapping their silverware from inside red cloth napkins. Kevin must not have paid any attention to Diane when they ordered because he was surprised to see that she was having only a simple tossed salad. He, on the other hand, had a plate of spaghetti, garlic bread, a tossed salad and an order of cinnamon bread sticks. He began to feel like a glutton, but said nothing as the waiter left and Diane answered Kevin's question.

"A woman who loves the man she's about to marry, that's who," Diane emphasized. "Look, Kevin, Lisa is a physician. She of all people will understand that you can't just pick up and go on holiday any old time you want. There are responsibilities to work, family and friends that have to be considered. Trust me, she'll understand. Just tell her you'll have your honeymoon when all this terrorist business has been resolved."

"And what if that takes years? I can't ask her to wait that long." Kevin whined.

Diane, ever the optimist, said, "Don't worry, Kevin, if you haven't solved this case by then, they'll probably fire you anyway. Then you'll have lots of extra time for a honeymoon."

"Yeah, in Cleveland," Kevin halfheartedly quipped.

Diane opened her purse and tossed a twenty on the table. "Lunch is on me. Maybe that'll help," she said.

"You didn't have anything but a salad, Diane. I'll pay for lunch."

"Do me a favor?" Diane asked, "Put your wallet away and stop moping around. Consider this an engagement present."

Kevin lowed his head, a little ashamed, ready for Diane's next lesson.

Diane got up from the table and grabbed her purse. As Kevin rose to meet her, she added, "Do you really think that a woman who has survived two attempts on her life will be angry because her honeymoon has been delayed?"

As the two of them headed to the door, Kevin answered Diane's question, "Yep".

•

Doug had been relentless over the next few days in his research of Aldo Veneto. He discovered that he was 73 years old, a widower, extremely rich but not ostentatious and generally well thought of in the area of Genoa, Italy. He was a prodigious philanthropist, seemingly always ready to help those in need, the father of three and grandfather of nine.

What piqued Doug's interest was a mention of Veneto's close-personal friend, a Frenchman named Antoine Rousseau. Rousseau's biography was virtually a carbon copy of Veneto's, at least in the important things. He was 72 years old, a widower, extremely rich but not ostentatious and generally well thought of in the area of Marseille, France. He was a prodigious philanthropist seemingly always ready to help those in need, the father of five and grandfather of fifteen.

Something seemed at bit unusual to Doug Bennett. *"How many rich European guys are quiet and unassuming? How many rich, unassuming European guys have rich, unassuming European guys as friends?"* he thought. Agent

Bennett had no proof, but his gut told him these guys could be part of the group they were looking for. He reckoned that these men, whoever they were, would need resumes just like Veneto and Rousseau if they were to pull off their plans without publicity.

Back in the office, Jimmy was as agreeable as ever. He thought Doug was on a wild-goose chase but said he would help him investigate, "for all the good it'll do".

It was getting very late, well after 9pm, when Doug asked Jimmy if he'd like to get something to eat. Never one to turn down food, the diminutive but pudgy genius agreed and offered to buy the pizza. "Why don't we go over to my place and finish this up, Jimmy?" Doug suggested, "I have a lot of the information filed away there."

Jimmy got up, picked up his laptop and said, "That sounds good to me, Agent Bennett, let's take your car and I'll take a cab from your apartment."

Since they were the only ones in the office, Doug locked the door and activated the security system as the two men exited the building. Kevin made it clear that he didn't want to explain to his bosses why the offices of the Tampa FBI had been broken into.

While they walked through the empty parking lot to Doug's car, Jimmy asked, "Where is that little memo with Aldo's name on it? We don't want to lose that."

"Don't worry; I've got all of it at home in my Megalomaniac file. I do most of my best work from home. You should try it," Agent Bennett said.

"I prefer the organizational atmosphere at the office;" Agent Forbes replied, "besides, my neighbors are far too boisterous for my taste. I could get very little accomplished."

After the two had picked up the pizza they drove the short way down Himes Boulevard to the Chesapeake

Apartments, a gated community, just north of MacDill Air Force Base. Doug, a long time bachelor, had an apartment with a balcony that faced a well-manicured lawn with a lake, footbridge and Texas-sized (and shaped for some reason) pool.

As they approached the door to his apartment something caught Doug's eye. It was probably nothing, but the two men sitting by the pool seemed out of place. They were both dressed in business suits and neither seemed to be in any way relaxing. They also seemed to be going out of their way not to look in the direction of Doug's apartment. *"Oh well,"* Doug thought, *"if it's us you're after, wait till we're done with the pizza."*

Doug opened the door and the two slipped into the apartment. Doug was not in the best of shape; a long day at work was usually enough to fatigue him. He dropped his keys onto the table by the door and plodded into the living room.

The apartment was clean and orderly, but sparse. The two bedrooms, one of which had been converted into an office, were roomy and on either side of the spacious central living room. There was a chocolate-brown couch, love seat and recliner, all facing a 48 inch plasma TV which sat precariously on a thin plank of wood held up by two cinder blocks. A coffee table sat before the couch and there was one end-table between it and the love seat. There were no decorations, per se, except one picture of what Jimmy assumed was Doug's family, over the TV, and an Oakland Raiders mug on the kitchen counter.

"Finally," thought Doug, *"I can sit on the couch and take off my shoes."* "Hey, kid, make yourself comfortable." Doug said, waving his hand in a welcoming gesture. "The kitchen table's got plenty of light if you want to work there. Right now, though, I wanna rest my achy-breaky feet."

Jimmy placed the pizza and the files they had brought with them onto the kitchen table. "Where is the case file, Agent Bennett? Is that it?" Jimmy asked, pointing to what seemed to be an identical file sitting on the floor by the La-Z-Boy.

"Yeah, that's the file, and you can stop calling me Agent Bennett, Jimmy. We're in my home, for heaven's sake. Call me, Doug!"

"Sorry," Jimmy said, taking a bite of pizza and wiping his mouth, "Is this all the information we have on this case, Doug? The memo? The research into Veneto and Rousseau? Everything?"

"That's all I've got," Doug said, sinking deeper into the couch with each word, "it ain't much but it smells like a good lead to me." Doug was still facing away from the kitchen when he thought he heard a funny sound behind him. He turned his head toward Jimmy and said, "Can't you relax a ..." Doug Bennett never spoke again, ever. The last thing he ever saw was the young, intellectual and usually frightened Agent Jimmy Forbes pulling the trigger of the gun that would end his life. What he didn't get to hear were Jimmy's comments as he killed his friend, "Sorry, Doug."

Agent Forbes walked immediately to the front door and opened it. Standing there were the two gentlemen that Doug had seen by the pool. They would take care of the cleanup.

Jimmy walked back to the kitchen table and picked up the pizza. He was hungrier than ever. Without a word, he walked past the two men, out the door and down to an awaiting car.

•

The next morning Doug didn't show up for work. When he was over an hour late, with no answer on his cell phone,

Kevin sent Bobby and Ali to check on him. About 30 minutes later, Kevin received a phone call from Bobby with the news that Doug had been murdered. "It was execution style, Kevin," Bobby said with tears, "they just shot him right in the head."

When Kevin heard the news from Bobby, he dropped to his knees, overcome with shock. Diane could see that whatever Kevin had heard, it must be tragic. She dropped her coffee cup to the floor and rushed to Kevin's side. "What is it?" she cried out.

Kevin's head was bowed in grief. He wasn't afraid to let Diane see him cry but he also didn't want to "lose it" at the office. "It's Doug," he said, then looked up at Diane, who was already crying, "He's been murdered."

Just then, Jimmy walked into the room. He saw Kevin slowly raise himself to a standing position with Diane draped over him, weeping. "What's happened?" Jimmy asked, knowing the answer but needing to act surprised and sorrowful, "Are you ok?"

Diane turned to Jimmy and related the news of Doug's murder through a veil of flowing tears. The three agents, without saying a word to one another, went about those things that were comforting at such a dreadful time.

A shroud descended over the office as each of them dealt with the news of Doug's death in their own way. Diane went right to the bathroom and wept, Kevin stoically sorted through the data, thinking of how hard it would be to tell Lisa, and Jimmy was apoplectic. "I was just with him last night!" Jimmy exuded, "Who could have done something like this? Why?" he said, crocodile tears welling up in his eyes.

"I don't know, Jimmy, but we're going to find out, I can tell you that!" Kevin seethed. Then he called Bobby and told him to tell Ali that they should let the lab guys process the scene and take the rest of the day off. They wouldn't get much done, anyway, he thought. He informed Diane and Jimmy of the same and then left the office in a huff. He knew he needed to see Lisa but she was at work. He called her and told her he'd pick her up after she got off work, about 6pm. He couldn't tell her on the phone.

Feeling the need to blow off some steam, Kevin went to the gym. In actuality, it was the local Bally's Health Club, but FBI agents insisted on calling it "the gym"; the other sounding too girlie. Kevin liked to use free-weights; none of that elliptical, ergonomic, Stairmaster machinery for him. He'd work out hard and then go to the speed bag followed by the punching bag, particularly if he wanted to ease built-up tension, as he did today.

He had worked with Doug Bennett for over three years and considered him a good friend. He was a hard worker, easy to be around, and an extraordinary investigator. Kevin couldn't think of a good reason for anyone to kill him; he didn't have any known personal issues, was always friendly and helpful and was the most likeable man he knew. Needless to say, Kevin gave the punching bag a rough going over, each punch a personal attack on whoever did this.

When he'd punched himself and his anger out, he headed for the locker room. His favorite part of working out was the sauna and steam bath afterward. He felt it was his reward for a hard workout; today it was just good medicine.

While he was sweating in the steam bath the door opened and another man entered. This was not unusual so Kevin just said, "Hey" to the man and continued his thoughts.

"Kevin?" the man said, "Are you Kevin O'Brien?"

Kevin couldn't see well enough to make out the man's features. "Yeah, I'm O'Brien, who are you?"

"Agent O'Brien," the man said, "I have come across some information that I believe would be relevant to your

Maelstrom case, as well as the death of the FBI agent last evening."

That was the wrong thing to say and the wrong way to say it. Kevin got up and kicked the door open to let out some of the steam. He wanted to get a good look at this man.

Quickly, the man said, "Agent O'Brien, please calm down. I assure you I had nothing to do with your friend's murder, but I believe I can help you find out who it was, if you'll sit down and act civil."

Kevin sat down, but he had no intention of acting civil, "Who are you?" Kevin asked, ready to punch this guy's lights out if he got a wrong answer.

"I'm with the CIA, Agent O'Brien. My name is unimportant but my information is. Shall I go on?" the man asked.

Kevin thought he sounded legit. "Go ahead," he said.

"During a recent investigation in Europe...I won't go into details, but the names of some interesting people have surfaced. These names belong to a couple of men that your man was investigating."

Kevin blurted out, "My man?"

"Excuse me, Agent O'Brien; I'm talking about Agent Douglas Bennett, the man who was killed in his home last night." The man paused long enough to assure himself that Kevin was still listening, then "These are very powerful men and extremely fond of their anonymity. I believe that it was Agent O'Brien's research into these two men that got him killed."

Kevin's head was spinning, partly from what he was hearing and partly because of the steam bath. "I don't suppose you're going to tell me these men's names, are you?" Kevin dubiously asked, "While you're at it, maybe you could tell me how the CIA knows more about the investigation of one of my men than I do?"

The man got up and opened the door again. Kevin was glad because he had just about had it with the steam. "I left a good deal of information in your car, Agent O'Brien. Please don't try to follow me; let's be professionals, shall we?"

"Yeah, let's?" Kevin responded, dryly.

"One more thing, Kevin," the man said before closing the door behind him, "I'm reasonably sure that one of your agents is a mole. As the information I've provided you will show, the hit on Agent Bennett was ordered from your office. I think we both know what that means. Good luck to you, sir." And he was gone.

Needless to say, Kevin couldn't believe what he'd heard from this...CIA agent, if that's what he was. However, when Kevin got to the parking lot and opened his car door, there on the seat was a Manila envelope marked "O'Brien". Considering that the trauma of losing Doug was going to be so heavy on everyone's mind, he knew he couldn't call the team together tonight. He headed for the hospital to pick up the only person who could help him think straight.

Chapter Nine

The Federal Reserve System (commonly known as the Fed) is America's central system of banking. Created in 1913 by the Federal Reserve Act—in response to a series of financial panics beginning in 1907—it is, ostensibly, responsible for conducting the nation's monetary policy, supervising and regulating banking institutions, maintaining the stability of the financial system and providing financial services to its depository institutions, the U.S. government and foreign official institutions.

According to its own official documents it is tasked with the additional responsibility of maintaining employment, keeping prices stable and keeping interest rates at an acceptable level.

In 1934, in a statement before Congress, Louis T. McFadden of Pennsylvania (former
Chairman of the Banking and Currency Committee for more than 10 years) had this to
say: "Mr. Chairman, we have in this Country one of the most corrupt institutions the
world has ever known. I refer to the Federal Reserve Board and the Federal Reserve
Banks, hereinafter called the Fed. The Fed has cheated the Government of these United
States and the people of the United States out of enough money to pay the Nation's debt.
The depredations and iniquities of the Fed has cost enough money to pay the National
debt several times over.
"This evil institution has impoverished and ruined the people of these United States, has

bankrupted itself, and has practically bankrupted our Government. It has done this

through the defects of the law under which it operates, through the maladministration of

that law by the Fed and through the corrupt practices of the moneyed vultures who

control it.

"Some people think that the Federal Reserve Banks are United States Government

institutions. They are private monopolies which prey upon the people of these United

States for the benefit of themselves and their foreign customers; foreign and domestic

speculators and swindlers; and rich and predatory money lenders. In that dark crew of

financial pirates there are those who would cut a man's throat to get a dollar out of his

pocket; there are those who send money into states to buy votes to control our

legislatures; there are those who maintain International propaganda for the purpose of

deceiving us into the granting of new concessions which will permit them to cover up

their past misdeeds and set again in motion their gigantic train of crime."

Andrew Jackson, in reference to the men who would create a Central bank in

America, put it more succinctly, "You are a den of vipers and thieves. I intend to rout you

out, and by the Eternal God, I will rout you out."

As Mayer Amschel Rothschild, one of the originators of the Fed, said, "Let me issue control of a nation's money and I care not who writes the laws." and more recently, Richard McKenna, former President of Midlands Bank of England said, "Those that create and issue the money and credit direct the policies of government and hold in their hands the destiny of the people."

Enter the Shadow men of Dark Island: Eight international heirs to the original idea of a New World Order. This "Elite Eight" as they surreptitiously refer to themselves are furtively pulling the strings on a national monetary collapse which will, they hope, lead to international financial chaos and the need for a "new" system of earthly governance. The hope is that America will begin to experience the riots and violent opposition to democracy which has inundated European cities for years. This will force the American government to unite with its European allies in order to centralize its financial, legislative and military power. Otherwise, America will join the likes of the Romans, Greeks and British who have watched their empires collapse under their own weight.

Of course, the Elite Eight are not doing this for humanitarian purposes. The consolidation of money within the countries of Europe and the United States has put almost unlimited power in the hands of a few. Assuming it works as planned, the consolidation of money (and the power that goes with it) will be almost worldwide. It will literally make these eight men (and those carefully chosen to succeed them) absolute masters of the earth.

Someone once asked, "How do you defeat an idea?" to which was answered, "With another idea!" The Shadow men of Dark Island were up to their eyeballs in an international conspiracy that would make Oliver Stone blush; yet, they experienced no angst, no fear of discovery and no concern for reprisals.

The very idea that conspiracy theories are so prevalent in modern times is not an accident; it is a well-thought-out arrangement by the very men of whom these conspiracies ought to be centered—but aren't! Aldo Veneto and Antoine Rousseau are keenly aware of this anomaly.

Meeting in Venice, Italy with Amal Singh, the newest and youngest member of the Elite Eight, Aldo and Antoine were tasked by Arthur Swift with providing a more lucid and detailed explanation to their latest colleague.

The three had arrived by water taxi to one of Aldo's many Venetian properties; this, a former luxury hotel that he had remodeled for his personal use. Resting on the Grand Canal, about halfway between the Santa Lucia railway station and the Saint Mark basin, Aldo's little getaway is the epitome of fourteenth-century Venetian Gothic architecture, with the thinner columns and elongated arches of the Byzantine age being replaced by ogees—a double curved window, resembling the letter S, formed by the union of a concave and a convex line—a style reminiscent of modern Arab architecture.

Being a man who enjoys his comforts, Aldo renovated the ancient edifice from within, leaving the outside to reconcile with its conservative neighbors.

While there is the occasional Renoir or Raphael painting on the wall and even a priceless (and as yet unknown) Bernini—the great sculptor of Baroque—depicting Joseph holding Jesus, Aldo's "crib" is twenty-first century all the way. It is filled with all the modern conveniences from electronics to solar power and dedicated to creature comforts for all who enter its plush environs. Even Amal, perhaps the richest man on earth, was greatly impressed, and after a short period of "relaxation" with one of Aldo's "women", was ready to hear what these men had to say.

Aldo, his health failing and his mind fatiguing, tried to use an analogy from his own life experience. "Amal, my young friend," Aldo said as he rested his hand on Amal's shoulder, "it is like religion. I know you are Hindu, but just for the sake of argument, let's say that the Christian Bible is the actual word of God."

"Heaven forbid!" Amal jokingly protested—he didn't believe in Hindu foolishness any more than these men believed in Christian foolishness.

Aldo continued after a smile and a short pause, signifying their mutually held belief that religions of all kinds were pure fantasy, "Ok," Aldo went on, "so, in this scenario, the Bible is the true word of God. There is only one God and his word is written for us in the Bible. Now, if there were no other religions to claim that there were other gods, or other books by other gods, then the reading and understanding of the Bible's words would be, as the Americans say, 'a no-brainer'. So, continuing with this analogy, how would the Devil get people to reject the word of God's truth in favor of a lie? The answer is, 'Introduce a new truth'.

"Hinduism, Buddhism, Islam, Christianity, Judaism, Sikhism, Shintoism, Rastafarianism, Scientology, Humanism and every other denomination, sect and splinter group imaginable. How the hell are you going to tell me which one is the 'real truth'? You can't!" Aldo had to rest a moment to regain his breath.

Antoine spoke up, feeling that Aldo was losing Amal, "And the point is…" he said, hinting for Aldo to wrap it up.

Aldo got the message. "And the point is," Aldo asserted, "that we can do the same thing with 'our' truth, as it were. All we have to do is to see that hundreds of conspiracies are running rampant across the international media landscape: Who killed JFK? Why is the government covering up the UFO landings in Roswell, New Mexico? Was 9-11 an inside job? The moon landings were faked in a movie studio! Who are these mysterious men of the Illuminati who are trying to control the world?

"You see what I mean, Amal?" Aldo added to sharpen his point, "The heightened awareness of global warming; the looming specter of global nuclear conflagration and the proliferation of international conspiracy theories let us hide in plain sight. We are the forest and we cannot be seen for the trees. It couldn't be simpler."

Antoine hadn't seen Aldo so animated since he discovered Viagra. "Maybe you should take a few breaths, my friend," Antoine suggested, "You're not as young as you used to be."

"No, Antoine, I am not," Aldo said with an air of resignation, "I don't believe I'll see the New Year, which is why it is so imperative that we succeed with the 'America plan' by the year's end; I'd very much like to see the baby being born."

•

Although being with Lisa has always been enough to keep even the most depressing emotions at bay, this night was particularly onerous. Having picked Lisa up at the hospital, Kevin headed straight to the Columbia Restaurant on Bayshore Boulevard. It was a favorite of Lisa's and it offered privacy for a frank discussion; a discussion that Kevin would hardly have thought possible.

"So, who's the mole?" Kevin muttered, almost to himself, "Ali would seem the obvious choice, but his

Christianity seems awfully real to me, and his wife died in the attack on New York. It just doesn't fit."

Lisa had no desire to paint with broad strokes, but Kevin needed a sounding board and she felt a duty to play devil's advocate. "Well, I've heard of many Muslim men who killed family members because of Sharia Law." Lisa almost winced from adopting this adversarial posture. She didn't have a racist bone in her beautiful body, but, there it was, she had to tell the truth.

"I know, honey," Kevin sighed, "but I just can't believe he's anything but what he appears to be. Besides, it would be pretty stupid to send an Iranian spy to America to spy on Americans for Iran? That would be like appointing Mahmoud Ahmadinejad as ambassador to Israel."

"Touché," Lisa said, glad he'd made the point. "Ok, so who's left? Diane? Bobby? Jimmy?" This last name caused them both to giggle a bit.

"Jimmy wouldn't know how to betray his country," Kevin guffawed, "he's afraid of his own shadow; I doubt he's got the guts to participate in much international intrigue."

It was true; Jimmy Forbes was not a man with the temperament or the intestinal fortitude to involve himself in something as primitive and precarious as murder, particularly not the murder of a friend and colleague. He was a man of "Letters", of intellectual thought and reason; he was a man of non-violence.

It was also true that he had killed Doug Bennett in cold blood.

His father, Senator Franklin Forbes, was a powerful representative of the great state of Pennsylvania. His 37 years of public service had been both long and distinguished; however, unbeknownst to the public, Senator Forbes had involved himself in some very nasty business, landing him snuggly into the pocket of an elite group of international conspirators for whom he would favor from time to time.

Jimmy's unlikely acceptance into the FBI had been no accident; it was carefully orchestrated by his father and a few well-placed assets. Jimmy's actions were not of his own choosing; they never had been. He would have been much happier in the library at Harvard, behind ivy-covered walls. It was at the insistence of his father—a man who always got what he wanted—that Jimmy entered what he considered to be a sham of a life at the FBI in the first place. His father demanded it! End of Story!

Now, Jimmy was killing for his father, a man that held his son's life as no more precious than that of his Rottweiler, a man who called his son coward and wimp.

While not generally inclined to concern that others might think him less than a man, Jimmy was not so impervious to the opinion of his father. It was primal in its nature and Jimmy was not immune to its primitive lure.

"Who else?" he asked Lisa, assured that Jimmy was a dead end.

"Well, Kevin," Lisa again felt the need to "run it up the flag pole", so to speak, "Diane is probably the most capable person in your office. You've said that on a number of occasions. Could she be in some kind of financial trouble that would leave her open to blackmail?"

"That's just it," Kevin said, "anything is possible, but my gut tells me that my people are honest and trustworthy. If I'm wrong then I need to find another career because in this job you have to develop very well-honed 'spidey senses', if you know what I mean?"

Grasping at straws, Lisa said, "Have you considered that this CIA agent, or whatever he was, could have either been wrong or just pulling your chain? The CIA is famous for being less than honest with other government agencies. Or have I just seen too many movies?"

Kevin smiled at his fiancé as the waitress brought their entrees. Lisa had Calamari—Kevin could never eat something that he thought would eat him if it were alive—and Kevin had New York strip, medium-well, with a baked potato. "How can you eat that?" Kevin asked with all seriousness. "Didn't you ever read 20,000 leagues under the sea?"

"As a matter of fact, I did;" she said, "this is my revenge. Remember, revenge is a dish best served cold...or hot, like this one, but you get the point."

They both smiled warmly at each other, welcoming the short break that innocuous conversation could afford them.

Kevin cut a small piece of steak, speared it with his fork and then thought better of it. He put his fork down and leaned forward to speak more intimately to Lisa. "I don't know what to do, Lisa," Kevin said with a sad, childlike expression, "we can't go on with Maelstrom while my people are under a cloud of suspicion, but then again, it's not like we can take a break. People are dying and lives are being ruined."

Lisa, already leaning over her Calamari to listen to Kevin's opining, recommended a good old-fashioned "mole hunt". "That's what they did on Mission Impossible," she said, "why can't you do the same thing?"

The reference to Mission Impossible made Kevin want to laugh. Everyone with a television set thought they knew how to try a case in court, take out someone's gallbladder, solve a murder case or find the infamous CIA, or in this case, FBI mole. *"However, life imitates art, imitates life,"* Kevin thought, *"perhaps a good old-fashioned mole hunt is just what the doctor ordered, literally."*

"Lisa, you're a genius!" Kevin whispered, loudly. "Maybe I need to watch Mission Impossible more often.

"Are you going to eat that tomato?"

•

The next morning did not leave enough time to fill the office with sunshine and rainbows. The death of one of their own had profoundly affected the office's esprit de corps. Everyone busied themselves with mundane tasks while no one really accomplished anything, and no one wanted to talk about Doug. Kevin realized that if, in addition to Doug's death, there was a traitor found in their midst, it would probably fracture any chance of real progress in the Maelstrom task force's mission. He had to find the mole but it was imperative that it be done with a degree of subtlety.

Lisa had been a wealth of information without even knowing it. Her reference to Mission Impossible got Kevin thinking about another movie he'd seen growing up; "Midway", with Charlton Heston (his favorite actor). In the movie, as in real life, the American code breakers, euphemistically known as "Magic" had broken the Japanese code. Admiral Yamamoto, fleet commander of the Imperial Japanese Navy, had a fleet of 200 ships and 100,000 men preparing to make an amphibious landing somewhere in the Coral Sea. The question was, where?

Joe, played by Hal Holbrook, intercepted a Japanese transmission that said the fleet would be directed to "AF". Joe thought "AF" was the Japanese code name for the island of Midway, but he had to be sure. So, he sent out a message, in a code that he knew the Japanese had broken, saying that Midway needed to replace its atmospheric condensers. The next day he intercepted a Japanese transmission stating that "AF" needed to replace its atmospheric condensers. Voila,

"AF" was Midway! That bit of information allowed Admiral Nimitz to catch them with their pants down and destroy virtually the entire Japanese carrier fleet in one fell swoop. At that point the outcome of the war in the Pacific was a foregone conclusion.

Kevin had an idea that something similar might expose the mole, assuming there was one. He contacted Asst. Director McCarthy and told him of his concerns, as well as his plan to deal with the problem. Director McCarthy agreed to assist him in his endeavor.

While they had been monitoring incoming phone calls to the office, it never occurred to anyone to monitor outgoing calls. McCarthy quickly remedied that situation, including cell phone and internet scrutiny. If a call went out or a message was sent from that office it would be intercepted. Additionally, each of the building's thirty-four employees would have their home phones, cell phones and home computers monitored. Nothing could be left to chance.

Kevin felt like a heel to some extent. If there was a mole he had to find them, but he hated that he had to treat everyone in the office as if they were guilty; nevertheless, it had to be done.

After calling an impromptu meeting of the team, Kevin prefaced his comments with a short litany praising Doug Bennett and the great loss they would all have to bear. Then, after some sharing of mutual remembrance, Kevin felt it was now or never.

"As you all know," Kevin began, "the business of this agency, and particularly this task force, has to go on. There are too many people counting on us for us to allow bereavement to act as a stumbling block. We'll have plenty of time to mourn Doug when this is all over." He waited a moment, just to see that everyone concurred. They seemed to. "I received some information last night that I believe will shed light on our search for this secret cabal of conspirators that Mr. Townsend alluded to in his documentation. It is my opinion that Doug was killed because he had uncovered something that could lead to this group's identification."

Kevin glanced at Jimmy, busy with his laptop, and said, "Isn't that right, Jimmy? Didn't Doug tell you that he'd uncovered something?"

Jimmy just about jumped out of his skin when Kevin called his name. "Oh," he stammered, "yes, yes he did, Agent O'Brien. We went over to his apartment and worked for a while, but nothing came of it. Later, after I'd gone, he called and said he had found some kind of link to some European guys, but he didn't tell me what it was about. He said he'd bring the information to the office the next day…but, there wasn't a next day." Jimmy sniffled a bit and then just dropped his head as if he was unable to say more.

"I'm sorry, Jimmy, I just needed to know." Kevin said. He then looked over the group at his table and laid the trap. "Asst. Director McCarthy informed me last night that, with the assistance of the CIA, he has identified the person or persons who are responsible for the death of Agent Bennett. He didn't tell me more than that; however, I've been instructed to be sure that everyone be in this office at 0800 sharp, tomorrow. The Asst. Director will be here personally." Kevin added this last statement to prime the pump of paranoia.

"Why would the Asst. Director want to meet with us?" Diane asked with a confused look. "If he knows who Doug killed why would he want to meet with us? It doesn't make any sense."

"Maybe he just wants to offer his condolences for the loss of one of our close friends." Bobby said, "Although, it is pretty weird, wouldn't you say?"

Kevin tried to read the faces of his team to see if he could detect any panic, but there was nothing discernable. "I don't know, Bobby. All I know is that we need to be here at 0800 tomorrow." He then dismissed the group until the next day, hoping that they would find it was all a mistake.

Chapter Ten

President Hamilton was all set to deliver his State of the Union Address in one hour. He'd practiced in front of his wife, his Chief of Staff and the mirror, the latter being the only one who smiled back at him. No one seemed to be happy with the decision he'd made regarding European and American unification, but he simply believed that it would be a mistake to give up so much of his country's freedoms for a safer and more prosperous future. It was never a good idea to deal from a position of weakness.

America, he thought, could ride out these rough times and emerge even stronger than before. Now, would the American people agree with him; he'd find out in an hour.

The second floor of the White House contains the living quarters of the President and his family. Although it is called the "Private Sitting Room" officially, Michael and Katie use it as their bedroom, as have many "First Couples" before them. Katie was quite adamant about bringing their personal bedroom furniture for use in the White House. "I could sit on someone else's couch," she said, "I can even eat off of their dishes, but I'll be damned if I'll sleep in their bed!"

The President had been fussily getting dressed for over half an hour and Katie, as usual, had to go in and see to it that he didn't go before the American people looking like an unmade bed.

"Mike, aren't you dressed yet?" Katie asked as she approached him like a mother hen. "And who taught you how to tie a tie? I assume that's supposed to be a Windsor knot, but if that's the way you tie it we could be in for an international incident." She grabbed his tie and began to reshape it.

"Honey," the President said, contemplative, "Do you think I'm making the right decision? I mean, do you think I have the right to make a decision that will so profoundly impact everyone in this country?" Michael Hamilton's decisions were final and he and she both knew it. He was just looking for some extra support. He got it, as always.

"I think the American people elected you for a reason. I happen to agree with that reason, so yes, I do believe you have the right to make this decision; furthermore, I believe it is your duty." She finished with his tie, "There, that's better."

"You're a good wife, Katie. I truly mean it when I say that I wouldn't know what to do without you. Thank you, sweetheart," Mike said as he kissed his wife, ever so gently on the lips. "Maybe later we can go in to the Lincoln Bedroom and add a trivia question to its folklore."

Katie laughed and said, "Yeah, how many Presidents have fornicated in the Lincoln Bedroom?" She giggled and added, "After this speech, I may be the only one you could get to go in there with you."

"Very funny," he said, "Go tell Harry I'm ready, and don't wear that perfume, it distracts General O'Malley."

"What a funny President!" Katie thought.

•

The Pomp and Circumstance that accompanies a State of the Union Address is laughable, at least that's what the current White House occupant believes. The Sergeant at Arms' introduction (twice); the long walk, shaking hands with all the people who wish you were dead; the continual applause with standing ovations from the President's side of the aisle, while the "other side" conspicuously remains seated. It's political from start to finish. Tonight; however, it would be different; it had to be.

Once the President had done the "dead man walking routine", as he called it, he shook hands with the Vice-President and Speaker of the House before turning and hearing, for the second time in less than one minute, "Mr. Speaker, the President of the United States!"

Michael Hamilton had been waiting for this moment for some time. He was sure that this was make-it or break-it time for his Presidency—Harry Cummings never let him forget it—but that didn't seem to matter as much as the content of his speech and his hope that it would spur the country to fight to remain an independent and unique symbol for the world.

After a few formalities; introducing a firefighter who'd saved a life, acknowledging a Medal of Honor winner and thanking the British Prime Minister, seated beside Katie and General O'Malley, President Hamilton got down to business.

"My fellow Americans, this State of the Union Address comes at a time of great upheaval for our people. We have been attacked in every way that a nation can be attacked and we have stood tall against a faceless and cowardly aggressor." (Standing ovation) "We have lost thousands of our fellow citizens to terrorist attacks while our financial system has been the target of that most modern of threats, cyber warfare! But even these pale in comparison to the devastation inflicted on the city of New York and its brave people." (Standing ovation)

"Some gifted and witty writers have even labeled this 'America's Year of Hell', and while there may be some truth to that, I prefer to think of it as America's greatest

test." There was a smattering of applause but no one really bought it.

"As most of you already know, the economy is in pretty bad shape. While we've tried to stabilize it with wage and price freezes, government loans and the grateful acceptance of international assistance, we still have a long upward climb back to national prosperity.

"The real crux of the matter is summed up in the recent offer by our European allies. They wish for us to join a conglomeration of nations from around the world that they say will stabilize our economy and protect us from military attack. They offer us a quick fix to the devastation with which we have had to contend these many months. But at what price?

"Are we willing to give up our national sovereignty that we may be spared the pain that will come with going it alone? Shall we tell our grandchildren that we had to give up on the idea of freedom because the going got too tough? Will we tear down the Lincoln Memorial, the Jefferson Memorial and the Washington Monument for fear they would be an embarrassing reminder of our national cowardice in the face of so great a challenge?" This elicited a less than enthusiastic response. National polls suggested that over 75% of the American people and over two-thirds of those in Congress were in favor of the "Euro-Union" as some were calling it. More than half of those in the President's own party were for the Union. The President was undaunted.

"I believe," continued the President, "that the darkness is almost over; that the light at the end of the tunnel is not an oncoming train and that with patience and a steady hand at the tiller, this ship we call America will find a welcome port in the storm! Thank you, and may God Bless America!"

All stood in respectful applause, but many, if not most, were less than hopeful of the direction in which the President was steering the country. Some wished him well, while others wished him ill. One wished him dead, and he would see to it that the President didn't leave the room alive.

●

Ali couldn't believe the events that had taken place in the last six months: the sniper attacks, the SAM attacks, the cyber attacks and Doug's murder, and of course, the attack on New York that had killed his beloved wife. Now, Kevin seemed to be suggesting that the agency thought that someone in their office could have been responsible for the death of Doug Bennett. What was happening?

Ali's road to the FBI had not been an easy one. He was an Iranian expatriate in a time when America's greatest enemy was the Iranian regime. It would be comparable to a Soviet defector being accepted into the FBI in 1960; however, Ali had shown himself to be an ardent supporter of the Capitalist system and the Democratic way of government. While he had been scrutinized extensively prior to his acceptance, he had passed with flying colors.

Once he entered the FBI Academy it became clear that he could be of great help in the fight against terrorism. He knew the culture, the language and the religion of Islam like no one else could, save for those raised within its unique environs. Once they realized his possible value, the CIA made a play for him but he preferred to stay with the FBI and protect America from within.

A few years after he graduated the Academy, Ali was sent to the New York office to assist in the investigation of terrorist activities in America, arriving a few years after 9-

11. His reception was chilly, to say the least. Ali understood why his fellow agents resented him; he represented everything they had come to consider their enemy, but within a month or two Ali had turned the entire office into his biggest fans.

His marriage to Karen and his acceptance of the Christian faith went a long way in making him feel more "American", something he desperately wanted to feel. He immersed himself in Western Literature, as well, reading Shakespeare, Dickens, Twain and his absolute favorite, Arthur Conan Doyle. Sherlock Holmes became such a hero to Ali that he would try to incorporate Holmesian techniques in his FBI investigations, including saying "elementary" a few too many times for his colleagues.

When Kevin ordered him transferred to Tampa, Ali was not a happy camper. He was very much in love with his wife and in many ways, dependent upon her; at least, from an emotional standpoint. He was an American, having attained citizenship before entering the Academy, and he was a New Yorker. Needless to say, his separation from New York and Karen had not been a welcome experience, but Ali knew it was only temporary; he'd be back in New York and in Karen's arms within the year. That, of course, would never happen now and Ali drove home to his place of residence—he shuddered at the thought of calling it his home.

If it could be agreed that George Carlin was correct, in that, "home is where your 'stuff' is", then Ali was glad to be home. He threw his keys onto the little dinette table and walked into the living room. He made some microwave popcorn and plopped down into his La-Z-Boy. It was 7:45pm, just 15 minutes until his favorite show was scheduled to air. Ali didn't understand the attraction so many had to these "reality shows" and he could just about stomach the "American Idol" type shows. Americans did seem to like some pretty superficial stuff, he concluded, but they were good people, overall, and assumed these shows were just escapist fare. One couldn't judge a culture by their media entertainment, he thought, otherwise the Japanese would have to be put in a collective strait-jacket.

No, Ali had a more sophisticated palette and in ten more minutes he'd be able to watch the show that was simply too good to be TiVo'd; reruns of the Dick van Dyke Show. The man was a comic genius and Laura Petrie was to die for! Mary Tyler Moore reminded him of Karen. She didn't look or act anything like her, but in Ali's mind, she was the spitting image. Watching the Dick Van Dyke show made him feel close to her and that was all that mattered.

The doorbell rang at five minutes till eight. Not at all pleased, Ali considered not even answering the door, but thought it could be important. So, he unloaded himself from his comfortable chair and walked to the door and opened it. There, on his doorstep, was a very sad and droopy looking Jimmy Forbes. He looked for the entire world like a lost child.

"Hey, Jimmy, what's up?" Ali asked, gesturing for him to come in. "You look like the proverbial lost sheep. What brings you over here?"

What brought Jimmy to Ali's apartment was a message he'd received about 30 minutes prior instructing him to come to Ali's apartment and kill him. Jimmy was not a brave man but had gotten in way over his head. He did not know how to extricate himself from so powerful a grip as these men possessed.

"Oh," Jimmy sadly spouted, "I just wanted to talk to someone about what's going on at work. Can you believe the convoluted situation that we're currently engulfed in?"

'That's our Jimmy", Ali thought, *"always the silver tongue."* "Come in and sit down," Ali said, "Hey, do you

like the Dick van Dyke Show? It's coming on right now!"

Jimmy had a small shoulder bag draped over his back. As he sat on the couch, he drew it off his shoulder and onto his lap. The theme music for the Dick van Dyke show was just beginning to play and Ali's eyes were affixed to his 52" Sony TV screen.

Jimmy unzipped his shoulder bag and slipped his right hand into its interior until he felt the cold steel contours of his Austrian-made Glock 19 handgun. He wrapped his hand around the non-slip grip and felt a tension come over his whole body. He couldn't believe he was about to do it again, and he kind of liked Agent Hussein. He was one of only a few people who seemed to accept Jimmy for who he was, not snickering at his odd manner of speech; nevertheless, orders were orders.

Ali was fixated on his television as Jimmy withdrew his weapon and placed it on his lap, still covered by the shoulder bag. Fully convinced that Ali would never see it coming, Jimmy pulled the gun out and pointed it at Agent Hussein's head.

Oddly, before Jimmy could pull the trigger, Ali suddenly slumped down in his chair as if he'd fallen asleep. Jimmy thought he was joking for a moment, but it seemed to go on for too long. "Ali?" Jimmy called out, resting the gun back on his lap, "are you ok?"

Ali didn't respond. He looked like he'd simply fallen asleep in his chair. *"How odd?"* Jimmy thought, *"I guess this will be easier than I thought."* He withdrew the Glock from his lap and aimed it at Ali's head, but just as he was about to pull the trigger he felt a strange sensation in his chest. It was unlike anything he had experienced before.

Had Jimmy remained conscious he might have noticed the tranquilizer dart protruding from Ali's neck? He also might have noticed the .38 caliber bullet hole in his own chest; the one that ended his life, but he didn't. Nor did he see the two men who came into the room moments later to "clean up" and "reinvent" the scene of the crime. He might have remembered them as the men he'd seen at Doug's place not long ago.

The two men moved quickly. They removed the dart from Agent Hussein's neck and removed any fingerprints from the Model 1905 Smith and Wesson M&P 38SPL Revolver that Ali had kept in his closet. He collected rare guns and this was one of his prized possessions. The gun was placed back in the closet inside the case from which it had been removed. The Glock 19 that Jimmy had brought with him was removed altogether.

One of the gentlemen accessed Ali's personal computer and typed a few letters. One, to Ali's deceased wife, telling her how sorry he was, and another to a mysterious Mr. Hasan, telling him that he was afraid the jig was up and he would have to flee before tomorrow's meeting at 0800.

The plan was as simple as it was ingenious. Within 20 minutes the FBI would be descending on this apartment with guns blazing. The gentlemen who sent these men were well aware that all the agent's phones and computers were being monitored. The FBI would arrive and find an unconscious Agent Hussein in front of a murdered Agent Forbes—complete with a bullet hole administered by one of Ali's prized guns—and question a confused Agent Hussein. When asked why he sent the messages referring to his escape plan and apologizing to his dead wife, Ali would have nothing but confusion and a lot of unanswered questions; sparse company to one in prison.

The FBI was in Ali's apartment ten minutes later.

●

Senator Malcolm C. Wooten was one of the, so called, "Lions" of the Senate. This colloquialism has been bestowed upon a slew of senators throughout American history, most recently, Sen. Robert C. Byrd of West Virginia and Sen. Edward M. Kennedy of Massachusetts. It is a term usually reserved for a senator who has served for multiple decades and is, more often than not, approaching retirement, death or both. Senator Wooten was not long for this earth, and if he had anything to do with it, President Michael Hamilton would soon be joining his august company.

Malcolm Wooten had been elected to the United States Senate in 1960. He'd come to the Senate as a young idealistic Congressman from the state of New York. Now, after over 50 years of senatorial service he was living his final year on earth watching his beloved country dissolve right before his eyes. The man he believed to be the major cause of its demise was now walking towards him, shaking hands with his fellow Senators and Congressmen. He would only get one chance to do this and he knew he had to make it count.

Senator Wooten's aging wife, Eleanor, as well as most of his children, grandchildren and great-grandchildren had lived within radioactive spitting distance of the "new ground zero" in New York. Now that Senator Wooten had been diagnosed with an inoperable brain tumor his only solace had come from the legacy of his progeny. Without them there was nothing to hope for, even in death.

Now, with the President fast approaching his position in the aisle, surrounded by seemingly well-wishing colleagues, Sen. Wooten reached into the pocket of his brown-tweed suit jacket and clutched the grip of his Ultra-Lite Taurus Model 94 snub-nose pistol. This small .22 caliber handgun was purchased 2 years ago by Malcolm's wife, Eleanor, whose Alzheimer's was just beginning to manifest itself. She had developed an inordinate fear of home invaders and wished to protect herself and her toy poodle, Penelope. It was Malcolm's son, Barry that had procured the weapon for his mother to ease her quickly diminishing mind.

Sen. Wooten, still confined to a wheelchair, had not been scrutinized by Capital security. The metal detector would be set off by the metal in his wheelchair and nobody was going to ask the legendary Senator from New York to stand up. They might as well strip search the President, himself!

Within moments, the President was standing in front of the dying Senator, extending his hand in greeting. In an instant of adrenaline-filled movement, the Senator reached up with his left hand and seized the President's right arm. At the same time, he withdrew his right hand from his pocket, firmly gripping his .22 caliber snub-nose weapon, and shoved its two-inch barrel into the left eye socket of the President. Then, with his last ounce of strength, and with all his might, he pulled the trigger.

When President Kennedy was assassinated, three years after Senator Wooten's election to the Senate, media coverage was in its infancy. The Zapruder film, which showed the gruesome death of the thirty-fifth President, hadn't even been viewed by the public until Geraldo Rivera showed it on ABC's Good Night America in March of 1975. Needless to say, times had changed. The close-up, digitally corrected and slowed down grimaces on the faces of those surrounding Senator Wooten would become the stuff of legend. So, also, would be the wrestling of the gun away from the fragile would-be-assassin as he wept in utter futility as Secret Servicemen quickly wheeled him out of the chamber.

The scene of a room full of Senators, Congressmen, Generals and Supreme Court Justices running around like ants on a hotplate while the Secret Servicemen gave the President of the United States the bums rush would never leave the consciousness of a frightened and ever confused public. Many began to long for the tranquility of days like 911.

Barry Wooten had not been a fool. The weapon that he had purchased for his frightened, senile mother had a special feature that saved the life of the President of the United States. When a special security key is inserted and turned a quarter-turn clockwise, the pistol cannot be fired or cocked and the gun's manual safety cannot be disengaged without another key's insertion and a counter-clockwise turn. Senator Wooten had been wholly unaware of this feature, lending whole new chapters to the conspiracy theories that would arise in the months and years that followed.

Although, none the worse for wear, the President had escaped the assassination attempt unscathed, if not unaffected. While he assigned no blame to the Secret Service and held no ill feelings toward the aged and hapless Senator Wooten, the President did, at least subconsciously, hold on to lingering feelings of culpability toward the European Union, whom he believed to be either directly or indirectly responsible for America's recent series of misfortunes. His future dealings with them would not be as cordial as before.

Chapter Eleven

The evidence against Ali didn't leave much room for speculation. He awoke just minutes before the FBI agents broke down his door. In his obvious confusion after having seen Jimmy lying dead on his couch with a bullet hole in his chest, Ali tried to revive him. When the agents entered the apartment, they found a forlorn and confused Agent Hussein standing over the fresh corpse of Agent Jim Forbes. His explanation to the arresting agents was less than believable, especially when the crime scene investigators found the murder weapon neatly tucked away in Ali's closet, free of all prints.

Kevin's "sting operation" hadn't gone quite the way he'd planned it; resulting in the death of Jimmy Forbes and the arrest for murder and conspiracy of Ali Hussein. Kevin's team, what was left of it, assembled at 0800 the following morning amid speculation of another agent's murder and yet another's arrest. Diane and Bobby were fit to be tied when Kevin walked into the office.

Diane accosted Agent O'Brien as soon as he entered. "What the hell is going on, Kevin? Is it true about Jimmy? Is he dead?" she whimpered.

Kevin sat his coffee cup on the table and loaded himself into his chair. He slowly lifted his eyes to the ceiling and responded with disbelief, "Yes, apparently so."

"Apparently so?" Bobby parroted. "Is that all we get? Where's Ali? Is he coming?"

Scuttlebutt in the FBI is no different than in that of any other career field. It can travel with the speed of light but is usually less than accurate in its course. Apparently, Diane and Bobby had heard about Jimmy's death but not who'd been arrested for his murder.

"Ali's not coming in today, either, Bobby." Kevin said. "He's been arrested for Jimmy's murder," he added with no pleasure in his voice. "Jimmy was killed in Ali's apartment, with Ali's gun and with Ali present and having no memory of the event. Apparently, he also typed a few rather incriminating letters, one indicating that he was preparing to flee the country rather than attend today's meeting."

To say that Diane and Bobby were dumbfounded would be an understatement. Their collective jaw drop could be heard in the next room. "Oh, pleeeeease!" Bobby oozed out. "There is no way that Ali could kill anyone, let alone Jimmy! This is Bullshit!"

Not knowing all the particulars and not yet having had the chance to talk to Ali, Kevin couldn't argue the point, only point out the obvious. "I agree, Bobby, but he has been arrested for the murder and everything I've told you is true, although, I can't even fathom Ali being involved in anything of this nature. He's no terrorist, I'd bet on that!" Kevin reiterated.

"You have bet on that!" Diane said. "I doubt the director would look kindly on you having assigned a terrorist to an anti-terrorist task force."

Kevin just looked at her. He would have protested her statement, saying that Ali was no terrorist, but they both knew that wasn't what she meant. "Well, then I think it's up to us to prove Ali's not a terrorist. I'm going to see him this afternoon. Maybe he can give us something to go on."

Bobby was chomping at the bit. "Wait a minute!" he called out in frustration, "I think we're missing the point here! The place to begin is not whether Ali is guilty or not, the place to start is, why was Jimmy killed? Just framing Ali for murder isn't going to help anyone's cause."

"Maybe they're just trying to disrupt our task force," Diane offered, "I mean, after all, we are tasked with stopping them. Maybe, like Doug, Jimmy was getting close to something."

All three agents were grasping at straws. Kevin didn't have any answers. "I suppose that could be it, but something doesn't smell right." Kevin said. "Why the big production? If they were on to something, why not just kill them both? If they thought Jimmy knew something that would implicate one of them, then they couldn't assume that Ali didn't have the same information. Even a disgraced agent can provide vital clues. Why not kill them both? It just doesn't make any sense."

"That's right!" Bobby jumped in, "The key to this has to be Jimmy, himself! They wanted Jimmy dead and they used Ali to cover up their involvement! It's the only explanation!" Bobby was quite animated. He was very close to Ali, even to the point of considering becoming a baptized Christian.

Kevin was equally sure of Ali's innocence which led him to a provisional agreement with Bobby. "If you're right, Bobby, then we've got to find out why they would want Jimmy dead. What threat was he to them that the rest of us were not?"

Diane had a thought. "You know, all this started at about the time we began to investigate the possibility of the existence of this 'European cabal', or whatever it is. Doug was killed shortly thereafter, and now Jimmy and Ali. It's awfully coincidental and I've never been a big fan of coincidence."

"You know," Kevin said with furrowed brow, "that was my impression, as well. Let's consider what Mr. Townsend alleges. If what he says is true, then it all fits together." Kevin pulled his briefcase across the desk and popped it open. He pulled out a file and flipped it open. After rummaging through it a bit, he pulled out a clump of loose papers, glanced at them a moment and looked up with a wide-eyed stare and said, "This has been one, big misdirection after another! Look at this!" he said, but didn't show them anything, it was just his way of getting their attention. "First, the Iranian connection to the sniper and SAM attacks. Townsend says the Iranians are being used by this mysterious European group to affect change in America. Secondly, the cyber attack; painstakingly disguised to look as if it were the Chinese. Now, Jimmy's murder made to look like the work of one of our agents."

Diane interrupted. "Boy, these guys are serious, aren't they?" This was a rhetorical question. "I don't know about you guys, but I'm for finding these assholes and nailing their butts to a cross!"

Kevin and Bobby were in complete agreement. It was time to stop pussyfooting around what seemed now to be the real issue; the deliberate and carefully planned attack on the United States by a European entity that was not motivated by religious fanaticism, but cold, unemotional self interest. There could be nothing so dangerous or nothing so difficult to prove; yet, that's exactly what they must do if they are to save their friend, Ali, and the United States, itself.

•

Lisa had just finished up with a difficult CT-guided lung biopsy on an elderly man when she walked back into her office and saw a package sitting on her desk. It was about the size of a shoebox, wrapped in beautiful Columbia blue paper (Lisa's favorite color), on top of which sat a single yellow rose (Lisa's favorite flower and second favorite color). There was no note, so her only clue as to its intention was that it was sitting on her desk.

A little wary of the mystery, but more curious than concerned, she lifted the rose to her nose and inhaled its aroma. After setting it to the side, Lisa carefully un-wrapped the "gift" and folded the wrapping paper neatly before opening the box. Inside the box were a number of small objects which were, at first, confusing. On top was a picture of a local Tampa church; Christ the King Catholic Church, to be precise. Written on the bottom of the picture, in handwriting she knew to be Kevin's, was the date of April 15th and the time of 8:00 am. Written underneath were the words, "Be there or be square!"

Beneath the picture of the church was a pair of American Airline tickets; round trip, open ended to Rome, Italy. The date of departure was April 15th.

Yet, one more item lay under the airline tickets. It was a single, gold, men's wedding band. When Lisa saw it, she put it all together and began to cry. As she sobbed with joyous anticipation she heard the obvious sound of a man clearing his throat. She spun her chair to the rear and beheld Kevin, kneeling before her, wearing a tuxedo and a silly grin.

"I know I've already asked this question, but I'd like to ask it again: Will you marry me, Lisa?" Kevin's eyes were filled with a yearning that Lisa hadn't seen before. She was overwhelmed by the moment.

Lisa rolled her chair toward Kevin and wrapped her arms around his neck. "Yes, Kevin, I'll marry you and never look back!" she managed to get out. Then, she pulled her head back a bit in order to look him in the eye. "But, if the date on the picture and the airline tickets is right, there may be a problem. That's two days from now, and there's no way I could get off that soon, particularly for a trip to Europe."

Kevin just loved to do this, "Welcome to the FBI, Lisa," he said, smiling from ear to ear.

Lisa wasn't going to accept that as an answer this time. "What is that supposed to mean? Did President Hamilton call the hospital administrator and get me put on vacation?"

"No," Kevin said, smiling like a Cheshire cat, "the Director of the FBI made the call. You are on a one month vacation beginning right now. Come on, I'm taking you to dinner," he said, taking her arm and leading her out the door.

Lisa was excited but dubious. "Kevin, I can't just leave without notice, there are scheduled patients to ..."

Kevin cut her off. "It's been taken care of, Lisa. Two additional radiologists are going to be here tomorrow morning to cover for you, now let's go!"

Lisa wasn't going to argue further. "Show me to the door," she yelped, "Boy, you really do have a lot of pull, don't you?"

"The better to impress you with, my dear," Kevin said, grabbing her jacket, "now, let's blow this Popsicle stand!"

So, out the door they went, leaving Lisa to ponder this amazing man she was about to marry and to wonder what the heck he meant by his last statement.

•

Ali Rajsanjani had been President Habibi's First-Vice President since he came to office. The office of First-Vice President of Iran was created in the revision of the Constitution of Iran in 1989 to take on some of the responsibilities of a Prime Minister, mostly leading cabinet meetings in the absence of the President.

In all, there are 10 Vice-Presidents, in charge of everything from nuclear energy to tourism. The First-Vice President is the chief organizer of the other Vice-Presidents. Ali Rajsanjani was a close personal friend of President

Habibi, growing up together with him just outside of Teheran. Having recently lost his wife to breast cancer, Ali had been in and out of his official duties for a few weeks, never quite feeling up to sitting in on mundane meetings, listening to the other Vice-Presidents prattle on.

The trappings of his office gave Ali a certain cache within the government, but his relationship with President Habibi added to his stature immensely. One duty that Ali had not been inclined to shirk was his role as intermediary with Arthur Swift, the man the President had relied on most to accomplish his objectives in Jihad America. Of course, neither he nor President Habibi knew the actual identity of Mr. Swift, referring to him by his nom-de-guerre, Mr. Peanut—Arthur Swift must have been in a jovial mood when he came up with that one. His correspondence boiled down to a few internet liaisons and about 5 telephone conversations that were scrambled, coded and muted to avoid any recognition.

The CIA had long ago caught on to the mutual admiration society between the Iranian Presidency and the European Union; they just hadn't pieced together the link-up with the terrorist activities occurring in America. Nor were they aware of the Elite Eight's existence and their lofty manipulation of the Iranian President—a situation that if known by the Supreme Leader or the Mahjis would lead to the immediate execution of President Habibi. Radical Muslim terrorist leaders didn't mind crawling in bed with the infidels to accomplish something, but Allah-forbid allowing the infidel to manipulate you.

Today's correspondence would be via telephone. Ali arrived at President Habibi's residence (the venue for all contact with Mr. Peanut) and was greeted warmly by ChalipA, Sadad's beautiful wife and best friend to his beloved, departed wife. "Hello, Ali, our dear friend,"

ChalipA said in greeting, "Welcome to our home. Are you well?" she inquired, sincerely concerned for his well-being.

"Thank you, ChalipA, you are a kind soul." Ali answered, entering the home. President Habibi was not home at this time, a situation which would normally be taboo—a man entering the home of a married woman with her husband absent—but no one questioned the integrity of either the President or his friend, the First-Vice President.

"I made you your favorite meal, Ali. It's waiting for you by the phone in my husband's office. The coffee has just been poured, as well." ChalipA said. Ali had always been fond of chelo kebab, the national dish of Iran. It consists of ground up lamb served on skewers over a bed of rice.

"ChalipA, you are too good to me." Ali said, ambling toward Sadad's office, "Did you see Ghahve-ye Talkh this week? For some reason I never got the DVDs. Of course, my wife usually took care of those things." Ali was referring to Iran's historical comedy series, roughly translated, Bitter Coffee, and distributed three episodes at a time. The show can only be viewed on DVD because of a dispute that prevented its airing on television.

"Yes, Ali, we watched it last night. Doesn't Siamak (Siamak Ansari, main character in the show, a historian who travels back in time to become a royal counselor.) remind you of Sadad? The resemblance is remarkable, I think." ChalipA said with a laugh.

Ali saw the resemblance as well. "I agree, ChalipA, but don't tell Sadad; he thinks Siamak is an idiot." Ali entered the President's office and closed the door. It would be another 10 minutes before he would receive the phone call. In the mean time, he would enjoy his chelo kebab.

Ali was quite satisfied with his corpulent form. Although he had been a ruggedly handsome and powerfully built young man, memories of those days seemed to have been from another life. Now, at the age of 69, the widower of a wife of over 50 years, his desire to stay fit and healthy was not a priority, enjoying the little things in life, like chelo kebab, were.

When the 10 minutes had elapsed, exactly on time, as usual, the phone rang and Ali answered with a simple, "Yes?"

Arthur Swift's voice was necessarily altered; making him sound like the nefarious character in those "Saw" movies. Ali, old enough to remember the old American spy thrillers, thought it was a hoot. He was thrilled to be involved in cloak-and-dagger.

"Mr. Vice-President, it is an honor to speak with you today," Arthur began, "The brave soldiers of the Iranian brotherhood have carried the banner of Islam with pride." Arthur nearly chuckled at his own words, but that's the way you spoke to these people. Their pride was off the scale. "Our mission is nearly complete. Soon the Americans will be part of the European confederation of nations and their support for the Israelis will be non-existent. At that time, I will see to it that Palestine is declared a State by the UN Security Council and Israel will have no choice but to withdraw from Jerusalem."

Ali was greatly pleased to hear this news. He had always wanted to live to see the destruction of Israel and the city of Jerusalem back in the rightful hands of Allah's children. Soon the Jews would have nowhere to go but back to America where they belong; if America still exists by then. "I am pleased, Mr. Peanut. What would you have me do to further assist you in this great undertaking?"

"Mr. Vice-President, you and President Habibi have done so much that it pains me to ask for just one more favor of you."

"What is it, my friend?" Ali felt benevolent, "We are here to serve Allah."

"*Gag me with a Ginzu*", Arthur thought, "Thank you, Mr. Vice-President," he said, "Iran is truly fortunate to have such great leadership. We have developed another weapon for use against the Americans that we believe will 'push them over the edge', so to speak. The resultant trauma will spread to Israel as well, I think."

"A new weapon?" Ali asked with surprise, "I can't imagine anything that could be used against the Americans that is not already being employed. Surely, the use of nuclear weapons is not an option; it would ignite a global conflagration."

"I assure you, Mr. Vice-President, this weapon is not nuclear. In fact, if all goes well, it will not only avoid inviting American retaliation, it could very well make American military power, ineffectual."

"We will deny you nothing if it furthers our plans to destroy the people of the Scriptures (Islam's term for Christians and Jews). Tell me about this new weapon, Mr. Peanut."

Chapter Twelve

The wedding of Lisa Martin to Kevin O'Brien was not an ostentatious affair, but neither was Lisa going to be denied her moment in the sun. Why Kevin had chosen to get married on the day when millions of Americans were scrambling to submit their taxes was anybody's guess. Most likely, it never dawned on him. Kevin was very intelligent and quite thoughtful, but his lack of understanding with regard to the contemporary social niceties left a lot to be desired. It was a personal failing that Lisa was happy to live with.

Dressed in her long dreamt of flowing white gown Lisa made the long, slow journey down the aisle of Christ the King Catholic Church and toward the man who waited nervously for the woman he loved. Lisa had never seen Kevin so handsome, yet, uneasy, as he looked right now. It filled her with joy and just a little personal delight to see him in such a vulnerable state as she glided down the aisle in view of a sea of tear filled eyes. She was sure that her parents would be very proud of her and she shed a tear for the sister who would never see this day, either for Lisa or for herself. *"Wish me luck, Tinker Bell"*, she thought to herself, using the pet name that her sister always hated.

When she reached Kevin, Dr. Henry James (a colleague and retired Radiologist who'd taught her everything she knows and the man she'd chosen to give her away), gave her a quick peck on the cheek and then placed her hand in Kevin's before being seated in the front row next to his wife.

The moment of truth had arrived. She was really getting married. She felt another twinge of sadness that her mother couldn't see her now, couldn't have known Kevin. She would have loved him so much.

As she stood there, arm in arm with Kevin, Lisa looked at the priest standing before them. She had never been much of a Catholic, at least, not since her childhood days of going to Confession to tell the priest something that she had "made up", standing proudly in front of her parents as she received her First Communion and feeling guilty about just about everything she did and thought. This was different; however, particularly because of the fact that her parents and her little sister couldn't be here; she felt proud to be standing, once again, in front of a priest to receive a Sacrament of the Church.

As the priest read the wedding vows and the two lovers parroted him, Kevin was so overcome by emotion that his eyes began to tear up. He didn't want to appear to be crying at his own wedding so he began batting his eyes as fast as he could, trying to stem the tide. He was successful enough to avoid embarrassment and stoically said his lines right on cue.

The rest of the wedding followed the usual script, ending with an ever so wonderful kiss at the end. Lisa wasn't prepared for a passionate kiss, just a quick peck on the lips and let's hit the road. Kevin apparently didn't have that in mind. He planted a kiss on her that made her legs sweat, starting a "way-too-long wait" for the honeymoon, at least, as far as she was concerned. Lisa was as pure and chased as any 21st century woman around, until Kevin arrived, that is, but she was also very passionate and very much in love with her husband. The reception couldn't go fast enough.

Later, when they were alone, Lisa tried out her new name. "Lisa O'Brien", she said, out loud, wishing to hear how it sounded. She tried it in a number of ways: "Dr. Lisa O'Brien; Mrs. Kevin O'Brien." Then she got silly with it, "The woman formerly known as Lisa Martin. I like that!

That's what I'll call myself, 'The woman formerly known as Lisa Martin'. How does that sound to you?"

Kevin loved the playfulness of Lisa's humor. She had her own mind and he loved it. He held her even tighter than before as the two of them rolled down the Courtney-Campbell Causeway in the back of a limo on their way to Tampa International Airport.

"Maybe I'm old fashioned," Kevin admitted, "but I kind of like the sound of Mrs. Kevin O'Brien, the most. It makes me feel like you belong to me, in a good way."

"Don't worry, sweetheart," Lisa said as she kissed him for the umpteenth time, "that's the one I like best, too."

•

The O'Briens arrived in the ancient capital of Italy on April 16th—seven months to the day since the first sniper attack, aimed, ironically, at his new bride. After checking in to the Rome Cavalieri, a posh and expensive Waldorf Astoria hotel, they went immediately to their honeymoon suite, the Napoleon, and didn't leave their king-sized "floating featherbed" until the following morning, when Kevin fought a pitched battle with Lisa in order to eat breakfast downstairs rather than order room service, as his new wife ardently suggested, nakedly. Kevin got his way only by telling Lisa that they had reservations for a guided tour of Rome, a lie that she didn't discover until the waiter had already brought the check.

Kevin simply needed to come up for air!

During breakfast, Kevin informed Lisa of another piece of information of which he had conveniently neglected to inform her; the wedding, the honeymoon and the month's vacation that she had so fortuitously received had not been without a price. Kevin had convinced his boss that his "honeymoon" would be a perfect "cover" for a more detailed investigation of this, "European Cabal", for lack of a better term, which he was convinced, was, at best, in cahoots with the Iranians, and at worst, orchestrating the whole thing from behind the scenes.

Needless to say, Lisa was less than pleased at this revelation, but she was also a practical woman. She was, after all, married and on an expensive honeymoon in Rome; neither of which she would have experienced any time soon had Kevin not pulled some strings. Also, while Lisa was a Wunderkind and a highly respected Radiologist in the Tampa Bay area, she was also an old-fashioned woman with no desire to be the "man" in her marriage. Kevin was a respected FBI agent, currently involved in a case that had serious national security implications. She wanted to begin her marriage supporting her husband, not complaining that she wasn't getting enough attention. She knew that Kevin was a good and thoughtful man; whatever he did, he did for a reason.

Now that they were out of the room, they might as well do a little sight-seeing, they decided; after all, Kevin owed Lisa the "guided tour" he'd promised her to get her out of the bed. They quickly discovered that they shared a fascination with historic places, particularly with regard to the Ancient Roman Empire.

They marveled at the precision and wherewithal that went into the construction of the Coliseum, also known as the Flavian Amphitheatre. Construction began in 72AD; two years after the Romans sacked Jerusalem and destroyed the Temple. It was with the proceeds of that profoundly far-reaching campaign that they built the Coliseum. This legendary edifice would be used for gladiatorial contests and spectacles; the re-enactment of famous Roman battles, animal hunts and even mock sea battles—in these cases, it was necessary to actually flood the floor of the structure in order to float the ships.

Naturally, they went to the famous Forum Magnum, or Forum, the one-time marketplace and center of public life in ancient Roman society. They had lunch at Armando's, a restaurant near the Pantheon, the "temple of the gods" and best preserved of the ancient Roman ruins, followed by a bowl of gelato (Italian ice cream) and a visit to Trevi Fountain, where they both tossed in coins to ensure they would return to Rome— or so goes the tradition.

After a whirlwind day, the happy but fatigued couple stopped at a café on the Via Alberto Cadlolo for a couple of lattes. It was within easy walking distance of the hotel and they just wanted to relax a bit. Kevin had not only spent the day enjoying his new wife's company but also the attractive view she provided him, dressed in a light-blue Cashmere sweater-dress that she must have been poured into, over which was a white Cardi sweater with a cascading open front. No supermodel could have looked more attractive. Kevin was about to suggest a return to the "floating featherbed" when Lisa's Blackberry went off.

"Oh, I'd almost forgotten," Lisa said, surprised that she had her phone with her, "I meant to leave this at the hotel." She pulled it from her small clutch and saw that it was a text message. "I wonder who'd text me now. No one I know would bother me on my honeymoon."

Almost as an afterthought, Lisa punched a few buttons and viewed the message. It said, *"Hello Lisa, I must say, I don't believe that Kevin has ever made a better choice than that of marrying you. You look absolutely stunning today, but it may be a little warm for the sweater. If I may interrupt your honeymoon for just a moment, would you please give Kevin the note that I placed in the right pocket of your very attractive white sweater? Enjoy your honeymoon and tell Kevin that the Venetian loafers are a little too touristy."*

Lisa, still staring agape at the message on the Blackberry, reached into the right pocket of her Cardi sweater and withdrew a folded piece of paper with Kevin's name written on it. Kevin was still unaware of the message on Lisa's phone, so she passed the phone to him so he could read it for himself. As Kevin read the text message he was stunned at its personal nature and filling with righteous indignation over the comments directed at his wife. Once Lisa realized Kevin had finished reading the message she handed him the note.

Both were dumbfounded at the placement of the note inside Lisa's right pocket; the same method used by the late Reginald Townsend. Who else knew that Mr. Townsend had communicated with Kevin via Lisa's right pocket?

Kevin unfolded the note and lifted it up to the street light's glow. The note was typed with no handwriting for a possible ID. It said, simply, *"Agent Bennett was on to something. That's why he's dead."* Then, underneath, was written a cryptic notation: *"Aldo Veneto is dying!"*

Kevin glanced at Lisa, still looking like the RCA Victor dog, and informed her of its contents, "It says, Aldo Veneto is dying. Who the hell is Aldo Veneto?"

Lisa answered this rhetorical question with a shrug. Then, she picked up her Blackberry and went to the internet. "Let's find out," she said, "if he's anybody of note he'll be in here." Lisa punched in the name of Aldo Veneto and got an immediate response.

"It says here that Aldo Veneto, from Genoa, Italy is one of the richest men in Europe. He is a shipping magnate, a philanthropist of some note, and it says here that while he's publicly low key, he is believed to one of the driving forces behind the original idea of the European Union. It also says that he has pancreatic cancer and is not expected to live much longer. Wow!" Lisa added, realizing that this is obviously the man the note mentioned.

Kevin had a cell phone, as well, but his was not a state of the art I-Phone or Blackberry, or whatever the newest phone was this week. He was the proud owner of one of the original Nokia cell phones. It didn't have access to the internet and when it was made, the concept of texting was not yet envisioned, let alone tweeting and twittering. Kevin was a 20th century man in a 21st century world. All he wanted out of his cell phone was to say "Hello", "Goodbye", and "Leave a message". Nevertheless, he punched it a few times and soon he was speaking with Diane Austin.

Kevin informed Diane of the contents of the text message and the typed note. "Get on this as fast as you can," Kevin ordered, "Find out everything you can about this Aldo Veneto and get back to me..." Kevin glimpsed his wife's raised eyebrows and continued, "Tomorrow!"

Lisa smiled.

•

The assassination attempt on President Hamilton had received all of the obligatory media hype it was due. "Experts" in forensics, ballistics, weaponology, psychology and historic context had examined the computer-enhanced assassination-attempt footage from every angle imaginable. Senator Wooten's life was scrutinized for latent homicidal inklings, the Secret Service and the Capital police were the subject of House and Senate hearings, and alarmists were calling for an end to the "risky" practice of Presidential public appearances. Even the famed fortune teller, Madam Wu, had made the talk-show rounds after predicting, just two months prior, that the President would soon "experience a frightening moment." However, with the general understanding of Senator Wooten's recent health woes combined with the death of his wife and family in New York, most people didn't overanalyze the attack on the President, giving it its proper standing as an anomaly, not the beginning of the end. Besides, most Americans had other things to worry about. The economy was still on life support; crime was still of major concern and the jobless rate stood at 32 percent.

While the President did get a bump in the polls after his adroit political handling of the assassination attempt, most Americans were still pro-Euro-Union and clamoring for the President to "see the light". Yet, President Hamilton stuck to his guns. He would not hand over one iota of American sovereignty to "a bunch of European low-life's that couldn't go 20 years without starting a world war!" This last statement was not meant for public consumption but was overheard by an enterprising young reporter for CNN. Needless to say, the President had some political fence-mending to do after that statement was relayed to the European leadership. They were tactfully understanding of the President's faux pas; but nonetheless, used it as leverage to convince the President to accede to their wishes, something that he simply was not prepared to do.

In a darkened, candlelit study on Dark Island, the men who would decide the fate of the United States were contemplating an ominous burden. The American President was a stubborn man and would have to be given another "nudge" in the right direction. The consequences could be dire, but the President was leaving them with little choice.

Tonight, the Elite Eight was seven. Aldo Veneto was at death's door and unable to make the trip. His friend, Antoine Rousseau was beside himself with grief, alternating back and forth between weeping and laughingly relating some past shared adventure between him and Aldo. "They will not make another one like him, I'll tell you that!" Antoine announced to the room. "The world will little mourn his passing and even less, appreciate the gravity thereof." Antoine loved to speak like a Shakespearean character. He'd always seen the theatre as his unrequited love.

"It is truly a black day for this august company, gentlemen," Arthur Swift injected, "but there are pressing matters that I'm sure the always attentive Mr. Veneto would wish us to address." He wanted to add, "*Aldo isn't dead yet, gentlemen!*" But he thought better of it.

Sir Harold Covington cleared his throat, announcing that he was about to impart a bit of British wisdom on the room. "Hear, hear, gentlemen, I must agree with my distinguished American colleague; there is a decision that we must make and it would behoove us to make it quickly. President Hamilton has exposed himself as an ardent right-wing ideologue and will not long be tolerated, even in America." Sir Harold tapped his Meerschaum pipe, emptying the ashes. He then inserted the pipe into his "special English blend" tobacco pouch to refill it. "The deployment of this weapon is not something that one takes lightly; nevertheless, it is necessary for the greater good of both Europe and America, and by extension, the world. We have no choice, gentlemen!" Sir Harold adamantly added.

Amal Singh listened to the arguments of Sir Harold and Arthur. He was not a man who lacked a conscience; he simply felt that in many cases, if not most, the "mindless rabble" as his father had referred to the general public, was incapable of making decisions for the greater good. It fell to those in positions of power to make those decisions for them. However, that was not the end of it, or so thought

Amal Singh: Those in positions of power were usually either elected officials, bent on reelection, or dictators who gave little or no thought to their subjects.

This, Amal felt, was the whole point of their "Elite Eight" establishment. He slowly arose and addressed the table: "Gentlemen," he said, "We cannot leave it to those in traditional positions of power to plan for an establishment of a worldwide governing body. Each man or woman in power, each nation and people on earth are too drunk with the memories of those who have gone before and the traditions that bind them together to think on the kind of grand scale of which only the men at this table are capable. It is with a full and generous heart that I urge you all to refrain from thoughts or actions which will continue to propagate the notion of national identity. It is the sharp knife that cuts the cleanest."

Amal sat down with the same quiet assuredness with which he had arisen. He turned his head toward Mr. Grant, the American.

Michael Grant was one of two Americans within the Elite Eight, but he was the only one who currently lived in the United States. Arthur lived on an island off the Grecian coast. "Gentlemen, the deployment of this weapon will have far reaching consequences. As a resident of Atlanta, Georgia, I have the most to lose with this plan's enactment. I must be given certain assurances if I'm to agree with this course of action, and as we all know, all decisions of the Elite Eight must be unanimous; Aldo's absence notwithstanding."

"Here it comes!" Herr von Graf said with a sarcastic tone.

Michael Grant would have none of that! "I resent your insinuation, sir, and demand an immediate apology! If your beloved Germany were the target of this dastardly weapon we would be hearing a chorus of Prussian expletives, I'd wager!"

"My beloved Germany was once the target of thousands of your American bombs, if my memory serves!" Herr von Graf shouted furiously, "Perhaps you should be a little less concerned with your precious Atlanta, Georgia and more concerned with the projected outcome of the New World Order we're trying to effect! No wars! No more poverty and little crime! Have you forgotten that this alliance will make the men in this room, virtual gods! You won't need Atlanta anymore; you can have Atlantis, for god's sake!"

Grant was seething. "Look, Wolfgang," he angrily pointed out, "your beloved Germany was the target of thousands of American and allied bombs because your psychotic leader, Adolph Hitler, wouldn't stop invading his neighbors."

Grant barely finished when Herr von Graf interjected, with some sarcasm, "It's just like an American to point out the obvious. You Americans have never dealt with enemy countries on your border. How easy it is for you to judge others while you are protected by two great oceans and bordered by the ever dangerous Canadians and the equally frightening Mexicans. It is a wonder you can sleep at night for fear of imminent attack!"

Wolfgang von Graf was the German version of Sir Harold; he was sixth generation noble, and heir to one of Germany's great fortunes. He was a veteran of World War Two, having lied about his age to fight for the man who had given him a reason to hold his head high again...Adolph Hitler.

His father, mother and both his little brothers were killed by allied bombing in the final days of the war, leaving Herr von Graf alone and bitter. With his family fortune tucked away in Swiss banks and he the lone survivor in his family, Wolfgang began post-war life with plenty of assets.

When he was presented with Aldo Veneto's idea for a united Europe, he jumped at the chance to create a Fourth Reich, with Germany as the powerful center piece. Veneto and his friend, Rousseau, had no idea that Herr von Graff fully intended to usurp power from their native countries of Italy and France. They were what he considered "useful idiots", helping him lay the groundwork for a powerful European Union with Berlin pulling the strings.

He had always resented America—a sentiment not uncommon in post-World War Two Europe—and felt that it was the German people, and not the Americans, who were providentially selected for world rule. He would need the help of the other European nations, but he felt that the rest of Europe had shown little ability to manage even their own affairs, let alone the world.

The online, Uncyclopedia, describes the British Upper Class—very much like the German Upper Class—like this: *The British Upper Class is not just a class-it is in fact a distinct species.* **Homo superior** *can be distinguished from the regular* **Homo sapiens** *by their stiff upper lips, wobbly chins, and strange distorted accents.*

Herr von Graff considered himself quite superior to other men, even the British Aristocracy, and looked at Michael Grant as an aristocratic wanna-be, having no natural breeding and a penchant for verbalizing his thoughts without the proper restraint. This, combined with his resentment and outright hatred of all things American, gave Herr von Graff a decidedly unsympathetic view of Michael Grant's opinion. He could just about tolerate Arthur Swift.

Arthur Swift, ever the ambassador of peace, called for composure. "Gentlemen, please, let's not have angry words with one another. I'm sure Mr. Veneto's condition, coupled with the gravity of today's decision has us all on edge." He turned to the man from Atlanta, "Mr. Grant, I'm sure Herr von Graf didn't mean anything personal." Then his eyes bathed all parties at the table. "Gentlemen, can we get down to business? The Iranian First Vice-President is awaiting confirmation."

"I believe we all understand the magnitude of our decision here today," John Devaney allowed, "I think we should consider bringing it to a vote," He quickly scanned the men back and forth before adding, "unless anyone has any objections."

No one did. The vote was unanimous. They would inform Vice-President Rajsanjani to expect delivery within the month. The American President, as well as the American people, was in for quite a shock. Soon, their whole society would be reduced to Third-World status, with all the rights and privileges, thereto. President Hamilton would preside over the end of America, as he knew it. It was a black day, indeed!

Chapter Thirteen

Diane Austin was celebrating—if you could call it that—her 31st birthday. She celebrated it with her Siberian husky, Nikia, and a bottle of Pinot noir. Most of her birthday had been spent researching Mr. Aldo Veneto and his apparent bosom buddy, Antoine Rousseau. They were quite a pair in European social circles.

Both men were roughly the same age, widowers, fathers and grandfathers. Both had been active at the onset of the European Union and they were each most noted as enthusiastic philanthropists. Aldo, from Genoa, Italy—most famous as the birthplace of Christopher Columbus—and Antoine, favorite son of Marseille, France had apparently been living together for the last 12 years. There had been some question about their homosexuality, but there was never any proof and neither man had been asked or had spoken of any such proclivity.

The two men fought in World War Two, on opposing sides. Their friendship began with a chance meeting in Athens, Greece when they were a mere 25 years old. They had both been instrumental in the establishment of the European Coal and Steel Community (ECSC) and the European Economic Community (EEC) in 1958 which led to the Maastricht Treaty in 1993, establishing the European Union, and the subsequent, Treaty of Lisbon in 2009, which redefined it.

While feeling no apparent antagonism toward their American liberators, both men had made it clear in the intervening years that they felt Europe needed to "spread its wings and fly again". It was their common belief that the continent that had civilized the world with its art, music and societal structure must never allow themselves to become internationally irrelevant; on the contrary, Europe should return to its historically justified position of world leadership.

Well into their sixties and mutually widowed, the two men established a common home and base from which to operate their respective business interests and philanthropic pursuits.

There was not much else of note. Diane was getting ready to call it a night when something struck her as odd. At the funeral of Reginald Townsend, some three months ago in Charlotte, North Carolina, Aldo Veneto and Antoine Rousseau had been spotted in the procession. That's not necessarily odd; they were all part of the Rich-Old-White-Man's Club, but also reportedly seen in Veneto and Rousseau's limo were five other "rich old white men", from various countries: Sir Harold Covington of London, John C. Devaney of Ireland, Arthur Swift of Chicago, Michael Grant of Atlanta and Wolfgang von Graf of Hamburg, Germany.

Diane had heard of the "Good-old-boy network" but this was ridiculous. All of these men were wealthy in the extreme. There was one from Chicago, one from Atlanta, Georgia and one each from England, Ireland, Germany, Italy and France; what could they all have in common that brought them to the funeral of still another wealthy old white man? It was just a gut instinct, but Diane thought this might be the group they were looking for. They certainly matched the description of Mr. Townsend's Euro-Cabal, a group in which Townsend claimed to be a member. Diane opened another bottle of wine and started researching the other men at Mr. Townsend's funeral. "Happy birthday, Diane!" she said to herself.

•

The next morning Kevin awoke to find Lisa firmly snuggled up against his body. To say the feeling was agreeable would be an understatement. He needed to go to the bathroom but didn't want to wake her; the way most of us do when our dogs or cats are resting on our laps. The cavalry arrived in the form of a gentle rap at the door, which forced Kevin to break Lisa's kung fu grip and put his clothes on.

Lisa barely even noticed as Kevin arose, donned his complementary Waldorf Astoria bath robe and opened the door. The man, well, boy, at the door was a courier with a large Manila envelope. He was dressed in what reminded Kevin of the old Bellhop outfits he used to see on TV as a kid. If he were in America it might have been comical, but in Italy, well, it was Italy. Kevin found his pants and pulled out a few Euros to give the boy. He thanked him with his best "grazie" and took the envelope. Lisa was awake now, sitting up in bed with her sleepy eyes affixed to his every move. "What's that, honey?" Lisa asked.

Kevin tossed the envelope onto the table and headed for the bathroom. On the way, he answered Lisa's question. "If I know Diane Austin, she's been up all night researching our little Euro-group. This is probably everything she came up with."

"Good," Lisa said, raising her voice so that Kevin could hear her in the bathroom, "I hope she finds something! These messages are getting a little creepy."

"You got that right!" Kevin hollered. The toilet flushed and the door opened. "Hey," Kevin said as he ambled back to bed, "you want to help me go through this stuff? It will go a lot quicker with four eyes than it will with two."

Kevin sprawled over Lisa like a bear. She mockingly screamed in terror, followed by a cute little giggle and a long good-morning kiss. "If you promise you'll keep doing that," Lisa sighed with pleasure, "I'll join the FBI."

Kevin put his arms around his lovely wife and held on for dear life. He whispered into her ear, "I'm sorry that I have to do anything but pay attention to you, but it's very important that I do a little snooping while we're over here. I hope you're not too upset."

"I'm not upset at all," she said, "You have a job to do and I wouldn't respect you if you didn't do it. Don't worry, you didn't marry a nagging wife, you married a partner."

That was all Kevin needed to hear. "Make you a deal," he said as he launched himself from the bed, "let's get showered...together, and go have breakfast before we bother with any of this stuff."

"If we shower together," Lisa said, "we may have to change that to lunch. Why don't you go first?"

•

When they got back to the room, Kevin snatched up the Manila folder and ripped it open, spilling all of Diane's research onto the table. "That was a superb lunch, wasn't it?" Lisa said as she sat down at the table, ready to work.

"Not as good as breakfast." Kevin said.

"I told you we shouldn't have showered together;" Lisa said with a sexy smile, then, "Let's get to work, huh?"

Kevin appreciated Lisa's supportive attitude. He knew she'd rather be shopping or sitting in a gondola in Venice. He gave her an appreciative look and said, "Remind me not to divorce you."

"What's a divorce?" she said, and reached into the pile for something to study.

After a short time, Kevin realized that Diane had really nailed it. She not only had the names of eight of the possible conspirators, but detailed biographies, addresses, phone numbers and, with the assistance of Interpol, a smattering of financial records.

Also included, were newspaper interviews with each of the men, at various times in their lives, as well as various local newsmen's presumptions about the collective activities of these powerful, yet low-key men. It seemed that many who knew them best were puzzled by their sudden departures, their unusual purchases or their abrupt changes in plan. There was nothing untoward, but to those who knew them most intimately, there were many puzzling behaviors. The clincher seemed to be that all eight of these men's bios rang alarmingly similar.

"If I didn't know better," Lisa said after looking over much of the information, "I'd say these guys were in cahoots. They all seem to abruptly leave their homes at an eerily similar time and return the next day. Friends and family members are all at a loss to explain where they've gone; and the men, according to most of the family members, are purposely evasive when asked to explain their absences."

"Sort of makes you think they're meeting somewhere, doesn't it?" Kevin asked.

"Either that, or they all have the same tee times." Lisa joked. "Here's something! Look," she showed a cut-out newspaper article to Kevin, "Aldo Veneto is dead. How creepy is that?" Kevin gave her a look of shared understanding. The message on the note had said, *"Aldo Veneto is dying."*

"When's the funeral?" Kevin asked, sort of, to himself, since he was now holding the article. After finding the details, he said, "OK, the funeral is tomorrow at 10am in Genoa, Italy. How much you wanna bet that all these men will be in attendance? It's not far from here." He looked at

Lisa with puppy dog eyes, still afraid he was pushing it too far, and asked, "How'd you like to go to a funeral?"

"As long as it's not mine, I can live with it. What are they wearing at Italian funerals these days?" Lisa inquired with her usual wry humor.

Kevin shrugged his shoulders and lifted his palms, face up, "Black?"

•

Agent Ali Hussein had been languishing in a federal prison cell for over a week. No matter what he said to the interrogators it sounded like he was guilty. No wonder, Ali thought, he couldn't figure it out for himself. Obviously, someone had framed him; there was no way he would have killed Jimmy and he certainly didn't write those e-mails they had told him were on his computer. The very idea that he would apologize to his beloved wife while she lay in her grave was...ludicrous! *Apologize for what? And who the hell is Mr. Hasan?*

Ali never felt so low in his life. He'd lost his wife, he'd lost two of his friends—one of whom he was accused of killing—and now he'd lost his career and probably his freedom. He kept going over in his mind the events of that night. He remembered feeling a stinging sensation in his neck just before he passed out, but there didn't seem to be any sign of a wound; at least, not now. He must have been drugged; there was no other explanation. But why kill Jimmy? Was it just to frame him for his murder? What would be the point? He was probably the least important of the Maelstrom Task Force. It just didn't make any sense.

Ali, however, was a man of faith. Even through these dark times he felt a certain peace. He couldn't explain it, but it was there, nonetheless. It was as if God was trying to make him stronger by piling all this sorrow onto his shoulders. Anyway, Ali felt that everything would work out in the end.

His cell measured twelve feet by twelve feet. It had the obligatorily uncomfortable cot with an itchy green military blanket. There was a toilet, a sink, a small metallic table (melded into the wall) and chair. His cell door was barred, giving him an excellent view of the dull gray wall across the narrow hallway. He had had no contact with any other prisoners and was glad of it. He was still an FBI agent and most prisoners weren't inclined to befriend such men, they were more likely to give them a shank in the back.

After a night spent wide awake and worrying about his fate, Ali rose from his bunk and listened to the sounds of the prison as it began another day that would be identical to the day before and indistinguishable from all those that would follow. Having seen men in prison in Iran, England and in the United States, Ali realized that there were some universal constants: prisoners were loud, vile and most inclined to listen to themselves talk. There were smile-less faces bent on instilling fear in those around them, mostly from a desire for self-preservation and a total lack of the kind of hope that was an essential part of any man's life.

Ali, however, would see none of these things. He was in solitary confinement. He could only listen as the morning greeted him with loneliness and the promise of more to come, perhaps a lifetime of it.

After his morning breakfast of slop, the guard came to his cell door and announced that he had a visitor. Ali was excited at the idea of anyone visiting him. He hadn't spoken to a caring face since Kevin had seen him the morning after his arrest. Since the guards thought he had killed an FBI agent they were less than thrilled to make his acquaintance. The fact that his name was obviously Muslim didn't help either. Although Ali had told them he was Christian and requested a Bible they brought him a copy of the Koran and a prayer rug.

"Bobby, are you a sight for sore eyes?" Ali said as Agent Wang approached his cell.

Bobby waited until the guard had opened the door. He then asked to be left alone with the prisoner. The guard locked the door behind him and walked off.

Ali was almost in tears. He didn't expect to have such an emotional reaction to Bobby's arrival. "Hey man," Bobby said, patting him on the back, "it's ok. We'll get you out of here one way or the other."

"So you don't believe I did this?" Ali whimpered.

"Of course not, Ali, everybody knows this is a frame-up! Like I said, we'll get you out of here if it's the last thing we ever do. Kevin is in Europe checking out the guys we think are responsible and Diane's tracking them like a bloodhound. Don't worry, just hang in there."

Bobby's words came as great solace to Ali. He'd begun thinking he would be in here for the rest of his life; a life he was sure would be a short one. It was good to know that his friends and colleagues believed in him; that was all he really needed.

"Now," Bobby said as he pulled up the old metal chair and sat down in a close face-to-face with Ali, "I want you to tell me everything you remember and everything Jimmy did while he was in the apartment."

Ali unloaded everything he had gone over in his mind since that night. He told him of Jimmy's odd arrival, which seemed strange to Ali, the stinging sensation in his neck just before he'd passed out, and then waking up to the gruesome scene of Jimmy's death. He didn't leave anything out, even adding a few things that he'd only just remembered.

Bobby wrote down everything Ali told him and promised that the "team" wouldn't stop working on it until he was out of jail and back at the office. As Bobby walked out the cell door, leaving behind a relieved but still forlorn friend, he asked, "Jimmy had never come to visit you before?" Then, he shook his head as if perplexed, and added, "That's strange. Hey, I'll see you later, and I'll tell the guard to get you a Bible."

•

Genova, the Italian word for the city of Genoa, is about four and a half hours from Roma, the Italian word for Rome, by train. The trip was long, dirty and famishing, with no food car, no on-board beverages and toilets that made a man glad he could pee standing up. Women, of course, squatted in all public bathrooms, unbeknownst to men. Rarely did a woman's behind come in contact with a public toilet seat, and Lisa was no exception.

Although they were not invited to the funeral, hundreds of people were in attendance and it was unlikely anyone would notice two funeral-crashers. Kevin wore a black suit, laughing when Lisa asked him if he had one. He told her, "I'm an FBI agent, sweetheart! Yes, I have a black suit."

Lisa was dressed in black, as well, although she had been unsure of its appropriateness, considering she wasn't family. Her jacket and mid-length skirt were quite tasteful and in no way showy; they didn't wish to be noticed any more than was necessary.

The internment was held in the cemetery of Staglieno, the largest outdoor sculpture museum in Europe. It houses one of the finest collections of late 19th and early 20th century Italian marble sculpture known to exist, and, although generally overlooked by tourists, was currently receiving a much needed restoration.

The funeral was an extravagant affair. Kevin didn't think he'd seen so many flowers in his life. They had arrived early and quickly made their way to the casket to "pay their respects". This allowed them to step back and observe those who came after them.

Kevin didn't have a photographic memory, but it was pretty remarkable, at least with certain things. Faces, for instance, were Kevin's forte. He could look at a picture of a suspect and never forget it. This came in quite handy in his line of work and particularly handy on this day. Before they'd left for Genoa, Kevin had committed to memory all eight of the Euro-guys that Diane had identified. As expected, all eight of them arrived to pay their respects; in the case of Antoine Rousseau, to break down into a crying jag.

They hadn't all shown at once, but they were all conspicuously present: Aldo Veneto, of course, made his appearance as the dead man; there was also Antoine Rousseau, acting like he'd lost his lover; Amal Singh, Arthur Swift, Sir Harold Covington, Michael Grant, John C. Devaney and last but not least, Wolfgang von Graf, looking bored with the whole thing. Of course, there were many rich people at the funeral of one of Europe's wealthiest men but Kevin was convinced that these were the men he was looking for. Now, all he needed to do was prove it. *Piece of cake*!

With a beautiful woman at his side, Kevin was able to poke around quite a bit; much more than even he thought possible. Lisa's beauty, sort of ran interference for Kevin's probing questions. Those, to whom he spoke, if they were men, were distracted by Lisa and were off-guard enough to shed some light on the eight men. The women were highly emotional and happy to talk about everything they knew, making them feel important somehow, that they would be "in on" the intimate details. Aldo was dead, after all, and this handsome young man was probably an American reporter or something. It was all quite exciting for many of them.

Kevin believed that he had learned what he needed to learn in order to conclude that these were the men of whom Mr. Townsend had referred. The rest would come down to investigative work; work that he was sure Diane and Bobby were busy with back in Tampa. Now, they would need to come up with some kind of "sting" operation to catch these guys red-handed. As usual, Lisa had been able to see things with a clear and unbiased eye. "Correct me if I'm wrong," Lisa said, "but didn't Mr. Townsend say that he was one of the 'eight', in the documentation you told me about?"

Kevin wasn't sure where she was going. "Yeah, so..."

"Well," Lisa went on, "didn't we just bury number eight? There was Aldo Veneto and seven others, right?"

Kevin still didn't see the point. "Yes, honey, there were eight of them. Now there are seven of them. What's your point?"

"My point is, if their group consisted of eight members before Mr. Townsend died and eight members before Mr. Veneto died, it stands to reason that they replace their members when they pass away." Kevin was beginning to see what Lisa was getting at as she finished her point. "Now that Aldo's gone, they're gonna need another member. Maybe you could figure out a way to compromise their next membership drive, if you know what I mean."

"Wow, my wife is smart!" Kevin thought, then said, "Lisa, my love, you're brilliant! That's the best idea I've heard all day!"

Back on the dirty train, but this time with a couple bottles of water and a few protein bars, Lisa whispered into Kevin's ear. No one could hear what she said, but whatever it was it led Kevin to revise his previous statement. "On second thought," he announced, "that's the second best idea I've heard all day!"

He couldn't wait to get back to the hotel.

Chapter Fourteen

Württemberg is an area of southwestern Germany near the Swiss border. After World War II it was divided between the French and American zones, forming two new states which were called Wurttemberg-Hohenzollern and Wurttemberg-Baden. In 1952 the two states merged into what is now, Baden-Wurttemberg.

The capital of this region is Stuttgart. It is well known as the "cradle of the automobile" and one of the most high-tech areas in Europe, with companies like Porsche, Daimler AG, Bosch, Hewlett-Packard and IBM—all with either world or European headquarters located within its unusually rolling hills.

About an hour away from Stuttgart is an area that the Romans called Silva Nigra, or the Black Forest. The Germans call it Schwarzwald, known for its dense forestry which virtually blocks out the sun. The Black Forest is home to the highest mountain in Germany, outside the Alps, with an elevation of 1,493 meters and is called, Feldberg. Not many people live in this area due to its harsh climate and inaccessibility to civilization.

One man; however, finds it to be the perfect spot to call home. He lives at the base of Feldberg Mountain in a small two-room shack that he constructed out of the local timber. While a highly educated and more than wealthy man, he finds the rustic confines of his "home away from home" to be just the ticket when preparing for a "gig", as he calls it, alluding to the American rock band lingo referring to a job.

Over 75 miles from anything that could be called civilization, it is the perfect place to construct weaponry and then test it with no concerns about nosey neighbors calling the police. Inside its unfinished log walls are located all the tools of death. There are rifles and pistols of every size and description, knives and sabers, bows and crossbows and explosive ordinances like C-4, dynamite and nitroglycerin. Even an assortment of poisons along with elaborate delivery systems can be found inside.

Also inside is a man; a very dangerous man. He is highly educated but his art is the death of human beings; he listens to Wagner while he sharpens his knives; he washes the blood off his hands and then writes poetry. He has no feelings to get in the way of his work.

You do not want to meet this man under any circumstances; no sane man would.

His name is Ernst Kruger but there is no one on this earth who is aware of it. The few people who have actually known him well enough to call him by name could be counted on the fingers of a one-armed carpenter with Parkinson's disease. To others he is simply known as "Tuefel", a nickname given to him by the last living person who knew his real name. The name stuck with him and has been his sobriquet for over twenty years. The German translation of the name Tuefel, or Devil, is testimony of his reputation by those who are unlucky enough to know him.

The description given of Lord Byron by Lady Caroline Lamb was that he was "mad, bad and dangerous to know," an apt description of Tuefel. He had been a highly trained member of Germany's elite Special Forces detachment known by the initials KSK. Ernst, as he was known then, was ejected from the KSK for being too violent. This is akin to being excommunicated from the church for being too kind.

Ernst left the military and its structure and entered a world constructed entirely of Ernst's wishes and desires. His training was still intact but he had no more use for rules and regulations; he'd make up his own rule of law.

Enter, "Tuefel", an alter ego erected by Ernst to remind him of who it was that he worshiped. Oh, Ernst didn't actually worship the Devil, per se, but no one who witnessed anything he ever did would have believed anything else. There was no compromise in Tuefel, nothing behind the eyes that someone could look to for mercy; no place to submit a final appeal for clemency before Tuefel ended your life with extreme prejudice. He was paid to end lives and end lives he would, for the right price.

Arthur Swift had met Tuefel's price and more. After a cool one million Euros was confirmed to be transferred into his Swiss account, Tuefel began his preparation for a new "gig".

•

When they had returned from Genoa, Kevin and Lisa went to one of the most famous restaurants in Rome, Sora Lella. It is located on a boat-shaped island on the Tiber River and inside a medieval tower. Well known as the hangout of movie stars like Marlon Brando, Sora Lella is the culinary delight of the Eternal City.

Lisa, as always, looked like she belonged in Sora Lella; Kevin looked like he belonged parking the cars. Even when he tried to "dress up", Kevin always seemed to look like a long-tenured professor at Cambridge University; intelligent, introspective, but wholly unconcerned with his appearance. Lisa, while having a natural elegance about her, didn't really put in the effort that her appearance might suggest. She was, simply, the epitome of class. It showed in her manner of dress, walk, speech and inflections. It was not meant at all pretentious nor was it perceived as such by those who knew her, it was, simply, in the end, Lisa.

After they were both seated and enjoying their Jumbo Shrimp Cocktails—Kevin couldn't eat at McDonalds without an appetizer of Shrimp Cocktail—Lisa's Blackberry played its familiar tune. Without thinking, Lisa reached into her bag and saw that she was being texted. Before she looked at the message, she, almost as a reflex, reached for her right pocket to see if there was another surprise. As it turned out, she didn't have any pockets in her exquisitely chic Italian night-dress, leaving her to punch a couple of Blackberry buttons to receive another ominous message from their "guardian angel".

Lisa didn't even look at the message before handing her Blackberry over to Kevin who looked at the message with stunned disbelief. "It says here," Kevin whispered, "that we did not go unnoticed at Aldo's funeral. It says that we may be in grave danger."

The meal was spectacular. Kevin's Tonarelli was first rate as was Lisa's Rigatone with seafood sauce. Both had the obligatory zabaglione gelato with strawberries and melons on the side. On the side is very big with Lisa.

The conversation was not quite as colorful as the meal. Both Kevin and Lisa were at a loss to explain their feelings. Who was this mysterious texter and note writer? He certainly had up-to-date information—right down to what Lisa was wearing—and for some reason, he seemed to be trying to help them. His first message led them to the Euro-guys responsible for America's woes, or so they thought, and the second message seemed to suggest that their trip to Genoa may have ruffled some Euro-feathers.

Kevin had no problem being in a perceived danger, but he wasn't prepared to put the life of his new bride in danger with him. Needless to say, the conversation over dinner took a decidedly unromantic turn. "I think you should go back to Tampa!" Kevin said for the third time, "We've seen what these guys can do. They killed Doug, they killed Jimmy and pinned it on Ali; it's just too dangerous."

"Look, Kevin, first of all, this message, as usual, was addressed to me." When Lisa got this look in her eye there was no arguing with her. Kevin figured that out after her first syllable but didn't interrupt his dynamic wife. "It doesn't say that you are in danger or that I am in danger, it says that "we" are in danger. What makes you think that if I return to the United States these guys won't come after me there? I've had my fill of fighting for my life! Now that you're my husband, I'd like to hang around with you and let you fight for my life, for a change."

Lisa's argument was flawless. She was right, of course. These men might well come after her in Tampa and him in Rome. They needed to stay together and fight this bunch of Euro-snobs with all they had; besides, he felt Lisa would be safer with him. Also, if he were brutally honest, he might be safer with her, as well. She seemed to see the landscape with a clarity that he didn't possess. He trusted her opinions and her instincts better that anyone he'd known. They would make a stand together.

•

The Al Qaeda navy sounds like an oxymoron, but they are thought by many terror experts to have just that. Not, perhaps as fearsome as the American navy but rumored to possess about 80 small, old freighters like the "Baltic Sky", a 2,000 ton coastal freighter that was seized by Greek commandos in 2003. Although the ship's manifest listed its cargo as fertilizer, the commandos found over 750 tons of TNT and over 8,000 detonators. Exploded under a bridge or next to another ship, 750 tons of TNT would do some serious damage.

These ships, many of whom are known to those in a position to care, would be seized, as was the Baltic Sky, if they ventured into a country's local waters, but in international waters they are usually unmolested. On this Labor Day, three 2,500 ton freighters were set to disembark their port in the city of Tyre, in Lebanon. Tyre, a Shi'a Muslim stronghold, is the home of over 60,000 Palestinian refugees. Hezbollah and the Amal Movement are the predominant political parties and they control the city to a large degree.

Tyre is most famous as the object of Alexander the Great's wrath. In 332 BC, Alexander laid siege to Tyre for over seven months, finally conquering the island by constructing a causeway from the mainland to the island. Over time, the very presence of the causeway itself caused sediment to build up and make the connection permanent.

This morning, well before thousands of Lebanese would arise and celebrate the holiday, Captain Faysal of the freighter, Nomad, was finishing his morning cup of Kafé Botz, or mud coffee. He had been up all night being briefed on the specifics of his journey and fighting a sinus infection that had tormented him for a week. Well over 60 years old, Captain Faysal had been travelling the world's seas for the better part of 50 years, beginning his nautical life at the age of nine. Today's launch would be no different to him than hundreds of those that had gone before, except that today he was coordinating with two other freighters and carrying a cargo that would put his ship and crew in great peril.

His cargo was unlike anything he had ever borne on one of his ships. Aside from the added complement of 15 non-sailing men assigned to him by the Lebanese government, was a series of large metal canisters that had to be loaded

172

with a crane. Of course, Captain Faysal would perform his duty as he always had, but he didn't like being in the dark as to his mission, or the contents of those canisters. He felt it showed a certain disrespect that so seasoned a Captain would be "out of the loop" on a mission that had obvious national security implications.

There would be no cell phone or computer communication during the voyage. The leader of the 15 man group which accompanied the canisters, a Colonel Haddad, would be in charge of the overall mission while Captain Faysal would command the Nomad for its journey. Clearly, nothing was being left to chance and Captain Faysal was no fool. He knew that this secret mission was both important—at least to the Lebanese government—and dangerous, as all secret missions with giant metal canisters were.

The Nomad would sail through the Mediterranean Sea, out the Strait of Gibraltar and into the Atlantic Ocean. It was important for his trip to take a little longer than would normally be necessary, according to orders. After about a week of Mediterranean meandering, the Nomad would head for the open waters of the Atlantic and its destination, 80 miles off the coast of Philadelphia, Pennsylvania, 3 weeks from the date of departure. There would be no communications between the Nomad and the other two ships which would each have different destinations and orders. The Captain was informed that he would be apprised of the exact nature of the mission once they were safely in the Atlantic Ocean. Being a man of duty, Captain Faysal set course without asking any probing questions. He was a patient man and knew he would find out soon enough.

•

It had been over two weeks since Kevin and Lisa had arrived in Rome and begun their combination honeymoon and investigation. Lisa's idea had gone over well with Asst. Director McCarthy and Kevin was informed that a plan was "in the works."

There had not been that much for Kevin and Lisa to do after the Bureau identified the men now known as the "Elite Eight"—a term that was discovered to be the group's personally selected moniker. Still on the public dime, Kevin decided not to waist the opportunity to wine-and-dine his new bride to the fullest extent possible, but within reason.

They traveled to France, Spain, Portugal and Greece, seeing the sights and enjoying each culture's culinary delights…until one day. Sitting in a gondola on the Grand Canal, in Venice, Lisa's Blackberry began to sound. Lisa reached into her pocket, drew out the phone and handed it to Kevin without even glancing at it.

Kevin took the Blackberry and checked the incoming text. Neither of them were surprised by the communication, they'd been-there-done-that, they thought; however, they were astonished by the message itself. *"Hello,"* the message began, *"Don't be startled, I am a friend. If you wish to have verifiable proof of the Elite Eight and their activities, return to your hotel where a message awaits you."*

They took the first train back to Rome and checked with the concierge concerning any messages addressed to either of them. A very pleasant man, but a bit confused, he knew of no messages that had arrived.

They returned to the room where they rested and showered for supper. Kevin assumed that their "friend" would make sure that the message was made known to them in some fashion. Why else send the text?

Kevin was correct. The message came when they had finished their dinner. As Kevin reached for the check, he noticed an envelope under the tray. It was sealed, but there was no name written or typed on the outside. Kevin opened the envelope and discovered a short note accompanied by what looked like a map, of what he couldn't tell. The note said, *"Follow the map and you will find your proof."* Kevin then looked at the map more closely and found it to be a map of one of the Catacombs of Rome.

The Catacombs are traditionally known as the underground burial chambers of the Christians during their Roman subjugation, but that was recently debunked when Jewish and even Pagan graves were discovered. The fact that most of the Catacombs were built under busy Roman thoroughfares lends more credence to the latter theory. If they had been situated under such a well-traveled area they would have quickly been discovered.

There are over forty catacombs in Rome alone, unbeknownst to Kevin, who asked the waiter where the Catacombs could be located. "Which one?" was the answer he received. A closer study of the map, by Lisa, showed that the map was of the Catacombs of Marcellinus and Peter, named for the two martyrs said to be buried there. The map showed the location as the Via Casilina, formerly the Via Labicana, near the church of Santi Marcellino e Peitro ad Duas Lauros.

"You read that like an Italian," Kevin said with surprise, "how'd you learn that?"

"Well," Lisa said, "I don't speak Italian, as you know, but every other word in medicine is Latin. I guess I just learned the conjugation."

Kevin got up and walked over to Lisa. He kissed her on the forehead and then stepped behind her to pull out her chair. He didn't always do this, but somehow it seemed appropriate to the setting. "From now on," he said, "you read all maps."

The sun was quickly fading to the western edge of the city of the seven hills. Kevin was anxious to investigate this latest clue, but thought it better to wait until morning. This would give them time to study the map in more detail and ask questions of the locals, if need be. Kevin had downloaded an English to Italian and Italian to English translation program to help him with the local dialect. It would surely come in handy while trying to decipher this map He grabbed a cold beer out of the refrigerator, sat down and got to work. Lisa was nowhere to be found.

As he studied the map, Kevin thought that it pointed to a specific grave within the Catacomb. He wasn't sure, but it had a kind of "X marks the spot" kind of a look. Cartography was never his best subject. "Hey, Lisa," Kevin called out toward the bathroom, "Come and take a look at this map! I think it's pointing at a grave!"

There was no answer from Lisa. He assumed she was doing some kind of "girl thing" and figured he'd better not bother her. After a while he began to wonder why she hadn't come out of the bathroom. They'd both showered before going out to eat and even Lisa wasn't persnickety enough to need another shower yet.

Kevin got up and went to the bathroom door. It was open. He walked in and saw nothing and no one. *"Oh, I thought she was in the bathroom"*, thought Kevin. *"So, where is she?"* He walked around the suite, assuming that Lisa was sitting on the couch, reading or something, but he didn't find her anywhere. *Could she have gone to get something to drink out of the machine? She's never done that before.*

Now, Kevin was beginning to get a little nervous. Maybe it was the note they'd gotten last week about possible danger, but he was starting to call her name in a raised voice that indicated his angst. "Lisa!" he called out, "Lisa, where are you!" he called out, louder.

A sudden rap on the door made him jump out of his skin. Hyperventilating, he opened the door to see the concierge holding up what looked like a letter. "Signore O'Brien?" he said, "This came for you just moments ago. I was instructed to deliver it at once."

Kevin snatched the letter from the concierge and without saying a word, slammed the door. This envelope looked strikingly similar to the one he received in the restaurant. Kevin ripped it open and found the typed note inside: *"Meet me at the Catacomb in 2 hours. Your wife is quite beautiful. Don't be late."*

Kevin almost passed out. His head started swimming and it became difficult to focus. His emotions had completely overwhelmed any rational thought. *"Oh, my God! They've got Lisa! If they hurt her, I'll..."* His thoughts kind of trailed off from there. Quickly, he ran to the table and took a good look at the map. He wasn't sure of his ability to find the Catacomb in time. He grabbed his jacket—the one with the Glock 23—and raced out the door and down the hall to the elevator. He was on the 16th floor but both elevators seemed to be well below him. *I don't have time for this crap!* He scampered into the stairwell and leapt four stairs at a time until he hit the lobby.

When Kevin burst into the lobby, he saw the concierge standing by the front desk. Wasting no time, he quick-stepped it over and asked him for help. "I'm sorry, but I need your help and I need it now!" Kevin pled, as he raised the map to the man's face. "You see this map?" he said.

The concierge nodded, wide-eyed. He wasn't sure that he might not have a mad-man on his hands.

"I need someone to take me to this location! Now!" he raised his voice to urgency. "Look, I'm an American FBI agent and someone's going to die in 2 hours if you don't get me to this location! Capisce?"

The concierge still looked a bit frightened but he seemed to understand that Kevin was in a hurry, not crazy. "Si Signore, I will help you," he said, and he flagged down a young boy. "Garcon," he yelled. "Go quickly and hail a taxi! Tell them it is an emergency!" He then looked back at Kevin and said, "Let's go, Signore."

Chapter Fifteen

Kevin and the concierge dashed out of the Cavalieri and into a waiting taxi. Amerigo, the name of the concierge, after looking quickly at the map, called out to the driver to head for the church of Santi Marcellino e Peitro ad Duas Lauros on the Via Casilina. He knew the Catacombs of Macellinus and Peter were close by.

Amerigo Lombardi was raised in Rome and had spent his whole life there. He'd always had a certain fascination with America and with Americans in particular. Amerigo felt that the United States was always getting the short end of the stick. Whenever another country is in trouble, America comes to the rescue; even if the other country is an enemy. Sure, they push their weight around a little too much, he thought, but America usually had good intentions, and with great power comes great error.

Another thing that drew him to Americans was the fact that his father had always dreamt of going to the United States. It was a dream that he knew would never come to pass, but he would do the next best thing; he'd name his son after America. So, Amerigo got his name from the man for whom, it is believed, America got her name, Amerigo Vespucci, the famed Italian explorer and cartographer. America is derived from the Latin, Americus, which means "work-power"—something Amerigo thought the United States had in spades.

The taxi driver made a beeline for the church as Kevin confided in Amerigo about the danger his wife was now facing. "Oh no," Amerigo cried, "Signora Lisa? She is in danger?"

Kevin just nodded. The taxi rounded a corner so quickly that Kevin and Amerigo were thrown together. Just as quickly, the taxi stopped. Kevin looked out the window and saw a beautiful Italian church which he assumed was the one they were looking for. He looked at Amerigo for confirmation.

Amerigo pointed to an area about a half a block away and said, "The Catacomb of Macellinus and Peter is there, signore, I come with you!"

"No," Kevin said, "this is as far as you go...but thank you, Amerigo, I'm in your debt." Kevin jumped out of the taxi and started walking toward the area that Amerigo had pointed out. He hadn't gotten two steps before Amerigo leapt from the cab and announced that he would not take no for an answer. "Besides," he said, "you will never find the grave without my help. This is too important to worry about fear. I will come with you and we will save the beautiful, Signora Lisa. Si?"

Kevin was appreciative of Amerigo's offer and simply said, "Si, let's go."

Amerigo led the way through an area known as "Ad Duas Lauros"; it is a complex that includes the catacombs, together with Helena's Mausoleum, a Basilica and the ruins of the cemetery of the "Equites Singulares". The entrance to the catacombs is through St. Paolo's church. Amerigo was well familiar with this area and this complex, having been a guide to American tourists as a young man; further reinforcing his fascination with Americans.

"This way, signore," Amerigo whispered, feeling that it was prudent to enter unannounced, "We must go through the church."

Kevin was in no position to question anything Amerigo said or did. He did not know this city, area or complex. He would have to trust that his new friend was leading him in the right direction. He followed Amerigo without comment.

They quickly traversed the block or so to the church and as they approached the front entrance Amerigo was surprised to see that the door was ajar. He looked back at Kevin, and with eyes which displayed uncertainty, said, in an ominous tone, "Signore Kevin, this door should not be open at this time. I think, maybe, someone is waiting for us."

Kevin was not surprised by Amerigo's statement. Obviously, whoever had taken Lisa wanted him to come in; nevertheless, Amerigo's statement was not a welcome one. "Let's go." Kevin quietly urged, and the two men opened the door and entered.

With over 4.5 kilometers of subterranean galleries on three distinct levels, the Catacomb of Peter and Marcellinus was vast, to say the least. With over 25,000 people buried here, finding one burial site could be impossible, unless you knew where to look, which, fortunately, Amerigo did.

After studying the map further, Amerigo saw that the "X" on the map—the place to which it was obviously directing them—was above the word, "Orpheus". He lifted up the map and motioned for Kevin to take a look. "This is the Orpheus," Amerigo explained, losing the whisper and raising his voice to a normal level, "it is approximately one and a half kilometers away. I used to take tourists there as a youth. If Signora Lisa is being held there, we had better move faster. It is a long way by foot."

Kevin nodded and the two of them began to walk at a brisk pace down the "corridors" containing paintings and frescos for hundreds of the "saints" that were buried here. Some were buried very simply, in what are called, "loculi"; others were buried in elaborate "arcosolia" and still others in "cubicula", small chambers with several burials.

As they walked, Amerigo explained that the "Orpheus" was actually a 4th century depiction of the early pagan/Christian view of Christ. It shows Christ sitting in a yoga type position, beardless, in Greco-Roman fashion, and holding a torch in his right hand and a Lyre in his left—with this he tamed the wild beasts. He did not know if there was any significance to this, but it was clear to him that the word "Orpheus" on the map could mean nothing else.

Moving quickly, Kevin and Amerigo paid little notice to the historical implications and religious underpinnings of the alcoves, niches and apses that they passed in their fevered trek to find Lisa. There were frescos of the Magi, a picture of Jonah being thrown into the sea, a painting of the Epiphany, as well as a slew of graffiti from worshipers over the centuries.

Soon, Amerigo began to display the signs of a man who was quickly approaching danger. He began to slow his pace and then started to creep along the side of the catacomb, motioning for Kevin to do likewise. As they approached a bend in the route, Amerigo stopped, knelt down, and raised his index finger to his lips in the universal sign to indicate that Kevin should remain quiet. Kevin followed Amerigo's instructions with patient anxiety.

"Signore," Amerigo whispered, "the Orpheus is just around this bend. We should approach quietly."

As Amerigo raised himself to advance, Kevin put his hand on his shoulder to stop him. In a hushed tone he said, "Let me take the lead, my friend." Amerigo relented and Kevin eased by him. As he passed him, Kevin whispered to Amerigo, "You are very brave, my friend. No matter what happens, I owe you."

Kevin crept up to the edge of the bend and peeked around the corner. He was able to see the niche that Amerigo had described to him. There was a depiction of a cross-legged man holding a torch and what he assumed was a lyre. This must be the Orpheus/Christ that Amerigo described. There was darkness within the recess of the alcove but Kevin thought he could make out the shadowed figure of a human being. He couldn't tell if it was a statue or a living person.

There was no cover from here on out, so Kevin flipped the safety lock on his Glock 23 hand gun and held it down with both arms extended, ready to rise up and assume a quick firing position. He turned his head to Amerigo and raised his hand up, palm out, to indicate that he should stay put. Quickly returning his hand to his weapon, Kevin began a slow forward movement, always keeping his back to the wall, eyes sweeping back and forth for any movement, ever listening intently for tell-tale sound. As he neared the apse that Amerigo had called Orpheus, Kevin could now clearly make out a person seated within the dark recesses. A pair of legs was becoming visible in what little light was present and Kevin was pretty sure they belonged to Lisa.

Overcome with fear for the safety of the woman he loved but also guided by his professional training, Kevin didn't race in to free her. He continued to move forward, back to the wall, eyes and ears alert for danger. When he'd come to a point that put him directly across from the niche, Kevin could now see that it was, in fact, Lisa. She was seated on a concrete bench, hands and feet tied and a blindfold over her eyes.

As he swiftly assessed the scene, Kevin sensed no fear from Lisa as she sat on the bench. She seemed calm; sitting with perfect posture, in what Kevin would later describe as a regal bearing. Even then, with fear and trepidation in his heart, Kevin could appreciate the fine qualities that Lisa possessed. He was very proud of her.

He couldn't see anyone else around, but Kevin wasn't stupid. Obviously, whoever had kidnapped Lisa wanted him to simply stroll over and untie her, putting them both in the perpetrators sights. By this time, Amerigo had joined him across from Lisa's position and whispered to Kevin, "I will untie her, signore. Cover me," he said, and slowly walked up to Lisa, whispering to her gently, "Signora Lisa, I am Amerigo. Your husband and I are here to save you."

Lisa sat even straighter. She seemed to become tense as Amerigo began to untie the cords that bound her hands. When he had freed them, Lisa reached up and pulled off her blindfold. Amerigo knelt and began to untie Lisa's feet as she caught her first glimpse of her husband; he wasn't even looking at her, he was looking down the passageway with his gun pointed in like manner. He still hadn't said a word.

"Kevin, I think he's gone," she said, "I haven't heard a sound for over an hour."

Kevin turned toward his wife as Amerigo freed the last of her bonds. Lisa jumped up and leapt toward Kevin, wrapping her hands around his neck and squeezing him so hard he had to pull away. "Hey, honey, don't kill me, I'm here to help." Kevin said with uneasy levity. "Are you ok?"

"Yes, honey, I'm fine," Lisa said, releasing Kevin from her grip and turning toward Amerigo, "Who are you?" she asked.

"This is Amerigo Lombardi, honey. He's the hotel's concierge and my new best friend. He guided me here." Even as Kevin spoke he was scanning the vicinity for anything unusual. "Are you sure there's no one here? This seems a little odd, doesn't it?"

At that moment, Lisa's Blackberry sent all three of them through the proverbial roof. Lisa wasn't even aware that she had her cell phone. The sound didn't seem to be coming from her person; it seemed to be coming from the back of the Orpheus apse. Kevin walked into the darkness of the niche and discovered that the familiar sound was emanating from a small valise resting on the floor under the depiction of Orpheus/Christ. He grabbed it by the handle and pulled it into the light.

Lisa's Blackberry could be seen in the front pocket of the bag, so Kevin withdrew it and checked for messages. Sure enough, it was a message from their "friend". It said, *"I'm sorry for the dramatics, but I needed your undivided attention. The information you need is within this satchel; put it to good use, and remember, you continue to be in great danger, as I'm sure you can deduce by the fact that I just kidnapped your wife and brought her here. It was quite easy. Watch your back!"*

Kevin was dumbstruck at the unmitigated gall of someone kidnapping his wife to make a point, but this was not the place to be pondering that question. The danger may have passed or perhaps not even have existed, but he wanted to get Lisa out of here, pronto! "Let's get out of here," Kevin said.

"Si, Signore Kevin, I'm in full agreement." Amerigo said with a grateful sigh. "Let's get back to the Cavalieri!"

The three then walked the kilometer and a half back to the entrance and out to the street where Amerigo quickly got them a taxi. "The Cavalieri," Amerigo ordered the driver as Lisa and Kevin emotionally embraced, "and step on it!"

Once they had returned to the hotel, Lisa, now fully aware of Amerigo's bravery, hugged him tightly and kissed him on either cheek. "Thank you, Amerigo," she said, softly, "You're my hero."

Amerigo turned beet red and lowered his head, humbly answering Lisa's comment, "Oh, Signora Lisa, it was nothing. I'm just glad you were not harmed." Then, to avoid being overcome by emotion in front of a beautiful American woman, Amerigo turned to Kevin and said, "Signore Kevin, please take her upstairs. I will have a delicious meal and a bottle of our best wine brought to your suite within the hour."

Kevin was truly grateful for everything Amerigo had done. "You are a good man, Amerigo. You have made two lifelong friends who will always be indebted to you." He took Lisa by the arm and led her toward the elevator, turning again to say, "Grazie, amico mio."

When they had returned to the suite, Lisa immediately jumped into the shower and Kevin delved into the oddly obtained information within the valise. Their "friend" was right; the valise contained pictures of the Elite Eight, travel vouchers, airline tickets, multiple memoranda and even a taped conversation of one of the groups meetings. It had times and dates of weapon deliveries as well as transcribed conversations between Mr. Arthur Swift and the Iranian President and First Vice-President, all verifying that it was this group of European elitists that had masterminded the whole thing.

Kevin was satisfied that he had all the proof he would need to convince Asst. Director McCarthy and President Hamilton that these men were to blame for the terrorist attacks in America. He was confused by the need for all the "cloak and dagger" but confident in the data he'd received. He was almost saddened because it would mean an end to their European honeymoon; there was no reason for his continued presence here.

He would certainly not mention any of this to Lisa until she'd had a nice meal, a few glasses of wine and a good night's rest. Tomorrow would suffice.

Chapter Sixteen

Diane was in the office at 0700 the next morning. She had received a cryptic phone call from Kevin the previous night informing her that he had new information and was sending it to her by courier. Diane knew that Kevin couldn't speak freely over an open telephone line and that the "new information" was probably significant.

She walked into the little kitchenette and started a pot of coffee. She still couldn't understand why she had started drinking this stuff in the first place. She'd gone her whole life without even tasting coffee—she started drinking it when she was assigned to the Maelstrom Task Force, for some reason—and now, here she was anxious for the pot to fill up.

There was no one in the conference room, so after she poured a cup of coffee she sat down in Kevin's chair—it was much plusher than hers—and contemplated a bit. She was 31 years old, the world was going to hell in a hand basket and she was still single. What that meant, only her mother could explain, but it meant something. She was still very attractive, or so she thought, but she hadn't been asked out on a date in months—and that was only memorable because her date had forgotten his wallet, so she had to pay for the meal. Actually, now that she thought of it, he had been one of the better dates.

Perhaps, even more than at home, she could concentrate best here at the office, particularly early in the morning when she was alone. She leaned back in the chair and took another sip of coffee. Too bad she hadn't thought to stop and get a bagel or a blueberry muffin on her way to the office; her stomach was growling at her.

Diane wasn't a feminist. She believed a woman should be paid equal to a man if she did the same job, but she was well aware that men and women were different and wasn't inclined to wish it were not so. She was a highly trained agent with a black belt in Tae Kwon Do but knew that if a good-sized man ever got a hold of her with ill intent, she was toast. She had a great regard for the abilities of the male agents with which she worked and appreciated that they treated her as an equal. In fact, she was treated with a great amount of respect as an agent and at the same time, as a woman.

The problem was that she knew she couldn't date a fellow agent—it wasn't just frowned upon, it was forbidden—and with the hours she put in and the places she frequented, she was unlikely to meet anyone who wasn't either a colleague or an ax murderer. She could go for a good ax murderer, but they were usually unattractive, to boot.

Her biological alarm clock had gone off a number of times, but Diane just kept hitting the snooze bar and going back into hibernation. The dating scene was not kind to a female FBI agent, no matter how attractive she was. How many times she would recall the odd looks on the faces of men who would ask her to dance or buy her a drink when they found out she was an FBI agent. Men wanted a woman they could protect, not one who could field strip a Heckler and Koch MP5 sub-machine gun. *"Oh well"*, she thought, *"maybe the courier will be a cute CIA agent."*

No sooner had she finished the thought, there was a rap at the door. Diane got up and went to the door and opened it. It was indeed, the courier…the female courier. "I have a package for Diane Austin. Are you she?" the courier said.

Am I she? Who talks like that? Diane mentally lambasted the young girl. "That's me!" she said, showing her FBI ID badge.

The pretty blond courier handed the package to Diane before saying, "Thank you, Ma'am."

Diane took the package and closed the door, a little harder than normal, and walked back to her coffee and comfortable chair. "Ma'am? When did I become a Ma'am?" she grumbled to herself. She dropped the package onto the table in front of her and plopped herself back into the chair. Not one for long bouts of self pity, Diane pulled the package closer and ripped it open. "I hope you found something worthwhile, Kevin," she muttered, "We could sure use the excitement."

•

Within a week of receiving the Elite Eight information the ball started to roll toward justice, at least, for some. Bobby went to see Ali in prison, just to cheer him up, when they were surprised by a visit from the prison's warden. He was dressed to the nines and walking rather sheepishly, for a warden. The guard who led him to Ali's cell opened the door and stepped aside as the warden entered the cell and withdrew an envelope from his suit's breast pocket. At the same time, he reached into the suit's right hip pocket and pulled out his glasses.

"Agent Ali Hussein," he began, now looking down the bottom half of his bifocals, "by order of FBI director Bernard Freed, by direct order of the President of the United States, you are hereby discharged from this facility, forthwith, and given your unconditional release as of this date, at this hour." He fumbled a bit with the paper as if the next part was particularly difficult for him to read. "And," he went on, tentatively, "I am to inform you that Director Freed, by order of President Hamilton, has requested that you accept his...and my...apology for any inconvenience this experience may have caused you."

Ali and Bobby just looked at each other, trying not to laugh, as the warden continued his rather uncomfortable oration, "Furthermore," he went on, "you are to be reinstated to your previous job posting with a promotion to Special-Agent—with all the rights and privileges thereto—and given back pay in the amount of 10,000 dollars."

The warden took off his bifocals and put them back into his pocket. He refolded the letter and, after inserting it back into the envelope, handed it to Ali. He turned and walked out of the cell, giving the order to the guard that Ali was to be released "at once".

•

Kevin and Lisa were still in Italy. Asst. Director McCarthy wanted Kevin to remain until he felt there was no more he could do. The Elite Eight were, after all, Europeans, and Director McCarthy thought Kevin should remain "in country", as he so melodramatically put it.

He didn't have to twist Kevin's arm, and Lisa was positively giddy. They were able to stay in Rome and Kevin was, at least temporarily, released from any current duties. This gave Lisa a chance to spend the kind of quality time with Kevin that she'd hoped for when they'd first arrived.

"It's so nice to have you all to myself." Lisa said as she watched Kevin put another log on the fire and return to the couch. "It's like a dream come true."

Kevin picked up his end of the cover and crawled under it with Lisa. "You realize," he said, "that it's May 15th. It's practically summer, and here we are sitting in front of a fire. It all seems so extravagant."

Their suite was luxurious, to say the least. It consisted of a bedroom (with the floating featherbed), a kitchen (which they never used), and the central living area with three Queen Ann chairs and a large, plush couch on which two people could comfortably recline. The only problem was that the color schemes were a little ostentatious. There were lots of reds, purples and oranges, mixed into an olio that was not pleasing to the eye; at least, not the American eye. Nevertheless, neither one was inclined to complain; they were living in luxury on the public dime, something that Kevin felt a slight twinge of guilt over.

Lisa pulled Kevin closer. "So," she cooed, "the air-conditioner is on, isn't it? Live a little!" she added with relish.

Kevin was far too content to argue the point. "You know," he said, "Ali's back at the office. I talked to him today and he's not resentful or angry in the least. Doesn't that surprise you?"

"Well," Lisa said, "I've never met Ali, but from what you tell me, he's a man of true faith. I suspect that's the reason he's so forgiving."

Kevin added with a contented sigh, "Yeah, I suppose so."

Lisa perked up and sat up a bit. "You know, you never told me why Ali was released. Did the information that my kidnapper provided prove his innocence?"

"As a matter of fact, it did." Kevin said, "There was a taped conversation between Michael Grant and who we believe is John C. Devaney, plotting the whole thing." Kevin rolled over, rested on his elbow and looked at Lisa with a sadness that made her comment.

"What is it?" she asked.

"It's Jimmy," Kevin said. "He was a traitor."

191

Lisa looked at him as though he'd just asked her for a divorce. "What? You mean the Jimmy Forbes you always talked about like he was your little brother? That Jimmy Forbes?"

Kevin dropped his gaze and dishearteningly nodded assent. "Apparently, he killed Doug and was about to kill Ali when they shot him and pinned it on Ali." Even as he said it, he couldn't believe it. It was like some kind of John Le Carre novel. "I don't think Jimmy was that good an actor. They must have had something on him or intimidated him into committing such a violent act. It just doesn't seem like something that he was capable of doing."

"If he killed Doug, than I'm glad he got what was coming to him." Lisa said with a tone inconsistent with her style. "Doug saved my life, and if Jimmy killed him in cold blood…well, I don't want to talk about it." Now Lisa was getting emotional.

"Let's not talk about it anymore," Kevin said, "we've got about 14 more days till we go back to Tampa. Let's make the most of them."

Lisa pushed Kevin onto his back and rolled on top of him. She looked down into the eyes of the man she planned to spend the rest of her life with. "I love you," she said, and added, "You know, we've never talked about children. Do you want children?"

You could have knocked Kevin over with a feather. Not that the subject didn't appeal to him, it's just that he was totally unprepared for it. "Well, sure I want children, honey," he said, "but is this the right time to discuss it? I mean, with everything that's going on?"

"Hey," Lisa said, "there's no time like the present." She could see that Kevin was tripping over his own thoughts. "That's ok, honey," she said, "We'll talk about it some other time. I know you've got a lot on your mind right now."

Now, Kevin felt foolish. "I'm sorry, honey," he said, "The answer is, yes, I'd love to have children, as long as they're yours. But you're right; this isn't the time for thinking about that. We've got to get back to America and put our country and our lives back together. Then, I want the picket fence, and the dog, and a passel of kids; and I want them all to look like you, even the boys...but, not the dog."

"That's reassuring," she said.

•

Now that the Nomad was well into its Atlantic journey, Colonel Haddad felt it was time to inform Captain Faysal of the true nature of their mission. The Colonel was much younger than Captain Faysal but his superior rank lent itself to a haughty attitude. He was also a fitness fanatic and felt distain for those who didn't take care of their bodies. He drank only bottled water and worked out each morning with fervor.

At six feet three, Haddad towered over Faysal, who was well short of six feet tall. While Haddad always looked like he'd walked off a photo shoot, Faysal was overweight, rumpled and rarely clean shaven. This really graveled the Colonel, who was a stickler for health, cleanliness and protocol. Captain Faysal was a seaman and not inclined to, what he called, "such superficial tripe". He didn't say these things around men like Haddad, but couldn't care less what the Colonel thought of him; he'd be gone soon enough.

Haddad called the meeting for 0700. It was now 0650 and he was the only one in the Captain's cabin—it was actually the Colonel's cabin since he'd purloined it as a perk of his superior rank. While technically not late, Colonel Haddad felt that an officer ought to be at least 15 minutes early for a meeting in order to avoid the usual delays that accompany any gathering of men, i.e. getting a cup of coffee, going to the bathroom, idle chatter, etc...

When the Captain and his First Officer entered the cabin, only 2 minutes early, Colonel Haddad lit into them. "Is this the way you run your ship, Captain Faysal? Did the two of you get enough sleep? Why don't you both sit down and I'll make you a nice cup of coffee!"

The Captain and Lieutenant Zamani endured the Colonel's sarcasm without comment. The two senior officers of the Nomad simply sat down and gave the Colonel their attention. There were no facial expressions of resentment at having been disrespected or childish comments which stated the obvious. They were here and so was the Colonel; now that he had established who was boss, the briefing could begin.

"As I'm sure the two of you noticed," Haddad began, "there were a number of very large containers loaded aboard this ship at the time of her launch. What you do not know, and must now be told, is that within these containers lay the hopes and dreams of every faithful Muslim in the world."

Captain Faysal didn't react, he just reached for the pot of coffee and began to pour himself and Lieutenant Zamani a cup; this was going to take a while.

"Since the Ayatollah Khomeini first freed us from the tyranny of the Americans and their puppet, the Shah, we have struggled to overcome their satanically provided technology which has enabled them to oppress our Palestinian brothers and prop up Allah's greatest enemy, the Israelis. The time for Allah's revenge is at hand!"

Captain Faysal was Muslim but had spent his entire life at sea. These kinds of religious pronouncements had never held much interest to him. His First Officer was in complete agreement but the two men never batted an eye as they

194

listened to the Colonel spew out Islamic platitudes, quite aware that the man simply liked to hear himself talk.

And so he did, "I assume you are familiar with the Shahab 3 ballistic missile?" It was a rhetorical question; the Colonel had no intention of allowing himself to be interrupted by something as banal as an inferior's reply. "Well, gentlemen, the containers we have stowed away on this ship hold the new Shahab 4 missiles. They, like the Shahab 3, are medium-range ballistic missiles, but are capable of traveling over 2,500 kilometers at speeds exceeding 7 times the speed of sound."

Now the Captain perked up. He'd never launched a missile from the deck of one of his ships. If the Colonel was suggesting a deck launch of a ballistic missile, this would likely be a one-way trip. America would quickly detect the location of the launch and destroy his ship with alacrity.

"Our mission, gentlemen, is to position our ships well off the coast of the United States, approximately 80 miles into international waters, and launch the Shahab 4, tipped with a special device called an E-Bomb and wait for America's demise."

Captain Faysal had heard enough to feel that he could ask a question. "Colonel, forgive me. I am a simple freighter captain and not familiar with this kind of weapon. What is an E-bomb and why will it destroy a country as technologically superior as America?"

"I'm glad you asked that, Captain." Haddad replied with relish. He really was glad the Captain had asked that. It gave him a chance to expound, and the Colonel loved to expound. "You see, an E-bomb is an Electromagnetic Pulse device which, when triggered over a country, at about 400 kilometers in height, will knock out all electrical power, from circuit boards to cell phones. It will make domestic communications impotent."

"How much of the country will this...E-bomb affect?" the young Lieutenant asked.

"We believe that one EMP will knock most of America back to the 19th century. We, on the other hand, have three ships and three EMP devices to assure the complete technological annihilation of the American people. The Nomad will position itself off the coast of Philadelphia, Pennsylvania, the Alvand, under the command of Captain Omidi, will position itself off the coast of Miami, Florida and the Moudge, commanded by Captain Mouradipous will position itself in the Gulf of Mexico off the coast of Brownsville, Texas."

Colonel Haddad was really feeling his oats. He stood tall and paced back and forth like a General reviewing the troops. While he did stop at times and fire a stern stare at the Captain and First Officer, Haddad was alone with his megalomania; he usually kept his eyes fixed on the walls. Faysal wondered if the Colonel was looking at his own reflection in the windows.

"At precisely 0700 Eastern Standard Time on June 1st, for Nomad and Alvand, and 0600 Central Standard Time for the Moudge, we will simultaneously launch the Shahab 4 missiles to optimum height and upon their detonation, America; from coast to coast, will have no electrical power. They will have no way to launch missiles or jet fighters; they will have no communication, perhaps with the exception of smoke signals, and there will not be a computer in operation anywhere on the continent. America will be totally without technology. As I said, we will knock them back to the 19th century." Haddad had a smile from ear to ear. His air of superiority was gone and in its place were visions of grandeur. If this worked as planned, he, as the man in command of the mission, would be a legend throughout the Muslim world. He would be imbued with the status of martyr and he wouldn't even have to die to attain it. He had always felt that Allah favored him, and now he could see clearly that he was correct.

Chapter Seventeen

It had now been over 8 months since the sniper attack on Lisa Martin had begun a period unlike that of any in American history. The death toll of those directly killed by foreign terrorist activity had topped out at over 25,000, not including the attack on New York, which was in a whole other category. Those killed by American criminals empowered by America's chaos was probably equal to the 25,000, though exact figures couldn't be obtained. The economic calamity that followed the attacks, coupled with the cyber-attacks on financial institutions, and, of course, the utter destruction of America's premier economic hub, New York, had put the country into a financial morass that would have seemed unconquerable. Yet, the American people had somehow withstood it.

There had not been a SAM attack on an American airline in over 3 months. No one had any illusions that the terrorists were gone, just that they seem to have run out of SAMs.

The cyber-war which America mistakenly believed was launched by China was beginning to smooth itself out, thanks in great part to the assistance of the Chinese people and the Chinese government. President Hamilton thought they just wanted to assure America that they were innocent, but the effect was the same. Thousands of computer "geeks" were dispatched throughout the country to de-bug the nation's computer systems and, with the help of an IBM genius, new anti-virus/anti-malware software was introduced that would prevent any such occurrence in the future, or so they said.

It was the destruction of New York City that had been the biggest blow to the American psyche, and in turn,

America; so many dead and so much lingering pain. In all, over 2 million people were killed in the initial blast, with just under 1 million dead in the ensuing months. Many "America haters" worldwide thought that the United States had gotten a little "payback" from their dropping of the bombs on Hiroshima and Nagasaki in World-War Two. Ironically, Japan was not one of those countries.

The Japanese were the most sensitive of all, sending doctors to treat the radiation burns and lingering sickness, helping to rebuild the communication apparatus, in neighboring New Jersey, and pouring in millions of dollars to the American economy to help prop it up. The American people were grateful and quite humbled by Japan's generosity.

In all, America had weathered the storm with a modicum of dignity, and, to a certain degree, growth. Gone was the culture that considered a drug-addicted actor or musician to be more important than a doctor or a farmer. Even the young people, frightened by the magnitude of the events, became better students and more responsible citizens. Inner city youth were still fairly lawless, but even they had come to understand that life was precious and that America wasn't invulnerable, leading many to abandon lives of idleness for a chance at a better life through education.

President Hamilton's poll numbers were becoming respectable. In the latest Zogby poll, the President had a 53 percent approval rating. That was remarkable considering the shape the country was in and its opposition to the President's stonewalling of the European Union. Americans were still partial to a man who "stuck to his guns" and although most disagreed with the President on the issue of the Euro-Union, most gave him credit for stating his position with firmness and then standing up to the mounting political pressure. From the perspective of most Americans, the country had indeed remained independent and the future looked...well, not bright, but hopeful.

Now that he was presiding over a nation that was, if not prospering, at least not coming apart at the seams, the President had a mind to avenge his countries ills. After long talks with FBI Director Freed, his Chief-of-staff Harold Cummings and the senior Senator from Virginia, Charles Huxley, an old and dear friend, President Hamilton had a plan. That plan would require that he consult the man in charge of the Maelstrom Task Force, FBI Special Agent in Charge, Kevin O'Brien.

Back in Rome, Kevin was taking a long, hot shower. He had just finished working out in the hotel's spa—Kevin hated that word—and was washing some of the ache away. Lisa was just finishing a bowl of mint-chocolate chip ice-cream and trying to make heads or tails of an Italian game show, with no luck.

Suddenly, Kevin's old Nokia cell phone went off. Normally, Lisa wouldn't have thought twice about answering Kevin's phone, but she hesitated for a moment, for some reason, before grabbing it and pushing the green button. "Hello, this is Kevin O'Brien's cell phone, I'm his wife, Lisa O'Brien—she loved saying that—may I help you?"

"Yes, young lady, may I speak with Agent O'Brien, please?" the voice on the other end said.

"He's in the shower. May I ask who's calling?" Lisa had always practiced good phone manners.

"Yes, this is the President," he said.

"The President of what?" Lisa answered, never letting it cross her mind that very few presidents just say, "The President" when asked who they are.

"The President of the United States," he replied, amused. Presidents never admitted it, but this kind of thing was one of the perks to the Presidency; the ability to "blow people's minds" when they called.

Lisa was no different than most people, who, when told that the President of the United States was on the line, assumed it was a joke. "Ok, sure, whatever," she said, "do you want me to have him call you when he's out of the shower or do you want to call back?"

"I'll call back in about 15 minutes, young lady. I assume he'll be out of the shower by then?" said the President.

Lisa wasn't amused; perhaps a little sarcasm was in order, "I don't know," she said, "he sure likes the shower. He may be in there for months."

The President, knowing that Lisa didn't believe him—and loving every minute of it—replied, "Well, I'll call back in 15 minutes and find out. Goodbye, Lisa O'Brien."

After she had hung up, Kevin came out of the shower wearing nothing but a hunter-green towel around his waist. Lisa was intrigued. Having never given the phone call serious thought, since she believed it to be a crank call, she forgot about it in lieu of other considerations, like Kevin in a towel.

She got up and walked over to her husband, who was still drying off his hair. Lisa reached for the fold in the towel and pulled it off of Kevin's still dripping wet body. Kevin was intrigued. Having never heard the phone ring in the first place, Kevin could easily massage his libido and Lisa at the same time.

The two came together in a passionate kiss as Kevin's cell phone went off again. The sound broke their concentration and reminded Lisa of the previous call. As Kevin reached for his cell phone, Lisa, jokingly said, "Oh, I forgot to tell you, the President of the United States just called. I told him you were in the shower. That's probably him calling back."

Kevin looked at Lisa as if she had just belched the Star-Spangled Banner. He picked up the phone and answered it. Lisa sat there with a smile on her face. It would be interesting to find out who this joker was.

Lisa's face began to take on a look of concern. Kevin seemed to be stunned but hadn't said a word, until..."Yes, Mr. President, this is Agent O'Brien."

Lisa flopped onto her belly and pulled the covers over her head. She had no intention of ever being seen again. Kevin continued his conversation in stunned disbelief. "Yes, Mr. President, I've led the Maelstrom Task Force since its inception. I believe we've made some significant headway."

The President agreed. "I realize we have you to thank for identifying the men responsible for these traumatic times, Agent O'Brien. The country is in your debt."

"Thank you, Mr. President, but there were many people involved, some of whom lost their lives." Kevin felt the need to point that out.

"You're absolutely right, Agent...may I call you Kevin?" the President asked.

Kevin's humor knew no bounds. He came very close to saying to the President, *"No, Mr. President, I prefer that you call me Special Agent in Charge O'Brien"*, but he thought better of it. "Of course, Mr. President," he said, not adding, *"May I call you, Mike?"*

"Kevin," the President went on, "you're absolutely right, and I promise you those men will not be forgotten." Then he got to the crux of the call. "The reason I've called you personally, Kevin, other than to thank you for your fine service to the country, is to ask your advice concerning a plan that I and others here at the White House have come up with. I believe it was your wife, Lisa, who first suggested that we may wish to plant our own man within this...Elite Eight, or whatever they call themselves. Is that right?"

"Well, Mr. President, she did suggest it first."

"I hear you are recently married, Kevin. May I offer my congratulations?" the President said. Kevin was moments from a stroke.

"Thank you, Mr. President. Lisa is a wonderful woman."

"She sure sounded like quite a girl when I talked to her earlier."

"I'm sorry for that, sir," Kevin said, red-faced, "she didn't believe you were the President."

Kevin could hear the President laughing on the other end of the line. "That's ok, Kevin, in fact, I get a kick out of people's reactions when I call them. Lisa sounded like a wonderful lady, I mean that."

"Thank you, sir," Kevin said, and then listened as the President detailed his plan to infiltrate the group known as the Elite Eight. He pointed out a number of ways that the Bureau could be of use in the implementation of such a plan. Naturally, Kevin was honored to be a part of it and told the President that he thought the plan was well thought out and if done right, could catch this Euro-trash, as the President referred to them, with their hands in the cookie jar.

After the two of them had hammered out the details of the plan, President Hamilton gave Kevin a little advice on his marriage. "Kevin, when Katie and I got married, over 50 years ago, my father gave me some advice. He said there were two things I needed to remember. One, that it's not the big things that trip you up: the mortgage, the car payments, it's the little things like toothpaste and toilet paper, because you never budget for them. And the second thing to remember, he said, is that one of these days, you're going to be in the bathroom, shaving, and your wife is going to walk in, sit down on the toilet and take a dump. When that happens, Kevin, the honeymoon is over. Talk to you again soon, son." And he hung up.

Kevin stood there like a Greek statue, naked and stone-faced. Lisa, realizing that the call was over, pulled the covers off her head and came up for air. "Oh my God! Was I just sarcastic to the President of the United States?"

Kevin, of course, thought it was hilarious. "I'm afraid you were, sweetheart, but I think he was impressed with you."

Lisa couldn't believe that she'd just spoken to the President, and talked to him as if he were a crank phone caller. "Remind me never to answer your phone again," she said. Then, a thought occurred to her, "You just talked to the President of the United States! I had no idea I was married to such an important man."

"Well," Kevin said, "now you can treat me with the respect I deserve."

Kevin was still standing naked before her and it did not go unnoticed by Lisa. She got up and finished what she'd started before the phone rang.

•

Falah Mohamed had escaped reprisal from the American infidels for over eight months. In all, he had personally been responsible for the destruction of over 10 planes and the deaths of hundreds of the enemy of Allah. However, the supply of SAMs had dried up and he was left to ponder his future as a soldier in the army of Islam. He could just find a rifle and start sniping Christians and Jews but was unsure whether he should strike out on this own or wait for orders that may never come.

He had not heard from his cell leader in over a month, just two days after his last use of the Surface-to-Air missiles. He had been told to "sit tight" and wait for orders, but the former Terrique Johnson was not inclined to patience. Although he kept his cell phone—the method used to contact him—close by and charged at all times, he was beginning to think he had been forgotten. Was this all there was? He was a soldier of Allah and willing to die in his cause; there must be something for him to do, someone for him to kill.

Since his conversion to Islam in a California prison, Falah had given up alcohol, the most difficult challenge of his Islamic walk. He was partial to Jim Beam whiskey and had spent many a lonely night ruing the fact that we could not enjoy its many pleasures.

One other thing that Falah had given up was the companionship of prostitutes. He was unmarried, and, in his line of work, not inclined to meet Miss Right. On this late May evening, Falah was strongly feeling the need, as he sat forlornly in this hotel room, of both Jim Beam and Miss Right...or Miss Wrong, for that matter. He just wanted to ease some of the tension he felt and whiskey and women were Falah's favorite two ways to ease tension; Allah would understand.

As he looked out the window of his second-floor Motel 6 room, he could see the women plying their wares on Hollywood Boulevard. He'd noticed them every night, in fact. Tonight, Falah would give in to his desires and relieve some of his angst. So, he left his room, after showering and dressing in what he thought was his "best look", and strolled down to the liquor store to buy a bottle of Jim Beam...and a couple packs of cigarettes, Allah wouldn't mind if he smoked a little, too.

The variety of prostitutes on Hollywood Boulevard was akin to the variety of breakfast cereals in an American grocery store; the pickings were virtually unlimited. There were black, white, Asian, Hispanic; tall, short, thin, fat and everything from repulsive to supermodel beautiful. The price was determined by any and all of these factors, as well as whether you wanted a "quickie" or someone to spend the night.

Falah, having more money than he needed and less companionship than he wanted, decided on an attractive blond girl to spend the night with him. Her name was Chastity—both knew it wasn't her real name—and she said it would cost an extra fifty for kissing. Prostitutes didn't usually like to kiss their "Johns", it was too intimate. Falah gave her the extra fifty.

Back in the room, Falah and Chastity drank Jim Beam and did a little "crack" that she had brought with her. Falah didn't think Allah would mind. Falah really missed doing crack-cocaine; it made him feel like Superman. It also made him a great lover, a fallacy that Chastity soon discovered, but of which Falah never caught on.

After a night of sex, drugs, and Gangster-rap, Falah and Chastity fell into a drug induced stupor and passed out, Chastity on the bed and Falah on the bathroom floor. More than four hours passed when Chastity awoke and went to the bathroom, only to discover Falah dead to the world on the floor. Not one for modesty, she simply stepped over him and sat down on the toilet.

After she'd finished on the commode, Chastity got up and stepped over Falah again, just as his cell phone went off on the nightstand. Falah was oblivious to anything, so Chastity picked up the cell phone and checked the message. All it said was, "President Hamilton". That was odd, she thought, but she'd seen weirder. She sat the phone down on the table and turned around, only to come face to face with a very angry Falah.

He slapped her on the face so hard it knocked her onto the bed. "What the hell do you think you're doing?" he screamed, "Who told you to answer my cell phone?"

Falah, in anger, reached to see the message on his phone. Once he saw it, he took a more civil tone with Chastity. "I'm sorry I hit you, but you should know better than to check someone else's messages. Are you alright?"

This was not the first time Chastity had been hit by a man...this week, so she thought nothing more of it. She started to put her things together—after all, the night was over, wasn't it?—and head for the door. She didn't get far, as Falah wrapped one of his seldom worn ties around her throat and squeezed with all his might. Chastity dropped to the floor of her own dead weight, literally.

Falah wasn't worried about the authorities finding a dead body in his room. He was leaving anyway and the ID he used to get the room was fake. Now, feeling a bit hung-over but invigorated by a new assignment, Falah gathered his things, including a pack of Marlboros—Allah wouldn't mind—and headed for his Jeep Cherokee. He needed to get to the ATM and then get something to eat; he had a long trip ahead of him.

Chapter Eighteen

It was three days until June 1st, the day their flight would touch down at Tampa International Airport. Kevin and Lisa, although grateful for the honeymoon and the excitement, were ready to get back to Tampa and begin a new life together, hopefully coinciding with the end of these terrorist attacks.

They had decided to spend their last couple of days sightseeing in Rome and relaxing by the Cavalieri's beautiful pool. Their first stop was Vatican City.

Although, located within the city of Rome, Vatican City is not under Rome's jurisdiction; it is considered a country in and of itself, complete with an Ambassador to the United Nations. Inside the Vatican City, is, of course, the Vatican itself. Built in 1506, the Vatican is the central core of the worldwide Catholic Church. Kevin and Lisa knew they couldn't leave Rome without seeing the Vatican's extraordinary array of museums which house the work of the greatest artists throughout history. Paintings and sculpture by Michelangelo, Da Vinci, Raphael and hundreds of others grace its ornate buildings.

Lisa was particularly stunned and awed by the Sistine Chapel in Saint Peter's Basilica, well known throughout the world as Michelangelo's masterpiece. The chapel itself, she thought, was much smaller than she anticipated. She'd seen many Catholic churches in America that were much larger, but its contours created a perfect synergism for the extraordinary artwork that had been meticulously applied by Michelangelo and recently restored by the church.

"Have you ever seen anything like it?" Lisa said with open mouth, "The pictures just don't do it justice."

"It's like God graffiti," Kevin said, "there isn't an inch of space that isn't art, and I thought it was just the ceiling," he added with mouth agape, "the frescos on the walls are more extraordinary than the ceiling."

Lisa had always been an art lover; always appreciative of the artists spirit within the work. This, on the other hand, was out of this world; probably, literally. "You don't have to be a Christian to appreciate the beauty and wonder of this," Lisa said, "but I'm sure it wouldn't hurt. It's like a pictorial of the entire bible, from the Creation, to Adam and Eve, to the miracles of Christ. I'm absolutely flabbergasted."

Kevin was no less amazed by the classic work of art. It moved him in a way he hadn't expected. "You know, I've always considered myself a Christian, but seeing something like this makes me feel close to God. Does that make any sense?" he said, turning to Lisa for approval.

Lisa didn't even look at Kevin. She continued to stare at the art all around her as she answered him, "Yes, Kevin, it makes perfect sense. It's as if God himself used Michelangelo to paint it."

There were many people around them, walking around the Chapel, gawking at the frescos and fiddling with their bifocals to get a better look at the handiwork of one of the world's great artists. One set of eyes, however, was not appreciating the artistry of Michelangelo but the movements of Kevin and Lisa. They belonged to a man that had been following them for a number of days, always being sure to remain invisible and ever aware of each of his two subject's manner and habit. Sometimes he would disguise himself, sometimes he wouldn't. Always, he would blend into his surroundings with his acutely honed ability to disappear from view while remaining quite visible; in fact, at times, downright flamboyant.

On one occasion, when Kevin and Lisa were strolling down a Roman street, he jumped out of a taxi, and right in front of them, yelled at the driver to such a degree that the police were called. He had spoken to Lisa on one occasion and had bumped into Kevin in a restaurant's men's room. The two of them had seen him on a number of occasions but his presence had not once registered in either one's mind.

Tuefel had been in Rome for over a week. When he was given a job to do, he did it with excruciating patience and attention to detail. Nothing could be left to chance and his targets could not be allowed to escape alive. Tuefel, however, was not a Muslim fanatic; he had no intention of being caught by authorities. Tuefel was a professional, and professionals got paid, and then enjoyed the fruits of that payment. The death of these two people would have to be done in a way that would allow his escape while providing none for his targets. Obviously, the Sistine Chapel didn't have the necessary criteria for such an endeavor, but Tuefel was patient and would wait until an opportunity presented itself, then he would quickly end their lives and head to the beaches of southern France for a little R and R.

•

After another delicious dinner, Kevin and Lisa returned to the hotel to spend the night relaxing. They showered, put on the hotel's complimentary his-and-hers robes, and sat down on the couch in front of the fire. Kevin opened a chilled bottle of Lambrusco and poured them each a glass before sitting down beside the woman the loved. "Did you know," Kevin said, "that the ancient Etruscans cultivated the grape long before the Romans became a civilization?"

Lisa turned her head toward Kevin and gave him a look that shouted, *"So?"*

Kevin laughed and said, "Amerigo told me. He said this sparkling wine was made in the province of Lombardy. That's where his family is from, the Lombardi's"

Lisa leaned over and kissed her husband on the cheek. Then she looked at him with all seriousness and said, "Wrap it up!"

They both laughed at Kevin's darling, but boorish attempt to play the tour guide. "Well," Kevin said, "I thought it might impress you."

Lisa's eyes smiled at Kevin. She loved watching him do just about anything. She rested her head back into the crook of Kevin's arm and let out a long sigh. "This is the life, isn't it?" she said with some sadness, "We'll be leaving this all behind soon for the mundane life of an American couple. Will we be able to stand it?"

Kevin took another sip of the wine. He didn't reply, he just looked at the fire and enjoyed his wife's presence and warmth. They were both happy to be at the stage where they could sit together without feeling the need to speak. It was, they believed, the mark of a happy marriage. Kevin broke the silence; however, and reminded Lisa that, in the future, when he was in the bathroom, shaving, he didn't want any company. Lisa looked at him, took another drink of wine and looked back at the fire. She had no intention of asking him what he meant. Some things were better left unknown.

Lisa had fallen fast asleep in the crook of Kevin's arm. He had long ago wished for another glass of wine but didn't want to disturb her in order to get it. Lisa's Blackberry came to Kevin's rescue, momentarily, as its outburst caused Lisa to snap to consciousness so quickly that she spilled her wine on her robe. "Oh dear," she said, wiping the red stain with her hand, "who the devil could that be?"

After hurriedly putting her wineglass on the table and continuing to wipe off her robe, Lisa scurried to the nightstand and grabbed her Blackberry. She punched a couple of buttons and retrieved her text message which read, *"You know where to look, don't you?"*

Lisa was still half asleep as she returned to the couch and handed the Blackberry to Kevin, "What the heck is this supposed to mean?" she said as she planted herself back in Kevin's embrace.

Kevin took the phone and read the message. He sat the phone down on the table and asked Lisa to sit up for a moment. When she did, Kevin reached his fingers into the right pocket of her pink wine-stained robe. Sure enough, he pulled out a typed note from their "friend". "I don't know about you," Lisa said, "but this is getting a little old, don't you think?"

Kevin opened the note and read it to himself as Lisa replanted herself snuggly within his arms. Moments later, Kevin practically threw Lisa off the couch as he rose like he'd been shot out of a cannon. "Oh my God!" was all Kevin could say. He repeated it three times before Lisa could get him to explain. "Here," Kevin said, handing the note to his wife, "read it for yourself!"

Lisa picked up the note and read it, *"Lisa,"* the note began, *"please tell Kevin that a rather monumental terrorist attack is imminent. Information has come my way which points to an E-bomb attack on the United States within the week. Two or three ships in international waters will launch the attack to be sure of its success. Good luck, Kevin, I hope you can stop this."*

Kevin was already on the phone to Diane. "E-bomb?" Lisa said to herself, at first, then louder, to Kevin, as a question. "E-bomb? What's an E-bomb?"

Lisa didn't have to get a reply because she overheard everything that Kevin said to Diane. "Diane, everything this guy has said has come true; I have no reason to believe this isn't true, as well! Contact Director Freed and tell him to get the Navy, Coast Guard, Special Forces, and anyone else he can think of, to scour the international coastline of the United States." Before Kevin hung up he reminded Diane, "We've got to stop this! If they succeed, the most sophisticated American technology would be familiar to Isaac Newton, and I, for one, have no intention of riding to work every day on Old Paint!"

•

The weather was perfect. Arthur Swift couldn't have picked a better time or place to hold an outside meeting of the Elite Eight. As he slowly made his way to the head of a long, ovoid Cherry-wood table—Arthur recently had his left hip replaced because of Necrosis—he pondered the scene before him.

There, already seated at the well-shaded meeting table, resting just yards from the shore of the St. Lawrence Seaway, were Antoine Rousseau, looking like a broken man; Herr Wolfgang von Graff, a vicious man that one did not cross; Amal Singh, a solid new member; Michael Grant, a fellow American but a bit of a tool; John C. Devaney, drunken Irishman; Sir Harold Covington, a good friend, but a bit stuffy, and a quite attractive young lady seated away from the table and looking like a queen about to take the scepter.

She was approximately 40 years of age but could have been taken for 30. Her complexion was creamy and tanned. Shoulder length and silky, her auburn-colored hair fluttered in the gentle late- spring breeze. She looked about her fellows with confident, blue eyes that had surely seen their share of suffering; her comportment was nothing if not resilient. She would be a great asset to their group as they went forward. Arthur had always thought they could do with a woman's touch.

The scene brought with it interesting memories of how it all had transpired. Arthur could well remember his election into the group, just over 45 years ago. He had been a young man then, reletively speaking, and idealistic as they came. His money had been made the same way the rest of these people had made theirs, by screwing everyone around them until they had enough to become philanthropists, and, at least as far as the general public, buy their souls back.

As he approached the table he wondered what Herr von Graff would have done, or would do now, if he only new that the man who was sitting at the head of that table was a Jew. For that matter, from the conversations that had taken place on Dark Island, he doubted anyone here, save Amal and Michael, would allow him to leave the island alive, if they knew. He was not about to tell them.

Dark Island was, today, quite bright and cheerful. The group had buried Aldo Veneto and was ready to move on to accepting a replacement for the group's eighth member. The temperature was a comfortable 72 degrees on this 30th day of May and Arthur was anxious to conclude their business and return to his island before the United States became a third-world country.

"Gentlemen, may I call this meeting to order?" Mr. Swift said, wishing to cull the other six members from their wanderings. When they had all been seated, Arthur, after remembering to praise Aldo Veneto, began his introduction of their newest member. "Gentlemen, I have the distinct honor of introducing our little club's newest, and first, female member, Deborah Hargett."

Miss Hargett approached the table and stood behind the only empty chair; it was obviously the chair they had provided for her. She stood straight up and with a firm, but friendly voice said, "Gentlemen, it is indeed an honor." Then she made an evident glance down at the chair in front of her and said, "May I?" in an unmistakable request to join the group by being seated. All heads nodded as Miss Hargett seated herself and without a word, turned her attention to Mr. Swift and the head of the table.

"Welcome, Miss Hargett, the honor is ours," he said, then addressing the group, added, "Now, Gentlemen," he paused a moment and turned to the newest member, "and Lady", then he turned back to the group, "the President's refusal to consider incorporation into our little confederation has left us with little choice but to escalate and expedite our plan. New orders have been given through our Iranian friends and our German..." he paused, "specialist...is busy at work."

Amal Singh spoke up, "Arthur, with the impending introduction of an EMP, why do we feel the need to further enhance the situation? Would we not do better to observe the consequence of this device's...application, as it were?"

Sir Harold was quick to address Amal's concerns. "An excellent point, Amal, but it was thought that this extra bit of pressure on the American political landscape might, push them over the edge, so to speak. Do you feel deeply about protecting this president?"

"Not at all," Amal replied, "it's just that sometimes less is more. We don't want to overplay our hands, do we, gentlemen?"

Amal Singh was, of course, of Indian decent, having been raised in the city of Agra; home of the Taj Mahal. He was the only son of one of the truly wealthy men in all of India, the famed oil baron, Patag Singh, the man who had single-handedly brought the Middle-Eastern oil magnates to the table with the South American oil magnates to create America's greatest nightmare, a colluding and anti-American oil conglomerate.

Amal inherited, not only his wealth—his father died in a plane crash when Amal was 19 years old—but his father's drive to make India a world player and an economic rival of America and Europe. He learned well from his late father that in order to "beat 'em" you had to "join 'em", or at least, "deal with 'em". It was Amal, chiefly, who was responsible for the fact that one cannot call an American company of any size without speaking to an Indian representative. Although not widely known, Amal Singh's net worth is more than that of all the other group members.

Arthur put the matter to bed. "Amal, Sir Harold is correct, you make an excellent point, but time is becoming a factor. I believe that President Hamilton has arched his back and borne his teeth. It seems to me, at this point, the more pressure he feels to relent; the greater will be his desire to fight back. The best thing for our purposes is, I believe most earnestly, to replace the man in the White House with a less combative sort. I feel sure that Vice-President Canton will see that America's only avenue for survival is to join us in our 'Union of the willing', as former President George H.W. Bush used to say. It's really just that simple." He looked at Amal with sincere respect. "Will you join us, Amal?"

Amal stood and faced Arthur. He bowed just a bit and said, "I will, indeed, Arthur. Let us be sure that this is our last adventure into American politics. It is a most distasteful place." And he sat down.

After Arthur gestured toward his Indian colleague with a slight bow of the head, he addressed the group as a whole. "Are we in agreement, then?

Now the nods were unanimous. The E-bomb would end America's reign as a superpower, leaving it malleable for future manipulation, the assassination of President Hamilton would end America's resistance to change, and with the removal of a few other obstacles—already in the works—things should stabilize in a very short time.

•

By order of the President, Coast Guard cutters, as well as a number of naval vessels, began a frantic sweep of America's coastlines from 150 miles off shore and in. Navy Seals, Air Force Paratroopers and Army Green Beret were assigned to the various ships to act as a SWAT team when a ship was discovered. Also, the FBI, CIA and Military Intelligence had all sent their best snipers in case of a need for a more "remote" response.

Kevin was satisfied that he had done all he could to prevent the attacks. The President had been notified and put every resource into finding the ships that would launch the EMPs. It was their last day in Rome so he and Lisa went for one more sightseeing trip, this time to the Bocca della Verità, located in a portico of the Santa Maria church in Cosmedin, in Rome. Being an avid fan of Audrey Hepburn and an ardent worshiper of Gregory Peck, it was something that Lisa had long wished to see. The Mouth of Truth, as most Americans know it, is most famous for its role in the movie, "Roman Holiday".

In the movie, Gregory Peck and Audrey Hepburn are both being dishonest with each other. When they visit the Bocca della Verità, Peck's character puts his hand in the mouth of the Poseidon-like Pavonazzetto-marble carving, which, according to legend, will lop off the hand of anyone who is lying. Lisa said she wanted Kevin to put his hand in the mouth of the carving and then tell her how much he loved her. Kevin playfully acted a bit nervous at the prospect of this but relented when Lisa promised him carte blanche back at the hotel suite that evening.

The two honeymooners decided to stop and have dinner before heading over to the church. Kevin hadn't eaten all day so Lisa agreed to stop for some real Italian spaghetti. Kevin didn't enjoy the meal; however, thinking it was plain and bland. American-Italian food was by far, better tasting, or so the two had long ago decided. "We should have gone to McDonalds." Kevin complained, "Are you gonna eat that tomato?"

After dinner they hopped in a taxi and headed for the Santa Maria church in Cosmedin. The driver spoke English and told them that it was likely to be closed at this late hour. You could see the Bocca della Verità, he told them, but probably from behind locked gates, putting to an end any chance Lisa would have of being sure that her husband truly loved her. "Now I suppose I've just got to take your word for it!" Lisa joked, "But, I'd still like to see it and get some pictures, if that's ok with you?"

"That depends," Kevin said, "on whether the arrangements have changed for later."

"Boy," Lisa said, rolling her eyes in mock disgust, "I thought I was a sex maniac."

Kevin called out to the driver, "Lead on, McDuff!" The cab driver hit the gas.

Chapter Nineteen

When they arrived at the Santa Maria church in Cosmedin, Kevin paid the driver and thanked him for his help. Lisa headed straight for the church, so Kevin had to catch up with her. "Hey, hold on," Kevin called out, "what's the big hurry?"

"I've got places to go and people to see!" Lisa yelled back. "Come on," she urged him, "we're burnin' daylight!"

"Burning daylight? Who are you, John Wayne?" he said as he hurried to join her.

Kevin finally caught up with his wife at the portico of the church. It was immediately clear that the portico, which houses the Mouth of Truth, was closed and locked. While told to expect this, Lisa was, nevertheless, disappointed. They walked along the outside length of the portico until they came to the Mouth of Truth, clearly visible from outside the gate. Lisa, while an intelligent and sophisticated physician, began to get downright giddy. She had always dreamt of seeing this famous landmark, mostly...no, totally because of the scene from the movie Roman Holiday.

Almost 6 feet in diameter and 7 inches thick, the Bocca della Verità, or Mouth of Truth was brought to Rome from what is now Turkey. Its actual function is a bit of a mystery. Some think it was the opening for a fountain while others believe it was a man-hole cover. The absence of wear around the holes—the two eyes, two nostrils and mouth—has led many experts to conclude that it could not have had water running through it, at least, not for very long.

The depiction is thought to be that of the god, Oceanus, because the bearded figure closely resembles a familiar bronze cast of the head of the Roman god of the sea. It has crab claws that look like horns, a fish on the left side, and the heads of 2 dolphins, as depicted in the bronze relief. To Lisa; however, it was the stuff of dreams.

"Well," Lisa whimpered, "I suppose the best we can do is to take a few pictures with it as a background." She lifted up her Minolta, with the zoom lens, and motioned Kevin toward the icon. "You stand over here and I'll get pictures of you, then I'll stand there and you can take a few of me."

Kevin did as he was told, feeling silly about the whole thing, a feeling he had no intention of relating to his wife. Lisa took a few pictures of Kevin and then handed him the camera as she moved in front of the Mouth of Truth. "Now me!" she said, giggling as she posed with various facial expressions.

"Excuse me!" The voice came from behind them. It was that of a rather bedraggled looking fellow, about 50, blond or white hair, hard to tell in the dark, and dressed like a janitor. The man smiled at them pleasantly and after a moment, said, "Would you like me to take a few pictures of the two of you?"

He must have read Lisa's mind. "Oh," she said to him, "would you mind?" She said this as she simultaneously handed him the camera and grabbed Kevin, pulling him toward the monument. "This is so kind of you." Lisa said.

"Think nothing of it;" the man said in an obvious Italian accent, "I work here."

The man took a few pictures of the couple as Lisa posed and Kevin stood still as a statue, a bored look on his face. "Hey," the man said, "I bet you'd like to take some pictures with your hand in the mouth, wouldn't you?" He could see Lisa's eyes light up, so he said, "Here, come with me."

He handed the camera back to Lisa and reached into his side pocket and pulled out a set of keys. "I don't suppose it would hurt too much for you to go inside for a few minutes. Don't tell anyone." He said with a smile.

As Lisa squeezed Kevin's arm with excitement, the man unlocked the gate and allowed the two of them to enter. Lisa walked quickly over to the larger than expected carving and stuck her hand in its mouth. "I swear that I love my husband and that I will never even look at another man as long as I live." The gods have little sympathy for liars, but apparently Lisa was being honest and she retained the use of her right hand.

Satisfied that she'd fulfilled her duty, Lisa said to Kevin, "Now you!" Kevin didn't roll his eyes but he wanted to. He walked over and put his hand in the god's mouth as Lisa gave the camera to the "janitor", hurriedly returning to stand by Kevin and make funny faces as he pledged his love to her with his hand in the "jaws of death". "Now," Lisa said, looking at Kevin with playful earnestness, "what have you got to say?"

Kevin looked at the "janitor", who was laughing at Kevin's discomfort, and said, "I swear that I love Lisa O'Brien with all my heart and will never look at another woman for as long as I live." Then, after retracting his non-severed left hand from the god's mouth, he turned to Lisa, now moving back to retrieve the camera, and said, "There, are you satisfied?"

"I don't much like your tone, young man," she said, "we come all this way and bother this nice man and that's the attitude you take? I'm very disappointed," she said.

Kevin was just about to make a snide comment, when the man dropped the camera onto the pavement and grabbed Lisa from behind. With his left arm clutching Lisa tightly, he produced what looked to Kevin like a hunting knife, and pressed it against her neck. "Please don't be alarmed, Kevin," Tuefel said, now in his native German accent, "I

222

just need to ask you some questions, if that's ok with you?"

He wouldn't get any argument from Kevin, not while holding his wife at knife-point. "What do you want?" Kevin asked, outwardly unemotional.

"I just need to find out what you and your friends at the FBI know about the people who sent me here. They are greatly concerned that you have been overly curious about their activities."

Although it was a warm evening, Kevin was wearing a wind-breaker in order to conceal his Glock 23. He knew that producing a weapon at this time would not be wise; this man was holding a knife ever-so-close to Lisa's throat. There would be no way to be sure he could shoot him before he struck a lethal blow.

"To what people are you referring?" Kevin asked, "My office is working on many cases." Kevin was stalling for time, but time for what he didn't know.

"Please, Kevin, don't insult my intelligence. The answers that I need from you are not vital to those who employed me, but they are very thorough people; I'm sure you understand."

Kevin looked at Lisa to see how she was holding up. She seemed calm, but obviously frightened. "What do I call you?" Kevin asked, again, stalling.

"I can't see the importance, frankly, but if you must address me by name, call me Tuefel."

That name had no more meaning to Kevin than if he would have said, Santa Claus; Lisa, on the other hand, understanding the translation, mumbled, just loud enough for Tuefel to hear, "the Devil."

"That's right, young lady, the Devil. It is a name that has been with me for many years and I must warn you, it is an appropriate moniker." He looked up at Kevin and said, "Kevin, I'm not known for my patience."

Kevin couldn't think of anything else to do; he answered the man's inquiry with a telling series of questions. "What is it that you'd like to know? That we are aware of the Elite Eight's existence? That we know all of the group's names and where they live? And, of course, what they've been doing?"

"Yes, in essence, that is what I wished to know. So," the man seemed resigned, "you are aware of much. My employers won't be happy about that." He reached into his belt and produced a Laser Max Sig Sauer P225 hand gun. It is equipped with an internally mounted laser sight which cannot be knocked out of alignment. When the "red dot" is on something and the trigger is pulled, the bullet hits the target. That dot was now on Kevin's forehead as Tuefel released Lisa and held the gun with both hands.

Kevin had been in the "business" long enough to know that this man had made a decision and was about to act on it. He knew this man was about to kill them. Quickly, as Lisa backed away from Tuefel toward her husband, Kevin started talking. "Tuefel, as I've told you, there's no reason to kill us. The FBI knows everything; as do the CIA, the OSI, the President and just about every agency in the United States except the Girl Scouts; even Interpol is well aware of the Elite Eight's crimes. The jig is up!"

Kevin hoped that this would confuse the man just long enough for him to act, but this was no ordinary hit man. Tuefel smiled at Kevin and replied, "Kevin, it is unimportant to me what happens to the 'Elite Eight', as you call them. I have no political leanings. I simply wish to get paid, and I have been paid, handsomely."

Tuefel eased up on his aim just long enough to say, "You know, the two of you are a cute couple. I have been watching you for many days and have come to admire you both. Also, I must admit, it is a shame to see the loss a woman as beautiful as Lisa. I assure you, this gives me no pleasure." He raised the gun and sighted Kevin's mid-chest.

Kevin knew it was now or never, so he dove to his right and pushed Lisa to the ground, while at the same time withdrawing his Glock 23 from his jacket. Kevin knew he had no chance but maybe this would give Lisa the time she needed to run, not that she would.

Kevin hit the ground, arms extended, with the Glock aimed at Tuefel's chest. Suddenly, Tuefel fell backwards as if he'd been jerked by something powerful. His gun clanked to the ground, bouncing a good distance away. As Kevin looked on, stunned to still be alive, Tuefel quickly rose up and confronted a black-clad man, approaching him from behind.

Tuefel reached into a sheath attached to his hip and withdrew the hunting knife that he'd held to Lisa's throat. The man in black leapt back as Tuefel swept the knife across his body, avoiding it by what seemed to Kevin like millimeters. Then, with speed that Kevin hadn't thought possible, the man spun in the air and delivered a round-house kick to Tuefel's knife-wielding left hand, knocking the weapon from his grip and sending it spiraling against the portico wall.

Now the fight was strictly hand-to-hand. As the two combatants squared off, Kevin dashed to Lisa's side and held her in his arms. He was trained in hand-to-hand combat, but Kevin knew he had to stay with Lisa. The two of them did not know who was fighting for them, but his assistance was deeply appreciated and profoundly welcome.

Tuefel smiled at the man in black, clad almost like a ninja, with black pants, shoes, shirt and pullover mask. Even now, Kevin's devilish wit reared its ugly head as he had a momentary thought that this man in black might be O.J. Simpson.

Tuefel rose up on his right foot and jumped into the air, simultaneously, and with great speed and force, stabbing his left foot at the man in black with a scissor kick. The man, rather than try to block the blow, dropped to his stomach, rolled over and whipped his right foot at Tuefel's legs, sweeping him off his feet. Tuefel landed on his back with a thud, but rose quickly to his feet in attack posture.

Kevin stood by, holding on to Lisa with one hand and his Glock with his other. He wasn't about to fire at Tuefel because he might hit the man who'd just saved their lives; besides, this guy didn't look like he needed any help.

Now it was Tuefel's turn to do a round-house kick. This, directed at the left side of the man in black's jaw; however, he missed as the man dropped to a squat position and then before Tuefel had landed, sprang forward and delivered a crushing straight-fist blow to Tuefel's chest, knocking him breathless. With lightning speed, the man spun around and took Tuefel's right leg out from under him, dropping him to his back. Now, with one quick thrust, he came down on Tuefel's throat with his elbow, effectively breaking his neck and ending his life.

Tuefel lay on the concrete in a heap, his head tilted to the side at an unnatural angle, his eyes lifelessly staring at the ceiling of the portico. It was a scene Tuefel had seen many times before only this time it was his eyes that blindly gazed into eternity, an eternity that, for Tuefel, was not likely to be a pleasant one. He would kill no more and the world was now a better and safer place.

The man checked Tuefel for a pulse. When he was satisfied that he was dead, he slowly rose to his feet and turned to face the stunned couple. Kevin stood, helped Lisa to her feet, and the two approached the man in black, if only to thank him.

When the man removed his mask Kevin couldn't believe it. The black-clad ninja warrior who had just saved their lives with a display of martial arts that even Kevin was unfamiliar with...was Mr. Townsend's valet.

"Agent O'Brien, I thought you could use some help, so I stepped in; I hope you don't mind," he said, "I wanted to make sure that nothing happened to you or your lovely wife."

Kevin released Lisa and approached the man with his hand extended. "No, sir," he said, shaking the man's hand, "I don't mind one bit." Then, with his head cocked to one side, just a bit, Kevin asked, "Weren't you Mr. Townsend's valet? Aren't you the man who took care of him when he died?"

"Indeed, I am, Agent O'Brien. As I told you at the time, I believe Mr. Townsend chose wisely."

Something about that had bothered Kevin at the time. "I never did understand what you meant by that, Mr....Wow, I don't even know your name," Kevin said with an ironic laugh.

"Stephen Boyd," he replied, releasing Kevin's hand, "I simply meant that Mr. Townsend had chosen wisely in his selection of the man to confide in. I didn't mean to seem overly dramatic." Mr. Boyd looked over Kevin's shoulder at Lisa and said, "Is she alright?"

"Thanks to you, yes, I think so. We owe you our lives, Mr. Boyd." Kevin said, still more out of breath than Mr. Boyd.

"Please, call me Steve. I work for a living, too," he said, echoing the age old military retort.

Lisa had now joined the party, wrapping her arm around Kevin's waste as she showed her gratitude, "Steve?" she asked, to which he nodded. "Steve, thank you for saving our lives; I believe that man was moments from killing my husband. I don't know how to thank you."

Steve bowed a bit, just for aesthetics, and said, "It was an honor, ma'am," and he left it at that; the classic American hero; humble and self-effacing. This guy was right out of a 1940's Hollywood script, except that he was real.

"Did you get my message?" Steve asked Lisa.

Now it made some sense. "So you are the one that kept sending us those messages?" Kevin asked.

Again, Steve simply nodded.

"How did you manage to get them into her pockets without us noticing?" Kevin had to ask.

Steve just smiled and said, "Trade secret, my friend, trade secret."

Kevin was just curious. You don't look a gift life-saving in the mouth. Lisa, on the other hand, did have one question she wanted answered. "Steve, again, we can't thank you enough for what you've done, but there's one thing I don't understand."

"What is it?" he replied.

"Why did you have to drug me and kidnap me in order to give Kevin the documents about the Elite Eight? A simple phone call would have sufficed."

Steve's face showed only confusion. "What documents?" he asked, "Kidnap you? My dear, I assure you I would never do anything to harm either of you."

Now it was time for Kevin's and Lisa's face to show confusion. "You mean, you had nothing to do with kidnapping Lisa and taking her to the Catacombs? And you didn't leave a valise filled with compromising information about the Elite Eight?" Kevin realized that Steve had already answered the question, but felt the need to hear it again, so that he could fathom it.

Steve had an economy with the English language. "No," was all he said.

Neither, Kevin or Lisa could imagine who would have or could have wanted to give Kevin the information about the Elite Eight. They assumed it was their "friend" who turned out to be Stephen Boyd. Now that they knew that it wasn't Stephen, it didn't make any sense.

Steve could see the consternation on the faces of his new friends. "I think I can shed some light on the subject, Kevin," Steve began, "as you can imagine, while Tuefel was stalking the two of you, I was stalking him. It was, I believe, he who kidnapped you and provided the information about their activities. He had no intention of hurting either of you until you had given the information he provided you to your government."

"But why would he do that?" Kevin asked. "He just spent 5 minutes questioning us about what we knew about them before planning to kill us."

"I believe," Stephen elaborated, "that he wanted to be sure you had delivered the information. He had no qualms about killing you both for money, but he didn't like the way his employers were manipulating Europe. He was not an extremely political animal, but he apparently did have his values."

"Go figure." Kevin said.

"Well, I believe the two of you have a big day tomorrow, so I'll take my leave of you. I'm glad I was able to assist you and I wish you both the best of health and the best of luck. Good day, madam," he said with bowed head to Lisa, and then he looked at Kevin, and with a slightly less pronounced bow of the head, simply said, "Agent O'Brien." Then he turned and was gone.

As Kevin and Lisa stood looking at each other in stunned disbelief, the sounds of Roman traffic began to get louder.

No one seemed to be looking in their direction and the "death match" they had just been involved in and witness to had not even caused a stir. Italians were a volatile people and loud noises and voices were not inclined to take them from their more pressing pursuits.

Nevertheless, Kevin didn't wish to hang around this dead man for long, so he grabbed Lisa and hurried to the street to hail a taxi. Stephen was right, they had a big day tomorrow and they needed to get packed.

Chapter Twenty

Captain Navid Omidi was an ardent and faithful Muslim. His ship, the Alvand, was the first that he could say, he commanded. Not yet twenty-five years old, he was young for command of his own ship, even a freighter. It paid to be well connected in Iranian society; doubly so in the Iranian military. Navid's father had been an Admiral in the Iranian navy during the war with Iraq. He had saved the life of a favorite of the Ayatollah Khomeini and been given command of a large section of the Iranian navy after the war. Since nepotism was not frowned upon in Iran, the Admiral put his son on the fast track to naval command, beginning with command of a freighter.

Neither, he, nor his son Navid could have imagined that in a few short months, his son would be given a mission that could change the face of Islam and perhaps even usher in the coming of the 12th Imam, the Mahdi, who was prophesied to return and destroy the Jews and Christians, before setting up an Islamic paradise on earth.

Navid, now fully briefed by the mission commander, Lieutenant Colonel Rostami, had positioned the Alvand 120 miles off the coast of Miami, Florida, as ordered. It was 2300 hours, May 31st, just eight hours until they would launch their Shahab 4 missiles and effectively castigate the southern half of the United States, if not more.

The men of the missile team, commanded by Lieutenant Colonel Rostami, were busy at work, constructing the deck-launcher for tomorrow's highly anticipated attack. Everything was shipshape and progressing as planned. The Captain went up to the top-deck to survey the progress. Rostami was his superior officer on this mission, but, of course, he had command of the ship. As he walked around the deck, Navid was feeling a bit puffed up concerning his role in so important a moment in history. He was already busily writing headlines in his mind, with himself as the beloved hero.

At about 2330 hours, Captain Omidi was alerted to something off the starboard bow. It was a faint light, quickly approaching from the west. Navid looked through his binoculars but couldn't make it out.

Seeing the lights of other ships was not unusual, but given the nature of their mission, Captain Omidi wasn't going to take anything for granted. Over the next hour, Navid kept a close eye on the approaching ship until it became close enough to identify. It was an American Coast Guard Cutter and it was headed their way.

Again, the sight of an American ship off the coast of Miami, Florida wouldn't normally be cause for concern, but this was not a normal time, anything but. The Captain, just out of prudence, called for General Quarters. Soon, as the Cutter neared, with obvious intentions of inspection or perhaps even boarding, the Captain called for Battle Stations.

Two teams quickly manned the two 20mm Oerlikon cannons and a third team manned the 40 mm Fateh-40 autocannon. The Coast Guard Cutter got close enough to clearly identify the Iranian freighter; yet, it suddenly, and without fanfare, turned around and headed in the opposite direction.

Captain Omidi was a little green, but even he didn't believe they could be so lucky. Here they were about to attack the United States and an American ship had inexplicably failed to check them out when they had the chance. Navid, a devout Muslim and strong believer in the assuredness of Allah's will, got down on his knees and thanked Allah for his mercy. He was also sure, more than ever, that Allah was watching over them.

If, indeed, Allah was watching over the Alvand, he was not alone. After calling the Alvand's position to Strategic Air Command at Homestead Air Force Base near Miami, the base commander scrambled a state of the art B3 Stealth Bomber to the scene. Now, as Navid gave thanks to Allah for all his mercy, the B3 was watching the decent of a 5,000 pound, bunker-busting bomb as it was laser guided onto the deck of the fortuitously stationary Iranian freighter.

When the bomb struck the Alvand, it did not immediately explode. It punched a hole in the steel deck plating and sank into its belly, waiting a full 2 seconds before exploding in all directions. The crew of the Alvand would have been better off if the explosion had occurred on deck, but as it was, the detonation from within gave the bomb's powerful yield nowhere to go. The Alvand and its entire crew were virtually disintegrated within 1 second.

The explosion could be seen for hundreds of miles and provided a spectacular light show for the people still awake on Miami Beach. One of the three Iranian ships had been found and destroyed, but there were still two more and no one knew exactly when they planned to launch their missiles. "From the looks of the deck," the Coast Guard Cutter's commander radioed in, "it won't be long."

•

After a month and a half of vacation, Kevin and Lisa were happy to be heading to Leonardo da Vinci-Fuimicino Airport for their midnight flight to Tampa. Since Rome is 6 hours ahead of Tampa time, the 13 hour flight should land them at TIA at about 7am, June 1. They were particularly happy when Amerigo volunteered to drive them to the airport and see them off. Since the incident at the Catacomb, Amerigo had been adopted by the two of them. They'd had dinner with him and his wife on two occasions and invited Amerigo and his family—he had four children—to visit them in Tampa after everything had cooled down.

Once on board, Lisa settled into her window seat and resumed the book she had been trying to read for over a week; Kevin simply relaxed with a couple of rum and cokes. After a few minutes of reading, Lisa lowered her book and looked over at Kevin, "Let's see if we can add this up," she began, "I've been shot at in the parking lot of Tampa General, attacked in my own home by a terrorist, kidnapped by a German hit man and held at knife point while I watched that same hit man try to kill my husband. Does that about sum it up?"

Kevin smiled at Lisa's attempt to see the absurdity in what had been truly frightening events in her life. "Yeah," he said, "that's about the size of it."

Feeling the need to say more, Kevin added, "I promised you that marriage to me wouldn't be boring, didn't I? Oh, by the way, I've contacted the Director (of the FBI), and he assured me that you can start collecting hazardous duty pay as soon as we get home."

Lisa looked at Kevin with mock scorn and said, "If it's alright with you, I'm going to retire from the Bureau as soon as we get back. I've had it up to here with kidnappers, terrorists and assassins. Not that I'm complaining," she added.

●

Now that the country was returning to a semblance of normalcy, President Hamilton decided to do a little subtle campaigning. After all, his numbers were up and the election was just over a year away. Not normally a "whistle-stop" kind of guy, Katherine had talked him into using the train to "go out there and meet the people", as Katie had put it. She was a big fan of President Truman and thought Michael could use a little of the "buck-stops-here" kind of press. He had, after all, stood up to mounting pressure to join the Euro-Union and she thought this was the perfect time to, sort of, milk it.

The idea was to use the Cardinal route—a passenger train route, mandated by congress and operated by Amtrak—to travel around the north, south, east and Midwest, beginning in Philadelphia and ending in Indianapolis, via Delaware, Washington, D.C., Charlottesville, Virginia and Cincinnati, Ohio. It would give the President the chance to show the people that he cared about their needs, while at the same time, giving Katie and him a little vacation.

After stops in Philadelphia and Wilmington, Delaware, the "Freedom Train", as President Hamilton's overly zealous campaign manager dubbed it, was passing through Washington on its way to its next stop in Charlottesville, Virginia. Katie was busy with a crossword puzzle, something her husband could never do, as the President read the Wall Street Journal—while there was no Wall Street, the publishers wanted to continue using the name. "Mike," Katie called out. She was always trying to involve Michael in her puzzles, "the clue says, 'You can't stand to have it'; three letters."

The President, his eyes glued to his paper, said, "Katie, why on earth you do those infernal crossword puzzles is beyond me. Why don't you go bake some cookies?" He loved to say stuff like that; it really graveled his wife, but in a nice way.

"You want some cookies?" Katie returned, "I'll bake you some cookies; filled with strychnine!"

"Hey," the President responded with a look of false concern, "don't say that too loud, the Secret Service will wrestle you to the ground and take away your crossword puzzle."

"Lap!" Katie yelled with enthusiasm.

Michael almost jumped out of his seat. "What?" he asked.

"Lap", she said, "the crossword clue. 'You can't "stand" to have it;' your lap!" She loved to figure out the double-entendres in crossword puzzles; Michael could do without them altogether.

President Hamilton continued to read his paper but couldn't resist the chance to poke fun at what she was doing; something he thought was a waste of time. "Here's one, Katie," he said, as if reading it from the Wall Street Journal, "a six letter word for peace and quiet."

Katie stopped looking at her puzzle for a moment, just to ponder Michael's question. "A six letter word for peace and quiet?" she repeated, then, "I don't know."

The President laid his paper down in his lap, looked over at his wife and said, "Valium, v-a-l-i-u-m, why don't you go take a couple."

"Oh yeah?" she said, "Well, let me tell you how I spell peace and quiet, d-i-v-o-r-c-e."

"Well," he answered back, "at least you know how to spell it."

Katie raised her hand and made a clenched fist, ostensibly to threaten the President with bodily harm. "I wonder how long it would take the Secret Service to get here once they heard you scream bloody murder?" she asked with mock wonder.

"Would you like me to scream bloody murder so you can time them?" the President said.

Katie looked back down at her puzzle, "No," she said, "but if I hear one more peep out of you, we're going to give them a run for their money."

Both of them settled back down to the mundane activities that gave them both peace of mind. They had very much enjoyed the time they'd spent together on this trip and today was one of the nicest days yet, but that was about to change.

While the train was still about 40 miles from Charlottesville, the President and Katie could hear the sudden outburst of urgent shouting from the Secret Service detail in the car in front of theirs. The train consisted of five cars; the engine, followed by the Press car, the Secret Service car, the President's car and ending, naturally, with the caboose—this was the car the President would speak from. It was draped with red, white and blue bunting to assure everyone that the President loved his country.

Michael had been President long enough to ascertain the difference between the usual raised voices and that of someone, particularly someone in the Secret Service, showing grave concern with something. He tossed the paper to the side and arose from his chair just as two Secret Servicemen burst through the door.

Neither the President nor Katie had time to question them before being unceremoniously stampeded into the caboose, pulled to the floor, and covered by the bodies of the Secret Servicemen and Servicewomen.

Once they were lying under a few rather heavy agents, the President managed to get out, "What the hell's going on?"

The agent to whom he had become the closest, and head of Presidential protection, Warren Jacobs, told him that there was a van up ahead, on the tracks, and on a collision course with the train. The President and Katie could feel the engineer apply the brakes and hear the screeching of metal to metal as brakes tried to fight the laws of physics and slow the 500 ton behemoth to a halt. Unfortunately, Falah Mohamed, moments from a 72 virgin orgy, was approaching at a rapid pace. He had filled his van with high explosives, straddled the track that it now shared with the oncoming Presidential train, and put the pedal to the metal.

There were four separate train cars in front of the President's when the van collided with the not-yet-stopped train, and exploded. The explosion, combined with the impact of the van at 70 miles an hour and the still moving train, lifted the engine off the track, pulling one car after another along a tortuous and grinding journey of twisting metal and disfigured people. It took a full forty-five seconds for the train and its contents to come to the end of its mangled course; forty-five seconds that seemed like an eternity to those who would die and those who wished they had.

When the frightening sounds of metallic disfigurement and earthen displacement had come to an end, only the sound of escaping steam could be heard over the muffled sounds of the mangled and misshapen men and women who moments before were healthy and happy.

When the President regained consciousness, some ten minutes after the explosion, he was surrounded by the sounds of labored coughing amid the acrid smell of burning oil. Around him was no discernable movement, but if there had been, he wouldn't have been able to see it.

He waved his hand back and forth in front of his face, trying to clear the air so that he could look around. Soon, he saw Warren Jacobs lying next to him. His eyes were opened, fixed and dilated; he was clearly dead. The sight of Warren's dead body brought home the possibilities to the

President. *"Oh no! Katie!"* he said to himself in a terrified moment of concern, "Katie!" he yelled, "Katie!"

Michael rolled over onto his stomach and lifted himself up on all fours. He began to crawl along the floor, feeling people as he went along. When he came across someone, he'd check for a pulse, see that they were dead, and move on. After coming across four dead bodies the President started to panic. *Could Katie be alive in this mess?* "Katie!" he called out again, feeling more and more frightened of the possibilities with each terrified scream. "Katie!"

Then he came upon his wife. He still couldn't see, but he'd been married to her long enough to know the feel of her contours, besides, she was the only one other than him not wearing a suit; even the Secret Servicewomen wore them. He rested his hand on her chest to see if she was breathing as he gently called her name again, "Katie, my love."

Her chest rose up and down, indicating that she was breathing, but she didn't answer his calls to her and he still couldn't see her eyes. He got himself into a seated position and pulled Katie's head and shoulders into his lap. As he stroked her face and hair, she seemed to come to consciousness, if slightly.

"Katie, can you hear me?" he said, calmly and with deepness of love. "Katie, talk to me?" he said.

"What happened?" she replied, barely audibly. "Did the Secret Service get mad because I threatened to poison your cookies?" The last couple of words came out in the midst of spastic coughs, and then the President could hear only the slow exhale from his lifelong love as the last and final breath passed through her beautiful lips. Katie was dead, and the President knew it.

His face dropped into the crook of his still wife's neck and he began to weep like he had never wept before. It came from an emotion more profound than sorrow. He'd felt sorrow before. No, this was much, much more menacing. It was the complete loss of any and all sense of well-being, coupled by a complete disregard for himself or his surroundings. The President knew that everyone in this railroad car was dead, and he knew that he was one of them.

The President was one of only three people to survive the attack and the only one who would ever walk again. He had broken his right fibula and he had a severe concussion, but he would survive, physically, at least. His state of mind would never heal; however, he had lost the only thing that he'd ever really loved.

•

Ali Hussein and Robert "Bobby" Wang had spent the day with Diane Austin in the FBI's Tampa office, working on the plan that the Director informed them, "came straight from the White House". The plan, now well into its fruition, called for the replacement of the Elite Eight's Aldo Veneto with one of their own, or at least, someone they controlled.

"I hear they sent a woman," Bobby said, "that ought to stir the pot a bit, huh?"

Ali tipped his head to the side and raised his eyebrows. "I suppose." he said without giving it much thought. Ali loved the Bloomin' Onions at the Outback Restaurant and he had gone through well over half of one in the last few minutes.

"Why don't you just forget the chewing and have a couple of those things surgically inserted into your stomach. Wouldn't that be faster?" Bobby complained.

Ali looked puzzled. "What? I really like these things." He said this with his mouth full of onions.

"Well," Bobby said, "then here's hoping you never get to like me that much.

"Are they ever going to bring the check?" Bobby impatiently clamored, ostensibly to Ali, but the air would have sufficed. "I need to drive you back to your apartment and then go all the way to Indian Rocks beach. I'm not going to get to bed until after midnight."

"You could spend the night at my place," Ali suggested, "unless, you've got some hot chick waiting for you at home."

"How would I get a change of clothes?" Bobby asked, "I can't go to work wearing these. I've had them on all day."

Ali put the last of the Bloomin' Onion in his mouth, wiped his hands on the napkin and picked up the check that the waitress had brought 15 minutes before. "I've got a washer and a dryer. You could have them washed and dried in one hour." Ali said, getting up from his seat to leave. "Let's go, man, Dick van Dyke is coming on in half an hour."

The two left the Outback restaurant in Clearwater and piled into Bobby's Ford Explorer. They had become the best of friends over the past few weeks. The death of Ali's wife had laid him emotionally bare. Doug's murder, followed by his arrest and incarceration for the murder of Jimmy Forbes had almost been more than he could take, but Bobby had been there as a partner and friend. Ali wouldn't forget.

Along the way to Ali's apartment, Ali thought he heard something out of the ordinary. He told Bobby to turn down the Billy Joel music and listen for a minute. "What is that?" Ali said.

"What's what?" Bobby answered, paying him no mind.

"Can't you hear that?" Ali said, concerned. Then, suddenly, Ali knew he had to do something quick. "Pull over!" he yelled, "Pull over, now!"

Bobby looked at him like he was crazy, but hearing the urgency in his voice and the seriousness in his eyes, he pulled the car over and into the Ben T. Davis Beach parking lot, just off the Courtney Campbell Causeway.

When the Explorer came to a stop, Ali called out to Bobby, "Get out of the car, now!"

Bobby had no idea what he was talking about but he certainly seemed serious, so after Ali made a quick exit, Bobby opened the door and got out. He was rounding the vehicle, about to ask Ali if he'd lost his mind, when the Explorer exploded, lifting Bobby into the air and hurling him about 12 feet. Ali had gotten far enough away that the explosion just singed his hair, but Bobby had taken a huge blow.

As the fiery Explorer lit up the night, Ali slowly rose to his feet in a daze. Although he had suspected something like this he was still momentarily unsure what had happened. Giving the blistering heat of the burning auto a wide berth, Ali eased his way around and into Bobby's line of sight. When he saw his friend lying splayed out on the cement parking lot, Ali felt a sickening presence in his gut. Was Bobby dead?

Quickly, Ali ran to Bobby's crumpled body and checked for a pulse. Thanking God that he felt one, he immediately called 911 and hoped that there was an ambulance available. Although Tampa had been "restocked" with emergency equipment, things were not what they once were. Many of the things that were formerly taken for granted, like ambulances, were in short supply and had to be used with prudence.

Luckily, it was a slow night in Hillsborough and Pinellas counties and emergency crews were dispatched without delay. Ali sighed with relief and sat down beside his unconscious friend to wait for assistance. He didn't dare move him for fear of exacerbating internal injuries or paralyzing him by inadvertently adjusting his position and finding out later that he'd broken his neck. Fortunately, the ambulance arrived quickly and Bobby was rushed to the hospital.

Ali rode with him in the ambulance, watching as the paramedics started IVs and cleaned his wounds as best they could. He needed x-rays, a CT scan and maybe an MRI, if there were any; not everything had been replaced, yet. Ali had a nasty head wound and that was the worry. He seemed to move his limbs well enough, but he was clearly, at minimum, concussed.

After being transferred to St. Joseph's Hospital in critical condition, Bobby stabilized through the night. He was taken off the critical list and started talking Ali's ear off by 4am. Ali didn't leave his friend's side the whole time.

Chapter Twenty-One

About 90 miles from Brownsville, Texas, Captain Akbar Mouradipous, of the Iranian freighter, Moudge, was in the last stages of preparation for his 0600 launch. As a weapons specialist, he had command of both the mission and the ship; an honor given to few captains in this circumstance. Having long ago gone to radio silence, the Moudge had not been in contact with the other two ships since they had synchronized their attack scenario. As a consequence, Captain Mouradipous was unaware of the fate that had befallen the Alvand and would soon threaten his ship.

Akbar was a man who followed orders, but he was also a man of action. He had long ago decided that in the event his ship was in any way compromised, he would launch the missile, regardless of the time, and with the Shahab 4 missile's deck launcher constructed and in place, he could launch the missile at a moment's notice.

The weather was fair and the sea was calm. Akbar was content that nothing could prevent his launch, just two hours hence, which he could not detect in time. With lookouts posted fore and aft and radar tracking any unusual movement, Akbar decided to get an hour's worth of sleep before the launch; he wanted to be at his most sharp.

It didn't take him long to fall into a deep slumber; he hadn't slept for over 24 hours. About 45 minutes into the last dream he would ever have, Akbar was awakened by a call from his radar room. "Sir, ship spotted and approaching our position at 32 knots!"

"32 knots?" the Captain thought, *"only an American cruiser could travel that speed, or would want to!"*

The Captain was right. An American, Ticonderoga class, guided-missile cruiser was headed his way at top speed. They had identified the Moudge as an enemy vessel and had orders to sink her with all speed.

Captain Mouradipous scrambled from his bunk and raced to the deck of his ship. "Report!" he screamed as he climbed the ladder leading to the main deck.

His First-Officer reported immediately, "Radar confirms! Ticonderoga class, guided-missile cruiser!" He turned his head in a swift gesture to the Captain, "It will be here in less than 5 minutes, Captain!"

The Captain knew exactly what to do. He charged over to the missile launcher and started barking orders to his men. "I want this missile airborne in less than 2 minutes! Is that clear?" Each of the five men of the missile team knew that if there was ever a rhetorical question, this was it. They wasted no time in uncovering the sheath on the missile and prepping it for launch.

The First-Officer, aware of their orders to launch at 0600, called out to the Captain, "Sir, do we not have to wait until 0600? It is only 0455, sir!"

"We don't have time to wait, Pavel," he shouted back, grabbing the wheel and turning the ship around to get a better launch angle, "we've got to get that bird in the air, and now!"

The USS Antietam was quickly approaching the Moudge's position and they were filled with bad intentions. The Antietam's captain was in no mood to stop and chat with the captain of the enemy ship, they had to be destroyed quickly, before they had a chance to launch their missile.

As soon as his ship was in range, Captain Hendershot ordered the launch of a Tomahawk missile from one of his Mark 41 launchers and said a silent goodbye to the crew of the unknown Iranian ship.

However, the crew of the Moudge was quite capable. They quickly detected the Tomahawk's launch and with the realization that they were all about to die anyway, launched the Shahab 4 missile moments before their ship became a burning tomb for all aboard.

"Missile launch!" the young radar operator of the Antietam called out over the intercom, "Missile launch!"

The Captain didn't have to be told that a missile had just been launched into the blackness of the early Texas morning, but he appreciated the decorum. The Shahab 4 was brighter than any star in the sky as it barreled upward at 5 times the speed of sound in an attempt to reach its designated height and distance for a rendezvous with destiny.

Fearing that just this sort of thing might occur, Captain Hendershot had seen to it that his ship was equipped with the newest class of Patriot missiles, and that they were ready for launch. His crew had been fully briefed and told to prepare for just such and eventuality.

The men manning the Patriot battery were well aware of the Iranian launch and of the consequences if it were to explode over the United States. They were oblivious to the shouted orders of the Captain because they were already activating everything needed for a quick launch.

Within 20 seconds of seeing the Iranian missile launch, the first Patriot missile lifted off to intercept the Shahab 4. Seconds later, the second Patriot was fired from the Antietam's deck, hot in pursuit. The crew stood in frozen silence at the sight of the two streaking trails of light pursuing the third, closing the gap ever so slowly, it seemed. They stared into the early morning darkness and prayed that one of the two Patriots would hit the mark, knowing they didn't have time for a third launch.

When enough time had elapsed for the men to begin to assume the worst, there was a collective sigh at the thought of the consequences of failure. There was a silence on the ship's deck which was deafening in its significance.

Then, just as their worst fears seemed to be a reality, they were rewarded for their vigilance. No one was sure which one got it, but one of the Patriots must have hit the target, causing an aerial explosion that sent the crew of the Antietam into hysteria. Everyone had been fully briefed as to the consequences of even one of the three missiles exploding over American soil. They were aware that the Air Force had gotten the first one; they wanted to make sure it was the Navy that got this one. There were still one remaining ship and one remaining missile, they all knew, but, so far so good, they thought.

•

In Teheran, President Habibi was having lunch with his First-Vice President. Both were aware that the attacks on America were to occur within the hour; 0700 eastern standard time in the U.S... Neither was aware that two of the ships, along with their Shahab 4 missiles, had been destroyed since there was no radio communication and it was still 45 minutes until the launches were scheduled to take place.

Since there was still much to do, and both men wanted to be at the Parliament building when the reports of the EMP attacks came in, they decided to have their meals served in President Habibi's office. Habibi had Jujeh Khoresht- a boneless chicken with garlic, tomato, and shallots in a fresh lemony sauce, while Rajsanjani had Khoresht Keimeh-cubes of beef cooked with yellow split peas in a cinnamon potato and onion sauce.

The two men had spent many hours eating together, worshiping together and governing together. While Ali was older than Sadad, it was Ali who looked to Sadad for guidance. Completely oblivious to Habibi's lack of true faith, Ali had considered his friend to be a pillar of strength within the Islamic faith, helping him to get passed the death of his wife and the debilitating depression that followed. Habibi, while not sharing Ali's true beliefs, did consider him a best friend and an admirable soul. He was an old family friend and he was concerned with his well-being.

"Ali, I think it is time you considered finding a new wife. It has been over a year since you lost your beloved Sasha; it is not good for a man of your age and position to be alone."

"I have thought much of this, Sadad," Ali said with a sad tone, "but her memory hasn't faded in my heart. I'm not sure I could truly love another woman as I did my Sasha."

Sadad poured another cup of tea for them both. "I'm sure ChalipA could find a good wife for you, Ali, she knows many women who have lost their husbands for the cause of Allah. I'm sure many would consider it an honor to marry a man of such important standing. Just say the word, my friend, and I will tell her to begin the search."

Ali smiled as if to say, *"We'll see"*, but he had other things on his mind. "Sadad", he said, "what do you think will happen when America is rendered cripple? Do you believe they will retaliate against us? Remember, they will still have a highly capable military force outside the continental United States."

Sadad laughed as he said, "Ali, I think America has always been a 300 pound, bully. Most bullies are brave because they have such an advantage that no one would dare to defend themselves, but we are going to shave a couple hundred pounds off this bully, and then we shall see what he does as a 98 pound weakling."

"I pray you are correct, Sadad, but our dealings with these Europeans have made me a bit disconcerted. They are no different than the Americans. They do not embrace Allah; in fact, most of the Europeans are godless atheists. What they do, they do for themselves and their desire to regain their prominence in the world. As America grows weaker, Europe grows stronger. Are we not simply trading in a bully 4000 miles away for one 1000 miles away?"

It was a valid point. Ali was always one to see with a discerning eye. "You are wise to suspect the Europeans, Ali, but remember, they have light-years to go in order to become a military superpower. We have the advantage of Russian influence and the prospect of our own nuclear program, which is only months from completion. Soon, we will be too powerful for the Europeans, Russians, or anyone else for that matter, to simply dismiss as a third-world puppet. We will have a seat at the table, my friend, and you and I will be the men who occupy that seat."

"Allah be praised," Ali said, tearing up, "let his will be done."

Sadad smiled at his old friend. He could care less about Allah's will, but if Ali believed it and the useful idiots within his government needed a crutch to lean on, so be it. The future is what you make of it, he thought, and in about 30 minutes the future was going to take a decidedly drastic turn in his direction.

●

The Nomad was 120 miles off the coast of Baltimore, Maryland. Its original position, off of the coast of Philadelphia, had too much traffic, so Colonel Haddad had ordered Captain Faysal to move south to avoid any shipping lanes.

Haddad had already seen to the Shahab 4's implementation and pronounced it ready to launch. Captain Faysal glanced at his watch and realized that in just over 15 minutes his ship would launch a weapon that would make them a target for any American warship in the Atlantic.

According to Haddad, the missile would attain an altitude of approximately 400 kilometers and travel about 400 miles due east. This would, according to Haddad, place the Shahab 4's EMP detonation about 250 miles from a point midway between Philadelphia and Baltimore.

Haddad said he was doing this as an insurance policy against miscalculation, since the EMP burst should take out the whole eastern and southern United States power grid, as well as any other electrical components, battery powered units, or circuit boards in a 2000 mile radius.

When Captain Faysal asked what protection the Nomad had against the loss of its own power, Haddad laughed and said something about a Faraday box. Captain Faysal had never heard of such a device or what its function could be, but Haddad seemed confident enough—something that always made Faysal nervous.

After scanning the immediate vicinity, the Captain, the lookouts and the radar operator found nothing of import within Nomad's "danger zone". Although he detected a heightened tension among the crew, everything seemed to be, "Go for Launch".

At five minutes, the countdown began. Colonel Haddad went over his last minute checklist and pronounced the missile, "Good to Go!" Captain Faysal maneuvered the ship into optimal firing position and awaited Haddad's ten-second countdown. Everything that could be done had been done; now, it was just a matter of waiting and hoping that nothing and no one prevented the launch.

•

Approximately, 50 miles NNW of Nomad's present position, the American Aegis Cruiser USS Lake Erie plodded along in the balmy air of an early June 1st morning. Its mission was identical to that of every other ship within 200 miles of the American coastline; find that third ship and prevent the launch of any missiles, by whatever means necessary.

The Lake Erie's Captain, Russell "Rusty" Grant had been commanding this ship for over 3 years. Based in Pearl Harbor, the USS Lake Erie had made a quick trip through the Panama Canal and around the Florida peninsula in order to patrol the North Atlantic for this third and, hopefully, last threat to national security. Captain Grant was "sharp as a tack and ready for action", or so he was described by his last commanding officer, Admiral Jacob Poindexter, the man who had given him this command.

Captain Grant was commanding one of the nation's most sophisticated anti-missile ships. Equipped with the modified Aegis Weapon System and the modified SM (Standard Missile)-2 Block IV, the USS Lake Erie can intercept a missile in one of two ways: a direct body to body hit between the interceptor and the missile or a near-direct hit where the high pressure heat and fragments penetrate the missile via blast fragmentation warhead.

In addition, America's defense capabilities include a system called the Passive Coherent Locator (PCL) that detects ship-launched missiles and feeds the tracking coordinates into the national missile-defense command-and-control for immediate response. This information would, theoretically, be instantly transmitted to the USS Lake Erie or any other ship with the capability of missile interception. The PCL system is networked with sensors from Maine to Miami and the defense platforms, like the USS Lake Erie, are "hot-wired" into its sensitive detectors.

●

Back on board the Nomad, Captain Faysal was in full missile-attack mode. All unnecessary electrical systems had been shut down, radio silence was in full effect and Colonel Haddad's Faraday cage, or whatever he called it, was fully activated. The Colonel's voice was now heard on the ship's intercom: "five, four, three, two, one...full systems launch!"

With that order, the Captain and crew witnessed an explosion of fire and fuel designed to break every physical law known to man and lift the 6,500 kilogram missile to a height of 400 kilometers and rocket it to over 400 miles above the American mainland, all at 7 times the speed of sound.

With the sun still nestled beneath the eastern skyline, the illumination was bright enough to burn out the retinas of some of the ill-informed crewmembers who stared at the conflagration without the proper eye shading. Shahab 4 was now streaking across the sky and there wasn't anything the Americans could do to stop it.

Colonel Haddad watched the missile for a few seconds, sat down on an old wooden chair and reached into his breast pocket. He withdrew a Cuban cigar and put it in his mouth, simultaneously flipping the top of his father's old Zippo lighter and igniting his symbol of success. The missile was away, the mission was a success; who cared what happened next?

●

Alarms were sounding all over the USS Lake Erie! No one had to inform Captain Grant that the Aegis system had detected a missile launch, but they did: "Captain, we have confirmed ship-based missile launch to a north-northeast position! Aegis systems are online and tracking!" The steady, but alert voice of Ensign Snodgrass informed the Captain of all he needed to know. Frankly, a quick glance to the north-northeast would have informed all but the blind of the missile's launch. The brightness could be seen for a hundred miles.

In these situations, the Captain is, in essence, extraneous; as he has no particular function within the defense mechanisms of the Aegis system. If the time were taken to wait for a human command to launch the interceptors, there would be little chance of success in any missile's destruction; people are simply not fast enough to respond in time. Fortunately for the American people, thought the Captain, the Aegis system was plenty fast enough.

Without the need for human intervention, the Aegis system immediately launched a cruise missile from the USS Lake Erie, specifically designed to intercept this type of threat. Technicians with banks of computers monitored the missile's chase of the Shahab 4. About 30 seconds after the USS Lake Erie's launch, there was an explosion. Most of the crew of the Lake Erie could see the explosion and began cheering loudly for the Shahab's destruction.

Captain Grant couldn't assume success so quickly, so he called out to the "geeks", as he called them, "I want confirmation of impact!" Then, after a moment with no answer, the Captain repeated, "Do we have confirmation?"

Ensign Snodgrass answered him, "That's a negative, Captain! We have negative impact on target!"

Captain Grant had not actually panicked since he was a young ensign and Admiral Farnsworth invited him to the "captain's table" for supper. Now, however, he went into full panic mode. "What? How could it have missed? What was that explosion?" he called out; all relevant questions, but not inclined to provide any assistance in the downing of a still live and quickly moving enemy missile.

"Is it going to launch again?" the Captain screamed. "It's going to launch again, isn't it?" This series of questions was ostensibly aimed at the missile geeks but the Captain would have been happy with anyone's response. As it was, his question was answered by Petty Officer First Class Anthony Gibson, "Aye, sir, it's going into full re-launch mode!" No sooner did the young Gibson finish his statement then there was the flash of bright light as another missile was sent in pursuit of the Shahab 4.

Chapter Twenty-Two

The flight to Tampa had been a long and uncomfortable one, at least for Kevin. He could never seem to get to sleep, despite drinking enough liquor to put everyone on the flight into a coma. His iPad only worked sporadically and the movies that had been shown on the flight were not to Kevin's liking, leading to comments like, "Does Jennifer Aniston have stock in this airline?" and "Can I have another Rum and Coke?"

Lisa was more patient with the discomforts and inconveniences that came with transcontinental air travel. She didn't get so impatient with things she knew were out of her control and with which she would not long have to contend; besides, she loved Jennifer Aniston movies.

"Kevin," Lisa said, for the umpteenth time, "how long are you going to lay there pretending you're asleep? Look," she pointed out the window, "there's the Florida coast. We'll be in Tampa in a few minutes."

Kevin turned his head just enough to indicate that he was still conscious. "How few minutes?" he said.

"Oh, stop being such a baby," Lisa admonished him, "If you sit up like a big boy, we'll get ice cream when we get off the plane."

Kevin didn't want to get up, but at that minute the pilot's voice came over the intercom and instructed everyone to fasten their seatbelts and prepare for landing. Kevin sat up, partly because of the pilot's instructions and partly because he was dying for some ice cream.

•

"What was that?" Captain Grant asked after hearing a loud "crack" in the distance. "Did we get it?" he asked, hoping his geeks would tell him they had downed the missile.

Moments later, he could see a flash of light all around, like a lightning strike. Although, unlike any missile detonation they had ever seen, many of the crew thought the Patriot had downed the enemy missile, giving rise to muted cheers. The Captain had never seen this before, either. The light seemed to spread out in all directions from the point of the missile's trajectory. He screamed to the crew, "Silence! That was no detonation, at least not the kind we're looking for!"

Moments later, every electrical system of the ship went into freefall. There were crackles and pops, sizzles and fizzes and a lot of glowing screens. Most importantly, there was no power to any ship system, whether it be propulsion, communication, weaponry; even watches and I-Pods were rendered useless.

Before he or anyone else could identify what had happened, most of the United States of America was literally in the dark. For those Americans who were early risers and had already heard the alarm clock, they would see their televisions glow eerily bright, whether they were on or off. As the electrical lines arced, the smell of ozone would become very noticeable and, of course, the electricity would be off. For those holding cell phone, MP3 players or IPods, they would begin to feel warm to the touch as the batteries inside overloaded.

When these early risers went to check their computers, they would see that they were "fried" with the loss of all data. After a cold breakfast they would hit the streets only to discover that there were no working automobiles, buses, taxis, trains, traffic lights, streetlights—or any other lights, for that matter—and unless their jobs consisted of lighting the gas lamps on a 19th century street corner, they probably have no real reason to go to work.

For those who aren't early risers, they are still asleep, because their alarm clocks didn't go off. They would later discover the devastating effects of rotting food, stuffy apartments and the local candle store.

On board flight 774, Rome to Tampa, the effects were a little more immediate and a lot more pressing. Electrical systems began shutting down all over the cockpit and cabin as instruments and communication suddenly disappeared. Lights, including those controlled by the back-up generator went out, as did the back-up generator.

Power throughout the aircraft was down and the plane began a quick decent towards a rapidly enlarging view of the ground. Kevin and Lisa, as well as all those around them, were in the dark, literally. Nothing that used batteries or electricity seemed to work, and since everything that functions aboard an airplane requires electricity and/or batteries, the prospect of a smooth landing was rapidly becoming, an impossibility.

This scenario was being played out on thousands of aircraft across thousands of miles of American airspace. Soon, those aircraft would be crashing into the ground, taking the lives of those on board, as well as anyone or anything that stood between it and its fiery destination. Kevin and Lisa were facing just such a prospect as flight 774 began a rapid decent with them inside.

"What's happening!" Lisa cried out, "Why did the lights go out!"

"It's even worse than that," Kevin called out as he reached for Lisa, "we've lost power! The plane is going down!"

"I can't see anything!" Lisa said, calmer but with urgency, "What are we gonna do?"

"I don't know, honey," Kevin said, unbuckling his seatbelt, "I'll see if I can get to the cabin!"

While all those around him were screaming into the sightless void of impending death, Kevin reached his right arm out to grab the seat-back on the other side of the aisle and launch himself toward the cockpit. He knew he was leaving his wife at a time when she needed him most, but Kevin would rather try to save her life than hold onto her as they plunged into a fiery death.

No one on the plane was thinking of unbuckling their seatbelts at a time like this, so Kevin had an unimpeded walk to the front of the plane. He'd reach out for each successive seat-back to propel himself forward; first right, then left, then right again, like a man climbing a horizontal ladder. About halfway there, it dawned on him. *This must have been the EMP! The bastards must have gotten one through!*

When he reached the cabin door he had to feel around for the knob. The plane was in a nose dive and everyone around him was screaming for God's help. He flung the door open and screamed into the cockpit, "Captain, the loss of power is due to an EMP burst! It was designed to destroy all electrical systems! Do you have conductive-textile technology aboard this plane?"

Captain Carlos Estrada was a moment from a few rapidly and Spanish-spoken Hail Mary's when Kevin's warning reminded him of something. *The Faraday box!* Captain Estrada called out to his co-pilot, also in the last moments of prayer, informing him of the possibility of the regaining of power. "Just cut the main line and set the auxiliary ports to nominal!" he screamed, hoping he remembered this procedure correctly. "Now, set the battery terminals to DC and hit restart!"

His co-pilot, Captain Justin Lantz, had no idea what the hell Carlos was talking about, but better to go down fighting, he thought. He did as Captain Estrada instructed and suddenly the engine turned over and power was restored to the airplane. That was the easy part, Carlos thought, now they had to pull the nose up before it impacted Disney World—at last check, they were over Orlando.

Kevin knew he could be of no further use in the cockpit, so he rushed back to Lisa, finding her tucked forward in the instructed crash position. He sat down, re-buckled his seatbelt, reached over to embrace his wife and began praying.

Giving the engines full power, the Captain pulled at the controls with all his might in an effort to raise the plane's nose. Intermittent sputtering of the engine made his job all the more difficult and siphoned much needed power from the engines at the most critical time. Nevertheless, when the plane had fallen to approximately 500 feet—a ridiculously low altitude for a passenger plane—Captain Estrada began to feel the nose rise, a little at first and then far enough to stabilize the flight pattern.

He'd done it! Flight 774 was back on internal power and just a few minutes from Tampa International Airport. Now that they had averted disaster, the Captain noticed something odd down below. "Justin," he called out to his co-pilot, "do you see any lights down there? The sun is rising but it's still early enough that there should be lights on all over the place. What did that guy say? An EMP?"

Justin responded with a "Yeah, that's weird, isn't it?" before Carlos also pointed out the lack of landing lights at TIA, or lights of any kind, for that matter. "There must have been some kind of a black out," Carlos said, "That's why there are no lights and why we can't communicate."

The two men were just happy their plane had survived and were anxious to land safely. Justin added, just before touchdown, "It's awful weird that there would be a blackout down there and up here at the same time, huh? Maybe that's what an EMP does?"

Kevin and Lisa, as well as all their fellow passengers, cheered when the wheels of the jumbo liner made contact with the pavement and the plane began to roll along the runway. Few had any idea what had happened but they were glad they would now get the chance to find out.

What the world would soon discover was the explosion of an EMP device over the Midwest United States at 0710 on June 1st, sending virtually the entire nation into a technological freefall of epic proportions. From central Canada to the middle of Mexico, including all of Florida, north to south, and from Maine to Phoenix, Arizona in the west, the United States was now operating with technology that would have been quite familiar to Benjamin Franklin.

Ironically, the only thing that saved Kevin and Lisa's plane, and a number of other things, which would eventually be discovered, was an invention by a contemporary of Mr. Franklin, a Michael Faraday. Kevin had been aware of its existence but was unsure if and how it was implemented on modern jets. He was glad that his plane had it and that the pilot was so quick to figure it out; most planes, even those with the technology, went down in flames.

In 1836, Faraday invented the device that would later bear his name, the Faraday cage or shield. It was designed to act as an enclosure against lightning strikes, but with the advent of electricity and the subsequent technological devices that followed, its invention took on an even greater significance. Still later, it became the answer to the problem of EMP during nuclear detonation.

A device lined with conducting material—any material which conducts electricity, like water or metal—blocks out external static and non-static electrical fields. One expert on such eventualities posited that a nuclear explosion, with its resultant EMP pulse, over the middle of the United States would damage every computer chip without protection in the entire lower 48 states from Mexico to Canada. Supposedly, these Faraday boxes, if properly installed, could protect from such a surge. Certainly, in the case of flight 774 from Rome, it worked.

Most of the aircraft; however, didn't have the Faraday cage installed and dropped out of the sky. Most of those that had the Faraday cage didn't fare any better than those that didn't, mostly because the pilots either didn't realize it, couldn't restart the engines, or once started, couldn't bring the planes out of their dives.

Needless to say, hundreds of thousands of people died from the thousands of airplanes and helicopters that fell from the sky on the morning of June 1st. The death toll was staggering to those who were aware of its enormous number, but there were no radios, TVs, computers, cell phones, or IPods from which to get the news. There were no planes, trains or automobiles in which to travel from one place to another to learn this startling information, and those whose job it was to count the dead and deliver such grim statistics, were doing so with pencil and paper.

This would not go on forever, of course, but those who for generations had depended upon such useful electronic devices as the telephone, the television, the oven, and the washer and dryer, just to name a few, were in for a long and difficult stretch.

Although the EMP was not directly injurious to humans, the aftereffects could be quite harmful. This would not happen immediately, but the loss of power would have a domino effect on every aspect of American society. First, the lack of communication would cause a general lack of coherence in society. There would be no refrigeration, which would quickly lead to warehouses full of rotting food. Those vehicles that could be salvaged would face the problem of pumping gas without electricity. There would be the obvious lack of sanitation, in that everyone's trash would pile up, and there would be no running; hence, no clean water, causing diseases from insects and animal infestation. There would be no ambulances or fire trucks to respond to emergencies, which would not be reported anyway, because of lack of communication.

The American people were about to get a quick tutorial on self-sufficiency that many thousands of convenience-dependent Americans were simply not willing to deal with. Thousands of people would soon take their own lives, many sitting alone in candle-lit rooms with warm booze and bong smoke. Most would not be found until the smell of death alerted neighbors to get together and bury the unfortunate man or woman, and then split their belongings.

The rule of law would quickly become a thing of the past. Policemen would have no cruisers in which to patrol the streets, and while some local police departments would go back to walking the beat, many more would simply abandon whole neighborhoods because they were too dangerous for police. Neighborhood watch groups would be established in many of America's middle class areas and would work well for most; yet, very few would venture out at night and most would arm themselves to protect their homes against invaders, as police assistance was unlikely.

•

The President was still recovering at Walter Reed Army Hospital in Washington, DC when the power suddenly went off. Not knowing exactly what had happened, the Secret Service, who were just outside the door of the still grieving President, came in to be sure he was ok. There was no immediate danger, but they weren't going to stand in the hall during a blackout; you never knew why the blackout had occurred.

It didn't take long; however, for a few particularly clever individuals in the defense department to realize what had happened. The fact that there was no working electrical or battery powered device, including automobiles; as well as the fact that planes were coming down all over the place, led them to the conclusion that this could only have occurred by nuclear or EMP attack. The lack of a mushroom cloud or the obvious destruction that would have taken place with a nuclear detonation— even one from some distance— brought them to the conclusion that this was an E-Bomb—a weaponized Electromagnetic Pulse device that must have been delivered in aerial fashion to have had such a widespread effect.

Now, the obvious question was, how much of the country was affected and how could they find out, given that there were no working communication devices. The answer was provided by the people at the NSA, the Defense Department's cryptologic intelligence agency. They, of course, have been well aware of the possibility of EMP attack for some time. The building which houses the highly secretive defense agency had been fully enveloped in conductive textile—a fabric woven with metallic strands to shield it from just such an attack; sort of a more sophisticated Faraday cage. Hence, the building was filled with useful items like computers, cell phones, satellite phones, etc..., so the President could speak to the West Coast and coordinate assistance for the rest of the country.

Apparently, the states completely unaffected were, of course, Hawaii and Alaska, as well as California, Oregon and Washington. Also, most of Idaho including Boise had been spared. The first thing the President ordered was for the Secret Service to transfer him to the NSA so that he could begin communicating with military bases in those unaffected states. Now that the EMP blast was over, there were no lingering effects that would harm any undamaged device or vehicle brought to aide in travel or communication.

The President's physician argued the point, but Michael Hamilton was a man of action, and action was what was needed right now. He would lose himself in the needs of the American people, even though he was going through every man's greatest nightmare, the loss of his wife. Some men say the worst thing that can happen is the loss of a child, but they're lying. Perhaps it is true for a mother, but not a father. The worst horror imaginable for any man who loves his wife is to lose her to accident or illness.

Michael Hamilton had just lost the other half of himself, his wife, Katie. He would never be the same again, and to his way of thinking, never care about anything again for as long as he lived...except his country. In what doctors would have prescribed, had they known its effect on him, the President would immerse himself in an emergency situation in which he was desperately needed to help save the lives of others and heal a gravely wounded country. He would have time to mourn later, and the later the better. He ordered the Secret Service to get him to the NSA building by any means necessary and with all speed, his fractured fibula and concussion be damned.

Chapter Twenty-Three

Kevin and Lisa returned to a city, state and country in immediate crisis. Kevin's warning to the President had apparently been enough to stop two EMP missiles, but not the third. Although, their home base of Florida had been stripped of all modern technology, at least there were enough states unaffected by the blast to provide some assistance. The FBI offices in the unaffected states were already coordinating with one another to begin the distribution of cell and satellite phones to some of the major offices; Tampa's being one of them. Kevin was informed via military transport plane that a shipment of electronic items were due in from California's Fort Ord by 0800 tomorrow.

In the mean time, Kevin and Lisa went to her condo and tried to make some sense of the situation. Obviously, Lisa was of no use in a hospital that couldn't do medical imaging, but she would report there in the morning, nonetheless, in case she could be of some use; she was still a licensed medical doctor.

Kevin would report to the Tampa FBI office tomorrow. Part of the cargo of the C-130 Cargo plane would be a number of Jeeps and Humvees. He, being a VIP, would have a Humvee delivered to his door in the morning. He would take Lisa to the hospital and then head to the office. The President was scheduled to call him at 1200 hours tomorrow and he wanted to have some answers to give him.

June 1st can be a particularly warm time in most places, but in Tampa, Florida, sans air-conditioning, it is unbearable, particularly if trying to sleep. Without even a fan to help cool them, Kevin and Lisa slept out on the balcony, quickly making the acquaintance of a number of other couples who'd had the same idea. As the night became still, the neighbors finally succumbed to fatigue and went to sleep, but Kevin was stirring. He glanced at his wife, sleeping like a baby, and thanked God for everything he had been given. With all that had occurred, Kevin was still optimistic that his country would come out on the other side of this ongoing tragedy as a stronger, wiser nation.

His restlessness was due to his concerns over a number of things: Would the President now succumb to what would surely be mounting pressure to join this...Euro-Union, or whatever they called it? Could the country survive the sudden loss of all electrical power, forcing everyone to adjust to a lifestyle without modern technology? Would the country submerge itself into a state of anarchy, with the law reverting to that of the old west? Somehow, Kevin thought not.

He had seen the way his neighbors had banded together in order to overcome the loss of power. Twice, just last night, people had come to the door asking if they could do anything to help. Their next-door neighbor, Helen, whom they had never met, brought a batch of cookies she'd baked before the EMP attack.

While cooling off on the balconies, he and Lisa had struck up conversations with others in the same predicament, and their attitudes were not those of people who were angry, or even distressed. They all seemed to think of this as something to overcome, and not alone, but with community effort. As Kevin finally drifted off the sleep, his arm wrapped firmly over his beautiful wife, he thought that this may end up being his country's finest hour.

•

Captain Faysal was not as happy as Colonel Haddad and the rest of the crew. The Faraday box—Haddad had explained it to him after the launch—had apparently worked. The Nomad was underway and at full power, steaming at top speed back to the Mediterranean Sea and home. The same could not be said for all the ships they passed on their frantic trek toward friendlier waters.

On their short journey, so far, they had passed a number of freighters, steamers, fishing boats, and even a few American cruisers and destroyers, obviously without power to move or launch an attack. The Captain was still dubious as to their chances of making it home in one piece, notwithstanding the celebrations that had erupted and continued even now. Normally, Faysal would have put a stop to them, but Colonel Haddad was the man who was leading the party; the Captain didn't feel he could usurp the Colonel's wishes. What the heck, he thought, if we don't make it back, at least the crew enjoyed their last moments with the feeling of victory. As the Nomad cruised toward home, they passed an American military cruiser. The name on the side could just be made out by his lookout; USS Lake Erie, it said. Captain Faysal was glad they hadn't had to contend with them.

•

When Kevin finally arrived at the Tampa FBI office the next morning, the place looked like Grand Central Station. Apparently, the C-130 transport had been filled with just about everything a busy FBI office would need: cell and satellite phones for everyone, as well as land lines for the office; new computers with all known information already downloaded; Jeep or Humvee vehicles for all agents and secretaries and large generators for the office, as well as smaller ones for the staff to take home with them.

To say that Kevin was surprised, as well as pleased, would be an understatement. The first person he met at the office was Sam Waters. He was seeing to the distribution of all the equipment and office supplies. "Agent O'Brien," Sam said upon seeing him enter the office, "you must have really impressed someone in Washington. Director Freed tells me that the President, himself, ordered this office completely re-equipped from stem to stern."

"Well," Kevin replied, sheepishly—Kevin now carried the same rank as Waters but old habits die hard. He was still a little intimidated by him, "I'm sure I didn't have anything to do with it, but it's great news, nonetheless."

"Tell it to the CIA, O'Brien!" Waters said, "Director Freed told me that the President was so impressed with you and your suggestions that he made sure this was the first office resupplied." Then Waters added, "He also told me that you should be expecting a call from President Hamilton at noon. What's your secret?"

Kevin didn't know how to reply to that last statement, so he ignored it. "Noon, huh? Well, I'd better get our side of the office in order." Kevin walked toward his bank of offices, acknowledging Agent Waters as he left, "I'll talk to you later, sir."

When he entered the Maelstrom Task Force's bank of offices, Kevin was pleased to see Diane Austin greet him at the door. "Kevin, welcome back!" she said, giving him a hearty embrace, "We missed you here at the salt mines."

"It's good to be back," Kevin lied, "one more week in Rome and I would have considered suicide. How'd you get here so early? What'd you do, sleep here?"

Kevin was joking but quickly realized, by Diane's expression, that she had, in fact, slept here. "You're kidding?" Kevin said.

"No," Diane said, "I was here all day after the power went off and decided that I would have a hard time getting anywhere, so I just stayed here." Then she put her hand on Kevin's shoulder and said, "But, thank God you got us these vehicles. Now, I get to go home tonight."

"I don't suppose they thought to resupply us with coffee makers, did they?" Kevin asked, already knowing the answer.

Diane did a half turn and pointed behind her. "As a matter of fact, they did," she said with a smile.

Kevin made a bee line for the coffee as he asked, "Have they sent cars for Ali and Bobby? They wouldn't let a little thing like an EMP attack keep them from coming to work, would they?" Kevin hadn't been informed of the attack on Bobby and Ali.

"Kevin," Diane said, "Bobby's in the hospital. A bomb exploded in his car when he and Ali were heading home from the Outback the other night. He's going to be ok, but it was close." Before Kevin could ask, she added, "Ali's fine. He's the one that heard something funny and made Bobby stop the car and get out. They were both out of the car when it exploded, but Bobby was close enough to have been injured pretty badly. He's going to be ok, though. Ali is with him, at least, that's the last I heard before the blackout."

"Well, I guess that's good news then?" Kevin asked, sardonically.

"At least he's gonna be ok," Diane repeated for clarity.

Kevin sat down in his chair, motioning for Diane to do the same. She sat down and rested her coffee cup on the table. Kevin took a drink from his cup and said, "So, these guys are trying to kill us now, huh?" He was talking to himself as well as Diane, he didn't expect an answer.

He got one anyway. "It looks that way," Diane said, "I just found out this morning that someone tried to kill the two of you in Rome. Is that true?"

"Yep, it's true. If it hadn't been for the help of Mr. Townsend's valet, they would have succeeded. Boy," he added with exuberance, "you shoulda seen that guy fight. His hands moved faster than I could see. It was like one of those Japanese Anime karate movies."

Diane got a look on her face that moved Kevin to comment. He could see what she was thinking. "Don't worry, Diane, now that they've accomplished their goal, I doubt if there will be anymore assassination attempts. They were just trying to stop us from stopping them. Unfortunately," he continued with a sad tone, "they seem to have succeeded."

"Oh, I don't know about that," Diane said, "We managed to stop two of them. That saved at least a part of the US from the effects of the EMP. It also gave us plenty of resources to help us re-21st century-ize us, if that's a word." It wasn't, but neither of them cared.

The two spent the morning reorganizing the office and seeing to it that everything was in working order. The GI's that had delivered all this stuff also removed the damaged equipment, making it easier for the two of them to straighten things up. The lights were a little dimmer than usual and things didn't happen quite as quickly as before, but otherwise, you'd never have been able to tell they had been "zapped", as Kevin was now referring to it.

Naturally, Kevin wanted to go and see Bobby and Ali as soon as possible, but he had to wait for the President's call at noon. He would be calling Kevin's new satellite phone, so he could be mobile, but Kevin thought the

President may want some information that only the office could provide. The call came at precisely 12 pm.

"Kevin, how are you? I heard you've had a harrowing couple of days," the President said, temporarily mindless of his own tragedy.

"Yes, Mr. President," Kevin said with sadness (he had been informed of the attack on the President's train that took the life of the First Lady), "we're ok, though. May I offer my sincere condolences to you on the loss of the First Lady? I can't imagine how difficult this must be for you, sir."

"It's going to take some time, that's for sure," the President replied, "but right now we've got things to do to keep us busy. Has everything been delivered to your office, Kevin? I want to be sure you want for nothing."

"Yes, sir, Mr. President, and we appreciate all you've done." Kevin said.

"I just wanted to be sure my favorite FBI agent and his co-workers were fully supplied. We have a lot of work to do." Before Kevin could reply, President Hamilton told him, "By the way, Kevin, I've seen to it that your wife Lisa has been supplied with a satellite phone and a Humvee. They were taken to the hospital and delivered to her there. All the phones have been loaded with every other phone's cell-number. That should make it easier to communicate. By the way, my personal number has been programmed into your satellite and cell phone. I want you to be able to call me at any time, night or day."

"Thank you, Mr. President; I'll try to put it all to good use." Kevin said.

"Kevin, there's one thing I need to tell you, and it's a bit disturbing," the President said, showing obvious concern, "Remember our little plan to infiltrate the Elite Eight by planting one of our own in their evil little group? Well, apparently we weren't fast enough; they have a new member already, and it's not the one we were planning to send."

"Do we know who the new member is, sir?"

"All I know is that it is a woman. That's all the information the NSA could give me. I'm hoping you can find out the rest, son," the President said, making Kevin blush just a bit when he called him son.

"I'll do my best, Mr. President," Kevin assured him.

"I know you will, Kevin," the President said, in goodbye. "Take care of that wife of yours, son, and appreciate every moment you get to spend with her; they only happen once. Goodbye." The line went dead.

Kevin was so moved by the President's obvious pain, and the guts he had to fight through it, that he became a little teary eyed. It was obvious enough to Diane—who had stayed for the conversation—that she made up some lame excuse so that she could leave him alone.

•

Over two weeks had passed since the devastating EMP terrorist attack had virtually crippled a once mighty country. The President's ankle had heeled up enough for him to walk without a cane and his concussion was forgotten. What wasn't forgotten was the loss of a lifetime partner and the desire to see that justice was done.

However, that would be for another time. Right now, the President would put all his energies into organizing the resupply of America. Now that Washington had been restocked with planes, automobiles, computers and phones, the business of helping the rest of the country could begin in earnest.

The response from not only the military bases, but of all the citizens of those states and areas not affected by the

EMP attack was staggering and heartwarming. People from Alaska, Hawaii, California, Oregon, Washington and parts of Idaho, were flying, driving, shipping, and in some cases, paddling supplies of all kinds to the rest of the nation.

The President had received calls offering assistance from Israel, England, Australia, Japan and even China within a few days. All were sending computers, generators, airplanes, and just about anything else the President requested. It would take a long time, but the country was slowly getting its legs under it and making new friends in the process. Many of those who had previously either feared, resented or just plain disliked the United States, were moved to assist America in its time of need. Most of South America, Europe, Asia—including many Arab countries, like Saudi Arabia, Jordon, Iraq, Kuwait, Dubai, Turkey and others—sent food, water, batteries, radios, televisions, computers and cell phones to information hungry Americans.

The outpouring of international kindness left Americans, Canadians, and Mexicans, all of whom needed and received assistance, with a new view of the international community. Maybe a New World Order was not what was needed. Maybe we just needed to change our attitudes about each other and realize that we're all on this big blue ball together. Maybe with the right kind of surgery, my Aunt could become my Uncle.

Needless to say, world unity would not be so simple, but the assistance that North America had received would go a long way towards easing much of the world's tension, at least, for a while.

President Hamilton had answered the call by the European Union for America's enlistment with a resounding, "NO! And don't ask again!" This time he could count on the support of the American people and those in Congress to back him up.

This country had gone through too much to consider relinquishing any of its sovereignty to anyone but those who had written the Bill of Rights. America had a long way to go, but she would continue until she was as strong as or stronger than she was before. This time; however, the President imagined, America wouldn't be the same superficial amalgam of money-grubbing sociopaths. The recent ills, he believed, would surely turn Americans from their selfish pursuits and into more of an attitude of community, the way he remembered, or, at least, thought he remembered America.

Chapter Twenty-Four

Diane Austin had a date.

It was a real date with a real man to a real restaurant. She met him two days ago when she was filling her Humvee with gasoline. She must have dropped her wallet because after she had finished filling the tank, she turned around and there he was, holding her wallet. "Did you lose this?" he asked.

It was just over a month since the EMP attack, a day the country had now dubbed, Black Monday. Gasoline was in short supply, but in supply. Many businesses had reopened, including gas stations and restaurants.

Once she saw that the wallet was hers, Diane thanked the man profusely and that was enough for them to strike up a conversation. He was a charming man and obviously honest; that was a pretty good start, she thought. About five foot, ten inches in height, Marco Eugene Barnett had jet black hair, well coiffed, blue eyes and a red, white and blue hat that said, "Kiss me, I survived Black Monday!" Evidently, Marco had a sense of humor, as well.

Before she left for work, Marco asked her if she would have dinner with him. Diane accepted and gave him her apartment's address.

Having not been on a date for well over a year, Diane was as nervous as a priest with Turret's syndrome. She went to the newly reopened mall and tried to find an appropriate outfit for the occasion, but nothing seemed to fit her fancy. She wanted to appear professional but at the same time, approachable—but not too approachable. She finally came home, empty-handed and decided on a blue pantsuit she'd only worn once.

While she looked forward to her date, part of her was sorry she'd ever accepted the invitation. Consciously, she felt that, perhaps this wasn't a good time to start dating. The country was a mess and she was very busy with the work of the task force. In truth, she was afraid of the possibility of complicating her life with another intimate relationship that would leave her unfulfilled and maybe even emotionally wounded. While she wasn't particularly happy, she wasn't in any particular pain, either. Sometimes, in the world of the discontented young woman, the absence of pain can be interpreted as happiness. Nevertheless, something inside her kept urging her to "give it another try"; so, she'd go out with Marco and see what happened, assuming nothing and expecting less.

At seven o'clock she heard a knock at the door. *"Hmm, punctual, as well,"* she thought. Diane grabbed her purse, took one last quick glance into the mirror and walked to the door and opened it. Marco looked very handsome in a pair of dress jeans and a yellow sports shirt. He had a light-brown corduroy jacket draped over his arm.

"Right on time," Diane said, walking outside and closing the door behind her. "I like a man who's punctual," she said, jokingly, attempting to hide her nervousness.

"I aim to please," Marco replied, much for the same reason, "Let's hit the road."

This kind of sophisticatedly rapid-repartee continued through dinner and well into the short drive back to her apartment—she lived just under a mile from the restaurant. Suddenly, the right front tire blew and the car began limping on the rim until Marco could pull over to the curb.

"Great!" Diane thought, *"Let's stretch this out a little while longer, shall we?"*

Marco got out and went to the back of the car to get the jack and the spare tire. He seemed to have an extremely difficult time getting them out, as the car jostled back and forth with every push and pull of Marco's attempt to wrestle the spare tire from the trunk. Diane considered getting out and seeing if he needed any help but didn't want to appear too unladylike, not that this relationship was going anywhere.

Finally, Marco seemed to have given up and walked around to Diane's window, probably to tell her that he could use some help. She opened the door to see if there was something she could do when suddenly Marco leapt on her, but it wasn't Marco! It was someone else!

The "someone else" tried to force her back into the car, but Diane was no fool. She dropped to the ground like ragdoll. If he wanted her in the car he'd have to physically pick her up and put her in there, which he then tried to do. Diane played dead. She acted as if she had fainted and the man thought he could do with her as he pleased, until he tried to do with her as he pleased. Then, Diane, the trained FBI Agent that I'm sure the attacker had not anticipated, jumped up, kicked him in the groin and gouged at his eyes with her fingers.

Unfortunately, at the moment he began to back away, pained and in fear for his safety, Diane slipped on some oil and came crashing down on her rear end. That was all it took for her attacker to recover and reengage. As Diane tried to rise up, a thunderous blow landed on her shoulder, knocking her off balance and back down to the pavement.

Dazed, but not deterred, Diane quickly lifted herself off the ground and kicked him in the shin. This seemed only to make him angrier. Breathing deeply, the obviously out of shape attacker reached down and picked up a tire iron. Diane knew she didn't have much chance if he hit her with the crowbar, so she pushed up with all her might and brought her feet under her body, ready to spring forward at her attacker, but unexpectedly, the man seemed to simply fly by her as if he'd been snapped back by a huge rubber band.

Diane, still perched in attack position, leapt to her feet and turned in the direction that her attacker had seemed to fall. What she saw was the man who had attacked her being pummeled by another man. That fight lasted about 10 seconds as her attacker dropped to the pavement, unconscious. All Diane could see of the man who had evidently saved her life was the back of his pants as he bent over her attacker to make sure he was unconscious, but alive.

When he turned to see if she was ok, Diane caught her first glimpse of him. He had short cropped sandy-brown hair, brown eyes and a ruddy-brown complexion, as if he'd spent a lot of time in the sun. As he approached her she could see the genuine concern in his eyes. This was not a man who was macho for macho's sake, he was just macho!

Although still a little dazed, she saw a big hand reach down to her and say, "Ma'am, are you alright?"

Diane reached up and took his hand and he lifted her to her feet. Once she was standing, she realized she had to look up to see his face. She was glad she did. When she saw his look of concern, mixed with a brow that curled over a stern set of man-eyes, she melted. If this man had asked her to marry him at that moment she would have said yes.

Diane was in a kind of dream world; partly because of the blows she had received and partly because of the man who had saved her. Suddenly, she had a thought, and a guilty one; "Oh my God," she said, racing past the man who'd just saved her, "Marco!"

She raced to the back of the car, fearing that she'd find Marco dead. What she found was nothing. "Where did he go?" She wondered, aloud.

"You mean the guy who was wrestling with the man who attacked you?" said the tall dark stranger, "He took off that-away." He said this while pointing into the darkness of Bayshore Boulevard.

Diane was stunned. "You mean he just left me to fend for myself? He just took off?" Diane wasn't speaking to anyone in particular when she added, "But this is his car!"

"Then why don't you let me take you home, Miss?" he said. She noticed that she'd gone from a Ma'am to a Miss in a very short time. He must like her, she thought. "I'd appreciate that very much," she said, as she took his arm and walked down the block to his car.

"That's a pretty big bruise on your face," the man said, "maybe we should take you to the hospital, just in case."

Diane wasn't one to go to hospitals, unless she was dying. "No, I'll be ok," she said, firmly gripping his arm, "just take me home; I just need a good night's rest."

After they had walked about a half a block, Diane looked up at the man who had just saved her life and said, "So, how long did you watch that man wrestle with Marco and attack me before you decided to play John Wayne?"

He laughed at her spunk and said with a wit she would come to love, "I just wanted to see how you handled yourself," he said, "I must say, not very well."

"I was just pacing myself," she replied, hormones coursing through her excited brain, "If you hadn't intervened, I was about to open up a can of whoop-ass on him."

He hadn't met a woman like this before, he thought, "You know, I actually believe you would have," he said, "Remind me never to make you mad at me."

Diane felt that she'd fallen in love the first moment she saw this man. She reminded herself, as he opened the door and helped her into his car, *"I'm going to have to remember to ask him his name."*

•

Things had gotten almost normal since Black Monday. Kevin had availed himself of a few GI's and a van, and moved most of his belongings into Lisa's spacious condominium. It would do until he could get the house with the picket fence he'd promised her. His three-room single-man apartment was not even considered by Lisa as a possible place of co-habitation; frankly, she didn't like to go in there. It depressed her.

Tampa General Hospital had not been returned to normal by any stretch of the imagination, but they had installed a new CAT scanner, MRI, and two Radiology rooms. She was back at work and doing what she had been trained to do. She promised never to complain about the repetitiveness of her job, and to be thankful that no one was trying to kill her.

After a long day at work, she was headed home, anxious to tell Kevin that she had read a CT of the Brain on Robert "Bobby" Wang, and that there were no abnormalities. Bobby had been transferred to TGH from St. Joe's because TGH had the CAT scanner. She learned that Bobby was to be released the next day. She'd also met Ali for the first time; she liked him immediately.

When she'd purchased her condo a few years ago, she made sure and bought one with a two-car garage. As it turned out, that was a wise move. As she pulled into her side of the garage she saw that Kevin was already home. She had picked up the ingredients for making his favorite meal, spaghetti and meat sauce with garlic bread, and was anxious to make it for him, as well as give him the good news about Bobby.

She entered the kitchen and put down the groceries, she then walked into the living room looking for Kevin. What she saw upon entering the room shocked her more than anything that had happened to her since the sniper attack, and that was a lot.

There, sitting on her couch, talking to Kevin and another man she didn't recognize was President Michael Hamilton. "There's the lady of the house!" the President said, as he got up to greet her. "It's a pleasure to finally meet you face-to-face, Lisa," he said as he shook her hand.

Lisa was dumbfounded. She must have looked it, because Kevin told her to sit down before she fell down. She sat down on the arm of the couch and said nothing. She probably couldn't have spoken anyway, but saying nothing seemed appropriate.

Kevin did the introductions. "Lisa, I'm sure you recognize President Hamilton," then he motioned toward the man sitting beside him on the couch, "This is Colonel Tamir Hofi, of the Israeli Security Agency, Shin Bet; he and the President are here to try and stop a full-fledged attack on the state of Israel by the Iranian and Syrian militaries."

Lisa still remained silent, unsure why the President and an Israeli agent would meet at her condo to plan the defense of Israel.

Kevin saw her stupor and explained further. "Honey," he said, "the President felt that this would be a good place to meet in secret. As far as the press is concerned—what press there is, nowadays—the President is recuperating from his injuries at Walter Reed. Even the Secret Service, minus two agents, believes he is still in Washington, and we'd like to keep it that way."

Lisa was still confused, but had found her tongue. "Well," she said, "can I get anyone a cup of coffee, or a drink? I know I could use one." She got up and walked toward the kitchen, turning to ask, "Mr. President?"

Michael hadn't had a drink all day and was inclined to accept. "Do you have any Budweiser, Lisa?"

"Yes, sir, I do," she said, before being interrupted with, "Please, Lisa, I'd appreciate it if you would call me, Michael. I'd like to hear my name spoken by a beautiful young woman."

Lisa knew instantly what the President meant by this last statement. He was longing for the sound of his wife's voice, a voice he would never hear again. He wanted to feel like a man for a while, not just a President. "Very well, Michael," she said, "Budweiser it is!"

Before she turned back to the kitchen, she asked Tamir the same question. "No, thank you, Mrs. O'Brien, nothing for me, please," he replied. Lisa walked into the kitchen thinking, *"I just love it when someone calls me, Mrs. O'Brien."*

Back on the couch, Kevin asked Tamir why the Iranians believed they could be successful in a war against Israel. "After all," he said, "nothing has changed as far as Israel is concerned. America may not be in a position to help much, but Israel has never had any problem fending off Arab attacks. What makes them think they can win now?"

President Hamilton was content to sit back and listen to Kevin and Tamir discuss the problem. He gained most of his knowledge and wisdom from listening, not talking.

"That is a very good question, Agent O'Brien," Tamir was comfortable, but would always act with a professional military manner, "and the fact is, I cannot give you a credible answer. This is the problem that confronts us." Tamir looked at the President as if to get approval to speak, and received it with a silent nod. He turned back to Kevin and said, "The Mossad—Israel's version of the CIA—

believes that the Iranian military is receiving help from an unknown source. We would like your help in finding out what that source is."

Lisa walked back into the room carrying two bottles of Budweiser, one for her and one for the President, and a rum and coke for Kevin. "Here you are, Michael," Lisa said to the President, eliciting a grateful smile, "and Kevin, I believe this is yours." She gave him the rum and coke.

As Lisa sat down beside Kevin, it occurred to her that she may not be welcome in a conversation that had obvious national security implications. "Should I leave the room, gentlemen?" she said, wide-eyed.

"That won't be necessary, Lisa," the President said, "I believe you've earned the right to sit in on any national security conversation. I hereby grant you a field-top-security clearance."

Lisa smiled warmly and humbly, dropping her eyes demurely, as if to acknowledge that she will treat anything said with the utmost confidence.

Kevin redirected his attention to Tamir. "Colonel, of course we would be willing to help in any way possible, but I don't understand how we could be of any more help to you than your own people, who have surely infiltrated the Iranian government and military."

"I appreciate your candor, Agent O'Brien," Tamir responded, "The President told me that you were not one to pull your punches." He paused a moment and then, "We believe that the help they are receiving is coming from the group that you have identified as, the Elite Eight. It is our belief that they are preparing to introduce a computer virus that would, if successful, render the Israeli military, impudent."

"Don't you have any way of combating a virus?" Kevin asked, "Can't you just see to it that your computers are protected?"

"I realize that this sounds like something that should be easily overcome, Agent O'Brien, particularly when we know it is coming; however, that is the problem with computer viruses, if you don't know what type of strain they are then you can't develop a resistance to them. From the reports we have received, which are sketchy at best, the virus they plan to introduce is like no other we have seen before."

Kevin saw his point. "Colonel, if they did wish to introduce a virus that would cause the kind of damage to your military infrastructure that you describe, how would they introduce it? Would someone have to physically download it into an Israeli computer?"

"We believe, that to do the kind of damage that would be necessary to impede the Israeli defense," Tamir paused just a moment, "yes, I believe someone would have to download it personally, but short of identifying that person and apprehending them before they could make the download, the prospect of success in stopping it would seem bleak."

Kevin and President Hamilton were well aware that the Elite Eight had only recently added a new "eighth" member. The information on her was limited, but she was thought to be the wealthy widow of a previous member. Kevin promised Colonel Tamir that he would do everything in his power to assist him in finding the virus and stopping it from being introduced.

Both Kevin and Colonel Tamir were a bit unsure why the President had made the trip to Tampa, and to Lisa's condo, for that matter. He and the Colonel could easily have met at any location and discussed this matter without involving the President. Lisa, on the other hand, knew exactly why the

President had come; he missed his wife and wanted to be pampered by a woman again.

Lisa did her best to give him what he wanted, and needed. She cooked Kevin's spaghetti dinner and served it to the President and Colonel Tamir. Apparently, this was the first time the Colonel had eaten spaghetti, and he loved it. The four of them sat comfortably after dinner, drinking Budweiser, rum and coke, and wine. Even the Colonel was talked into a couple of glasses of Pinot Noir.

When the President and the Colonel were leaving, after spending the night—the President in the spare room and the Colonel on the couch—Kevin assured Colonel Tamir of his unquestioned assistance and Lisa gave the President a much appreciated hug. Kevin understood the nature of the President's attraction to Lisa, so he felt no jealousy. He couldn't imagine what he would be like if he lost Lisa, and they had been together only a short time, the President and the First Lady had been married for over 50 years.

Chapter Twenty-Five

Since the EMP attack, the usual meeting place on Dark Island had been thought to have been compromised, but as it turned out; Frederick Gilbert Bourne had a great fear of lightning strikes and had constructed Singer Castle with Michael Faraday's concept of conductive textile in mind.

There had been some minor damage to outlying devices, but those within the castle itself, and particularly in the Library, were unaffected. This would be their third gathering since the death of Aldo Veneto and the installation of Deborah Hargett.

Mrs. Hargett, the wife of the late, Admiral Jonathan Hargett, one of the founding members of the group, had been a Godsend to the aging group's morale. While the widow of a man who, if he was still living, would be almost 90 years old, Deborah Hargett was only now turning forty. Her marriage to the Admiral had been quite scandalous in high society circles, but the arrangement had worked out well for the both of them.

While the Admiral got to entertain with the beautiful Mrs. Hargett on his arm, as well as enjoy the occasional sexual dalliance—he had been over seventy-five and not in the best of health—she got to enjoy the protection that the Admiral's money and position afforded her. Additionally, upon his death, she inherited his entire estate. He had no living relatives, since the tragic loss of his whole family in a boating accident some years earlier, and Deborah was his ticket to a happy final few years on earth. "You can't take it with you!" the Admiral used to say, and as it turned out, he was right.

"Gentlemen," Mrs. Hargett spoke up, "as you can see before you, I have prepared my special Cranberry and white chocolate cookies for your after-dinner treat and, of course, a glass of wine; Chateau Margaux, 1787."

The mention of this expensive wine drew a gasp from even these most wealthy of men: "I will not tell you how much I paid for it at Christie's, gentlemen, but suffice to say, none of you could afford it." This remark drew a variety of snickers, giggles and belly laughs. Nothing was beyond the purses of these men and they all knew it, so did Mrs. Hargett.

Sir Covington lifted his glass in toast as all the others did the same. "To our lovely Deborah, and the sunshine she has brought into our lives," he said, bringing a few "hear-hears", a couple of "to Deborah" and one sound that no one would own up to.

Arthur Swift, acting in his usual roll as unofficial chairman, brought the meeting to order. None were too happy with the President's reaction following the EMP attack on America: "The man's out of his mind," Herr von Graf bellowed, "and now the whole damned country with him! He absolutely refuses to see the benefit of American inclusion in our Euro-Union! We've killed his people, blown up his planes, sabotaged his financial centers and virtually destroyed his country's technological prowess; not to mention an attempt to kill him! What the hell's wrong with his man?"

Sir Harold piped in. "Perhaps his reaction is like that of a man being tortured. In many such cases, the man being tortured responds with an attitude of unquenchable indignation. It may well be that this President has gotten his feathers ruffled and doesn't like the feel of it."

"Translation," the Atlantan, Michael Grant injected, "he's got his panties in a bunch!"

There were laughs all around, but Sir. Harold didn't appreciate it. "Crudely put," he said, "but accurate."

"I'm afraid, gentlemen, and lady," Arthur said, "that our most pressing issue today is the computer virus that Amal has acquired for us. The Iranian president has been of great use to us and would now like us to reciprocate."

"Reciprocate? Are you kidding me?" Mr. Devaney howled, "We've twisted ourselves around like a pretzel for the Iranians! Why should we take the risk of nuclear war for a bunch of Allah-worshiping camel jockeys?" He gave a quick glance to Amal, and added, "No offense, Amal."

Amal was a patient man, but he felt the need to clear up a few matters. "I am not a Muslim, Mr. Devaney, nor am I Arab. I am from India and my religion is Hindu, not that I take any of it very seriously, but just to clarify."

Arthur tried to bring the conversation back to the subject at hand. "Amal assures me that the Israelis will have no ability to respond, once this virus is introduced. With America out of the way, there should be no danger of proliferation. Israel will be unable to activate their so-called, Sampson option." (The Sampson option is believed to be Israel's version of the 1960's cold war acronym, MAD-Mutually Assured Destruction, in which it was believed that neither side would launch a nuclear attack because of the assuredness that they would be destroyed in retaliation. In Israel's case, they have simply made it known that "if they go down, you go down", inferring that if Israel is ever overrun, they will not hesitate to launch a nuclear attack at whoever is overrunning them.)

"I think we should give them what they want," Sir Harold said, "Israel has been nothing but trouble since we were foolish enough to allow them to establish a state. The world will be better off without their stiff-necked and bullheaded attitudes. Can you imagine what would happen in the Middle East? There would be immediate peace and terrorism would grind to a welcomed halt. I say we give it to them!"

The consensus of opinion seemed to favor the implementation of Amal's virus into the Israeli military complex. Most of those in the room believed that the prospects for peace far outweighed any possible adverse reaction by a helpless state of Israel; those that were unsure about the plan were not adamant enough to overturn the prevailing opinion. In the end, all eight members voted to have Amal's virus introduced into the Israeli military weapons system, and by their best man. This was too important to leave to just anyone, it had to be done by the man they all called, "The Situation".

This moniker had been earned and given long before anyone had heard of the television show, "Jersey Shore". The man known as the "Situation" had been doing important jobs for this group for over 20 years. He was so named because whenever they had a "situation", this man could handle it.

Ironically, no one had ever seen this man and no one had any idea where he lived, what nationality he belonged to, or even if he was, in fact, a he. The money was deposited and the job was done and that was that. No questions, no problems.

•

No sooner had the President and Colonel Hofi gone; than Lisa's new cell phone went off. "Nobody knows this number but you," she said to Kevin, "who could it be?"

It wasn't a call, it was a text message, and not being used to this new phone, Lisa had a heck of a time retrieving the message. Finally, she pulled up the text and couldn't believe her eyes. *"Hello again Lisa, I trust that you are well,"* it said, *"I have some information for Kevin concerning the virus that he and the President discussed last night. I would have put the information in your pocket but I think I'm long passed surprising you. Tell Kevin to call President Hamilton, the information you need is in his right jacket pocket. Don't be a stranger, your friend."*

When Lisa gave the phone to Kevin and he read the message, he was confused, "I don't get it. If this is Stephen Boyd, why doesn't he just say so? He did identify himself as the 'friend' in all these pocket messages, didn't he?"

"That was my impression," Lisa said, "but the only other person to send a message to me was that evil Tuefel, the man that tried to kill us, and I don't think he'll be sending us any more messages."

Kevin didn't want to spend time analyzing things. He called the President immediately. The President, who was still in a car on the way to the airport, read the caller ID and answered appropriately, "Kevin, I asked you to call me anytime, but I didn't think it would be so soon," he said.

Kevin appreciated the President's humor, but this wasn't the time. "Mr. President," Kevin began, unsure exactly how to phrase his next remark, "would you be so kind as to look in your right jacket pocket and tell me if there is anything in there?" Straight and to the point is always best.

A few moments passed and the President, who'd obviously found the note, said, "There sure is, Kevin, what's it all about?"

Kevin thought an explanation was in order. "Mr. President, while Lisa and I were in Europe, we received a number of messages in just this manner, though up until now, in Lisa's pocket. When we were attacked in Rome, the man who came to the rescue identified himself as the man who was sending us these messages. He said his name was

Stephen Boyd, but for some reason he didn't identify himself this time. Perhaps the message in your pocket will identify him. What does it say, sir?"

"Well, before I read it, Kevin, perhaps you can tell me how someone got a message in my jacket pocket?"

"I have no idea, Mr. President," Kevin said, "He seems to get a kick out of reminding us how elusive he is. I realize it's a bit disturbing, but he has been a great ally, and it does get your attention, doesn't it?"

The President had to reach into his shirt pocket and retrieve his bifocals. He opened the once folded note and read it to Kevin, *"Good day to you President Hamilton, I'm a big fan. The information I'm about to give you is as sure as the information I gave you concerning the EMP attacks. A man who calls himself, believe it or not, 'The Situation', has been commissioned to introduce a viral infection into the Israeli military apparatus. I do not have his identity, but I can tell you that he will plant the virus personally and that it will be within the next three days. My contacts tell me that he is an Egyptian double agent in the Mossad. Good luck, sir, and take care of young Kevin for me, will you?"*

"That's it," the President said after finishing, "is it of any help?"

"It could be, sir. Is the Colonel still with you?"

"No, Kevin, he said he had a date, believe it or not?"

"A date? You mean a date, date?" Kevin asked.

"That was my impression. He gave you his number didn't he? Why don't you just call him? I'm sure he'd be very interested to know that the Mossad has an Egyptian spy onboard."

"Yes, Mr. President," Kevin said, "I'll call him immediately."

"Keep me posted, will you?" said the President, then added, "It's funny, Kevin, you seem to have a way of attracting people who want to help you. I think that's a great gift, and in your line of work, very helpful. Talk to you later, son. Goodbye."

Kevin called Colonel Hofi and told him of the message's contents. Though startled, Tamir didn't seem surprised. Kevin just assumed that this was the way of things in the world of international intrigue.

●

When Kevin arrived at the office, he could see that Diane was walking on air. She was not one for displaying her emotions, especially as they pertained to her personal life, but it was hard not to spot the twinkle in her eye and the spring in her step. Kevin just smiled and didn't ask any questions; she'd tell him when she was ready.

Having visited Bobby in the hospital and hearing the latest report from his wife, Kevin wasn't surprised to see him at work, but he was quite pleased. Ali had stayed with him throughout the whole thing. One couldn't ask for a better friend. It was good to have the whole team in one place for a change, though it did emphasize the loss of Doug, and even Jimmy, poor soul.

As they all sat down in their customary positions around the table, Diane asked to be excused for a moment. Assuming she had to use the ladies room, the rest of them just sat there, drinking coffee and chatting about football— Ali was a big fan of the Tampa Bay Buccaneers. When she returned, she was carrying what looked like a cake of some kind, but when she laid it on the table and said, "Welcome back, Bobby!", the three men looked like they'd been asked to solve Rubik's cube, blindfolded.

It was, indeed, a cake, but it looked as though someone had run over it with a lawn mower and then given it to a couple of monkeys to play with. "What's that?" Kevin had to ask.

Diane was smiling from ear to ear. "That's Bobby's cake! It's called a Car-bomb cake! Doesn't it look like it was in a car bomb? They're all the rage in Afghanistan's CIA offices!"

Bobby saw the humor right away and picked up a spatula. "Should I use this, or do you have a shovel I could use?" He grabbed a plate, slopped some of the cake on it and grabbed a plastic fork. "Hey, I don't care what it looks like," he said, "as long as it tastes good."

Since Bobby had almost lost his life in a car bomb, this kind of seemingly tasteless humor would not be easily understood by the average person, but for those who deal with life and death situations on a daily basis, it is cathartic. Everyone in the room was still mourning the death of Doug, and even Jimmy. All had felt the gut wrenching pain that came when they were told of Bobby's critical injuries, and all were tense at the prospect of future attacks, but to react in any other way was to bring unwanted and even dangerous emotions to the surface. This was, by far, the best response to the possibility of ill-fated futures.

The four of them enjoyed Diane's car-bomb cake and spent a therapeutic hour of reminiscing and fellowship before getting back to work. Diane even told them about the man she'd met the other night; although, not mentioning the circumstances that had brought them together. She was excited and clearly hopeful of tonight's date.

Chapter Twenty-Six

Two days after the President and Kevin had received their message, a man of medium height and build, dark complexion, and a black moustache entered a room marked, "Top Secret" in the Israeli headquarters of the Mossad. He was carrying with him a small device that he called a "thumb drive", what most now call a "flash drive". It is a device, about the size of a man's thumb, capable of storing the contents of the American Library of Congress. The components of even the most virulent virus could easily be stored within its diminutive contours.

The man carrying this device was not skulking around; he was exactly where he had been every day for the last 5 years, working in the counter-intelligence section of Aman, the Mossad's military intelligence section. It was about lunch time and most of the section's employees had already headed off to the cafeteria. The man that everyone knew as Ephraim Dagan had been dieting for over two weeks and preferred to keep working rather than break for lunch. He said it was easier to diet when he stayed busy.

Now that he was alone, Ephraim reached into his pocket and pulled out his "thumb drive". It had been loaded with the most vicious and destructive virus that had yet been conceived, at least, according to the Indian sounding man who had hired him to download it into the main computer. It was just business, Ephraim said to himself, just another "situation" for him to make money. This would be the easiest of them all.

•

President Hamilton was back at the White House and was being informed by his CIA chief, Richard Ames, that there was a serious buildup of troops at Israel's border with Lebanon, Syria and Egypt. Apparently, there was a buildup of tanks, armored vehicles and troops, as well as a large number of planes fueling for takeoff. Satellite imaging showed that Iran, Syria and Egypt were readying a plethora of missile systems, all, ostensibly, aimed at Israel.

America wasn't in tip-top shape at home, but she still had a formidable fighting force all over the world, especially in the Middle East. The USS Ronald Reagan was stationed in the Persian Gulf and the USS West Virginia was steaming there with all speed. Whatever happened, the United States would be in the middle of it; the President only hoped they wouldn't be in the middle of World War III.

The President was keenly aware of the threat to Israel and had no intention of letting them "go it alone". He had given standing orders to shoot down any and all aircraft which were deemed offensive to Israel. If that ruffled the feathers of some in the international community, so be it; he would not stand by while a country the size of Rhode Island was viciously attacked by their "mentally unstable", he believed, neighbors.

The President actually considered the possibility that his actions, or lack of them, could trigger the last war ever fought on earth. He knew the Israelis would not go down without a fight, and perhaps a nuclear fight, but right now, all he could do was hope and pray that cooler heads prevailed. The President was not inclined to believe they would.

•

President Habibi was beside himself. Not only were his troops ready for battle, but Syria and Egypt reported themselves ready, as well. He knew there was a risk in this Israeli attack, but he had received confirmation from Mr. Peanut that the virus had been deployed and that, while Israel would be able to respond with tanks, artillery and troops, their missile program would be useless to them, and if all went according to the predictions of Mr. Peanut's people, their aircraft, as well.

Ali was, of course, playing devil's advocate. He spent the morning pointing out everything that could possibly go wrong: the Israelis could have their nuclear and conventional missiles on separate linkups; the virus might not work as planned; Israeli tanks and artillery could do plenty of damage and the United States still had plenty of military power in the region.

Sadad thought he was an old mother hen, but tried to allay his fears by using Ali's great faith in Allah, a faith that he did not share. "Ali," President Habibi said, "do you think Allah would let us fail at this point. Look, America has been decimated, Israel has been vilified in the international community, we've introduced a terrible virus into their military computers and we have the most sophisticated assault group in the history of Islam. You must have faith, my friend. I promise you, Allah will not let this campaign fail."

"I hope you are right, Sadad," Ali responded with weak hope, "but if this fails..." Ali's thoughts trailed off into the obvious.

At the Israeli border, Iranian General Rahman Tehrani, who had been picked to lead the attack on Israel, was going over some last minute details. His second in command, Colonel Saeed Jafari, was considered the most capable of

Tehrani's missile-defense team. "General," Colonel Jafari said, "everything is proceeding as planned. If all goes well, we can launch the attack in 15 minutes."

"Well done, Colonel," the General replied, "just think of it, soon we will be standing in Jerusalem and the Israelis will be either dead or second-class citizens, as they should be."

"It will be glorious, sir," Jafari answered with an exuberance that came from both the excitement of being part of such a monumental day and his great desire to kiss the butt of General Tehrani, "you will go down as the greatest military leader since Saladin!"

General Tehrani had been thinking the same thing. "It is not important who gets the credit, Colonel, only that Allah's will be done," he said.

Twenty minutes later, with the blessing of his staff, General Tehrani ordered the attack to begin. Without delay, Iranian and Syrian tanks started rolling into Northern Israel from Lebanon and Syria. Their orders were to bypass the Golan Heights and swing around in an all out assault on the city of Haifa, while simultaneously, an Egyptian and Iranian assault force would sweep up from Egypt into southern Israel in a two-pronged attack. One force would plow through the Gaza Strip, taking Ashquelon and Oiryat before marching into Jerusalem. In-between the two was the city of Tel Aviv, which would be easily overrun once they had surrounded it.

The Israeli army engaged the invading forces in the north near the city of Akko, and in the south, throughout the Negev Desert and the Gaza Strip. The forces arrayed against Israel were formidable, to say the least. For every tank the Israelis had, the enemy had three, with the same ratio applying to artillery and troops; but Israel had been in this position on many occasions, sending the Muslim invaders home with their tails between their legs.

On the Israeli side, the battle was not going well. The north was experiencing heavy losses as enemy troops were only miles from Haifa. In the south, a desert war was being fought with tanks, and Israel was at a distinct disadvantage. It was time to soften up the enemy's flank with an aerial assault.

Colonel Navah ben Wiezman, the man that former Prime Minister Benjamin Netanyahu described as "the fox you don't see coming", was busy directing a counter-attack in the north. He decided that, "if you can't outnumber them, then out fox them". He ordered his tanks and artillery to pull back, allowing the enemy tanks and troops to move closer to Haifa...and farther away from the Arab artillery's ability to protect them. In American football parlance, the Arabs were outkicking their coverage. This strategy had been used to great effect in the Six-Day war, and Wiezman thought it would work here, as well.

Not know for their patience in battle, the Iranians, Lebanese and Syrian field commanders continued to chase the Israelis further and further into Israel, all believing they were routing the enemies' armies. Like a moth to a flame, the soldiers of Allah were hell-bent for leather in pursuit of their own destruction.

The tactics seemed to work, as Syrian and Iranian tanks were now "out in the open" and beyond the protection of artillery fire. Colonel Wiezman couldn't believe they had fallen for the same trick twice. "Don't they study their own history?" he asked a subordinate. "It's as if they think we don't have an air force!"

Ironically, that's exactly what they thought. The Muslim leaders were going on the assumption that the virus had been implanted successfully and that Israel could not respond with missiles or air power. It was another in a long line of Muslim military mistakes which had led them to defeat in just about every battle they had fought for over a century.

The Colonel ordered all fighter aircraft to scramble and "put them out of their misery". Soon, Israeli fighters were flying sorties over defenseless tanks and troops, destroying the tanks and sending the troops running for cover. Within an hour, the assault forces in the north were decimated and Wiezman could concentrate his forces in the south.

With the brunt of the enemy tanks rolling through the Negev Desert like a hot knife through butter, the Colonel thought it best to respond with a missile barrage. The chance of collateral damage in the desert was negligible and he didn't have enough tanks or fighters to defeat such a large invasion force, so he ordered the Arrow anti-missile interceptors to stand by in case of a missile attack—which he was surprised hadn't started already—and launched the Delilah missiles at the Iranian and Egyptian tank force. The Delilah missile is designed to seek out and destroy moving targets; perfect for defense against these fast moving behemoths.

While the Iranians, Egyptians and Syrians were not known to have a formidable naval presence, they had sent a number of "destroyers" to the port cities of Haifa and Tel Aviv, hoping that the Israelis would be "distracted" by the other military assault modalities and not pay them much mind. However, the Israelis are nothing, if not thorough; destroying every ship that threatened Israel with their Gabriel long-range anti-ship missiles, which use a technique called sea-skimming to find and destroy enemy ships.

In a monumental victory for Israel—a day that would "one-up" the Six-Day War with the moniker, the "Six-Hour War"—the Iranian, Egyptian, Syrian and Lebanese armies were routed by the Israeli army, navy and air force. The jubilant Israelis were puzzled as to why the enemy had not launched a missile or a plane in a coordinated attack.

General Tehrani had the same questions, but he asked them while flying into a rage. "What the hell happened?" he screamed at Colonel Jafari, "They weren't supposed to be able to launch missiles or use the weapons systems on their planes! What the hell is going on here?"

The General would continue in like manner for over an hour before working up the courage to call Iranian President Habibi and tell him of the devastating defeat. President Habibi treated General Tehrani in the same manner in which Tehrani had treated Colonel Jafari. No one in the Muslim assault force was anything less than devastated by the defeat, and most were embarrassed, to boot.

President Habibi intended to have a long talk with Mr. Peanut; Mr. Peanut intended to have a long talk with "the Situation", and Colonel Tamir Hofi, of Shin Bet, intended to give his best agent, Captain Josef Goldberg, a promotion to Lieutenant Colonel. It was Goldberg, after all, who had spotted Ephraim Dagan attempting to download a virus into the Israeli defense computers, not only stopping him, but allowing the Colonel to turn the tables on the Iranians.

Once Dagan had been discovered, he cooperated with Israeli requests to report back to his "people" that the transfer had been successful—with just a bit of persuasion—then Colonel Hofi made sure that one of his field agents in Iran downloaded the virus into the Iranian defense computers. While attacking Israel, the Muslim military had no idea that they would be unable to launch missiles, use their jet fighters or communicate with their commanders in the field.

It had worked like a charm and saved his country from certain annihilation. Colonel Hofi flew immediately back to the United States to take care of some unfinished business, not the least of which was to thank the President and Agent O'Brien for their help.

•

On the night of August 15th, Kevin and Lisa invited Diane and her new fiancé to dinner. The country had spent almost eleven months in a combination of Limbo and Hell; never sure what tragedy would befall them next. On the bright side, Task Force Maelstrom was in its final weeks of preparation for what President Hamilton called, "Project Payback".

Maelstrom was just a small part of the President's plan, but Kevin and the team were anxious for the chance to give rather than receive. Kevin contacted Stephen Boyd, who'd called him after the Six-Hour War to congratulate him on his handling of the situation in America.

Stephen was an extraordinary man. He was obviously an exceptionally skilled fighter, as he showed in Rome, but he was also an accomplished businessman, entrepreneur and loyal aide to the late Reginald Townsend. Kevin could never get him to come clean as to whether he had been the man who'd sent all those messages. He tried to thank him for all his help but Boyd simply brushed off any attempts to show his appreciation by saying things like, "You and your wife were very brave," or "The Lord helps those who help themselves."

Kevin wanted to see if Stephen could help them locate the most likely meeting place of the Elite Eight. The President felt he had enough proof of their complicity in many of the attacks that they could be brought to trial.

Obviously, they were too powerful to allow themselves to be extradited to the United States from Europe, but the President wanted to send them a message that he was on to them and would seek justice.

Stephen was not of much help. He said that the Elite Eight, of which his former employer was a one-time member, was not in the business of being brought to justice. He suggested that Kevin tell the President to concentrate his anger on the Iranians.

When Diane arrived for dinner, she was alone. Kevin felt a knot in his stomach as soon as she opened the door. *"Oh no, don't tell me you broke up,"* Kevin thought, *"You've been so happy, lately, I'd hate for that to change."* Kevin's humor; however, never took a break.

"Where's your future ex-husband?" Kevin said, as Diane walked passed him into the living room, "Should I change the table settings?" Diane walked back to Kevin and punched him in the stomach, playfully.

"Very funny," she said, "he said he was running a little late and would be here by eight."

As Lisa came in and gave Diane a big hug, Kevin continued his playful attack. "Are you sure he didn't say he was going out for a pack of cigarettes?"

"Don't listen to him, Diane," Lisa said, leading her over to the couch, "he hasn't had his medication today. Kevin, go take your pills!" she added, indirectly telling him to shut up.

Kevin got the hint. "I'm just kidding, Diane, I'm sure he'll be here...eventually." Well, perhaps he didn't get the hint. "Can I get you something to drink?" he asked, "Beer? Whiskey? Hemlock?"

"Kevin, will you shut up!" This time Lisa decided to go the direct route, and this time Kevin got the point.

Lisa had dinner ready at eight, but Diane's fiancé still hadn't arrived. Now, Kevin began to feel a little guilty. His humor was usually designed to lighten the mood and make people feel comfortable, but sometimes he was a little too quick to speak and too slow to think.

At about 10 minutes after eight the doorbell rang. Kevin breathed a sigh of relief as he walked to the door. When he opened it, standing in front of him was Colonel Tamir Hofi of the Shin Bet. "Colonel," Kevin asked with surprise, "what can I do for you?"

"Well, first of all," Tamir said, "I wanted to thank you for the tip you gave me about the Egyptian double-agent. We were not only able to stop him, but we managed to turn the tables on the Iranian war effort. I'm forever in your debt."

"Well, I was lucky enough to have received a tip from a friend," Kevin said, "I'm glad you were able to put it to good use."

Tamir smiled back at Kevin in obvious appreciation, but he looked a little uncomfortable, as if he wasn't sure if he should stay or go.

Kevin asked, "Colonel Hofi, you said there were two things. What's the second?"

"Well," the Colonel said, "I was invited to dinner."

Kevin, of course, had no clue. "What?" he said, " I'm sorry, Colonel, but I'm having guests for dinner tonight; maybe another night. *Why's he inviting himself to dinner?"* Kevin wondered.

Tamir just stood there, frozen into inactivity by Kevin's statement. "I'm sorry, Agent O'Brien," Tamir said, "but I was asked to come here by my fiancée, Diane Austin."

When Kevin's mouth hit the floor, you could actually hear it in the other room. "Oh," Kevin sputtered, realizing his mistake, "Oh, Colonel, come in, please? I'm sorry, I didn't make the connection. Come in, please?" he repeated, moving out of the way so Tamir could enter.

By this time, a rather tipsy Diane had made her way to the door. When she saw Tamir, she wrapped her arms around his neck and squeezed. "What took you so long, Tamir? I thought you were going to stand me up."

"I'm sorry, Diane, I was speaking on the phone with the President. I didn't want to tell him that I had a hot date."

"That's the story of my life!" Diane said, escorting Tamir to the dinner table, "Every time I think I've found the man of my dreams, he tells me he's got a meeting with the President of the United States."

For a moment, Tamir didn't realize that Diane was joking. When everyone else started laughing, he did the same, but he was still unsure why. *"Does this happen to her a lot?"* he wondered. Tamir was raised in a small Israeli town and wasn't up on all the many forms of American wordplay.

The look of confusion on Tamir's face made Diane laugh all the more. "Sweetheart, I'm only joking!" she managed to say, "You're the only man I've ever loved." The alcohol was making her a little too wordy, but this was a true statement; Tamir was the first man she had ever fallen in love with.

Over the course of the evening, Diane regaled Kevin and Lisa with the details of the night she and Tamir had met. Lisa was shocked that Diane had been attacked, but then bowled over by the romantic ending. "So," Lisa said, "what happened to Marco?"

Diane, who had now reached her limit, said, "He just took off! I never saw him again!"

Tamir was still a little stiff in front of Kevin, but after a few drinks he was a little looser. "I had no idea when I reached down to help her up that she was part of the Maelstrom Task Force. She didn't look like an FBI agent, she looked like an angel."

The thing that made this so touching was the fact that Tamir said it matter-of-factly. He wasn't trying to say something romantic; it was simply what he thought at the time. The obviousness of this made both Diane and Lisa cock their heads and say, "Aaah" at the same time. Diane tilted her head into Tamir's shoulder and smiled at the thought. "That's sweet," she said, "my knight in shining armor."

Tamir didn't know what that meant, but he rightly assumed it was good. Kevin extended his arm in Tamir's direction and as he shook his hand, said, "I'm very happy for the both of you. Take care of her, will you? We're very fond of her down at the office."

Tamir smiled, understanding that it was not something that required a response, just a knowing smile.

Lisa had not even asked the most important question, at least, most important to her. "Have you set a date?" she asked, her eyes already filling with images of the romance of a wedding.

"Yes, we have," Diane said, "we decided to get married on the one-year anniversary of the day America was attacked."

Even Lisa was surprised at that. "Black Monday?" she said, "You're going to get married on Black Monday? Why?"

"Because," she said, "September 16th was a red-letter day in American history and it created the Maelstrom Task Force which led me to Tamir."

Kevin couldn't help himself. "Diane," he said, "technically, September 16th could be described as a day that America will never forget, but I don't think the term 'red-letter day' is an appropriate way to refer to it." He tipped his bottle of Budweiser and drank the last of it before adding, "Why don't you get married on September 26th? Now there's a red-letter day for you!"

Only Lisa was aware that September 26th was Kevin's birthday. When she saw the looks of confusion on the faces of Diane and Tamir, she said, to Kevin, "If they want to get married on the anniversary of a disaster, either date would suffice."

Then Diane had another thought, "Oh, and it won't be Monday this year, it will be Tuesday. So, technically, it won't be Black Monday, after all, it will be White Tuesday." Diane smiled in a way that only she and Lisa could understand, thinking of things that only she and Lisa could think.

Kevin and Tamir had thoughts that only men could understand; that of confusion.

Chapter Twenty-Seven

Jodi Rowe and Phyllis Smith had the singular distinction of being the only two-man cockpit crew in the United States military manned solely by women. Both pilots carried the rank of Lieutenant Colonel and both had graduated from the school famously known as, "Top Gun".

The aircraft in which they had just lifted off was called the B-2 Spirit. It was one of 20 USAF Stealth bombers capable of carrying the heavy load that Rowe and Smith had laden aboard their vessel. This newer version of the familiar "Stealth Bomber" from the first Iraq war had the same configuration which gave it the appearance of the "Bat Plane" and the ability to slip behind enemy lines without being detected. This two-man craft was over 20 years old and could carry loads in the tens of thousands of pounds rage. For this mission, the cargo was limited to three 5,000 lb. Guided Bomb Unit-28's (GBU-28). These three bombs use the laser guided "smart bomb" technologies which allow them to penetrate hardened targets before exploding. They can penetrate over 100 feet of earth or 20 feet of concrete before going off, making them ideal for use as "bunker busting" munitions.

While their mission will be a long one, Rowe and Smith are very much up to the task, having been two of the Air Force's "guinea pigs" in "sleep cycle research", a program designed to improve the crew's performance on long sorties. Highly automated, the B-2 Spirit is unlike other two-seat fighters or bombers in that one crewmember can sleep, prepare food or use the lavatory while the other monitors the aircraft's functions.

For the almost 16,000 mile journey from their home base in Australia, the B-2 Spirit would have to refuel two times. This "in-flight refueling" (IFR) was necessary because the B-2 Spirit could travel only about 6000 miles on a tank of gas, and because the aircraft's mission was too secret to allow the plane to land on foreign soil; not that they could have received permission to do so, regardless.

Jodi and Phyllis were well known in the close-knit world of American fighter and bomber pilots. Carrying the unwelcome nicknames of Tweedle Dee and Tweedle Dum, the two pilots were chosen for this mission for a number of reasons: first, they were both extremely good pilots, the most important criteria for the mission; secondly, both had performed well in sleep-cycle research—this was going to be a long flight and the Air Force didn't want their pilots falling asleep in mid-flight and thirdly, both wanted to go. As a matter of fact, both Jodi and Phyllis begged to go on this mission.

Jodi's father had been one of the doomed firefighters who had lost their lives when Tower Two came down on 911 and Phyllis just thought it would be fun: As she put it, "If you can't drop bombs on Iranians, what are bombs for?" She didn't really think this way, but American fighter and bomber-pilot humor was notoriously foul.

The fact was; both women were happy to be serving their country and doing what they believed to be an important duty in a difficult time. Although, they both had personal feelings concerning the mission, they were foremost, professionals, and they had a job to do.

After they had travelled approximately 5,500 miles, Rowe maneuvered the aircraft in position to receive the "flying boom", a rigid, telescoping tube that the operator on the Boeing KC-135 Stratotanker—the flying gas station—

extends into the Spirit's fuel receptacle to provide it with enough fuel for the second leg of its mission.

As the 200,000 pounds of fuel was pumped into the 150,000 pound bomber, Lt. Colonel Jodi Rowe went over everything on the checklist and pronounced her craft to be in ship-shape. Their mission was a go and both women were anxious to get on with it.

After the flying boom was retracted, Rowe acknowledged the completion of the fuel transfer, "IFR compete, drawing back from boom," she said through her headsets, "Did you check the oil?" she asked.

Captain Johnson, the pilot of the Stratotanker responded, "Yeah," he said, "we changed the oil, gave it a lube job and I even fixed that squeak you guys were complaining about."

"Thanks, Captain," Jodi said with joviality, "that had been driving us crazy."

The Stratotanker began to pull away. "Good luck, ladies," Johnson said, "We'll see you on the return trip. Give 'em hell!"

"Will do," Lt. Colonel Rowe responded, "Will do."

•

It was now 3 months to the day since America had been devastated by the Iranian EMP attack on June 1st. Colonel Haddad had become the toast of Teherani society—at least, the upper social strata—after he was identified as the man who brought America to its knees. Captain Faysal was given a cursory "pat on the back" by the Ayatollah, but was not considered much more than the "getaway driver". This lack of acknowledgement was ok with Faysal, as he was not interested in such superficial goings on, anyway; he was just happy to be allowed to return to his ship and resume his quiet seagoing lifestyle.

Contrary to Islamic Fundamentalist propaganda, not all of Allah's "heroes" have to wait until death to enjoy the debaucherous lifestyle that is promised to those who kill for the sake of "Allah's will". Drunken parties filled with prostitutes and "sex slaves" from Europe are reserved for those that Allah has chosen to lead "his" people. Power corrupts and absolute power corrupts absolutely is a tenet that applies equally in all societies, including Islamic.

Haddad was still half drunk as he lifted himself off of the satin sheets of his ritzy government-paid-for hotel room in Dubai. He had been given carte blanche by President Habibi for a two-week vacation in the Arab "Las Vegas". Dubai, of the United Arab Emirates, was home to more millionaires, per capita, than anywhere in the world, and its boisterous way of life attested to it.

The two women that Haddad left lying naked in his bed had been kidnapped as part of what the world knew as "white slavery". They had both been taken from their homes in Moscow as teenagers by the Russian Mafia and sold to the Muslim slave traders for use in circumstances such as this. Both had long ago given up any hope, or even desire, to escape the daily abuse at the hands of men who could and would treat them with cruel passions.

Now, as he contemplated his soon return to Tehran and a future in the Iranian hierarchy, Haddad picked up a half-full bottle of Chardonnay and walked out onto the balcony of his 12th floor high-rise luxury hotel room. The view was magnificent, with the hundreds of modern and well-lit hotels, casinos and condominiums spread out before him like array of Egyptian harlots beckoning him to sample each one's sensual pleasures.

As he slowly paced back and forth, appreciating the view below him, Haddad pondered the mission he'd just completed. *"These Americans are such fools,"* he thought, *"and cowards, to boot."* It had now become clear who was responsible for the EMP attack on America. *"We attack them and they do nothing; we try to kill their President and they do nothing. They are truly paper-tigers and it's about time someone exposed them for what they are."*

In the suite behind him, the two young girls, still unconscious from the effects of drugs, alcohol and sexual abuse at Haddad's hands did not feel the sharp sting of the tranquilizer darts that pierced their skin and assured them a further two hours of sleep. Furthermore, Haddad was unaware of the single black-clad figure that had entered his suite, being sure to place the "do not disturb" sign on the room's outside door knob. He was only aware of his throbbing headache and the way he was likely going to feel in the morning.

As Haddad turned to return to the bed, he was confronted by a black, ninja-like figure, standing directly in front of him. He did not have long to reflect on this unexpected development before he was stunned into unconsciousness by a powerful Taser gun. When he awoke, some 15 minutes later, he found that he was tied securely to a chair, still as naked as he'd been when he got up from the bed.

Sitting in front of him was a tall, brown-haired Caucasian man, dressed in black leotards and smiling from ear to ear. "Hello, Colonel Haddad, my name is Stephen Boyd," the man began, "As you may have surmised by now, I am an American. As you may also be aware, my feelings for you are not what you would call, warm and fuzzy".

Fear had a way of heightening the senses, even through alcohol. Haddad was beginning to realize that he was in serious trouble. This man looked fully capable of doing him bodily harm, and what's worse, very likely.

"I can see by the look in your eyes, Colonel Haddad, that you have also come to another rather important realization; the realization that you are about to die a most unfortunate, and I assure you, a most horribly painful death. The question is, how?"

Haddad's eyes were as big as saucers but Stephen had been sure to gag him with a special rubber ball, designed for just such an occasion. He could make certain sounds but none that would not be interpreted as the Colonel's moans of pleasure as he continued abusing these young girls. Needless to say, Haddad was becoming well aware of this and began to lose control of his bowels.

"Colonel," Boyd said, crinkling his nose to show his disgust, "I would have been glad to take you to the bathroom rather than see you degrade yourself like this. What would President Habibi think if he could see you now?"

Haddad's eyes were streaming with tears and the look of a man silently begging for mercy. He would receive none from Stephen Boyd; his orders did not call for mercy, his training did not allow for sentiment and his temperament was not inclined to forgiveness. "Well, Colonel, how do you think you should die? We are very high up in this building. I suppose a 12 story fall would do the trick, but that wouldn't satisfy my desire to see you suffer."

Boyd dropped his head and shook it back and forth. "You see my problem, Colonel?" Stephen said, being sure to create as much terror in Haddad's mind as possible. "Wow," Boyd said as he got up from his chair, "you are ripe!" Haddad's loose bowels had begun to run onto the floor of the balcony. "Hey," Boyd said, turning back toward Haddad, "I've got an idea!"

Stephen walked back and forth in front of Haddad, who was now clearly crying. "Colonel, I must say I'm surprised at you." He reached down, pulled his knife from its ankle-sheath and stepped closer to the man who'd killed thousands of his countrymen. He "aimed" the knife, point first, at Haddad's genitals, saying, "It don't think you're going to have much use for those anymore, Colonel, I think I'll remove them for you." He moved the knife closer to Haddad's "package" before adding, "From the looks of things, Colonel, you won't be missing much."

If this went on much longer, Haddad would have a heart attack, and that wouldn't be justice, now would it?

Stephen Boyd was a highly trained former American special-forces soldier, and a man that, if he had a beef with you, would be dangerous to know. He was also a professional with no bent toward emotionalism. While he would have loved to stretch this out, he decided that it was time to end this.

"Colonel Haddad," he said, "you are responsible for the deaths of hundreds of thousands of people in my country. While I realize that a military man must do his military duty, I have learned that you took great pleasure in your work, as you apparently do with your sexual abuse of young girls. I have no desire to exact revenge on the crew of the Nomad or its Captain. I believe they were doing their duty as soldiers, but I have a bone to pick with you. I find you guilty of the murder of almost a million Americans, and on behalf of all those who lost their lives because of your EMP device, and because of the joy that you seem to derive from it, I sentence you do death. The sentence will be carried out immediately."

Stephen Boyd pulled out his Walther P22 with the threaded barrel and screwed on its matching silencer. Not a vindictive man, Stephen, nevertheless, got a slight thrill seeing Haddad's face as he watched him withdraw the instrument of his death.

"I must say," Boyd said, "if I had the time I would have loved to continue this for a few days, but as it is, I'm going to have to wrap this up." Stephen lifted the gun and gave Haddad a professional "double tap"; one bullet to the chest, followed by a quick bullet to the forehead.

Haddad was dead and good riddance. Now, Stephen walked into the suite where the two girls lay, still unconscious on the bed. He reached into the desk and, with gloved hands, withdrew a writing pad and pen. After scrawling a quick note, he reached into his "bag" and pulled out a few items, dropping them onto the table beside the note, then, he was gone.

Eighty minutes later, when the two girls awoke, they would find Colonel Haddad's naked, bound, bloodied and soiled corpse sitting slumped over in a chair on the balcony. They would also find 4,000 dollars, a couple of forged passports and a note that read, "Take this money and these passports and go home. You are free!"

•

The United States was approaching the one-year anniversary of the beginning of the terrorist attacks that almost sent her spiraling into a national abyss. Culminating with the EMP attack on June 1st, America had seen its position as a world power not only shrink, but virtually disappear.

Yet, here it was, almost one year later, regaining much of its strength and prestige through the help of some family, some friends and some unlikely acquaintances. The family was comprised of the unaffected states and territories like California, Oregon, Washington, Hawaii, Alaska and parts of Idaho. Also, there were many military and civilian entities, like the NSA, that had been prepared for an EMP attack and were largely unaffected, leaving them in a position to render assistance to the country following the attack.

On the friend side were most of Canada, Israel, Australia, New Zealand, England, Ireland, Wales, Scotland, Japan, most of Western Europe, South Africa, a few countries in South America and even Saudi Arabia. These countries, along with the few states unaffected by the EMP, rained technology into the continental United States in massive quantities. It seems that when America was in trouble, all the assistance they had poured out over the years had not been forgotten after all.

Odd acquaintances and old adversaries were turning into allies, as China, North Korea, Russia and Venezuela also filled their cargo ships with everything from computers to washing machines to automobiles. Not all that America received were simple gifts. Much was loaned with the understanding that, once back on her feet, America would repay with interest. Nevertheless, the help was given and appreciated by a humbled and spiritually renewed nation.

Even New York, much of which was still radioactive, had found new homes with the breaking of ground for the "new" Wall Street in New Jersey and the relocation of most of the national media into upstate New York. The city of Washington, DC had received a slight makeover but was quickly becoming the vibrant hub of international politics for which it had been known these many years.

Main Street, USA had also begun to see the stirrings of life that had for so long been the heartbeat of the nation. Movie theaters, restaurants, gas stations, night clubs and retail stores were opening and thriving as Americans began the attempt to replace that which they had lost.

There was a resurgence of patriotism throughout the country and a renewed appreciation for the blessings that Americans previously took for granted. Church membership and attendance was drastically up, as well as membership in new and old civic organizations like the Elks, Moose, Knights of Columbus and such, but with no membership restrictions and a rededication to community service.

With the help of the Canadians and the British, American television and radio stations had begun broadcasting in over 32 states, with other states being added weekly. The content of the broadcasts were much less hedonistic and far more compassionate and humanitarian than had previously been the case. Most Americans were feeling fortunate to be eating good food, drinking clean water and living in warm, dry homes. The thought of superficial, self-centered programming aimed at degrading the human soul with violence, pornography and decadence was not now in the realm of the American mindset. The hope was that it would never return.

Racism, the bane of American culture since its inception, had, at least for now, seemed to become a thing of the past, as concerns for the color of another man's skin seemed as superfluous as for that of his hair color. Small differences seemed to matter less and less, as Americans had all been subjected to a year of traumatic events that shook them to their core and produced, for those that survived, a kind of new love of country, community and family that had been squeezed out of them by a self-indulgent culture and lifestyle.

Americans stopped thinking of themselves as somehow better, or more deserving that others, and other countries stopped resenting Americans for their seeming privileged existence. For once in a very long while, the whole civilized world seemed to be on equal footing and began to take steps to bring about a "new" United Nations that could truly address the problems of the world; like poverty, famine and war. Even Europe began to drop their insistence on uniting Europe into a mega-state and started to consider a change in behavior and economics as the best solutions to the problems of mankind.

Leading the way into this hopeful future was a renewed leader of the regenerated United States of America, President Michael Hamilton. After watching his country absorb blow after blow, and still remain standing at the end, he gained a new confidence and a purpose that he thought he'd lost with the death of his beloved, Katie.

With his popularity at an all time high, President Hamilton had convened an international panel of leaders from every corner of the earth. The leaders of America, China, Russia and India, among many others, had come to the unshakable understanding that they were living in a dangerous world and that if this kind of thing could happen to a country like America then it could happen to them. Most felt it was time to stop the madness and begin a dialogue designed to promote an international "live and let live" agenda. This once seemingly naive objective seemed to be within the realm of possibility. There would obviously be stumbling blocks, but a world united against violence could force nations that were less than enthusiastic to succumb for fear of alienation.

But these were projects and hopes for the future. President Hamilton had proclaimed September 16th as America's "Remembrance and Renewal Day". It would be treated as a kind of second Independence Day throughout America, with fireworks, cookouts and memorials to those who had been lost. To demonstrate its new commitment to openness and trust, most of the members of Congress threw a "backyard barbeque" on the National Mall with everyone invited. President Hamilton had commuted the sentence of the dying Senator Wooten and invited him to be his special "unarmed" guest at the barbeque.

Not everyone was thrilled by these new developments. A small group of people sitting at a table in the library of Singer Castle on Dark Island were in particular disagreement.

"How the hell could this have happened?" Herr von Graf hollered. He looked at Amal Singh and shouted, "Singh, you were supposed to see to it that Israel went down! Apparently, this "Situation" of yours isn't so trustworthy after all! What do you have to say for yourself?"

Amal remained deadpan; he showed no reaction at all to von Graf's verbal attack. Arthur Swift was not having much success in easing the tension at the table, but, as always, he tried. "Please, please, Herr von Graf, this is getting us nowhere. Let us try to remain constructive and not lash out at one another."

"Put a cork in it, Swifty!" Michael Grant shouted in response, "He's absolutely right! What the hell happened?"

It seemed that the only member of the Elite Eight who could bring these angry men into a state of calm was Mrs. Hargett. Rising from her seat at the head of the table, she did just that. "Gentlemen, may I speak?" she said, calmly, as an example to the others. The men began to quiet down and give Deborah the courtesy that she had requested. All seven were, at least to some extent, taken by Mrs. Hargett's charms and she had been careful to milk it for all it was worth.

"Gentlemen," she began, "I too am angered by the lack of success that Mr. Singh's operative was able to achieve, but let us not forget that his was not the first attempt to manipulate the American President to join our little, Union. I believe there is plenty of blame to go around and I accept my portion of it, as all of you should accept yours. The question is, where do we go from here?"

"Biological weapons," Herr von Graf said, calmer now, "We should use biological weapons and bring the United States to its knees."

"Are you out of your mind?" Arthur Swift said, finally losing his cool, "We want America to join the Euro-Union, not destroy the country and the people! Are you a madman, Herr von Graf?"

"You may call me whatever you like," von Graf said, "but it is clear that what we've done so far has not worked. We need more drastic measures. I'm sure we can use targeted bio-weapons; the kind that will only infect a particular race, like the blacks."

"Gentlemen, and Lady," Sir Harold Covington piped in, "I don't think biological weapons are the answer. Besides, they could get away from us and infect the whole world. What we need to do is latch on to these new international feelings of good will. The whole world seems to be ready for a single government and leader. Why don't we work from within this new framework and try to steer it in our direction?"

"That will never work, Sir Harold," Antoine Rousseau pointed out, "Hell, with the way things are going now, President Hamilton would be the new leader. I'm not sure Herr von Graf's idea of a biological weapon is the right choice, but we must do something to stifle this new international initiative of cooperation, if we don't, all of our efforts could be for naught."

"What do you suggest?" Herr von Graf's sarcasm was obvious, "Should we join hands with the President and sing Kumbaya?"

Deborah Hargett rose to her feet. "Gentlemen," she said, "do you remember our last meeting? Do you remember the wine I served at that time?" She was speaking rhetorically, "Well," she said, reaching into an ice chest at the side of her chair, "I have outdone myself this time."

Deborah pulled a bottle of wine from the chest and set it on the table in front of her. She looked over at Antoine Rousseau and asked, "Would you do the honors, Antoine?"

As Antoine took the bottle and opened it like only a Frenchman could, Deborah walked over to a buffet table and picked up a tray of appetizers. She walked back and placed the tray at the center of the table. "Bruschetta, gentlemen," she said with a certain pride, "it will go well with the wine."

Rousseau had finished opening the wine but only now noticed the contents within it. "Oh my God," Rousseau said with an orgasmic sigh, "This is Chateau Lafite, gentlemen, 1787, the most expensive bottle of wine in the world. I tried to buy it at Christie's once and was outbid. This bottle of Bordeaux was sealed before George Washington was sworn in as President of the United States."

As Antoine poured each member a glass of the finest wine in the world, Amal passed around the Bruschetta—an Italian delicacy of grilled bread, olive oil, red pepper and tomatoes; a perfect appetizer for a one-million dollar bottle of wine.

Deborah was now walking around the table as she continued. "Now, gentlemen, Herr von Graf's suggestion of a biological weapon is, I believe, too dangerous for our purposes; however, I have a suggestion."

All the men were listening intently to Deborah, as they always did, but even a rich man won't turn down a free meal. As they ate the Bruschetta and drank the Chateau Lafite, Mrs. Hargett outlined a plan of her own. "Have any of you heard of a delightful little parasite called a pinworm?" This too was rhetorical. "Well," she went on, sauntering around the table, "these tiny fellows aren't very dangerous in their present form, but with the assistance of some remarkable biological engineering, they have been transformed into the most terrible and fearsome little predators on earth; kind of like piranha, but for the human body."

Von Graf jumped in, "How would we introduce such a parasite, Mrs. Hargett?"

"Into the water supply, I would think," she said, adding, "We could put it in their Cheerios."

This elicited a good laugh from the group as Arthur asked, "What, exactly does it do, Mrs. Hargett?"

Deborah smiled. "That's the best part, Arthur. Let me explain?" she said, now standing directly behind him. She put her hands on his shoulders and continued, "Once the eggs have been ingested, they are carried through the stomach and into the Duodenum, the first section of the small intestine, where they hatch. As they migrate through some 22 feet of small bowel, they grow rapidly, moulting twice as they grow to adulthood; male and female.

"Once they reach the Ileum, the last part of the small intestine, they mate, whereupon the males die and the females settle in the Ileum, Caecum and appendix. The marvelous part of all this is that all this happens in a matter of minutes. Then, each female lays between 11,000 and 16,000 eggs, literally introducing hundreds of thousands of genetically engineered pinworms into the small intestine and colon."

"Sounds pretty gruesome, if you ask me," John Devaney said with a grimace, "Is there a way to counteract the effect?"

"No," Deborah further explained, "Once the pinworms have been introduced, nothing can stop them short of complete removal of the digestive tract." Mrs. Hargett got a nasty looking smile on her face as she went on, "But that's not the best part, gentlemen. These products of genetic research are not just a bothersome parasite, leaving the colon after a few days, these little guys not only don't leave the colon or the small bowel, they turn around and head in the opposite direction, and the best part is, they eat their way through the small bowel to do it."

Mrs. Hargett smiled a snide smile and added, "Most people would be in horrible pain about 30 minutes after ingestion and quite dead within an hour, and their deaths will be painful and gruesome, as Mr. Devaney suggested."

Herr von Graf laughed a bit and said, "Mrs. Hargett, I had no idea you were so brutal. We certainly picked the right woman for the group, but are you sure these little parasites will do the trick?"

Deborah Hargett smiled at Herr von Graf and as she passed him on her way to her seat, patted him on the shoulder. She reached her seat, picked up her purse and began walking to the large Mahogany double-doors that served as the entrance to the library. She opened the door, turned to the group and said, "I don't know, Herr von Graf, but as you are the first test subjects, I'm sure we will know in a few minutes."

Mrs. Hargett left the room and closed the door on her way out, leaving a stunned group of men to wonder what she meant by her last statement. Then, the first of them began to feel a certain twinge of pain in his abdomen. Soon, all seven would understand the meaning of Mrs. Hargett's parting words as the severe abdominal pain and the frightening realization of impending death seemed to coincide.

Deborah Hargett walked briskly to the helicopter that had landed only moments before. As she strode towards the means of her exit from Dark Island, a well-dressed male figure emerged from its belly and met her with a handshake and a kiss on the hand.

"Is it done, Deborah?" he asked her, taking her hand and escorting her to the helicopter.

"Yes, Stephen," she said, "it is done."

Deborah Hargett and Stephen Boyd boarded the copter and it lifted off for Toronto Pearson International Airport. They would be taking separate flights from there.

"We appreciate everything you've done, Deb," Stephen said, about halfway to Toronto, "Mr. Townsend would be grateful."

"Anything I can do for Uncle Reggie, Steve, you know that," she said, "I never liked those sons of bitches anyway."

Chapter Twenty Eight

The new parliament building in the Iranian capital of Tehran was one of the showcase centers of the "new" Iran. Built of polished white marble, the pyramid shaped building could house the entire national government structure of Iran. That government structure was built around an Islamic theocracy, with the Supreme Leader, the Ayatollah Ali Khamenei—not to be confused with the original Ayatollah Khomeini from the 1979 Iranian revolution—as the de facto dictator.

Iran, of course, like all theocratic dictatorships, offer its people the illusion of parliamentary government structure, with an Executive, Legislative and Judicial branch of government, but it is the Supreme Leader and his cadre of Allah's finest who truly govern the country.

The Executive branch consists of President Habibi and his slew of Vice-Presidents, ten in all, including the First Vice-President Ali Rajsanjani; the Legislative branch consists of the Parliament's 290 members, or majlis, the Guardian Counsel of 12 judges and the Assembly of Experts with its 86 clerics; finally, the Judicial branch consists of the head of the Judiciary, appointed by the Supreme leader, and his appointees, the head of the supreme court and the chief public prosecutor.

Since the dedication of this enormous structure just over a year ago, there had yet to be a meeting of the entire government; tonight would be the first. Except for President Habibi, who was meeting with the Syrian ambassador this evening, everyone would be on hand to hear the inspiring words of the Supreme Leader.

By any Western standard, nothing of substance would be communicated to those seated in the great hall, but it would give the Supreme Leader a chance to feel important, spouting meaningless gibberish to a captive audience. Many of those in the room were enraptured by the slightest vocalization of their Supreme Leader, Allah's version of the Pope, but most were a little more sophisticated, realizing that the speech was all politics; necessary politics, but politics just the same. They were glad to be there for their own personal status, but would be glad when they could go home.

Once the "Assembly of the People" had been seated in the "Hall of Allah", the Supreme Leader entered the stage and walked to the podium. The anticipation was palpable, as it always was when the Ayatollah spoke, giving many of the assembled government leaders a glimpse into the mind of a man that was surely sent by Allah.

"My fellow soldiers in the war for eternal peace," he began to the hushed assemblage, "Our struggle against the Zionist regimes in Israel and America has been long and hard. The martyrs of Allah have given their lives in Jihad against the infidel American horde, but they have sent more than their share to the infernal reaches of hell. America, the great Satan, has been reduced to nothing more than an annoyance; an annoyance we will soon rid ourselves of."

The congregation rose up as one. The applause was defining until the Supreme Leader raised his hand to silence them. "However," he said, "we have been betrayed by one of Satan's henchmen! Just as we were prepared to launch a full scale attack on Israel, we were betrayed and left with hundreds of dead Islamic soldiers where there should have been dead Israelis."

The Supreme Leader was preparing to announce that the war with Israel was not dead, just about to take a different form; that of nuclear annihilation. The Shahab 4 rockets had been fitted with nuclear tipped missiles and would be ready for launch by the end of the month. At that time, he would go on to say, the destruction of Israel in a nuclear conflagration would usher in the 12th Imam—the Islamic messiah—and mark the advent of global adherence to Allah's teachings.

The Supreme Leader had much more to say to his ardent followers, but he would never get the chance because Jodi Rowe and Phyllis Smith were, at that very moment, laser guiding two 5,000 pound bunker-buster bombs into the side of the beautiful symbol of Iranian government.

When the first bomb ripped through the roof of the pyramid, it continued to travel through the air, then, after striking the floor of the parliament building, continued on through the ground for another 25 feet before exploding. The resultant explosion lifted most of the assemblage of leaders out of their seats and sent them hurtling toward the ceiling, while at the same time, the shock wave sent the roof caving in toward those lucky enough to have remained seated.

This violent explosion resulted in the entire building's collapse and the death of all but two of the 475 people in the "Hall of Allah". Those two people were the only members of the Iranian government left alive, except for President Habibi, but they would not be alive for long—or in one piece. Moments later, the second 5,000 pound bunker-buster bomb plowed into the debris of the once pristine structure and after digging into the ground for 75 feet or so, exploded and sent all that was left of the Iranian parliament building and its fragile human visitors into an unrecognizable amalgam of mortar, marble and pulverized human remains. No one within the building would or could ever be identified.

Approximately, 30,000 feet above Tehran, Jodi and Phyllis loaded up another bomb.

•

In an area known as New Tampa on a street called Tampa Palms Boulevard in a small building called Temple Ohev Shalom, Tamir Hofi was attempting to put on his tuxedo, with little success. In his whole life, Tamir had never worn a suit, and these cuff links were driving him crazy; not to mention the cummerbund—what was that all about, anyway?

He was to be married in just over an hour and he was sweating profusely and just barely breathing. His Best Man was doing his best to calm Tamir's nerves, but it was not helping. "Tamir, you're going to get married, not infiltrate a Syrian army barracks, relax," Kevin implored him, "I'm married, and it's not that horrible."

"That's easy for you to say, Kevin," Tamir was now quite comfortable with Kevin and considered him one of his best friends, "You didn't have to get married in front of my mother. She's just now beginning to call me by my first name, instead of her 'little mutton chop'. She thinks I'm 12 years old."

Kevin wanted to laugh but Tamir's look didn't invite humor, he really looked scared. "Hey," Kevin said, "do you love Diane?"

Tamir stopped fidgeting for a second. "Yeah," he said.

"Do you want to spend the rest of your life with her?"

"Yeah,"

"So, what are you worried about? What's the worst thing that could happen?" Kevin asked, hoping Tamir would see the foolishness of being nervous on such a happy day.

Tamir wasn't buying into it. He looked at Kevin with a "Duh?" kind of look, and said, "That my mother interrupts the ceremony to remind everyone that a 12 year old boy has no business getting married, and to a Shiksa!" (Shiksa is a term the Jewish use for a gentile female.) "You have no idea what she's capable of, Kevin. Ever since she got here from Rosh Pina—Tamir's home town of about 2000 people, just north of the Sea of Galilee, overlooking the Golan Heights—she's been crying and asking Jehovah, 'Why me, Lord'. She's acting like this is the end of the world."

"Tamir, all you have to do is get through today; after that, you're mother will return to Israel and you and Diane can live your lives in peace. You need to keep your eyes on the goals above your head and not on the obstacles at your feet." Kevin had heard that somewhere and thought it sounded cool, but Tamir would never buy it.

"Perhaps you're right, Kevin, but my mother is one of those mothers that make the Jewish people famous. If she's not complaining about something, she's trying to feed you. Sometimes she even complains about the food she is feeding you."

Kevin had no intention of trying to get between a boy and his mother. He decided to go for the jugular. "Tamir, when this day is over, you will be able to lie in a bed with Diane every night for the rest of your life." Kevin was not opposed to drastic measures, and by the look in Tamir's eyes, he'd had a breakthrough.

"You make a good point, Kevin," he said, a smile slowly engulfing his face, "You make a very good point, indeed."

•

"Do you think his mother likes me?" Diane said, as Lisa tried to work on her hair.

"Will you hold still, Diane?" Lisa said in frustration, "This isn't easy, you know."

"Do you think he's having second thoughts? I know men usually have second thoughts." Diane was just a little nervous. "You know, Lisa, I could use some Champagne. Would you like some Champagne?"

"If you don't hold still you're going to go down the aisle looking like Harpo Marx! Now, sit still!" Lisa was about to whack Diane with her own brush.

"His mother doesn't like me, I can tell. Did you see the way she looked at me? Talk about daggers!"

Lisa thought she had been nervous before her marriage but this was otherworldly. "Diane, if you sit still I'll see to it that you get some Champagne." She looked over her shoulder at Diane's sister, and said, "Karen, will you please go get a bottle of Champagne and a few glasses before your sister goes into orbit?"

A moment later, as Karen headed out the door, Lisa called out to her, "Maybe you should bring a couple bottles of valium, too!"

"Very funny," Diane snorted, "I seem to have some faint memory of your wedding. Wasn't it you who threw the wedding bouquet to the priest?"

"That wasn't nerves," Lisa said, "that was just bad aim."

"No," Diane said, "bad aim was when you got yourself turned around and kissed the best man instead of Kevin. That's bad aim!"

"If you don't shut up," Lisa warned, "you may consider yourself lucky to look like Harpo Marx."

Karen was just returning with a bottle of chilled Champagne. She had already opened it and was pouring them each a glassful. As she reached to hand Diane her glass, Lisa suggested that it might be quicker and more effective if she were to simply give her the Champagne intravenously.

•

President Habibi's wife, ChalipA, hadn't heard from her American "pen pal" for some time, so she was pleasantly surprised when he sent her an urgent message; however, when she saw the message's instructions for her to meet him at a small cafe on the outskirts of Tehran, she was frightened, but titillated all the same.

She had never done anything like this before, especially with her husband in the house; not that he'd notice she was gone, or even care. He seemed to have other things on his mind lately, and with the big speech coming on TV in a few minutes, he probably wouldn't notice if she left the house in a mini-skirt. "I'm going to the market, Sadad," ChalipA said as she brushed by him, anxious not to be late for her moment of intrigue.

"Make sure you're back by eight, ChalipA, Ali will probably come by after the Supreme Leader's speech, and I need an excuse to give the Syrian ambassador. The man smells!"

ChalipA gave her husband a cursory answer and headed out the door. She was anxious to see what her internet friend looked like. She'd always imagined him looking like Charlton Heston but she would be satisfied with Omar Sharif.

The fact was; Sadad never listened to the Supreme Leader's speeches live; he always recorded them with his new TiVo device and watched them later. The speech was set to begin in just a few minutes, so the President set the recording time and happily decided to watch the speech when he returned from seeing the Syrian ambassador.

As the meeting with the Syrian ambassador was not scheduled until 7pm, and ChalipA was out of the house, Sadad decided that, "While the cat's away, the mouse could play." He went into the den where the 52" flat-screen, plasma television was set up. He rummaged through the seemingly endless montage of electronic components until he found the control pad for his 1980 Atari 5000 system. There was nothing that calmed his nerves and excited his completive juices more than a brisk game of Miss Pac Man. He was sure that he was better at this game than anyone in Iran, and he was going to continue to hone his skills to make sure it stayed that way.

After Blinky, Pinky, Inky and Clyde had gone down for the count, the phone rang and President Habibi answered it in a huff; he didn't like to be interrupted when he was "rolling".

"What is it?" he barked, "I'm very busy!"

The man on the other end of the line didn't speak the same language as President Habibi, so he had no idea what he had just said. In the only language he spoke, and one in which he knew the Iranian President to be fluent, he said, "Hello, President Habibi, am I interrupting you?"

It was not a usual occurrence for Sadad to answer the phone and be spoken to in another language, particularly, English. Was this Arthur Swift? It didn't sound like Arthur Swift. "Is this Arthur Swift?" he said.

"I'm afraid I'm not familiar with Arthur Swift," the President of the United States said, "My name is Michael Hamilton. Are you familiar with that name, President Habibi?"

Sadad had heard that name a thousand times but not without the word "President" attached to it. "I'm afraid I don't know that name, now what do you want?"

"I'm sorry, President Habibi, it's my fault for not making myself clear. My name is President Michael Hamilton. I am currently the President of the United States of America. Does that name ring a bell?"

Sadad had never received what the Americans called a "crank call" before, but obviously that had changed. "I don't know who you are, but I have the ability to trace this call, my friend. You could be in for more trouble than you wish."

"President Habibi," Michael said, "I assure you that I am the American President and I intend to prove it to you in a moment, but...excuse me, Mr. President," Michael interrupted himself, "What time do you have?"

Now President Habibi was more confused than ever. "What are you talking about? Who is this?"

"Again, President Habibi, excuse me. My late wife, Katie bought me a Rolex about a week before she died; I was just trying to see if it kept the correct time."

Just to humor whoever was on the other line, Habibi looked at his watch and said, "If you must know, the time in Tehran is 6:29 pm. Is that helpful?" Habibi knew this couldn't be the President of the United States, but he sure had a lot of gall.

"I'm only asking because at this very moment, about 30,000 feet above your head, a stealth bomber is being piloted by a couple of rather disagreeable women. At precisely, 6:35pm, Tehran time, they intend to release a very large and particularly destructive 5,000 pound bomb and laser guide it into your living room."

Habibi was surer than ever that this was a crank call, but he started sweating just the same. "I don't believe you are capable of such an act in my own capital city. I think you are some kind of a ..." Habibi was interrupted by the sound of an enormous explosion, then moments later, another similar sound.

President Hamilton could hear the explosions on the phone. "The sounds you are hearing, Sadad," Michael gleefully explained, "are the sounds of two 5,000 pound bunker-buster bombs destroying your new parliament building and everyone inside. Am I beginning to get your attention, Sadad?"

Habibi turned to his left and looked out the bay window toward the parliament where the Supreme Leader was giving his speech. He could see a large plume of smoke rising from the location of the new parliament building, a building he could no longer see.

"What do you want?" he screamed into the phone. "You are not a murderer are you? Would you kill my wife and children as well? Are you a butcher?"

Calmly, President Hamilton said, "You don't have any children, Sadad, you're too self- centered to care about anyone but yourself, and ChalipA is not at home right now. She's on her way to meet one of her computer pen pals at a cafe outside the city. The pen pal is, of course, one of my men. I just wanted to see to it that she was safe before..."

What the President's last words to Habibi were, only he knew; Habibi didn't hear them. Jodi and Phyllis had dropped their last bomb and were now headed for a rendezvous with the Stratotanker. They had had a full day and while Phyllis monitored the plane's systems, Jodi was making them both a nice cup of coffee.

Chapter Twenty Nine

It took three glasses of Champagne and a threat of serious bodily harm from Lisa, but Diane was finally dressed for the wedding. Tamir would become weak at the knees when he saw her.

Kevin had plied Tamir with booze, as well. He was now standing beside Kevin at the altar, awaiting the entrance of his soon-to-be-wife. When the wedding march began, Tamir looked at Kevin with a "Is it too late to back out?" kind of look, and then trained his eyes on the parade of young girls as they led the way for Diane's highly anticipated walk to the altar.

When he finally caught a glimpse of her, Tamir was dumbstruck. Diane had always been a beautiful woman, but now she was transformed into an angel, gliding down the aisle with the grace of a ballerina. Her dress was white ivory chiffon with a starburst of seed beads. Sleeveless and strapless, the gown accented Diane's lovely figure with an A-line configuration, starting at the top and expanding outward until it touched the floor. Behind her was a Cathedral train, held off the ground by a couple of exited 10 year old girls.

When Kevin saw Lisa, he remembered his own wedding and how beautiful she had looked, very much the way she looked right now. He felt the chill of goose bumps for a moment, just thinking about how happy he was with Lisa. He hoped Diane and Tamir would be so happy.

Even Tamir's mother began to shed tears of happiness as she watched her Shiksa-soon-to-be- daughter –in-law walk down the aisle. She had come to terms that her son's wife was not Jewish...yet!

The wedding went off without a hitch and Kevin and Lisa were reunited on the way to the reception at the Hyatt Regency in downtown Tampa. They waited until Diane and Tamir had dodged the storm of uncooked rice and jumped into the limo that Kevin had decorated for them. It had about 10 empty coffee cans attached to the rear bumper—Diane's favorite, Maxwell House—plenty of crape paper bunting, the words, "Just Married" painted across the rear window, and the name and phone number of one of Tampa's prominent divorce lawyers written on one of the side windows. Kevin thought it was funny; Lisa didn't.

At the reception, Kevin danced with Diane; Tamir danced with Lisa; Lisa danced with Kevin; Bobby danced with Ali; in short, everyone danced with everyone. Presents were offered to the young newlyweds, envelopes of money were handed to them from people they barely knew, pictures were taken by professional and non-professional alike, Diane learned to dance to Jewish wedding music and fun was had by all.

When the reception was over, at least the part that included the newlyweds, Diane lined up to throw the wedding bouquet. She was determined not to throw it to the Rabbi or to his wife of 37 years. She stepped upon a chair and faced away from the young, anxious girls, then she flung the bouquet over her shoulder and directly into the hands of Tamir's mother, who had been the widow of Tamir's father for over 20 years. Mrs. Hofi looked stunned as Diane's body filled with adrenaline, readying her for "fight of flight". Just when she thought she'd better run like crazy, Mrs. Hofi burst out laughing. Diane breathed a sigh of relief but was still prepared to make tracks, when Mrs. Hofi, seeing the humor in it all, came over to Diane and gave her a warm embrace. "Welcome to the family, Diane," she said, "Now you have family in Israel."

Diane lit up like a Menorah. She turned to Tamir, who was beaming, and said, "Hey, let's go start the honeymoon, huh?"

Tamir didn't have to be told twice. He scooped Diane up and led her out of the Hyatt Regency and into the getaway limo. The couple turned and waved one last time at the screeching crowd before jumping into the limo and speeding off to a honeymoon in Miami Beach. It wasn't a long drive from Tampa and Tamir had family there. He got a great deal on a time-share.

Once they had gone, Kevin and Lisa, still arm in arm, walked back into the ballroom. Diane and Tamir may have been gone, but that didn't mean they couldn't still have a good time. They thought a few slow dances would be just the ticket, until Bobby decided to cut in.

He tapped Kevin on the shoulder, and when he turned around said, "May I cut in?"

"How original", Kevin thought. "I suppose so," he said, noticing Ali standing right behind Bobby, "Hey, are you guys planning on dancing with my wife all night?" Kevin said this with a jovial tone, implying humor, but he was serious. He wanted to be alone with his wife; yet, he correctly supposed that to be difficult at a wedding reception.

Kevin relented. "Go ahead, Bobby," he said, "but we're going to have to get you a girlfriend."

While Bobby danced with Lisa, Ali filled Kevin in on Bobby's recovery. Apparently, there would be no further need for medical treatment but the doctors thought he should be monitored for any post-concussion symptoms. He and Bobby had become roommates and shared a beach house in Treasure Island. Now that the Maelstrom Task Force had disbanded, Ali knew that he would have the unwelcome time to mourn his wife. Bobby was a good friend and his devil-may-care attitude helped keep the moods from getting too morose. Kevin thought they were lucky to have each other; however, he thought they should both go somewhere else and be lucky to have each other. He tapped Bobby on the shoulder and said, "Bobby, take Ali and get lost."

Kevin took Lisa in his arms and began a slow dance. They were so happy to be together and to have all this terrorist business behind them that they could have just popped with joy. Lisa held Kevin closely but then seemed to have had a thought occur, "Ok," she said, leaning back a bit and looking up into Kevin's enamored eyes, "let's go over this again: first, I get shot at by a terrorist sniper, then, that same sniper comes to my condo and tries to kill me in person, then I'm kidnapped by a professional hit-man, followed by a follow-up encounter with said hit-man, who holds me at knife point and tries to kill my husband."

Kevin looked like he was about to respond when Lisa held up her hand to indicate that she wasn't done. "Hold on," she said, "Then, we lose power in our airplane and almost plummet to our deaths, followed by a fun four months without much electrical power. Does that pretty much sum up the last year of my life, or am I missing something?"

"Well," Kevin said, "you did get married this year, didn't you?"

"Yeah," she said, "that was pretty cool, but I'm not sure it compares with having dinner with the President, who, by the way, asked me to call him, Michael."

Kevin winced a bit and said, "Yeah, I seem to have some faint memory of that, but trust me, he's too old for you. It'll never work out."

"Why not?" Lisa asked, playing straight man, once again.

"Because," Kevin said, assuming Lisa would be expecting one of his funny retorts, "I love you with all my heart. Nothing could ever make me give you up."

Lisa's eyes moistened.

"Besides," Kevin said, "the President already offered me 10 million dollars and two weeks in the Lincoln bedroom. I turned him down flat."

The two went back into a warm embrace, but soon Kevin noticed something familiar out of the corner of his eye. When he looked back to see what it was, he came face to face with Stephen Boyd, and Stephen was looking directly at him.

"Sweetheart," he whispered into Lisa's ear, "you're never gonna believe this." Lisa looked up to see Kevin starring at the man who had, not long ago, saved their lives. Why he was there; however, was anyone's guess?

The two walked over to greet him and ask him why he was here, but before they reached him he turned and walked out the ballroom door and into the main lobby of the hotel. Naturally, Kevin and Lisa followed him, as they suspected he wished.

In the lobby, Stephen turned and approached them. He put out his hand to Kevin and said, while shaking his hand, "It's good to see you, Kevin," he glanced at Lisa and said, "and you, as well, Lisa."

"Excuse me for asking, Stephen," Kevin said, "but why are you here?

Stephen didn't mince words. "I'd like you to come with me for a moment, Kevin." He turned to Lisa and said, "You don't mind, do you, Lisa?"

"Of course not," Lisa said with a slight bow of the head, "You won't keep him too long will you?"

"I promise you, Lisa, I will have him back to you in 15 minutes," Stephen said, and he led Kevin away.

As he and Stephen walked to the elevator, Kevin asked, "What's this all about, Stephen?"

"I'd prefer to show you," Stephen replied.

When they had reached the 10th floor, Stephen led Kevin out of the elevator and down the hall to room 1025. With his electronic key, Stephen slipped into the room, followed by a curious but trusting, Kevin—after all, the man had saved his life on more than one occasion.

When they entered the main sitting room of the suite, what Kevin saw made him do a double-take. There, sitting before him, looking as healthy as a horse was the "late" Mr. Reginald Townsend. "It's good to see you, Kevin," he said, "You look well."

Kevin wasn't sure what had happened. "I was just about to say the same thing about you, Mr. Townsend. As a matter of fact, you look surprisingly well, for a dead man."

Mr. Townsend laughed and said, "It's this new low-carb diet; it's made all the difference."

"Well," Kevin said, "whatever the reason, I'm glad to see you're alive. Now some things are beginning to make sense. It was you who sent me all those messages, wasn't it? They always seemed to me to be written by an older man; it just didn't sound like the kinds of things Stephen would have said."

"That's very astute, Kevin," Mr. Townsend said, "but then you always were very astute." He motioned for Kevin to sit, "Have a seat, Kevin; there are a few things I need to speak to you about." Then he looked at Stephen and said, "Stephen, would you leave us alone please?"

Stephen didn't say a word. He just walked out the door and closed it behind him.

"Would you like a drink?" Mr. Townsend asked, "Perhaps a cup of coffee?"

"No thank you, sir, I had about all I can stand at the reception," Kevin said, "but I would like to ask you a question. Why did you fake your own death? What was the point of having me come all the way to your home so that you could die on me?"

Mr. Townsend was seated in a red Buckingham Bordeaux Queen Anne Chair. It was his favorite chair and he had it brought to wherever he traveled. He leaned forward and rested his elbows on his knees. He looked down at the floor for a moment, seemingly to ponder what he was about to say and then raised his head to look directly into Kevin's eyes. "Kevin," he began, "as you know, I was a member of the Elite Eight for over 20 years. I joined their little club with the best of intentions. We would help to feed and clothe those in the poorer countries of the world; sometimes we would assist in the event of a natural disaster; we even saw to the overthrow of a few particularly malevolent tyrants, like Idi Amin and Saddam Hussein."

"Saddam Hussein was overthrown by the US military. They found him hiding in a spider hole. Remember?"

"So it would appear, Kevin," Mr. Townsend said, "Did you ever wonder why a man who had no weapons of mass destruction would allow himself to be overthrown rather than just admitting he didn't possess these weapons. That's all he would have had to do, isn't it?"

"Yeah, I suppose I wondered about that. Why? What did you do?"

"We convinced him to stick to his guns and not let America push him around. We also convinced him that America would never actually invade his country; that Bush was just bluffing." Mr. Townsend snickered a bit and said, "And he bought it, didn't he?"

Kevin was a little surprised by Mr. Townsend's admissions, but not astounded. "So," he said, "what made you fake your death?"

"Well, the 'organization', for want of a better term, began to get this idea of uniting all of Europe, North America, Russia and a few other countries, into some kind of an international mega-state that could be controlled by a few well-chosen leaders. Of course, we would be those well-chosen leaders, and we would set the agendas for their countries and the world at large."

"And you became uncomfortable with that prospect." Kevin said, matter-of-factly.

"Exactly!" Mr. Townsend said, "I wanted to do my part; all rich people want to be philanthropic, if only to allay some of the guilt they have for the means in which they became rich, but then Arthur and his little group began to get greedy. I could see that their plan was, in fact, to literally control the world and become, in essence, world dictators. I simply couldn't go along with it."

The fog was lifting. "I see," Kevin said, "so you wanted to get out, but in organizations like that, you can't simply resign and go about your merry way. It's like the Mafia, you can't quit, at least, not without a trip to the morgue."

"As I said, Kevin, you're very astute. I realized that the only way out was to fake my own death, and having the FBI actually witness my death would add credence to its reality."

"That's why you couldn't just send me the information. You wanted me there to witness your death."

"Precisely, Kevin," he said, "but there was more. As I told you before, I am a man who does his research. I was very impressed by you and what I believed were your, shall we say, latent abilities. I thought you were the best man for the job."

"What job is that, Mr. Townsend, to expose the Elite Eight's activities?"

"Partly, but much more," Townsend said, leaning forward a little further, as if to confide, "Yes, I wanted to take this pompous little gang of Hitlers down, which I knew, with my help, you could do, but I'm also thinking of the future."

Townsend sat up straight and looked at Kevin. He smiled a sort of, "knowing smile" and reached for the little "I've fallen and I can't get up" device around his neck, only when he pushed the button he wasn't summoning an ambulance, but Stephen Boyd. Moments later, Stephen entered the room and stood by the door, awaiting Townsend's instructions.

Townsend addressed Stephen as he entered, "Stephen, my boy, has everything been arranged?"

Stephen bowed his head in assent. He then walked over to the bed and retrieved a briefcase, not un-similar to the one he had given Kevin back at Townsend's home. He carried the briefcase over to where Kevin was sitting and sat it on the floor beside his chair.

"Will that be all, sir?" Stephen said, and when he had received non-verbal confirmation that it was; in fact, all, he went to the door, opened it, and stepped out into the hall, quietly closing the door behind him.

After the door closed, Kevin found that he was more curious about Stephen and his relationship with Townsend than that of the contents of the briefcase. He asked, "Mr. Townsend, why does a man with the kind of obvious talent and abilities as Stephen Boyd, follow you around like a little puppy dog? Frankly, it's a little disturbing."

Again, Kevin seemed to have tickled Townsend's funny bone. "I suppose it does appear strange, Kevin, and I will explain, but first, I have a few things to say to you before I go."

Kevin didn't respond other than to make it clear that he was listening by intensifying his stare.

"Kevin," Townsend continued, "I'm not a young man, and while I am, no doubt, still among the living, that condition may soon become a thing of the past. Forgive me, I've seen too many cloak and dagger movies; what I mean to say is that I am dying. I have advanced pancreatic cancer and my doctors give me very little time."

Kevin, for some reason, had become attached to Mr. Townsend from the beginning. "I'm very sorry to hear that, Mr. Townsend, I truly am."

"You know, Kevin, I actually believe you," Mr. Townsend said, moments before a rap at the door. "Come in!" Townsend called out towards the door, "Kevin, I hope you don't mind, but I think what I'm about to say concerns Lisa, as well."

At that moment, Stephen stepped through the door with Lisa closely in tow. Both Kevin and Lisa looked at each other, neither knowing why she was there or what Mr. Townsend was up to.

Stephen, without being told, picked up another chair and placed it beside Kevin's, facing Mr. Townsend. "Lisa," Stephen said, "would you like to have a seat?"

Lisa, obviously confused, walked over and sat beside Kevin, resting her hand on his as she sat down. "What's this all about?" she asked, to which Kevin replied with a shoulder shrug.

"Lisa, I wanted you here with Kevin to hear what I'm about to say." He looked back and forth at the two of them and continued, "Kevin, the briefcase at your feet contains everything that I own. Except for a small stipend for myself, to get me through the last week or so of my life, everything that I own is now yours."

The stunned and confused looks on the faces of Kevin and Lisa were so evident, Townsend didn't feel the need to point them out, only continue to explain. "You see, I have no living family and I have long wished to give my estate to someone I believe to be worthy of it and mature enough to handle its enormous responsibility. As of now, the two of you are the sole owners of my home in North Carolina, a private island off the coast of Aruba, numerous businesses around the world and more cars, limos, jets, and yachts than I care to count. Oh, and about 250 billion dollars, give or take."

Normally, when someone gives you 250 billion dollars, you say, "Thank you!" or "Thank you for the 250 billion dollars!" For some reason; however, Kevin couldn't seem to come up with the right words to express his deep... "What in the hell did you just say?" Kevin said, instead.

"Which part?" Townsend said, enjoying the couple's confusion.

Kevin sensed that what Mr. Townsend was saying was factual, but trying to fathom its implications was something else, altogether. He was not sure how to take this news. It was more than he could process. "Mr. Townsend, you don't have to..."

Townsend jumped in: "Don't tell me I don't have to give you this, or that you aren't worthy, or whatever it is you wish to say! The fact is, all of my worldly goods are now exclusively in your name. If you wish to give it all to charity, be my guest, but I hope you won't."

Townsend again leaned forward to better display his seriousness. "Kevin, Lisa, I'm not leaving you a lot of money. I'm not making you rich. I'm giving you a responsibility to your fellow man. The kind of money and power that is contained within that briefcase is an onerous thing. I believe that alone, Kevin would be unworthy and

344

unable to handle this great responsibility, but with the help of you, Lisa, his lovely and wise wife," he gave Lisa a quick, appreciative glance, "he will, I believe, be up to the task."

Townsend looked up at Stephen and said, "Stephen, shall we go?"

Stephen helped Mr. Townsend into his wheelchair and turned it toward the door. After he opened the door, he turned the wheelchair around in order to better maneuver his way out. Townsend looked at the young couple and with a tear forming in his eye, said, "I don't think I could have made a better choice. Goodbye, Kevin; goodbye, Lisa; God bless the both of you."

As Stephen pulled the wheelchair into the hall, Kevin had to ask, "Mr. Townsend, you forgot to tell me about Mr. Boyd, here. Why does a man of his ability and intelligence act like a valet?"

Townsend smiled warmly at the young man. "Kevin, sometimes Stephen does little jobs for me. You are correct; he is a man of extraordinary abilities, abilities that may now be exercised by his new employer...you!"

Townsend leaned forward, ostensibly to whisper something Boyd couldn't hear, though he obviously could, "Haven't you ever wondered how the Americans 'accidently' found Saddam Hussein hiding in a spider-hole in the ground? And haven't you ever wondered who was able to place all those notes in Lisa's pocket and that of the President without being detected? Stephen here, used to be the leader of Seal-Team Six."

Out in the hall, Mr. Townsend lifted his right index finger into the air and motioned for Kevin to come closer. He leaned forward as Kevin leaned down to let him whisper into his ear. "Kevin," he said, "who do you think killed Bin Laden?"